I0614018

Readers love M. King's
Breaking Faith

"Sensual, moving … If you enjoyed *Brokeback Mountain*, you will love Breaking Faith."

—Renee Knowles, www.reneeknowles.com

"…brilliantly written, with stunningly well-drawn characters… superlative… I couldn't put it down…"

—Dear Author

"…a wonderfully written, intense story … an incredible honesty … This one will stay with you for a long time to come."

—5 Stars, Rainbow Reviews

PASSING SHADOWS

M. KING

Dreamspinner Press

Published by
Dreamspinner Press
5032 Capital Circle SW
Ste 2, PMB# 279
Tallahassee, FL 32305-7886
USA
http://www.dreamspinnerpress.com/

This is a work of fiction. Names, characters, places, and incidents either are the product of the author's imagination or are used fictitiously, and any resemblance to actual persons, living or dead, business establishments, events, or locales is entirely coincidental.

Passing Shadows
Copyright © 2012 by M. King

Cover Design by Mara McKennen

All rights reserved. No part of this book may be reproduced or transmitted in any form or by any means, electronic or mechanical, including photocopying, recording, or by any information storage and retrieval system without the written permission of the Publisher, except where permitted by law. To request permission and all other inquiries, contact Dreamspinner Press, 5032 Capital Circle SW, Ste 2, PMB# 279, Tallahassee, FL 32305-7886, USA.
http://www.dreamspinnerpress.com/

ISBN: 978-1-61372-769-0

Printed in the United States of America
First Edition
September 2012

eBook edition available
eBook ISBN: 978-1-61372-770-6

"Man is a substance clad in shadows."
—John Sterling

CHAPTER ONE

THE tree grew at the edge of the parking lot, in the narrow, scrubby strip of grass that bordered the street. Tommy guessed it had to be one of those little touches to smarten up the neighborhood: just a single birch tree, its slim trunk encased in a black iron railing. The bark looked gray between the bars, and though the last wreaths of April snow still clung to the ground, the pale branches had started to put out shoots, tiny gleams of acid green in the dismal air.

He blew into his gloved hands and watched his breath curl in the cold. He'd spent the last six years further south, where the weather tended to be slightly less vicious, and returning to Havre had come as something of a shock. To do with way more than the wind chill, sure, but it still felt weird.

Everything felt... big. Strange. Even the familiar things seemed different, dislocated somehow, like he was just moving between them the way he moved in a dream. Tommy stepped back into the lee of the bland square building that abutted the lot, and leaned against the wall. This time last week, life had been nothing but routines and repetitions. He'd got used to that a long time ago, but he had never imagined it would be so hard to shake off.

Two days. Not that long at all. He was still giddy from his homecoming, unexpected and unprepared for as it had been. Walking into his mother's place—the house that had never been his home but that he was now supposed to live in, like he belonged there—had felt surreal, unnatural. Oh, they were pleased to see him... shocked, maybe, but pleased. Everyone was so loudly, ostentatiously *nice*, until the initial surprise wore off, and then no one knew what to do with him. It was awkward, and it didn't feel real.

Nothing, he reflected glumly, had felt real until he got back here. Back to *him*.

He looked up at the sound of a familiar engine. A dark-brown 1980 Chevrolet pickup coasted into view, and, a broad smile washing over his face, Tommy glanced at his watch.

Damn, it's only 5:20. Guess you couldn't wait either, huh?

He and Brett had said good-bye last night, on the steps of his mother's house, and Tommy had known then he'd made a mistake. He'd gone to Brett's the minute he got off the bus… before his mom, before anything. Just gravitated right here, to this square box of a building that didn't look like anything special from the outside yet held everything within it. He should've insisted on making Brett's place his registered address right from the start, instead of the so-called family home.

Still, no use complaining now. He'd promised to come by. Six o'clock, they'd said, and from the looks of things, Brett had been just as impatient as him.

The Chevy eased into a parking space next to a green Hyundai. Tommy bit his lip in anticipation. His grandmother had bought that Chevy for him—thirdhand and pretty decrepit, even then—on his seventeenth birthday. She could never have known it would come to mean so much, a kind of symbol of… well, everything, he guessed.

Brett hopped out of the Chevy, his hospital work clothes half-hidden by a heavy coat, though Tommy could still see those horribly sensible shoes. He'd lost count of the number of orthopedic clog jokes he'd made over the years. Brett turned toward the condo, red-brown hair tousled, and for a moment, Tommy felt as if the breath had been choked out of him, like he was struggling for air under the weight of dark, murky water.

Don't be so stupid. You only saw him yesterday.

Days didn't seem to come into it, though. Time didn't really matter. It hadn't for so long, because it had been passing in a totally different way. Those long creaking seconds, sprawling out endlessly and then whispering away in the cracks of the hours, never leaving a trace of where they'd been. He shivered, but it was okay, because Brett had caught sight of him, and now he grinned, jogging across the lot.

"You're early," he said, teasingly reproachful.

Tommy said nothing for a moment, lost in hazel eyes bright with excitement and the way the wind had pinched roses into Brett's cheeks and nose. He leaned in and planted a kiss on that supple mouth, the coldness of skin against the warmth of breath.

God, I missed you.

"I couldn't wait. And, anyway, Lila kept wanting me to help her with her algebra homework. You know I suck at math."

Brett smiled. "You don't give yourself enough credit. C'mon. You hungry?"

Tommy gave a noncommittal grunt and followed him inside, up the stairs to the cheap apartment Brett rented. Somehow everything seemed to fall away. The suffocating sense he'd felt over the past forty-eight hours since his release—that it must all be a dream, that he'd wake up and find himself back in his cell—lessened, and as Brett unlocked the door, Tommy hung close to him, like he made it all real. Perhaps he did. He'd been the lynchpin that held everything together for so long now, the one solid thing that the rest of the universe bent and warped around. Tommy rested his chin on Brett's shoulder, taking in his scent, overlaid with that vague hospital smell of disinfectant and liniment. He nipped the back of Brett's ear, making him shiver and jab the key at the scratch plate instead of the lock.

"Hey!"

Brett's body tightened, and it was easy for Tommy to see just how much he'd been missed while he was away. He kind of liked the knowledge, even tainted as it was with so much regret. Brett aimed for the lock again and missed a second time, his hand shaking a little as his breathing grew fast and shallow.

"Sorry," Tommy murmured, not meaning it for a moment.

He should be here, he thought ruefully. *They* should be here. The knowledge—the desire—grew heavier with each passing second.

Tommy reached around, slipped his hand over Brett's, and guided the key into the lock. The door swung open with the weight of both their bodies against it, tangled in a kiss. Relief flooded Tommy; no more of the dim, stilted awkwardness of his mother's house, with everybody tiptoeing around him and nothing but the endless phone calls to break up the empty daytime hours. He'd been grateful for them at first, after the crazy hysteria of his unexpected arrival and the impromptu celebratory dinner, but they quickly grew wearing. And however nice it had been fielding calls from friends and well-wishers, and taking some quiet time while everybody was out at school and work to consider his new position, Tommy knew he'd just been treading water until he got back here.

"H-hold on," Brett managed, groping for the keys that still dangled from the door.

Tommy pulled back while Brett shut and locked the door. He slid the chain on and turned to Tommy with a sheepish smile.

"So, what? You miss me or something?"

He said it with a breathless twist of laughter to the words, but something deeper lingered in his gaze. Tommy laughed all the same. Brett had got so good at keeping things light, steering them away from the rocks, even when it hurt him to do so. Tommy knew that. It used to cut so deep every time he came down for a visit, and in every call, every letter…. Tommy pulled him into a hug, tight enough to feel the hardness of Brett's chest against his own and the tension in his back and shoulders. Brett loosed a harsh breath as he clung on, and it broke damply against Tommy's neck.

He recalled, last year, helping a friend who'd been studying some distance-learning course in literature. Shakespeare had been a part of it, and some half-remembered line drifted back to him. *Lips like pilgrims…*. It seemed they sought each other that way now, Brett holding him and locking onto his mouth, tender but tentative, as if he was scared of putting too much pressure on him. Tommy let his lips part, eager to show him that couldn't happen, that this was all he'd wanted, and a stifled moan left Brett as the kiss deepened. He tasted faintly of coffee and fruit-flavored Life Savers, and he moaned again as he knotted his fingers into Tommy's hair. He tugged gently on its thick black weight, a small, familiar gesture that finally broke the floodgates.

Six years was a long time for anyone, and it left a lot of things locked up below the surface. The kiss grew deeper, harder, laced with desperation and threaded through with impatient hunger. Tommy ripped the gloves off his own hands to focus on the strictures of Brett's clothes, and they backed clumsily into the room, shedding the first of the many layers the Northwestern climate demanded. Brett cursed as he nearly tripped over the coffee table.

"We could slow down," Tommy suggested warily, not really wanting to.

"Like hell," Brett muttered, toeing off the ghastly white-soled shoes. "I couldn't sleep all of last night, thinking about you. Are you okay?"

"Mmn."

It wasn't quite a yes, a no, or even a dismissal. Tommy had no desire to expand upon that, so he hoped Brett would take the hint, and kissed him again. After all, it always used to be a good way of distracting him from asking difficult questions.

Six fucking years….

It *was* a long time. Of course he wasn't okay. And last night had been terrible. His brother Robbie, all of fifteen now, didn't want to share his room but had no choice. Everything was awkward and difficult, and Tommy hadn't been able to sleep anyway, too overwhelmed and turned around by it all, no matter how brain-meltingly tired he felt. That house wasn't his home, and he wished that, even if he hadn't listed Brett's apartment as his registered address, he'd at least begged to be allowed to stay last night. In hiding… perhaps never to surface again.

He caught Brett's wrists, pulling him toward the bedroom as he raised his eyebrows suggestively.

Don't make me say it. I don't wanna beg.

He flattered himself that Brett understood, that the way they tumbled through the door and landed on the soft mattress came from some sympathy, some wish to soothe his troubled spirit.

It wasn't necessarily the case.

"Fuck it… want you," Brett whispered, his voice taut as he tugged at Tommy's belt. "Been thinkin' about it all day. Damn nearly sent some poor guy to Orthopedics instead of Orthotics, I was that distracted."

Despite the rush of it, the pent-up need of year after year that didn't feel like it would ever be fully slaked, Tommy frowned. "Huh. What's the difference?"

"He needed a back brace… not surgery."

"Oh."

Brett pulled the hospital shirt over his head, flung it away, and turned his attention to Tommy's fly. Tommy winced. He didn't want to start thinking. Not now. He wanted to just fall into it the way they used to do, and prove that something more than the routines and dependencies of what life had become still bound them together. The breath whistled through his teeth as Brett's fingers trailed the waistband of his pants. Only… the room seemed so big. Everything, just so… bright. New.

Tommy reached for Brett, clutched at him, pressing tight against him. There had been a time he'd wanted to blot himself out, exist nowhere except where Brett touched him, as if he could be remade that way, cleaner and better. He couldn't make it feel the same now. Even intimacy seemed like separation.

No…. That's not true. It just feels like that. Just feels….

"You all right?" Brett pushed Tommy's hair back off his face. "You're shaking."

"I'm fine," Tommy muttered, inwardly cursing his traitorous flesh. Last night, even that one brief fumble they'd managed before heading over to his mother's had reduced him to tears. He'd wanted this to be like it used to feel: strong, familiar, endless, and natural. "I just… well, it's been a while."

Brett curled around him, his whisper settling magnetically on Tommy's ear.

"Yeah. That's why I wanna, uhmm, *feel* you. I bought… y'know. In the drawer." Brett nodded to the nightstand. "So we can. If you're okay with that?"

"But...," Tommy began, not sure how to voice it, especially given his sudden light-headedness, "you said you, uh, didn't. Y'know, when I was... away. Um. Are you sure you want me to—"

"Look in the drawer," Brett repeated, a slight flush rising to his cheeks as he sat back and stripped off the T-shirt he'd worn under his hospital uniform.

Curious, Tommy tore his gaze from the supple cambers and planes of Brett's chest, and the pattern of moles sprinkled across his arms and ribs. He kicked off his jeans, stood to open the nightstand, and peered into the drawer.

"*Oh.* Rii-ight...."

A grin slipped over his face, the knots of worry and the insecurities somehow all a little less threatening. He glanced over at Brett, who looked slightly embarrassed among the rumpled covers.

"Well? I said I missed you."

Tommy, still grinning, picked the lube and the newly bought condoms from the drawer. Trust Brett—imperfectly amazing, unconditional, wonderful Brett—to give him something to smile about, something to bring him back to center.

He thought of the night a lifetime ago when he'd taken Brett's cherry. How he'd tickled and wrestled and goofed with him until they got mixed up in each other, laughing like children. How it had melted everything away. He should have known that he had nothing to live up to, nothing to be judged on.

Never with you.

Tommy climbed back onto the bed and knuckled his way up Brett's body.

"Oh, I know you missed me," he teased, "but when did Doc Johnson get to be your new best friend?"

Brett's blush deepened to an attractive shade of pokeberry red.

"Shut up."

"You're gonna have to give me a personal tour of that toy drawer, darlin'. I mean it. Really. I can only imagine what—"

"Seriously... shut up."

Tommy laughed and turned his attention to Brett's nipples, pleased to find the action did exactly what he remembered it doing. Brett twisted beneath him, fingers digging into Tommy's shoulders. Soft laughter and half-formed cusses whispered between them until Tommy felt himself laid out on the sheets, layer after layer bared to the bone, deconstructed and defenseless. Hazel eyes, trusting and sincere, welcomed and enticed him as their foreplay turned serious.

He didn't know what he'd worried about; there wasn't anything outside of this. Nothing that could hurt, scar, or wound. Brett rolled over for him, all warmth and comfort laced with the heat of need, and Tommy kissed his nape as he slowly settled himself, listening for that sweet, rough little gasp that Brett always made. It didn't seem like six years since he'd heard it last. Tommy tossed the lube to the pillow and covered Brett's hand with his, fingers sliding over and over through the valleys of his knuckles as they moved together. The sound of his name on that mouth made him weak, yet stronger than he'd felt in a long time.

Need was need, though, and the sweetness grew hot quickly: a fierce, driving intensity. The bedsprings dissented loudly, and Brett flung his free hand out, catching at the headboard where it slammed against the wall. They bucked and heaved as one body, too far gone for anything but perpetuating this desperate catharsis. Tommy, vaguely aware of getting his foot caught in the boxers still tangled around Brett's ankles, screwed his eyes tight shut.

Oh, God.... Not yet. Please not yet.... One times seven is seven. Two times seven is... is fourteen. Yeah. Three sevens are twenty-fucking-one, four sevens... oh, twenty-eight. Giants v. Patriots, 17-14. Colts v. Bears, 29-17.... Five sevens... oh, boy.

He cried out—pretty certain of that—somewhere after nine sevens and another run of Super Bowl scores, and he heard the crescendo of Brett's guttural moans a little later, then soft whimpers as they parted. Tommy leaned down to toss the condom into the trashcan by the nightstand. Blood rushed to his head as he decided he couldn't possibly get up ever again. A contented groan and a rustle of covers signaled Brett rolling over, and after a struggle with his recalcitrant muscles, Tommy hauled himself up. He collapsed back against the pillows, flushed, burning, and floating on air. Brett gave him a beatific smile and reached out to pat Tommy lazily, his fingers meeting the cotton T-shirt which had, in the heat of their enthusiasm, somehow never been discarded.

"Take that damn thing off," he muttered, plucking at the fabric.

Tommy chuckled wearily and obliged, then tossed the shirt to the floor. Brett made a satisfied little noise in the back of his throat and dragged himself across the bed. He palmed circles over Tommy's body, as if celebrating the touch of skin on skin. Tommy draped an arm around him and pulled him closer. Not something he usually did, but he didn't feel quite ready to let Brett go.

Not just yet.

"Mornin', boo."

Brett Derwent stretched sleepily against the mattress, not quite ready to open his eyes. Not just yet. The warmth of the bed enfolded him too completely, and he wasn't sure that—if he admitted to being awake—he wouldn't find all this proved to be a dream. Reality could get sneaky like that.

Only.... *Wait a minute.*

Brett cranked open one eye, squinting in the yellow morning light.

"What'd you call me?"

A soft laugh rippled over him like calico. Tommy pressed up behind him and planted a kiss on the point of Brett's shoulder.

"You heard. How're you feeling?"

Slowly, Brett heaved up the other eyelid and did a quick mental check of himself. Two arms, two legs... ears, nose, and mouth all still there. Yeah, he was—oh, okay. *Ouch.*

"Good," he said, shifting a little. "Though I may never walk again."

"That mean you're gonna stay here all day?" Tommy asked, fingers tracking up Brett's stomach, tugging gently on the treasure trail of red-brown hair he found there. "'Cause that might not be smart. I wouldn't be able to control myself."

Brett tried to think of something funny to say as Tommy kissed his neck, but his brain felt decidedly fuzzy. The past few days had been too full of impossible things, not least the fact of Tommy's presence. Brett had been prepared for the parole process to take months, for there to be endless waiting before his release. He hadn't expected for a second just to open the door of his apartment and find Tommy standing there, looking lost and hopeful, but that's what had happened.

Funny how two days could feel like a lifetime and a split-second, all at once.

He'd tried to preserve the memory, the way they'd held each other—uncensored by regulations for the first time in so long—but it had disintegrated too quickly, washed away in the whirl of activity, of letting Tommy's family know he'd come… home.

Last night had been the first night they'd ever spent together, which was pretty damn momentous if he thought about it. Well, not the *first* night, but the first real, proper one, perhaps. Certainly the first in six long, dry years, and the first one that could have really been called normal.

The first time ever, in a real bed, that they hadn't had to worry about Brett's parents coming home, or Tommy needing to leave before dawn to get out to work or back to his place to get his siblings ready for school.

Those kids are teenagers now. God.

Brett wriggled a little in Tommy's arms and reached up to bat the questing, pinching fingers away from his nipple.

"Quit it. For now."

Tommy stroked his palm over Brett's chest one last time before he released him, and Brett clambered slowly out of the bed. He paused before he stood just to look at Tommy. His hair spilled out on the pillows, an inky backdrop to his high cheekbones, hard jaw, and dark eyes. Despite his mixed ancestry—Canadian, American, and Chinese, as well as Nakoda—he had fully enrolled tribal status now. Brett had to remind himself of that; it seemed strange to think of him that way.

Strange to think of him as Indian, by technicality and by identity, when he'd always been just... well, *him.*

Brett shook the thoughts as Tommy raised one lean gold-brown hand and rubbed it lazily over his shoulder, bobbing up to start the day with a kiss: chaste, on account of the morning breath. Brett traced his thumb over that square chin, rubbing against the prickles of beard growth and the fullness of his lower lip.

"I still can't believe you're here," he murmured, sorely tempted to call work and tell them he'd woken up with leprosy, or maybe the Ebola virus.

Tommy smiled, though his eyes grew a little clouded. Brett knew better than to push it. Reluctantly, he tore himself away, his attention lingering for just a moment on the tattoo that covered the top of Tommy's left arm. Prison ink. He'd got it done his third year inside, strictly against the rules. Brett remembered being so mad at him—not just for the infraction, when he'd promised to try and keep a clean conduct record—but for how easy it would have been to pick up an infection. Conditions were hardly sterile, and the way the ink got applied—jerry-rigged machines made of guitar strings and pen casings, and who knew what in the damn ink—made Brett queasy just thinking about it.

That wasn't what he hated most about the thing, though. He knew what it meant. The tat showed a dragon, snarling and foul, bursting through an inexpertly drawn rip in the skin, the symbol of the single, terrible moment when the beast broke out, ravaging and destructive.

Like it had the night Tommy's father died.

TOMMY stretched, luxuriating in the size and softness of Brett's bed. Sure, it had given him backache, but it felt so good. Everything felt good, even the soreness and twinges in his muscles and each one of the marks Brett had left on him. Tommy didn't recall him being so... demanding before, but maybe that was down to enthusiasm. Anyway, all kinds of stuff happened if you bottled shit up for long enough.

He thought of the last time they'd shared a bed. Stolen time while Brett's parents were out at work, when they could pull the drapes tight and pretend it was nighttime instead of midafternoon. Long, lazy kisses, and Brett's unquenchable delight in all the things that had been so new and beautiful. *He* had been that way too—all bright and idealistic, ready for the whole world—and then Tommy had managed to fuck it up.

It seemed like such a long time ago, and it *had* been a long time. But it hadn't been normal time. It hadn't passed like time between two people usually did, with the crushing weight of days and weeks and the chores of daily life. Instead, it felt as if they'd been suspended in some weird kind of limbo, not quite able to change but not quite able to stay the same.

Tommy realized with a kind of sinking dread that this probably would end up being the first day of the rest of his life.

That being the case, he ought to get up.

He yawned and glanced at the clock. He couldn't believe he'd fallen asleep again. He'd heard Brett leave for work, been aware of him saying that he should make himself at home, stay as long as he wanted and all of that. He'd just been too blissed-out to actually move.

Tommy rose, showered, and, towel wrapped around his waist, padded back into the bedroom to poke through Brett's closet in search of clean clothes. He knew Brett had kept some of his old crewnecks… kinda sweet, really. He snagged one and pulled it on, choosing an elderly flannel shirt to layer up over the top. It still fit well enough, though he was a little broader than he'd been last time he wore the thing. In a mild flash of mischievous kink, Tommy retrieved Brett's boxers from the floor at the foot of the bed and tugged those on too. He buttoned up his jeans and puttered about the apartment for a while, taking care of a couple of chores. He dumped the laundry in the hamper, washed a few dishes, and just enjoyed the sense of being in Brett's space.

It might not be much, but the apartment had a hell of a lot more going for it than Tommy had been used to in the past few years. He leaned on the windowsill in the living room, gazing out at the infinite sky and the hazy mountains, distantly banded above the neat, plain, crowded grids of Havre's streets. For a moment, Tommy fought hard against the desire for a cigarette. He'd started smoking—and quit—in prison, never appreciating before how such a simple action could so calm and soothe torn nerves.

Don't know why you're so fuckin' nervous, ya jumpy little faggot. You never do anythin'.

Tommy started from the window, almost looking over his shoulder. The voice—the memory—came from too far back to touch him. He knew that. Even so, his pulse skittered, and, as restful and safe as this place had been, he suddenly needed to get out. Fast.

Tommy threw on coat, boots, and gloves and, without a backward glance, let himself out of Brett's apartment. He jogged down the stairs and out into the icy street, appreciating the sharp, excising precision of the wind.

The relief of it wore thin as he walked.

CHAPTER TWO

TOMMY'S mother, Mei, had chosen well when she moved the family. Where their old place had been a dark, dull building plagued with damp and probably held together in parts only by decades of really terrible wallpaper, the two-story rancher she'd found looked clean, bright, and cheerful.

Like a Stepford wife.

Tommy quashed the thought as he walked up to the back door, wondering if she'd remembered to leave it unlocked for him. She'd promised to get a key cut, but he knew she worked long hours at the dry cleaner's, so she probably wouldn't have a chance for a while... or something like that, he imagined.

The door swung open as Tommy reached for it, and he found himself face to face with Scott, his twin brother, scowling and looking harassed. Barefoot, in Nike sweats and an old T-shirt that appeared to have oatmeal on it, Tommy suspected Scott had never looked more like him. They weren't identical—Scott most resembled their mother and Tommy took after the other side of the family—but, in that moment, it felt like looking down the years into a mirror.

"Where the hell w— Huh, I don't even have to ask." Scott's gaze raked succinctly over his brother, and he lowered his voice. "Laid much?"

Tommy grinned. "You're just jealous. What're you doin' here, anyway?"

Scott brandished a bottle of cough medicine. "Katie woke up sick, so Mom called and asked if one of us could come over and watch her—on account of *somebody* not being home—but Karen's at her sister's, and Atian's got the same thing, so I figured I might as well bring him over."

"Oh." Tommy let the dig slide. "You need a hand?"

Scott didn't respond at first. Tommy looked at his brother, trying to read the expression in those inscrutable dark eyes. Scott had always kept himself locked up tight; they'd both learned to do that at an early age.

Light rain began to fall, the kind Tommy remembered their mother used to call dragon rain: supposedly auspicious, not that she took much of an interest in superstition. The scar beside Scott's right eye—the kind of thing that used to happen in their house if you didn't learn to keep your head down and your mouth shut—twisted as he screwed up his face.

"Huh. Yeah." He rubbed his free hand over the soul patch he'd started to grow, still little more than a conglomeration of coarse hairs clustered together on his chin for comfort. "C'mon."

Tommy stepped into the narrow hallway. Like the whole house, it had been painted in a glossy, neutral yellowish-cream, the woodwork picked out in a brilliant white that would never turn buttery with nicotine. The chaos of kids' boots and shoes lay stacked up by the door, a muddle of coats and jackets taking over the rack and spilling eternally to the floor. From the living room across the hall, the TV blasted out some psychedelic cartoon show.

Katie, their youngest sister, was snuggled into the large couch and sharing a blanket with Scott's son, Atian. Due to certain accidents of parenting, little more than a year separated the two kids, and Tommy wasn't sure whether Katie, at seven, really understood that Atian was technically her nephew. She probably regarded him as her cousin, or maybe some kind of extra brother, he supposed. He didn't know how she thought of Scott and his wife either, or—for that matter—*him*. She'd only been a baby when he… left. Seeing her grow up in photos, or during the very occasional visit Mei would bring the kids 250 miles down to Deer Lodge for, really wasn't enough.

Plates of snacks and juice boxes littered the coffee table, and, seeing his father, Atian picked up one of the cartons and waved it.

"Da-aaad… need more juice."

"Sure, I'll go get it." Scott stood the cough medicine on the coffee table and collected the empty juice boxes on his way to the kitchen. "You guys see who's here?"

Katie turned and knelt up, peering over the back of the couch, her small fingers digging into the dark blue chenille upholstery. Her straight black brows drew together over deep brown eyes very like Tommy's, and then she smiled.

"Tommy!"

"Hey."

He grinned and started to move in to give her a kiss on the cheek, before he thought better of it and settled for ruffling her hair.

She seemed damp and a little feverish, and promptly broke into a short coughing fit. He rubbed her back and sat down on the couch, silently overwhelmed when she climbed into his lap and put her arms around his neck.

"I threw up," Katie said grimly. "*Really* lots… so Mom said I had to stay home." She fingered his hair thoughtfully, smoothing it neatly against his borrowed shirt. "We're watching TV."

"Yeah," he agreed. The cartoon show had gone to commercial; a trailer for a new Disney movie blared. "You feeling better?"

Katie played with his hair some more, turning shy.

"Mm-hm."

Tommy supposed he flattered himself if he thought she really remembered him. He was just some random interlude. Someone associated with occasional road trips and commissary candy bars eaten in the visiting rooms… maybe a voice on the phone. Not much else. He glanced at the bottle of cough medicine on the table.

"Were you guys meant to have some of that?"

Atian grumbled, twisting in the blanket. He looked very like his mother. A small, round face with the same lively, high-set eyes, but he showed none of the mild physical markers that Karen had of fetal alcohol effects. Tommy knew how proud she was of that, how she hadn't touched a drop of liquor since her first pregnancy test and had stayed almost teetotal ever since. Just to be on the safe side, she said, and he took that to mean they planned more kids. Scott stayed tight-lipped on the subject. With Atian's school already talking about ADHD and the economy in the toilet, he probably thought they had enough on their plates.

"Don't wanna," he complained, acknowledging Tommy's presence for the first time. "I don't need it. I don't wanna. Won't!"

He delivered the last word in a rising wail that brought on another coughing fit. Scott reappeared, armed with juice boxes and a spoon, and shot Tommy a grin.

"You hold his nose. I'll pour the stuff in when he opens his mouth."

The idea didn't go down well with Atian, who shrieked hoarsely and flung himself off the couch, making a run for the door before colliding with a dining chair and bursting into frustrated, angry tears. Scott scooped up his son, rubbing away the pain of the bump and kissing him. Atian was still yelling, mixed in with coughing and explosive sneezes.

Katie cuddled closer to Tommy. He didn't want to disturb her, so he just sat and let the TV play on while Scott took his son for a bath and a proper nap. Katie's breathing settled into a steady rhythm, rattling a little with stuffiness and the roughness of the cough.

Tommy hardly dared to breathe, just holding her. It didn't seem possible that someone this small could open up so much in him, make him feel as if he stood on the edge of something steep and infinite. He remembered Katie as a baby: rosy-gold and delicate, made of tiny perfections.

She's still perfect. Thank God.

HE PICKED up a text from Brett at lunchtime: just a few words, an abbreviated and thinly veiled check on how he was doing. Tommy tried to take it as kindness, genuine concern—the way he knew Brett meant it—but it still stuck in his throat a little, coming too hard on the heels of so many well-wishers' phone calls and so much solicitous fussing.

He helped Scott with the kids, played endless games of snakes and ladders with Atian, told story after story…. They had barely sat down before the rest of the family began to trickle home.

"Hi, honey." Mei kissed Scott's cheek as she paused by the front door to shed her coat. "Thanks for taking care of things. How are they?"

"Feelin' better. No more throwing up. Fevers are down. It's prob'ly just gonna be a twenty-four, forty-eight-hour thing."

Tommy lingered in the doorway. His mother looked tired. That didn't surprise him, but it wasn't just that. Beneath the tiredness, he saw something he still wasn't used to seeing: confidence. It had taken a long time. For years, every time he spoke to or saw her, she'd seemed as bowed, as diffident as she used to be, and he'd always thought it was his fault somehow. Brett said she'd been hostile, angry. Hard to tell whether that was because of him or just what had happened, Tommy supposed.

Mei glanced at him and smiled tightly.

"Hey," he said, not sure if he should move toward her, if she'd kiss his cheek too.

"Hi."

She lowered her gaze, stepping neatly to the side and bending to receive Katie's sleepy hug.

"Mommy!"

"*Uci!*" Atian yelled, skidding on the laminate floor in his socks. He carried on a high, excited chatter, jumping and tugging at Mei's sweater.

Tommy watched them all swirl past him into the living room, a montage of sound and movement. He tried not to feel crushed, though it pulled at him like lead.

In the kitchen, someone had turned on the radio. A tinny dance track pounded, and Robbie and Lila—his last two siblings, home from school—started to bicker with well-practiced ease. Tommy took a breath and turned to follow the noise, joining them all in the bustle and chaos of dinner… even if he wasn't really with them.

At thirteen, Lila had already started wearing more makeup and jewelry than Tommy thought she should, though he didn't feel he could comment.

"Monkey Butt!" she yelled at Robbie, who'd been halfway through taunting her about some guy at school.

Baby's first crush. Aw, cute.

"Enough!" Mei and Scott both snapped, in a kind of parental chorus that crossed generations.

Tommy smiled to himself and slid onto one of the stools by the breakfast bar. So different from his first night back, when they'd all celebrated with takeout and cheap champagne. Laughter and shocked elation and Brett, sitting next to him, apparently knowing more about Tommy's family than he did.

"So when's Brett coming over next?" Lila wanted to know, when they all sat down to eat.

Tommy stared at his plate of bacon and cabbage. The question hadn't been directed at him.

"Weekend, I thought," Mei said. He looked up, catching her glance at him. "Unless he said different to you?"

Tommy shook his head. Last night, in all truthfulness, really hadn't seen much talking. Robbie started to make a mumbled comment to that effect, stopped by what Tommy recognized as one of Scott's trademark under-the-table ankle-breakers.

"You and Atian are staying tonight, though?" Mei asked, switching her attention deftly to Scott.

"Well, I—"

"It's silly to go back if Karen's still in Harlem. Stay, yes? Atian can share with the girls for tonight, and you can have the couch."

"*He* coulda had the couch," Robbie muttered darkly, glowering at Tommy.

Tommy said nothing. He wasn't entirely sure whether Robbie being mad about sharing his room was a simple case of adolescent territory, or any one of a dozen other things he could have resented.

Even as a little kid, Robbie had been hard to figure out. He'd seemed to find it worryingly easy to shut himself down, go inside his own head and hide there, curled away from the world. Tommy wasn't sure that was a good thing, though it had usually kept him out of harm's way, more or less.

Now Robbie's scowl looked a little too familiar, colored over with bitterness and suspicion, and that stung worse than Tommy had expected it to.

"Robbie!" Mei reprimanded sharply.

His small dark eyes widened, and his narrow mouth twisted into a protestation of innocence.

"What? I'm just sayin' that—"

"That's enough," Mei snapped, and the grumbling dropped in volume, if not intensity.

Tommy focused on his food. It was easier that way.

Not as if I like it either… Monkey Butt.

He let it all wash over him: Robbie's complaints, Scott's attempts to weasel out of staying, Lila's protestations at Atian sleeping in the room she already had to share with Katie. It all melded into something messily beautiful, in its own way, but Tommy couldn't help feeling like an outsider.

Later that night, once Mei had got her way, with Scott and Atian settled in to stay, yet more cough medicine duly spooned down the kids, and Lila properly chastised for a detention her mother had just found out about, Tommy stole a quiet moment to call Brett.

He sat on the airbed he'd been given on the floor of Robbie's room. The vague odor of old socks mingled with the miasma of adolescence and unfinished homework. A few soccer posters had been pinned to the walls; Tommy noted them with mild concern. No brother of his ought to show such flagrant disregard for the NFL.

Maybe he's still young enough to turn.

"Hello?"

It seemed weird to hear that uncertainty in Brett's voice. For the past six years, every call Tommy had made to him had been preceded by an automated message asking him if he wanted to accept collect charges from the penitential facility. He'd always have known exactly who was calling.

"Hey." Tommy reached up and tucked his hair behind his ear. "It's me."

"Ah...." Warmth washed through Brett's voice. "The underwear thief."

Tommy smiled. "Didn't think you'd mind."

"I don't. How're you doing? You okay?"

Very briefly, the question prickled at Tommy, but he pushed it aside. He glanced at the door. Robbie would still be clogging up the bathroom, which left him plenty of time to talk.

"Mm," he said. "Tell me about your day."

"Huh?"

The airbed squeaked under Tommy as he moved, stretching his legs out on the dark blue carpet.

"Y'know. Like... like we used to."

A small silence hung on the line. "Used to" seemed odd, he guessed, when this had been their routine as little as a week ago. But, hearing the soft expulsion of Brett's breath, Tommy knew he understood. Brett started to recount a summary for him—light and simplified and tailored to make him smile—and Tommy shut his eyes, lost in the familiar rhythms of it.

A phone call like so many others, but yet so unlike. No timed cut-outs, no other guys milling around, no one watching or listening or recording his calls.

It felt good.

CONSIDERING how slowly, how clumsily, those first few days passed, Tommy reckoned he coped pretty well. Time meant something different outside, and you had to get a handle on that. Something you could hold onto or spread your fingers and let fly like dust. Not something that breathed oppressively down your neck and taunted with its inevitable, inexorable movement. Strange, because it got so easy to lose track of it, minute to minute. He guessed if there were country miles, there were probably prison hours.

Not so, out here.

He had a meeting with his parole officer that he needed to attend. It meant going into town—all those crowds of people, mixed up and uncontained—though Tommy still found going from room to room slightly overwhelming if he didn't concentrate. The PO, Ethan Myers, gave him forms to fill out and a short, very earnest interview about what he planned to do with himself.

"What are you going to do for work?"

The office wasn't far from the courthouse and the sheriff's department, which Tommy recalled in distant, clouded memories that seemed to echo through a tunnel in his head. Myers had a potted cactus on his desk. Tommy stared at it while the guy shuffled forms and made notes in margins, his cropped, graying head bent over the paperwork.

"Says here your old boss in Burnham said he might be willing to take you back," Myers said, glancing up at Tommy with sharp, dark eyes. "You follow that up yet?"

The cactus didn't have spikes, more like a fuzz of spiny hairs covering its length. It sat in a pool of pea gravel, in a little white ceramic basin. Tommy blinked.

"Uh… I called. He said the position's filled now."

"Oh. That's too bad. You'll get something, though, I'm sure. You got… uh, yeah. Your carpentry qualifications. You did very well on the ed program."

Tommy curled the corner of his mouth in acknowledgment. Yeah, so he had a piece of paper with his name on it. That wasn't going to suddenly open up the Burnham job. Filled? Sure. They could just as easily have claimed economic slowdown, or maybe something on the company's insurance policy. He knew what people thought. What he'd always be in this town.

"And you're resident at your mother's place?"

"Mm-hm."

Myers's pen hovered over the page for a few seconds. Then he glanced up at Tommy again, coolly inquiring.

"And how's that?"

"I-It's fine. I mean, it's only been a few days, so.... Uh. We're a little cramped, but it's fine."

Damn.

Tommy dropped his gaze and looked down at his hands. He'd always had a living from them, and it showed. Calluses and short, spatulate nails... the occasional tear or scar. But they always healed. Myers cleared his throat.

"Oh. Well, that's good. And you, uh, you have a—"

Tommy looked up. "My partner works at the hospital. He's a physical therapy intern. Got an apartment down by Rotary Park. It's all in the file."

He kept his tone even and enjoyed the flicker of surprise that crossed Myers's face. The PO shuffled through the papers, checking the facts.

Didn't expect that, huh? Asshole.

More questions followed, assessing his attitude, his awareness of the parole conditions... the suitability of his current circumstances, as Myers put it. Yet another report would come after this, part of the deadweight of paperwork that tracked Tommy everywhere he went these days. He left, with another appointment booked for a couple of weeks' time and a vague, rootless desire to either get drunk or hit something. He'd made it halfway to Brett's place before he really knew where he was heading. Embarrassed and flustered, Tommy stopped, stood on the sidewalk for a moment, then turned abruptly and dove into a diner.

He sat and nursed a cup of coffee. Back toward the wall, the window to his side, he studied the door. Outside, a spring wind bowled down the road and tossed the last of winter's debris before it... shredded ends of plastic bags, crumpled leaves, and the grit that would soon grind away the snow. What the hell had he been thinking? He'd been going to Brett's every night for the best part of a week. He couldn't keep running to him like this. Tommy glanced at his watch.

Three fifteen. What would he do? Sit outside Brett's door and just wait for him to come home?

Probably. Shit, what the hell is wrong with me?

Tomorrow would be Saturday. Brett had talked about spending at least part of the weekend together. He'd drop by in the afternoon to say hi to Mei and the kids, which Tommy gathered had become something of a tradition in his absence, and in the evening, Brett's parents wanted to take them out for a meal. Their way of being nice, Brett said, and Tommy had to admit they did seem like nice people. They'd come down to Deer Lodge with Brett one Christmas, all determinedly nonjudgmental and crisp with brittle cheerfulness. He remembered Brett making kind of a point of holding his hand.

Tommy dumped more sugar in his coffee, because he could.

"FOR the hundredth time, they are not going to hate you!"

Brett caught up with Tommy as they walked down the path to the Chevy. Tommy turned, wary and tight with discomfort. Brett reached out and straightened his tie. The suit didn't fit well and had definitely seen better days, but he found the effort Tommy had made to impress touching all the same, especially as *he'd* only bothered to sling a jacket over a shirt and chinos.

"They will. They probably already do…. They didn't even meet me until I was already in prison."

Brett tucked Tommy's hair back into place behind his ear, dimly aware that Mei and Lila were still watching them from the porch, waiting to wave them good-bye.

"My parents don't hate you," he murmured. "It's just dinner… they're only trying to be kind. You know that."

Tommy didn't look convinced. Brett resisted the temptation to kiss him and jerked his head toward the truck.

"C'mon. We don't wanna be late. Wave to your mom."

"Like a good boy," Tommy muttered through clenched teeth, raising a hand to Mei as Brett unlocked the Chevy.

He'd have to get himself a new car, he supposed, now Tommy was back. Or, rather, *a* car. Despite the fact that Brett had officially bought it, saving the truck from sale to some stranger after Tommy's sentencing, it had never really felt like it belonged to him. It had always been Tommy's—his space, and their secret place, during that first long summer—and it seemed only right he had it back now.

As soon he was ready, anyway.

They climbed in, and after a couple of moments' spluttering, the engine rolled over smoothly. Brett pulled away, catching sight in the rearview of Lila and Mei going back indoors. Beside him, Tommy slumped in the seat and sighed.

Brett bit back a momentary flash of irritation. Tommy had been like this all day, and this scratchy, touchy petulance didn't suit him.

"Look, if you *really* didn't wanna go...."

He let himself trail off, not having meant to voice the thought in the first place. Tommy shifted, picking at a loose thread on his cuff. He grunted something unintelligible.

"What?" Brett glanced over at him. "Hm? What?"

"I said, it ain't that, it's... it's just knowing how they're gonna see me. Y'know? How everybody does."

Brett frowned, idling the Chevy past the neatly trimmed lawns and vinyl sidings of the suburbs. A kid, maybe ten or twelve, cycled by on a green bike.

"What d'you mean? How they see—"

"You *know*, Brett. You know. I'm your lost cause."

Tommy crumpled in the seat, scowled at his cuff, and kept on tugging at the thread. Brett's thoughts drifted back to a warm day in August, the sound of a patrol car's tires on the dirt, and his stupid, impulsive panic. He and Tommy had already been apart then, all choked up in the aftermath of that dumb, bitter fight that Brett knew *he'd* started, even if he couldn't remember how.

It had all stopped mattering the second he heard what had happened. He'd dropped everything to find Tommy... dropped his whole life, just to help him, and he hadn't even thought about what he was doing.

He wondered—not for the first time—how things would have been different if he had managed to get Tommy over the border to Canada that day. They probably would have ended up in different prisons, for a start. Brett pulled the truck over, near a line of white trellis panels that bordered somebody's backyard, and left the engine running.

"You're *what*?"

He tried to inject a tone of disbelieving sarcasm into his voice, tried to give the impression that Tommy had just said something unbelievably stupid that he couldn't possibly understand, but it didn't work. He heard himself just sound so very tired.

Tommy glanced up, dark eyes fogged and dim.

"You heard," he muttered. "I always will be. Your boyfriend, the jailbird...."

"Tommy—"

"The killer."

Brett winced, recoiling from the word, and cursed himself because he knew Tommy had seen him do it. For one brief, horrible moment, a sick look of triumph crossed Tommy's face. Brett let out a long breath and gazed out at the road ahead. The dusk had drawn in, heavy and abrasive, likely to bring with it further snowfall. The road looked greasy, with ice toward the edges, tire tracks and salt worn down the center, black stains in a frozen landscape. Brett unfastened his seat belt and turned to Tommy, still slouched, staring morosely at his lap. Brett leaned his temple against the headrest.

"Don't do this. Please?"

"The one who wrecked your life," Tommy said, in a bitter monotone.

The words oiled their way under Brett's skin. With slow and careful consideration, he scrunched up a hand and hit Tommy on the arm, hard, with the side of his fist.

"No!" he snapped, glaring at Tommy when his head jerked up, alarm in his eyes. "You don't.... Just don't. Don't you *dare*. You don't say that... I don't wanna hear that shit! Understand? It's not true."

"But...," Tommy started. Then something in his expression hardened. He shook his head. "Nuh-uh. 'Cause... you'd be a doctor by now, if it wasn't for me. If you hadn't spent your college fund on the fuckin' lawyer, if—"

The first flakes of snow began to twirl on the breeze, batting softly against the Chevy's windshield. Brett's fist curled on the cheap fabric of Tommy's jacket.

"Shut up! I'm not listening to that crap. Tommy, it's bull and you know it. Please don't," he added, tone sliding from anger to anguish. "Please? Just don't."

Tommy looked at him for a moment. His gaze flickered, and his fingers slipped over Brett's clenched hand.

"I'm sorry."

Brett nodded once, swallowing heavily. "Just quit it. Now. All right?"

"All right."

"Thank you."

Brett gave the jacket a little shake, feeling Tommy's hand squeeze his briefly. He smiled and hoped that fixed things.

Just for now.

The restaurant wasn't far: a little way out of town on Highway 2. Havre didn't offer that much in terms of dining experiences, but Ballard's Grill would at least be comfortable, and less full of boisterous kids than Pizza Hut.

Tommy barely said a word, tense and silent for the rest of the drive. Brett left the radio to play and hoped the banalities of a local talk station would fill the silence. The Chevy's headlights lit up stretch after blank stretch of road, eerie in the murky, yellowish dark, and a light snowfall waltzed in the beams.

"I look like I'm going to a court date, don't I?" Tommy blurted.

Brett glanced over at him. The dashboard lights and the dappled shadows of falling snow played on his face, and Brett felt a tug of want, despite all the messy, broken ends of things hanging between them.

He's here, and he's mine. Shit... I'm never gonna get used to this.

"You look fine. The suit's actually kinda hot," he added helpfully.

Tommy shot him a reproachful look, though Brett caught the half-hidden smile at the corner of his mouth. Hard to stay properly annoyed with him when even his bitching and whining ended up as self-mockery. Brett turned his attention back to the road.

"Anyway," he said, "nobody'd even care if you showed up in a feed sack. They want to see *you*."

Tommy groaned. "Huh. Evaluated, assessed and picked apart...."

"No! God, how many times? It's just... dinner." Brett stopped, aware he'd started to sound irritable again, and that wouldn't help. "It's gonna be fine," he said evenly, unsure who he was really trying to convince with the words. "Don't worry. I won't let 'em get rough."

"My hero." Tommy snorted and stared out of the window.

Brett shook his head but drove on in silence.

CHAPTER THREE

MONICA DERWENT checked her lipstick in the rearview mirror. The last time she'd gone out for a meal like this—one of these "meet the parents" deals that were so fraught with potential awkwardness—Brett had been in high school, dating a girl with pretty blue eyes.

Monica supposed, if she was truly honest with herself, she'd known then that something wasn't right.

"Well, I know *that*," she said, glancing briefly at her husband. "I guess I'd been expecting it too. It was just the way it happened. I... never expected all the police cars."

Stephen chuckled softly and touched his wife's shoulder. She smiled, reaching up to give his fingers a light squeeze.

"You look beautiful," he said.

Monica smiled. "Are they late, or are we early? I wouldn't want to be sitting around for—"

"I think that's them now."

She looked where Stephen pointed. The Chevy pulled into the parking lot, and Monica took a deep breath.

"Right. Well, I guess we'd better—"

"Mo? Remember what we said?"

"Hm?"

"Gently."

Monica flashed her husband the best semblance of innocence she could muster. "Of course!"

She eased her ample figure—smart in a tailored black pantsuit with a pretty green blouse and the devoré scarf Brett had bought her last Christmas—out of the car. Stephen locked up, immaculate as ever in a dark blue suit. His gold-framed glasses had steamed up a little in the cold. He dropped an arm around her shoulders, and they watched the Chevy's two occupants get out—Brett first, still evidently saying something, then Tommy, who nodded in apparent agreement and fiddled with his tie. He turned, following Brett with both his body and his eyes, and the Derwents watched their son pause, one hand trailing on the truck's hood before he caught at Tommy's sleeve. Their faces drew closer together. Brett said something, and Tommy smiled. Monica tightened a little.

"Mo…," Stephen murmured, singsong but serious.

"I know, I know." Monica exhaled. Her breath clouded in the icy air. "I'm just not used to it yet."

Stephen kissed her hair. He gave her a brief, comforting squeeze, and Monica shuffled her feet in the gray, sludgy snow. The fresh fall had added little to the overall depth. Still cold, but the weather had started to soften. With luck, they'd seen the end of the storms this season.

"Mom! Dad!"

Grinning, Brett bore down on them. Tommy lagged behind like a frightened puppy. Stephen hugged his son, exchanged the usual familiar greetings—how was he, he looked well, really good to see him—and Monica smiled at Tommy. He hung back, weight on one foot almost as if readying to run, and returned her smile with a nervous grin.

"Hi, Mrs. Derwent."

"Monica. You know that, Tommy."

She leaned in to kiss his cheek and could have sworn the breath hitched in his throat. He tensed, stiff and unresponsive, and Monica feared she'd done something she shouldn't have. She patted his arm, and, after the briefest of awkward moments, Tommy gave her a small, shy smile. They shuffled around, him shaking Stephen's hand—thank you, he wasn't too bad at all, yeah, good to see you too—and Monica flushed with warmth as Brett hugged her and kissed her cheek.

"Hi, honey... how are you?"

"I'm all right," he assured her, and she believed him.

They hadn't seen much of Brett since Tommy got out, but Monica had been there when he first heard about the parole decision, and to her eyes, he'd only been shining more every day since.

"Is he...?"

She framed the words quietly, almost lost in the cold air. Brett understood and nodded.

"Fine," he murmured, glancing at Tommy and apparently satisfied that Stephen had him distracted. "Kinda overwhelmed still. Take it easy?"

Monica rubbed the back of Brett's arm reassuringly. "Of course."

He smiled, and his happiness bounced back over her like firelight. Monica pursed her lips. Nobody should really be allowed to have the effect on her that he did.

Ballard's, as a restaurant, strove for a better reputation than its squat, slightly grim exterior suggested it deserved. A neon sign in bilious green and Barbie pink broke up the cedar shingles and concrete at the front, while, inside, the décor ran to a kind of cookie-cutter sophistication lent by beige walls and generic abstract canvases. A faint waft of grilled steak and apple-scented air freshener assailed them as they entered.

While they waited to be seated, Monica watched the way Tommy's gaze flitted around the room. It was either her imagination, or she'd caught him checking out the exits. She wondered if he knew he was doing it; if he found it happened every time he entered a space. Maybe it had become subconscious now, just something you did. Plot out what threats, what problems lay in store and how to escape them... every minute a potential flashpoint.

Brett had said something along those lines not long ago, despondent after spending too much time surfing those god-awful websites for prisoners' families. *Oh, Mom, what am I gonna do? Says here a guy can get institutionalized in as little as eighteen months. What if he comes home crazy?*

She'd hoped never to have to wipe his tears again. Even so, Monica had found she couldn't hate Tommy. Oh, she'd expected to, and maybe she'd latched onto the idea of it for a while.

Six years ago, her son had been at the beginning of everything. A bright future, a good premed program, and then it had all changed, in one single breath. It was the secrecy, Monica thought. That was what had hurt. Thinking she knew him, and that he believed he could talk to her about anything—hadn't she said that, time and again?—and then finding that he'd lied to them… that he'd been lying for years.

She had *wondered*, of course. The girls Brett had dated in school never seemed to last long, and the one longer-term girlfriend he'd had hardly seemed to make an impact on him. She'd assumed he just hadn't met the right one. She might have contemplated the possibility that he wasn't all that interested, but… well, even if she *had*, she hadn't expected the way they'd find out. To learn that, for the best part of a year, he'd been seeing someone in secret—and not just any someone.

Monica didn't consider herself a snob, but she'd always thought Brett would go for a… a person from a background like his own. Not that class mattered, of course, but having things in common was important, and she couldn't understand what he could possibly have had in common with Tommy.

She remembered the way Brett had first poured the story out, teary and gulping with embarrassment and shock, the red marks from plastic restraints still on his wrists when they picked him up from the sheriff's office. It was the kind of phone call she'd never imagined getting. Words that buzzed in her head and seemed to make no sense, even on the third hearing. Attempting to aid and abet… it didn't mean anything. Then she'd seen him, tottering out to the front desk once he was released without charge, and the world had fallen in on itself, leaving her blind to everything.

He'd tried to explain, that day, and she hadn't wanted to hear. Being angry—feeling betrayed—had been easier, because that way he couldn't hurt her anymore. And yet Brett had needed her, needed comfort, and Monica had seen how much he... well, she'd seen the extent of things, and she'd tried to adjust.

She'd thought she'd be helping him recover from one bad decision. The more he talked about Tommy, lancing the burden of his guilt, she'd thought it must have been some cock-led adolescent thing, some stupid infatuation with an unsuitable, dangerous person. She'd been so angry, not just at Brett's idiocy, but at the thought her boy should have felt forced into something like that... only it hadn't been that way at all.

She knew that when Brett told her he planned to use his college fund to pay for Tommy's defense. She'd been furious. So much yelling, and for the first time in his life, Brett had met her, inch for inch. He'd yelled right back at her—right back at his father too—and he'd been so damn stubborn, and Monica had no choice but to watch as he parceled up his life and gave it, neatly packaged, to someone she regarded as a complete stranger.

Yes, she'd hated Tommy then, although they'd never met. The idea of him, the secondhand notions and stories... but she'd stayed quiet. Watching Brett lose his future was bad enough without losing him as well.

Still, she hadn't known what to expect when they went down to Deer Lodge. Some wild, crazy kid, maybe, condemned by his own pride... anything except the quiet, tired-looking young man in the prison-issue clothes, with shoulder-length hair and dull, closed-off eyes.

She remembered Brett holding his hand, and Tommy looking nervous and hesitant, even as he gripped back, like Brett was the only thing in the room worth holding onto.

It would have been so much easier if she could have looked at him and seen a killer.

Instead, the very absence of that steel worried Monica. It was as if—whatever had happened that night, beyond the loose details given in the allocution of Tommy's plea bargain—it had burned everything out of him, and she struggled to see a monster in someone so lost.

He'd been coming back, Brett said, over time. Slowly. Of course, it had been six long years of hard work for both of them.

She'd tried not to judge.

Now, they sat in a large booth—dark brown leatherette and a beech veneer table—and perused laminated menus. Tommy looked faintly stunned. Brett and Stephen had already started into a well-worn dialogue about the appropriate treatment of elbow injuries. More specifically, the treatment of a reminder of Stephen's old kayaking hobby, which always returned to plague him in the damp. Brett complained he didn't give it enough support; then Stephen protested he didn't need it, even as he winced…. It kept them occupied and, Monica suspected, probably related to some obscure father-son bonding ritual.

She caught Tommy's gaze across the table.

"It *is* nice to see you. Both of you," she added.

"Thank you. I'm just…. This is still new," he confessed, and Monica saw in the subtle twist to his body that he wanted to turn to Brett, to pull him into the conversation.

"I'm sure it is. It'll get easier, though. You'll see. How's your mom? Brett tells me you're staying at her house."

"Uh-huh." Tommy colored a little. "We, uh, well, I…."

"Very sensible, I thought," Monica volunteered charitably.

She had, after all, already heard the speech from Brett. How it wouldn't have been fair to ask Tommy to move in with him right away. How they should take it all slowly, not pile on the pressure.

Very noble sentiments. Wonder how long it'll last?

Tommy looked relieved. "Yeah. Well, I'm still lookin' for work. My parole officer says it shouldn't be a problem, with my, uh, qualifications and stuff…. I figured if I don't find anything in Havre, I might try ranch work. Either way, I'll get something."

Monica nodded and smiled encouragingly.

Is he telling me he intends to be able to provide for my son?

They ordered. She couldn't help but notice how Brett pointed out both the steak and the grilled chicken, offering a choice between two things instead of the whole menu.

The conversation ranged politely around the food, the décor, the weather…. Eventually it ended up on Tommy's family—or "the kids," as Brett always called them—and it was him, not Tommy, who talked about their latest escapades and achievements.

"So, Katie's recital's next week," Brett said. He glanced between his parents and Tommy. "You guys gonna come?"

"Of course," Stephen said genially. "Gotta swell the ranks, right?"

"Mm," Monica agreed.

Had she been especially concerned about grandchildren, she supposed the sprawling and extended second family Brett had acquired would have gone some way to damping any disappointments. She and Stephen had both been introduced to Mei Hawks and her kids. And her kids' kids. There had been a barbecue one summer about a year into Tommy's sentence. Brett had tried to bring everyone together, reconcile and smooth away differences and misgivings.

Monica recalled large quantities of charred meat and an unfeasibly small woman, looking pale and gaunt in the midst of all the bustle and chatter. Her children: Scott and his wife—neither of them more than kids themselves—and their baby son. His in-laws, Karen's parents, were an Indian couple whom Monica found dour and expressionless, with their other daughter and her own brood in tow. No husband, but a four-year-old girl and a baby. Then there were Mei's youngest three, ranged from nine to two at the time.

She'd found it all—found *them*—broad, foreign, and unsettling. It had to do with Mei's cool distance, the way the kids acted up... with Karen's dark, angry mood at some insignificant thing, bringing drama to the table that Scott glossed over with blue jokes and big smiles. Worse, the way Brett fitted in. He'd been working a crappy job at an old folks' home, scrimping to replace the college money he'd blown on Tommy's defense lawyer, but—however Monica tried to look at it—he wasn't the same as those people. He was different. He was... her boy.

She remembered thinking that.

This is not my son. This is not what we meant for him.

He'd been just one month away from going to Washington State, enrolling in his premed.... Yet there he sat, as if he'd never meant to be anywhere else. He swilled beer and laughed at titty jokes, talked fluidly, and looked so totally at ease that it daunted her.

They had been, Monica at last understood, foolish thoughts. Now she could admire her son for all he'd done, every bridge he'd built and hand he'd held. He had been stronger and more mature than she'd realized, and she was filled with pride for that. For him. So Monica smiled, and she would go to the damn kid's recital, and probably prickle with tears just like she used to when it had been her baby up there, looking petrified and clutching a violin he could barely scrape four notes out of.

She cleared her throat.

"Um. Ranch work, you mentioned, Tommy. That something you'd like to do? In the long term?"

He looked up guiltily from his dinner, and for a moment, she thought maybe she saw him a little like Brett did. A handsome man, lean and tautened by life but not yet badly careworn. Something in the lift of his glance, perhaps, made him seem oddly vulnerable, as if she'd caught him off-balance. She noticed that telltale little shift of his weight against the chair, the top half of his body inclining slightly to Brett again.

"I guess I don't really know," Tommy said. "I never planned much ahead before. Usually just figured somethin' would show up."

The simplicity with which he said it tugged at Monica's heart, but it also worried her.

"Uh-huh?" she prompted, raising an eyebrow.

Tommy shrugged a shoulder dismissively.

"Well… yeah. Y'know. We had food and a roof, so I didn't really…." He stopped, gave her another small, shy, uncomfortable smile. "I did some work on the ranch at Deer Lodge, and it was pretty good. I like bein' with the animals."

"Mm?" Monica dug her fork into her pasta.

"It's, uh, restful. They're… unconditional," Tommy said, glancing back down at his plate. He chuckled dryly. "My gramma used to say I oughta learn to ride for the rodeo."

"No way!"

Monica blinked. She hadn't even been aware of Brett listening, but he left off from his conversation with his father to poke Tommy's arm.

"Broken and fractured bones, torn muscles and ligament damage... you'd deserve every single one, and there's no way you'd get free physio off of me."

"Aw, not even massage?"

The look that passed between them could have blistered paint. A slight flush started to rise along Brett's cheekbones, and Tommy smiled. Monica exhaled softly.

A smile like a sunny day with ice cream. Ouch.

Stephen nudged her elbow gently, a reminder that her mouth was hanging open. She shut it as Tommy looked away and cleared his throat.

"So, uh," Brett said, the blush fading but the traces of a smug leer clinging to his face, "I read in the paper they're talking again about whether Highway 2's gonna get four-laned."

"Yeah," Stephen chimed in, after a beat. "I saw that. Figure they're gonna have to, if there's gonna be oil production down at Fort Peck. State of that whole corridor's pretty bad. You know how many wells they're putting in on the reservation?" he added, looking at Tommy.

Tommy shook his head, and Monica thought she saw a flash of resentment in his eyes.

"No," he said shortly. "I don't really know the area. My grandparents lived in LP Town... Lodge Pole, I mean. That's Fort Belknap rez, not Peck."

Monica prodded the toe of her shoe into her husband's ankle.

"Oh. Right." Stephen nodded thoughtfully. "Well, they're still gonna have to four-lane. I mean, all those trucks'll be comin' through...."

Monica groaned inwardly.

Eventually, the meal ended, not quite as awkwardly as it had begun.

Outside the restaurant, in the biting, metallic chill of the night, Monica hugged her son and glowed quietly when his "Thank you, Mom" brushed her ear. He kissed her cheek before he pulled back, eyes bright.

Monica held out her arms for Tommy, surprised by the way he filled them. No reserve, no offishness in his embrace. He just seemed… grateful? Relieved? She wasn't sure, but he kissed her too, all guileless elegance and, it seemed, genuine affection. He shook Stephen firmly by the hand once more and—so very soon—it was all over.

They got into the car, and Monica relaxed into the warmth of the upholstery, leaning her head back against the seat.

"Okay?" asked Stephen.

Across the parking lot, the boys—*her* boys—climbed into the Chevy.

"Mm," Monica said, gazing dreamily at them. "As long as I don't think about the butt stuff, I'm fine."

CHAPTER FOUR

BRETT woke with a start. The night creased around him; that thick, soft darkness that comes with the earliest part of the morning and hides things in its folds, muffling and distorting shapes and senses.

He'd grown used to fitful sleeping. In the few weeks Tommy had been home, Brett would wake at intervals throughout the night, as if he needed to check he hadn't vanished. Sometimes, he wasn't there. It had scared him at first, but then he realized that Tommy was in the habit of getting up, rising to pad around the apartment like a caged tiger or just stare out of the windows at the stars.

Brett didn't know whether he'd always done it or if this was something new, something he had yet to work through. Maybe he did it because he *could* wander if he wanted.

Maybe I snore.

He yawned hugely, scrubbed at his hair, and reached out to Tommy's side of the bed, expecting to meet with cooling sheets. He was already squinting into the dark to see where Tommy had gone. Instead, Brett's fingers touched cold, clammy skin. Tommy whimpered under his touch, thrashed once more against the mattress and cried out—a harsh, wordless groan that had Brett instantly alert and petrified.

He reached for Tommy again, trying to calm him, and caught an elbow in the face for his trouble.

"Get the fuck off of me!" Tommy yelled, sitting bolt upright, moving from sleep to panicked wakefulness in a split second.

"It's me! Tommy…! Ow," Brett added, still clutching his nose. "What the hell?"

He removed his hand from his face and squinted at it in the gloom, not seeing blood, but seeing worse when he looked at Tommy. He was flushed and panting, his hair damp and his eyes wet.

"You have nightmares?"

Tommy shook his head and swung his legs out of the bed. He wiped his face on the back of his hand—a hand that Brett saw tremble. He moved toward him, fingers barely grazing Tommy's arm before he pulled away, shaking off the touch abruptly. He rose and walked unsteadily to the bathroom.

Brett leaned back against the pillows, pretending the rejection hadn't hurt. But all the same he sat and waited for Tommy to return, to slide back under the covers. Brett touched his face, cool and damp where he'd splashed cold water on it.

"Tommy?"

Tommy leaned over and kissed him, just a soft brush of his lips at first. Slowly, he brought one hand to Brett's jaw, deepening the kiss into something more… not tender, Brett realized with faint surprise, but thorough. Methodical. Brett let him do it, staying supple and passive and letting Tommy take whatever he needed from him. However much he wanted answers, they could wait, he told himself.

For now.

"I love you," Tommy whispered against his mouth. "I love you so much."

"Love you too," Brett said, as Tommy folded against him.

He held him until the shakes stopped, and stared at that hateful tattoo. It seemed, for a moment, to twitch under Brett's fingers, to coil like a living shadow.

Gradually, Tommy's breathing calmed, and Brett thought maybe he was falling asleep again. He tried to move, to free the arm caught under Tommy and assuage the pins and needles that crawled through his flesh.

"Brett?" Tommy sounded sleepy, though his palm tightened against Brett's chest.

"I'm here." Brett gave up the idea of moving, gritting his teeth against the sore protests in his limbs, and tried to blank out the images in his head.

He should have expected Tommy's nightmares. He had, in a way. He'd read enough, prepared enough, that he knew what kind of marks the time would have left on him. But it didn't stop Brett wanting to know, desperate to see inside the landscapes of his dreams.

There had always been things they didn't talk about. Things they probably never would. But he wanted—*needed*—to know. What stalked those hidden places? Brett imagined the slimy brickwork of endless dark alleys, the repeated gunshots echoing over and over, what must have happened in those moments that Tommy had never really remembered. That he said he didn't remember properly, not even now.

Maybe they came back to him in the night, fully and vividly, with the choking, bitter reality of dreams... only to be lost when he woke. Maybe the things that came back were the years before that, the years Martin Hawks had terrorized his family: the violence, the uncertainty, the fear. Brett pictured him—a figure only in silhouette, for he'd never met the guy—striding through Tommy's head, but he knew he'd never understand it, even if he tried. He'd never know what it had been like, or how it had finally all collapsed, splintering into vicious pieces.

Perhaps it wasn't anything to do with Martin. It could just have been the joint. Brett hated to think that, but found it hard not to. Tommy had been so lucky: a plea bargain with ten years for voluntary homicide, and even parole on sixty percent of that time. He'd served the whole thing at the Deer Lodge state pen, with no transfers, no great dramas or disasters. Well... none that Brett knew about, though he remained painfully aware that Tommy hadn't told him everything. He remembered that first visit at Deer Lodge—those goddamned five-hundred-mile round-trips that had killed him almost as much as the waiting—thinking he saw bruises on Tommy's neck, but being too afraid to ask.

Shit, come on... pull it together.

He knew it had been bad. It wasn't *supposed* to be easy. Yet Tommy had survived... *they* had survived. Maybe not unscathed, but unbroken.

"Brett?" Tommy murmured again, lifting his head a little.

"Hm?"

"You're breathin' hard. Whassa matter?"

Brett exhaled slowly, unaware he'd worked himself up so much. "Nothing. It's… it's all right."

"Oh." Tommy snuggled against him, not showing any sign of going back to sleep. "Hey… you remember what you said?"

Brett blinked, not really concentrating. "When?"

"Before. The other night… 'bout new starts."

"Oh, yeah. Uh-huh."

Everything… here on out, it's a new start. His pledge of faith, a desperate attempt to make them both believe they could begin again, clean and fresh. He'd known as soon as he said it he was bullshitting. Even as Tommy kissed him and said yes, everything would be different, Brett knew he didn't really want that. It wasn't possible… they should build on the roots and binds that had grown with time. Sure, those ties had formed strangely. Six years should have seen them slide from new-kindled, desperate passion to regular, comfortable intimacy, butterflies of excitement with every meeting giving way to the predictable security of seeing each other every day. Not this… this web of things, light as silk and tight as iron, confusing and wrought with stolen time.

We're gonna make it count.

That's what Tommy had said, leaving unspoken how much they'd missed, the things that could never be replaced… and the things that could never be forgiven. Brett tipped his head slightly, Tommy's hair tickling at his neck. Under the covers, a little footsie action started, and Tommy found the sensitive spot above Brett's hipbone, massaging slow, even circles with the heel of his palm.

Brett bit back a sigh of pleasure. "Hmn… what were you gonna say?"

New starts. There'll never be anything new while we're here. This place.

"Well, I was, uh, t-thinking…."

Tommy faltered, and, for Brett, it meant the green light to a thought he'd barely had the courage to skirt around before. He frowned in the dark, aware of the numbness in the parts of him that Tommy was still lying on turning to a cold, fiery pain.

"Mm?" Brett prompted, gently pulling his arm out from under Tommy and trying to clench life back into his hand.

"Yeah. Um… y'know. It'd be… good. Startin' over," Tommy muttered lamely, adjusting his position.

Brett twisted his mouth. Tommy was acting weird. Well, that only confirmed it, didn't it? They had to get away. Brett wondered how the hell to ask the question. He felt Tommy's gaze on him, hungry and somehow frustrated.

"Uh-huh. It would. So… what?" Brett swallowed, working up the guts to say the words. It ought to be easier in the dark. "I mean, if you want… if you're still having trouble finding work, or you're not happy…."

"Brett—"

"We could go somewhere else. It wouldn't be a problem."

I said it. Shit. It's out there now. Brett held his breath, waiting for a response from Tommy, but scared of hearing it. After a moment, the breath whistled low between Tommy's teeth.

"*What?*"

"Wait… wait, listen. Not yet, I know. I know there's…. We said we'd wait, I know, and I'm not putting pressure on you. You've got your family here, and there's the parole conditions, but if it would help… if you wanted to give it a try…. I was thinking somewhere like Bozeman, even Billings."

Silence in the dimness. Tommy moved, hauled himself up on his elbow and left a chasm between them on the bed. Brett fought the urge to turn on the lamp; he didn't want to see Tommy's face. Better this hidden, grainy darkness, safe in the blurred blues and grays of the night, at least until he knew how Tommy would react.

"With you?"

Brett let out a breath too soft to be the laugh he wanted to give. "Well, yeah, with me. If…. I mean, I know it's a big step and it's kinda sudden, but...." He stopped, the amusement dying when Tommy didn't say anything. Suddenly, Brett wished he'd kept his mouth shut. "You can forget I said anything if you want."

"No, I...." Tommy tailed off, as if he wasn't sure what to make of it.

Brett silently cursed himself a dozen times over. *So fucking stupid...!* He should have known better. Waited. Kept it to himself 'til he knew what Tommy really thought. Dropped it in, casually, sometime it didn't matter. Not now. Not like this.

You idiot... d'you even know how stupid you are?

The bedsprings creaked gently as Tommy lay back, firmly on his own side of the mattress, hands behind his head. Brett looked up at the shadows on the ceiling and tried to pretend he didn't mind that Tommy had moved away. He pulled the covers up and turned over.

"Either way," he said, straining his eyes to make out the knots in the wood of his nightstand, "it will get better. Easier. I mean, it's just a matter of time. And we're pretty expert at that, right?"

He heard Tommy chuckle grimly, but he didn't really reply. Brett turned his head a little.

"Night, baby."

He closed his eyes as he felt Tommy's fingers brush across his shoulder.

"Night, Brett. Sleep well."

"Mm," he grunted noncommittally and burrowed down.

He wished he'd never mentioned Bozeman.

TOMMY left early the next morning. Brett got the feeling he'd have liked to slip out undetected, but, as he had his own early start ahead of him, Tommy would have had to struggle to leave him slumbering. Besides, Brett found the bed turned cold quickly without him.

"Mornin'," Brett said, peering sleepily through the open bathroom door.

Tommy didn't close doors if he could avoid it. He also spat in the toilet when he cleaned his teeth, not the sink. Brett wished he knew why. His gaze trailed slowly over Tommy's broad shoulders, lingering on the shaded cleft of his lower back, the waistband of... *my boxers? Again? Hm.* The fabric rode low on his lean hips, tenderly cupped that perfect ass, flared just so over the tops of those long, long legs. Firm, well-muscled thighs tapered through the intricate collection of planes that formed his knees to packed, solid calves, strong ankles, and those rawboned, arched, beautiful feet.

Brett had never paid much attention to feet before. He wondered—savoring those precious few seconds before Tommy turned around and acknowledged him—why he suddenly found these so interesting. Because they were a part of Tommy, presumably. The particular heat of his body, the smell of his skin. The taste of him. All his imperfections and his uncertainties and his maddening, impossible warmth: everything that made Brett feel so small, stupid, and lumbering.

He's home, so why can't I stop holding my breath?

Tommy glanced over his shoulder, still wiping traces of shaving foam from his neck. He turned, smiled tightly, and tossed the towel into the laundry hamper.

"Hey. Did I wake you?"

Brett shook his head. "I have to get going anyway. Want breakfast?"

"Nah. I ought to go. Stop eating all your food," he added, maybe in a half-assed attempt at humor.

"Listen. Tommy—"

"I don't wanna hold you up."

Brett wanted to jump in front of him, hurl himself into those loosely cabled arms, even grab Tommy by the hair and scream "Talk to me!" right down one of those neatly formed ears, but he didn't. Brett wondered why. Possibly he wasn't awake enough, or still embarrassed by last night: stupid questions and bad reactions in the dark. Perhaps he should blame the years of practice, being mindful of what he said and how he said it. Maybe he'd just got too damn tired of trying. It felt like that, as if all the fight had left him in one breath, and he was sagging on his feet like an empty punching bag.

"All right," he said, resigned. "Take care."

"Sure, babe."

Tommy dropped a quick peck to Brett's cheek and touched his arm briefly, just a gentle squeeze. Then he passed by, back to the bedroom, and started to dress, all calm efficiency and no apparent concern. He'd gone by the time Brett got out of the shower.

PHYSIOTHERAPY wasn't what Brett had planned to go into. For as long as he remembered, he'd wanted to be a doctor. Mainly to do with the sense of achievement, he guessed, of helping people and making a difference. Sure, it was idealistic, but there were worse ideals to have. Brett had been prepared for the massive amount of study, the financial and physical drains, and his parents had been so proud.

Of course, recouping the money that had gone on lawyers took a while and—by the time Brett was ready for college again—the gleam had rather rubbed off the idea of a premed. The study for physio still took long enough, though he'd managed to shave off a little time and money by starting his training through part-time and correspondence courses, and, had Tommy got out just a little earlier, they could have celebrated Brett's new clinical internship together.

Brett pushed the thought from his mind as he paced down the shiny, clean halls of the Northern Montana Hospital. He'd grown used to doing that—used to leaving all his thoughts of Tommy at the door— but it wasn't as easy to do now. Just knowing he was walking around somewhere in the same city made it seem like Brett could feel him, a constant presence, a faithful shadow at his side.

Brett quickened his stride as he swung a left by the sign for the radiology department, not looking at where he headed. He felt at home here. Sure, he still languished at the bottom of the heap, and much of his week seemed to comprise "Dump It on the Intern" days, but he worked with a supportive and friendly team, and he'd have the opportunity of choosing a specialism—and a better pay bracket—way earlier than he would have done as an MD.

Brett pushed open the swinging doors that led to the PT department savagely and stomped down the corridor. He didn't know why he was still worrying about Tommy. He'd expected him to have nightmares. Once, during one of those early visits, Brett had asked if he had them, prepared to help him talk it out, be a shoulder for him to cry on, so to speak. Tommy just shook his head and said he didn't need another damn therapist.

Fine. So who held you in the night? Who stopped the shaking, baby?

Brett nodded at Cathy, the clinic receptionist, behind her little glass window. She gave him a quick wave, phone clamped to her ear, pen and a sheaf of paperwork in her hand. He shook his head as he turned the corner and slipped into the break room, still trying to clear his thoughts. Brett knew enough pop psychology to realize that these sudden, sour flushes of jealousy and irritation toward Tommy stemmed more from his own guilt than anything else. His tall, green-eyed guilt.

Tommy knew about Nick. He'd always known—always said he didn't care, that itches needed scratching and that, frankly, it would probably be good for Brett to spread his wings a little bit. It hadn't been anything more than that, not really…. Whatever Nick would have liked, Brett had made it clear from the outset that there wasn't anything between them but sex.

They'd met at college. He'd explained the ground rules—explained about Tommy—and Nick had tried to understand. Maybe he even had. In any case, it had been easy enough to forget with him. Just for a little while. Easy enough for Brett to pretend that he didn't need anything except the physical stuff, and that all the smacking of pelvises, the hickeys, and the grunting would do him just fine.

Not that *that* was everything there had been with Nick. Not exactly, if Brett was honest enough with himself to admit it. Still, it had been almost enough, for a little while. They'd become good friends, and Brett had to admit that had lent something comforting to being with Nick, but it hadn't lasted. The sexual side had waned, though the friendship remained. Brett had a card from him on the mantel in his apartment, sent when he heard about Tommy coming home. *Congratulations*. He'd shown it to Tommy, registered the wry, slightly sarcastic smile when he read the message:

Happy for you, bud. Send a picture—wanna see what I was always second best to! N xx

Brett couldn't believe he'd been so stupid as to mention Bozeman. Too damn soon. Too much. He grabbed a cup of dishwater coffee and flung himself onto one of the saggy gray couches, glancing at his watch. He'd just wanted Tommy to know, even if it took that much, he'd do it. In a heartbeat.

Last night swirled behind Brett's eyes. Not just the bad dreams, but the nights before, and the nights to come: different, physically, to how it used to be. He'd changed, he knew that. More confident in his own body now, more… experienced. He had Nick to thank for that, mainly. Maybe Tommy sensed it, because something dark and fraught lingered in the way they touched each other. Brett had thought it wasn't anything more than having been apart so long, but it didn't feel soothing, the way it once had. It felt—oh, it still felt right, like nothing else really existed—but something clouded and complicated tainted it. Tainted them.

Shit, I wish I could afford a vacation….

A shadow fell across the low Formica table.

"Morning, Brett. You with us?"

Brett blinked. The coffee had gone cold in front of him. "Oh. Sorry, Elaine…. Morning. How are you?"

He looked up. His boss—her jaw-length bob parted at the side and carefully fluffed up, washed through with an ash-blonde dye to disguise the gray—smiled at him, the powder already settling into her crow's feet. Elaine started each and every day starched and pressed, perfectly primped and presented and, without fail, had creases in her tightly buttoned white smock by lunchtime. A silver crucifix glinted against the darkly tanned skin of her décolletage, and her expression softened as she leaned forward a little.

"Are, uh, *things* okay?" she asked conspiratorially.

He had to smile. "Things," with Elaine, meant a kind of team leader shorthand for anything from car trouble to mental health and, in Brett's case, what she referred to as "his complex home life." She knew about Tommy. Of course, the whole damn state did, however lucky they'd been in avoiding too much publicity. There had been reporters, both local TV and newspapers, and a bunch of people from the students' association at MSU, wanting to make him into some kind of gay martyr. Brett hadn't spoken to anybody. He knew Mei had thought about it—for the money, he supposed—and he knew she and Scott had fought over it. He'd won, thankfully.

"Sure," Brett said hurriedly, aware he'd been drifting off again.

Elaine didn't look convinced.

"Are you sure? You're sure you don't want to take that time off? Kathleen's maternity cover's in, so—"

"No. Thanks, I'll save it."

"Well, so long as you're with us. It must be… distracting."

She said it kindly, her tone suggesting that she really was worried about him, not just his work performance. Brett smiled again.

"I'm fine. Really. So, what's the briefing for today, boss?"

BRETT struggled to keep his mind on work, regardless of what he'd told Elaine, and risked totally missing the point of a video presentation on lymph drainage. He sleepwalked through the day—mainly paperwork and assisting with an elderly patient's post-hip-replacement therapy—and found he longed for it all to end. A weird sensation when Brett had spent so long throwing himself into his job and actually enjoying it.

Finally, he left the hospital and drove out to Mei's place. Her car wasn't outside, but the living room window was open, and music drifted on the air. The kids should be home, and so should Tommy. Brett's pulse quickened a little in anticipation; silly, but he couldn't help it. He parked the Chevy, wondering if it was really the prospect of seeing Tommy or apologizing for last night that had his stomach in a knot.

This has gotta stop. It's stupid.

Brett climbed out of the truck and went to ring the doorbell. Lila answered, dressed down—for her—in embroidered jeans and a pink cami under a black shirt, her hair pulled back and her makeup minimal. A huge zit weltered by her nose.

"Hey, Lila."

"Brett!" She smiled at him, but the light soon dropped from her eyes. "Tommy's not here."

What? Where the hell is he, then?

Brett bit down the first swallow of panic.

"Well… I didn't just come here for him. How are you?"

She shrugged briskly, ushered him in. The music—much louder indoors, rap and hip-hop—seemed to be Robbie's choice.

"Mom's not back until late. She's got a *date*," Lila added, her voice dripping with sarcasm. "Tommy's s'posed to be watching us. Ha… hey, can you keep an eye on Katie? I'm gonna be in *so* much crap if I don't finish my homework."

Brett nodded dumbly, still stuck somewhere around that first sentence. Mei? Date? Lila smirked, patted his arm, and wheeled off. She snatched up the phone and a bag of chips before she headed upstairs. *Yeah. Homework. Right.* Brett felt moved to say something, but she wouldn't have listened, and, as had always been made gently but irrefutably clear to him, he wasn't actually family.

He found Robbie in the living room, music up to eleven and the TV on, and Brett didn't even want to get into it. He'd seen it before. After a little while, everything would shut off and Robbie would slouch out of the back door and disappear with his friends. Only this time, Mei wouldn't be here to yell at him as he stomped off down the path.

Who in the heck is she dating? Since when? What did I miss?

Brett found Katie in the kitchen, sitting at the table, an array of coloring pens in front of her and the yellow one clutched in her fist. She looked up and smiled as he entered.

"'Lo."

"Hi, Katie. So, you're drawing, huh?"

She nodded. Her straight black hair, cut to jaw level with heavy bangs, was pinned back on one side with a barrette clip. The clip had a plastic ladybug on it and was already sliding gently down toward her right ear.

"Can I see?"

She nodded again and patted the table beside her. Brett sat down in the chair next to her and looked at the paper.

"Aw… pretty flowers, Katie."

"They're Daddy's."

The breath leaked slowly from Brett's lungs. *Aw, crap.*

He licked his lips nervously. "Like, uh, like the ones you take up to Highland Park, huh?"

Katie appeared to consider this for a moment. Then she wiped her nose on the sleeve of her sweater and shook her head.

"Nuh-uh. When we go, we put white ones. It makes Mommy sad. So… sometimes I draw pictures with colors for the flowers… 'cause the colors are pretty, and that makes people happy. They're like flowers for Daddy, but they're happy flowers. Y'know?"

"Uh…." Brett winced, considering the potential minefield before him. "Yeah."

"Even if they're not really real flowers," Katie added with a thoughtful frown, "'cause he prolly couldn't smell them anyway, right? But he'll know that I drew them. *I* think he will."

The tip of her tongue poked slightly from the corner of her mouth as she put down the yellow pen and reached for the green, carefully coloring in the stems of her flowers. Brett swallowed heavily, trying not to imagine the little girl clutching her mother's hand as they stood by the graveside of a father she'd never known.

"Uh. That's really nice," he managed.

"Yeah." Katie nodded proudly. "My Daddy likes flowers, I think. Guess he must."

She couldn't remember him, surely. She'd been a baby. No way she could have understood, growing up with the specter of Martin's death, of Tommy.... Brett fought down the urge to ask probing questions. He was no counselor.

Katie looked up at the sound of a truck outside.

"D'you think that's my mommy?" She clambered off her chair and went to peek. "No, it's not. It's Tommy."

Brett's gut did a tiny, halfhearted flip-flop.

God, I don't know how he ever did any of this.

He ambled out onto the porch in time to see Tommy drop lightly from the cab of a flatbed Ford. He looked furious, tight-lipped and scowling. The driver hopped out after him, left the engine running and followed Tommy into the front yard, still talking in a low voice. Indian, with short-cropped hair and a dark, closed-in set to his face, the newcomer didn't look all that friendly. A tattoo trailed down the lower half of his neck. From all Brett could make out, it looked like a medicine wheel with two feathers. The guy caught sight of him and, with a short bark of laughter, said something to Tommy. Brett didn't catch all of it, but he heard the word "apple."

Tommy's scowl deepened. He glanced up at Brett, showing no recognition whatsoever, then turned abruptly and scuffed his boot at the grass. Brett swallowed the greeting he'd been ready to give, along with his pride.

The Indian guy reached out and tapped Tommy on the back, a sharp blow with the heel of his palm. Tommy whirled around, his face close to the other man's, his shoulders tense. Brett strained to catch what they said. He couldn't hear over the thrum of the Ford's engine, but Tommy looked seriously pissed. He stuck one hand into the pocket of his jeans and brought out a fistful of bills, which he shoved gracelessly at the Indian. The guy took the money, curled his mouth into a hard, unpleasant smile, and climbed back into the truck. He pulled away, and Tommy slumped up the path, his scowl spreading out into a tight, flat mask of displeasure. Brett waited until Tommy's foot hit the first step.

"What was that all about?"

The words burst out, harsher than he meant them to be. No "hello," no smile of greeting. He kicked himself mentally as Tommy glanced up through his lashes with a sour sneer.

"Lane Harding. He's just a... jerk."

"That you give money to?"

The stair creaked under Tommy's weight as he paused, then swung around the newel post, coming to lean heavily on the rail beside Brett. He stared out at the street. The tarmac appeared oily in the chill of the coming dusk. Lights burned in the windows of a few other houses, just the odd yellow glow shaded by drapes or shades. People in this neighborhood seemed careful of their privacy. The buildings were packed a little closer together than aesthetics required, though the architecture was bright and clean. Something of a 1940s Sears catalog could be seen in the gables and neat porches, and, come the drier weather, men might well come out and hose down the sidings, while kids washed cars and mowed lawns. A car alarm squealed somewhere in the distance, and a succession of dogs began to bark at the noise.

"I know him from the joint," Tommy said quietly. "The lodge and the talking circle... an' that Four Winds thing."

He mumbled it like it was an embarrassment, something he didn't want to admit to being a part of, but Brett knew better.

"Oh. That's, like, the thing for, uh, traditional rights and education, isn't it?"

He grappled uncertainly with the words. Tribal blood quantum rules meant that, though Tommy had only one-quarter Nakoda ancestry, he could still enroll and—at Brett's suggestion—he had, though he'd grumbled about it in the beginning. It yielded few concrete benefits, though it had enabled him to make the most of the prisoner support programs and gave him, supposedly, a sense of identity, of pride and belonging intended to help him. It *had* helped, Brett believed, though he'd struggled a little when Tommy began to get involved with the prison sweat lodge, and phrases like "walking the Red Road" started to appear in his letters.

Tommy nodded. "Uh-huh. Only, you kinda need to make sure they're, uh, all there for the same reasons. Y'know?"

Brett pressed his lips together, concentrating on nipping them between his teeth in the hidden and—above all—silent space of his mouth.

"Like I said, Lane's a jerk."

"Like *I* said, you gave him money."

Tommy looked at him in surprise. Brett lifted one shoulder in a semiconciliatory shrug.

"I'm sick of not asking questions, Tommy. Sick of watching what I say and letting things slide. What'd you owe him for?"

Tommy's expression hardened slightly. A chilly void slimed its way through Brett's insides, but he stood his ground and stared Tommy down. Eventually, he got his answer.

"Gas."

"Gas?"

"Uh-huh. He ran me down to Hays, for a job interview. Don't say you coulda run me," he added.

Brett closed his mouth, barely aware he'd started to shape the words.

"You were busy," Tommy said reproachfully. He rubbed his knuckles along the side of Brett's hand where they still both leaned on the rail: a small, tender gesture of appeasement.

Brett loosened his fingers, relaxing into the contact.

"So," he said, breaking to clear his throat as Tommy's hand enfolded his, thumb tracing lazy circles on his skin. "How come he's such a jerk?"

Tommy sighed. "Ah... I got all the garbage, that's all. Thinblood this, apple that. Just stupid stuff."

"Apple?" Brett frowned. "Oh... red on the outside—"

"White inside, yeah." Tommy looked out at the street and puffed out his lips in a short, resigned breath. "I don't know... I'm not even all *that* red to start with."

A sardonic smile touched the corner of his mouth, and Brett tried to mirror the gesture. It wasn't that he didn't believe Tommy so much as he was aware of his ability to bend the truth by omission, to make out—simply and elegantly—that things were fine, when they clearly weren't.

Brett thought back to that first summer, how he'd seen the welts and the bruises on Tommy's body and told him he shouldn't take it any longer. In thanks, Tommy had pushed him so far away they'd almost lost everything. Brett leaned into him, seeking the solid warmth where his upper arm touched Tommy's.

"C'mon," he said after a while. "We oughta go check on Katie. And maybe think about dinner."

Tommy ducked in to press a quick kiss to his cheek, drawing a shiver from Brett that had nothing to do with the chill on the air.

"I love it when you get all domestic."

CHAPTER FIVE

TOMMY couldn't remember the last time he'd seen his mother in a skirt. The black fabric swayed gently around her knees as she moved, and he could picture it swirling if she danced. Would Ron take her dancing? The question bothered Tommy, almost as much as the fact Mei had started to date at all.

According to Lila, it hadn't been going on that long. A few mentions of his name here, a dropped reference to a shared lunch there.... Ron Ephraim owned the electronics store four doors down from the dry cleaner's where Mei worked, and Tommy couldn't help wondering how long he'd been waiting to put the moves on her.

She looked happy enough, he told himself. The skirt whispered against her legs, and her hair shone with some new conditioner that smelled like coconuts. She'd left the top two buttons of her blouse—white cotton shot through with silky, ivory stripes—undone, and Tommy averted his gaze as she swept past him. He had no desire whatsoever to peer down his mother's cleavage.

Instead, he frowned down at the plate he held in one hand and the circular motions he was making on it with the dishcloth.

"Did you have a good time?" he asked.

Mei drew herself a glass of water from the sink and leaned against the counter. Traces of an unfamiliar, carefree smile still clung to her face.

"Hm. Yes," she said, after an apparent moment of consideration and a sip of water. "Yes, I did. Thanks for watching the kids."

Tommy shrugged. "It's good spending time with them."

Only a partial lie, really... he'd spent time with Katie before bathing and tucking her in. Robbie had disappeared into the night a while ago, and Lila was shut away somewhere either on the phone or the computer. He'd read Katie a chapter of a Harry Potter book, and, sleepy and on the edge of dreams, she'd said she loved him just before he turned out the light. Tommy kept the memory close to his chest, cherished and tightly held.

Mei took another sip of water. "You didn't miss going to Brett's, then?"

Tommy caught the barb in her voice, but he wasn't quite sure what she meant by it.

"I told you, I don't mind watching 'em."

"'Cause you're spending a lot of time there. He ask you to move in yet?"

Tommy blinked. Mei had applied a lot more makeup than normal this evening. The combination of eyes lined precisely in a dark chocolate brown and mouth painted glossy caramel, set against pale powder—and the blush she'd got from a night out and a few glasses of wine—made him think of a china doll.

"N-no," he said, after a beat. "We were gonna wait. Not rush things."

She giggled. A pretty sound... or it should have been. Tommy put away the plate he'd been drying, struggling to remember which cupboard it went in.

"I, uh, had somethin' to eat," he muttered. "D'you want coffee?"

"Mm. Thank you."

He had to reach past his mother for the cups. Mei stretched out a hand, stroking his hair, suddenly serious.

"Poor baby."

Tommy flinched. She sipped her water again, leaving a pale, sticky lip print on the glass. Her gaze trailed darkly over his face, fingers coming to pat his cheek.

"Mom...."

"You have a home here, you know. You do know that, right? For as long as you want it."

Yeah, an airbed on the floor of Robbie's room. That's great, Mom. Thanks.

Tommy swallowed down the impulse to say it. "I know," he said instead, peeling her clammy hand off his skin and giving it a gentle squeeze. "Thanks."

"S'what Mommy's here for, honey."

She giggled again, and Tommy turned to make the coffee. He rolled his eyes heavenward.

The kettle purred and bubbled to itself as the water came up to boiling. Steam wreathed the kitchen, making transitory patterns on the doors of the melamine cupboards.

Poor baby.

Tommy tried to ignore the thought, but it was already gnawing at him, even as he reached for the tin of powdered coffee. He had nothing to offer Brett, he knew that. No job, no income, nothing except more obligations and needs. So, however much he missed being with him, Tommy wasn't ready to take that plunge. Not yet. Not like that. Only... had he made it that obvious?

Am I that pathetic?

He cleared his throat. "So, ah... Ron takin' you out regular now?"

"Would you have a problem with it?"

Tommy dumped spoonfuls of the sour-smelling granules into the two mugs, followed by the freshly boiled water, and stirred. Bubbles eddied on the coffee's surface, and he tried not to think of how he hated it when she pushed back at him like this. She used to do the same thing with Martin: a question for a question, never just a straight yes or no. Tommy wondered why. It had to be either a refusal to make a statement, never committing to anything, or maybe it was her way of fighting. Whatever it was, it used to make him hit her more.

"No," he said. "Of course not. I just wondered."

"Does it upset you?"

Maybe she just enjoys seeing how far people'll go.

Tommy shook his head. "No, it's.... I think it's good. You deserve somebody to treat you nicely, take you out places."

He passed her one cup of coffee, took the empty glass from her and turned to wash it. The silent question hung between them: *Is that what it is?*

"Ron's a nice man," Mei said at length, and she blew on her coffee to cool it.

"Ah-huh." Tommy shook water droplets from his hands.

She adjusted her weight against the counter, flexing one slim ankle. Her high-heeled shoe clicked on the linoleum floor.

"He's kind, respectful… considerate."

Tommy nodded and reached for his own coffee. An image sprang into his head, unbidden, of a balding man in middle age, red-faced and sweaty. His pudgy fingers worked at the buttons of Mei's blouse; meaty, uneven lips smeared over yellow teeth and thick glasses magnifying pale, bulging eyes. He would be paunchy, smelling of Old Spice, and the hair on the backs of his wrists and fingers would be dense, wiry, and gray.

Mei sipped her coffee. "I asked *him* to dinner, you know. He kept buying me sandwiches and cups of coffee, but he wouldn't take it any further. Not without a little nudge. He's very sweet like that."

Tommy swallowed, the coffee too hot on his mouth, slicing his throat.

"Does he know about… uh, about D-Dad and… everything?"

He screwed up his eyes for a second, ready for the sound of the shot, but the memory just turned over sleepily, tugging at the surface of his mind like a fishing float on still water. Tommy frowned. Mei gave another little laugh, incongruous and not quite pleasant.

"Honey, *everybody* knows. The whole damn Hi-line. You made the papers all the way to Idaho."

Tommy rocked back against the sink. He remembered asking Brett what had happened with that. He'd hated to think that he had inflicted all those newspaper and TV people on his—no, *both* their families. Brett had said it wasn't a problem, but he used to say that a lot, and Tommy could never be sure how often he really meant it. Even so, he'd have expected his release to generate a little bit more interest. Sure, the date had been changed at the last minute, but…. Tommy guessed that, after the initial shock of the crime, no one had really cared what he did, or what happened to him. He became a hypothetical, a case in point, raised up for water-cooler talk or small-town newspaper editorials and opinion pieces, and forgotten again.

A statistic, not a person.

He watched his mother drink more of her coffee. The pinkness had begun to fade from her cheeks. High on the kitchen wall, above the door that led to the living room, the clock that had once belonged to Tommy's grandmother struck eleven. It did so silently, its black feather hands stifling even the sounds of their own movement.

Robbie would probably be back soon. Either that, or not back at all. Tommy had no idea where he'd gone… where he went, almost every night. He supposed he could try and do the big brother thing and ask, but he hardly found himself in the position to instill respect in anybody right now.

"I-I should probably turn in," he said, swallowing the last of his coffee.

"Job-hunting again in the morning?"

He nodded. "Ah-huh."

"When's your next appointment with your PO?"

"Wednesday."

Mei cupped her mug in both hands, peering at him over the rim. She suddenly looked so serious.

"You know, Karen was saying she has an uncle, got a little horse ranch, could probably do with some help."

Tommy squirmed. "I don't want charity, Mom. And I never w— I don't really have that kind of experience," he corrected.

He'd worked on the prison ranch. Twenty cents an hour for shoveling shit and lifting bales. It could have been worse, he guessed. But he didn't know if that's what he wanted to do… *in the long term.* Brett's mom had asked him that, hadn't she? As if he knew how to make plans and look ahead, and didn't seem to spend all his time treading water. Tommy sighed.

"Where's the ranch?"

"Not far from Poplar, I think."

He frowned. "What? No way! That's more than two hundred miles, Mom! I'd have to apply for all kinds of crap if I wanted to move—"

Tommy stopped abruptly. *We could go somewhere else. Bozeman... or Billings.*

No. That... that wouldn't work. He couldn't leave. Why would she even suggest it? To say something like that.... Imagined-Ron lurched around his head again, chuckling sweatily and pawing at Mei's breasts. Tommy blinked the thoughts away.

Stupid.

"It's just an idea," Mei said quietly. "I don't know. You don't need to get so defensive when people try to help you."

"I'm not getting def—" Tommy bit the word off, hearing a familiar pattern in his voice. "Sorry, Mom. It's just that I don't know if that's possible. It's a long way... I'd have to talk to Myers before I even know whether I could apply."

She shrugged one shoulder, and Tommy glanced at the clock again.

"Well... g'night," he said.

After a moment, he darted forward and kissed her cheek before heading upstairs. She smelled of perfume and coconut, and her powder felt silky to the touch.

"Night, honey," Mei said.

She didn't even turn her head.

Tommy lay on the airbed in Robbie's room—trying not to move because every breath, every twitch of a muscle made the thing squeak like a drawn-out fart—and thought about leaving. It presented an extremely attractive prospect. Just picking up a bindle and walking out, away from everything, had always seemed like a good idea.

As a boy, he'd had a red plastic case, probably originally intended for storing paints or something in. Tommy remembered packing it with a spare pair of underpants, a bar of chocolate, his favorite comic books, and Droops—the flop-eared plush rabbit that he'd had and adored until it got passed down to Katie—and storing the whole thing under the guest bunk beds at Gramma's. His running away case, he'd explained to her when she found it. She'd hugged him, very tight. Funny, Tommy realized, that he'd chosen to store it there, instead of at home.

"DOES that hurt?" Brett asked.

Braden Solberg screwed up his eyes and shook his head. His narrow body quivered and, with a frustrated yelp, he toppled backward, thin hands clutching at the chair meant to support him. Brett caught the boy and rocked back onto his haunches, balancing Braden's weight against his own. Not hard to do, because the kid barely had enough meat on him to feed a flea, apart from the swollen, hardened muscles in his legs.

At ten, Duchenne muscular dystrophy hadn't yet robbed Braden of his ability to walk or stand, but the progress of his decline was painfully obvious. The physiotherapy couldn't cure him or delay the inevitable, but it gave him a lifeline, a set of goals to achieve and a way of measuring how hard he fought. Brett supported the kid under his arms, taking care not to harm his delicate ribs or nudge the back brace that laced around his curved spine.

"That's right, you're doing great," he said as Braden wobbled. "Yeah, take hold of the chair, now stand up. That's good… don't push it. And don't try to pull yourself up. Just use your arms to support and balance yourself. I've got you. I'm not gonna let you fall…."

"Remember to say when it hurts, Braden," put in Elaine, propping up the wall beside them and jotting something down on her clipboard.

Brett wasn't sure if the notes were on the patient or him, but he nodded to his boss and leaned a little closer to Braden's ear.

"You can just say it to me if you want," he whispered. "I won't tell. You're being really brave."

Braden relaxed from the exercise with a sniff.

"My legs are sore."

Brett bit his lip. "Yeah… I bet they are. You think you can do one more?"

"Maybe," the boy said hesitantly.

He set his jaw and tried again. Brett knew how painful the swollen muscles in the kid's legs must be. One of the ways the disease ate away at Braden's flesh was to harden it off first, like blight setting in to destroy a crop of tomatoes. He'd done well to stay out of a wheelchair so far, and—the longer therapy could keep him using his legs and feet in as normal a way as possible—a chance remained that they could delay the unavoidable decline.

The next set of exercises worked Braden's ankles. When standing, he tended to hold his feet oddly arched, walking on so-called "Duchenne's tiptoes" due to the contracted muscles around his heels. With Elaine dictating supervision and coming to kneel in front of Braden as he lay on a support mat on the floor, holding his hands and telling him how well he was doing, Brett helped him through the program.

He kept smiling and kept his touch gentle, and tried really hard not to think that this boy would most likely be dead before he reached twenty-five.

After they'd finished, he spent a little while talking sports and schoolwork with Braden, while Elaine popped down to the hospital cafeteria to find the boy's mother. She cared for him full time—on her own, since her husband had left them—so no one begrudged her a quiet latte and a blessed slice of time away from his illness.

Joking and buoying Braden up while they waited came naturally; Brett supposed from all the practice he'd had with prison visiting. It wasn't much different: keep talking, keep smiling, and for God's sake don't think about what might happen tomorrow.

After the Solbergs had left, Brett stood at the sink, rubbing antibacterial alcohol gel into his hands. Elaine's shadow fell over the brushed stainless steel, and he looked up.

"You're very good with him."

"Hm? Oh… thanks." Brett blinked as he worked the gel under the nails of his left hand.

The minute he'd stopped focusing on Braden, life had started to press in on him again. He cast around for something—anything—to push it away.

"Do you want any help with the hip replacement guy?"

"Mr. Landis? No, thank you. Peter wants you for some paperwork, though. Patient assessment notes, I think."

Brett groaned inwardly. *Yep. Dump it on the intern.* "Sure," he said brightly. "Anything else I can—"

"No, you're fine. Um... Brett?" Elaine called him just as he turned to leave. He peered back at her, hair already unruly, her smock creased and rumpled. Hard to believe she headed up the whole clinic.

"Yeah?"

"You think about your specialization yet?"

"Uh...." he began, mouth slack. He'd barely settled into the internship. "Not really, why?"

Elaine smiled. "Let me put it a different way. Are you thinkin' about pediatric physiotherapy? Or do you want to focus on sports-related work, maybe look at your own practice in a few years' time?"

Brett pivoted slowly on his heel. "Uh, I don't really... the pediatrics is pretty rewarding, I guess, but—"

"I'm glad you think so. Because if you did want to consider it," Elaine said airily, "there might just be an opening coming up in the department. In the, uh, future. Y'know."

She smiled at him again, and Brett's pulse did a little happy dance in the roof of his mouth. *Did she just offer me a staff job?* He turned his head and attempted to look unconcerned.

"Oh.... Well, I... I'll definitely keep that in mind. Thanks, Elaine."

"Good," she said, patting him on the shoulder as she passed him. "You do that."

A slow grin spread over Brett's face. For the rest of the day, not even mountains of paperwork could dampen his spirits, and he left work buzzing with elation. Brett had got out to the parking lot before he realized that, although he'd started thinking of Tommy, it was because he wanted to tell him what Elaine had said. It wasn't any kind of grim, dark thought… just the impulse to share something of his day. Brett started the Chevy, thrilled with the idea of that. For the first time in so long, a *normal* interaction. He grabbed his cell phone, letting the engine warm up as he dialed Tommy's number.

"Hey! It's me."

"You sound cheerful."

"I had a good day…. Listen, are you busy? Can I come over?"

Brett heard the crackle on the line of Tommy moving into another room, and something that sounded like a door closing.

"Uh… yeah, or I could meet you somewhere. How 'bout that?"

Brett frowned. "Tommy, is everything—"

"Everything's fine. Just a little bit crazy. How about Draper's? My treat. Beer and pool. Like a proper date."

Though loath to argue with a proposition like that, Brett was unconvinced.

What are you hiding?

"Okay," he said warily. "Want me to pick you up?"

"I'll meet you there."

Brett's frown deepened. "Well… all right."

"Good. You can tell me your news."

DRAPER'S occupied a great position for catching highway traffic, not far from the train station. Owned by new management, who'd revamped the place for a more contemporary look, it had initially attracted a lot of the wrong kind of attention in town. The local clientele had greeted the tall, wraparound glazed panels on the upper floor with quiet derision instead of architectural awe. That made sense to Tommy, Havre being famed for thunderstorms that could rage for hours and make even the sturdiest windows shake. Still, the place had a good bar and a comfortable atmosphere, so the question of just when all that oh-so-modern glazing would crash down to the sidewalk generally got relegated to quiet interest instead of loud, jeering debate.

Tommy waited, shoulders propped against the damp brickwork, the cold seeping through his battered cotton jacket. Summer would be here before long. Another few weeks, and the wide, flat, desolate fields that islanded the city—or the nearest Havre was to one—would be drenched with gold. Funny, really. Tommy used to like driving past the vast expanses of wheat fields, with their muddy, muted colors and endless spaces. The way the sky came down so far it seemed to ripple through the stalks almost made it feel like flying. Then, on rare days of August sunshine and bright, cloudless beauty, the drab palette of spring and winter disappeared, shot through with such intensity of gold and such vivid blue sky.

Didn't feel that way now. That kind of space made him nervous, left him feeling vulnerable and exposed. Weird how things changed. Like the walls, he guessed. Tommy had hated them, to start with. After the first year, he stopped noticing them, and, somewhere a while after that, he realized he'd begun to depend on them. They marked life up. Kept things in, sure, but kept other shit out.

He shifted against the brickwork. Working on the ranch had helped. He supposed he'd have to look into what his mother had said about this place in Poplar. He probably didn't have a shot at it, and, even if he did, there wasn't a chance in hell he could hold that down. There'd be too much to fix up, too much expense in the move, not to mention the permissions he'd need from the parole board, and Brett would.... Tommy suppressed a shudder. Brett would blow his top. Nearly 250 miles. That figure held too much significance for them, completely ignoring the practical problems.

Anyway, Tommy didn't want to be that far away. Not again. Not after everything he'd already missed. Lila and Robbie, almost grown up, Katie and Atian soon to follow... he couldn't give that up, and he didn't see why Mei had even mentioned it.

Unless....

Tommy glanced up, hearing the Chevy's approach, and the world got a little cleaner. The truck pulled up, every crunch of the tires and creak of the gearbox familiar. Brett hopped out, crossing the lot to greet him with a smile and the brief, reflexive touch of his hand to Tommy's sleeve.

"Hey."

"Hi," Tommy said, darting in for a quick kiss and enjoying the look of surprise that flickered across Brett's face.

It amused him, in a strange kind of way. During visits, Brett had always been happy to touch him—happy to kiss him, even in a room full of people—yet he rarely went for public displays of affection these days. Strange, Tommy thought. Still, public was different to prison, wasn't it? The big, wide, real world.

"So," he asked, as they headed inside, "what's your good news?"

"Well, it's not so much *news*... just kinda positive, maybe. Elaine—y'know, the department head?—kinda hinted she might have a place on the team for me. Once I've chosen my specialty, fulfilled all the criteria, of course. So…. Yeah. I was pleased."

Brett grinned sheepishly. He walked close, the smell of his aftershave all spice and lemons in the dusky air. It filled up everything, though it occurred to Tommy he still didn't know what the damn stuff was called. He'd have to find out, for Christmas… birthdays. Stuff like that.

Do we even have an anniversary?

"Well, that's great," Tommy said, realizing he needed to respond. He frowned. "So, that'd mean what? You have to finish the internship and apply, or it'd be like a promotion?"

Brett leaned on the green leather-topped bar. "Just a Coke for me. I'm driving."

Tommy smiled. He remembered a time they'd both drive up to Beaver Creek Park or Fresno Reservoir every chance they got. Bottles of beer glinted in the sunlight, abandoned on the hood of the Chevy while they made out in the grass. All those hazy, lazy moments of stolen time, perfumed with Brett's skin and the weed Tommy used to smoke… all those little ways he'd had—those ways he'd *needed*—to push life back to the boundaries of his existence.

He ordered the Coke and a beer for himself. A soccer match played on the TV above the bar, reminding him of the posters on Robbie's wall.

"…so I'd still have to complete the internship first, but I'd have a good shot at it," Brett was saying. He'd evidently been explaining in great detail. "It's just a question of what I'm really planning for… long term, kinda thing."

Tommy felt churlish for not listening.

Long term. There it is again. Seems everybody thinks like that except me.

Brett sipped his Coke, and Tommy caught his expectant sideways glance.

He swallowed his mouthful of beer. "Ah-huh?"

"Yeah. Well, I gotta pick a specialism. So, either I stay with the hospital, or I can look at sports therapy, something like that, look at setting up my own practice in a few years…. There's a lot of, uh, options. What d'you think?"

Tommy paused, the bottle halfway to his lips. Somewhere in the tumble of those very earnest hazel eyes, he saw what Brett was really asking. His own practice could take him anywhere. There would be opportunities, markets to follow, and maybe it would be better suited to a bigger city. Like Bozeman. Perhaps even a totally different state. Tommy frowned.

"'Bout how many years are we talking?"

"Five. Ish."

"Oh."

Tommy nodded slowly. About the same time as his parole would finally be up, then. Coincidence? He doubted that. Brett was still watching him, his gaze tracking nervously over Tommy's face.

"So, you see my—well, it's not exactly a problem. I mean, I don't have to decide right now. There's plenty of time, but it's… open. Y'know?"

Tommy looked away, hearing Brett's words—all those perfect, dreamy plans—trip over him like ripples on a lake.

"Either way, it'd be more money... a lot more autonomy, if I work toward my own practice. I could look at getting a bigger apartment, uh, well... pretty soon, and...."

Brett trailed off, the note of hopeful optimism in his voice lingering in the stuffy air. Laughter echoed from further along the bar, winding around a cheesy country song.

"Mm," Tommy said. He swigged his beer, and couldn't remember the last time so many people had wanted different pieces of him.

When he'd been inside, something he'd loved best about Brett was the fact he never talked about "one day." Tommy had seen guys drive themselves half-crazy with thoughts like that, and plenty more with girlfriends—and a couple with boyfriends—who did it for them. A dangerous thing, because the more a man built a world like that in his head—some nice little single-story rancher, maybe, not too far out of town, with a view of Bear Paw and room for a dog in the yard—the harder it got to admit that it wasn't real. And the more you clung to a dream, the more life you squeezed out of it.

No, they hadn't done that. Brett had always focused on the future in terms of weeks and months, dripping the outside world in with little snippets of news and anecdotes. Things he'd done at work, stuff about the kids and Scott... discussion about current affairs. Brett had kept him anchored, kept him sane, and only now did Tommy start to understand how much it must have cost him and how hard he'd been clutching his own dreams.

He blinked, aware of Brett watching him, waiting. The air wavered a little between them, and the room felt closer than it had before. A tiny bead of Coke clung to Brett's barely parted lips, and Tommy wondered why he bothered fighting the urge to reach out a thumb and swipe it away. He wanted to... wanted to so much. Only, there were other people. Not many, but more than enough, and he found himself very aware of every look, every face, every glance. People, and the *noise* from the TV, and the color and movement, and all that shit that had never been a problem before. It wasn't a problem now, he told himself. It was fine.

Everything was fine.

"Good that you got time, though, right?" he said, glancing back down at the bar. "That you don't need to rush."

Tommy stared at the wood, lacquered with polish and spilled beer.

You fucking coward. After everything he's done for you, and you can't even give him this? Not even a promise?

Brett said nothing for a moment. Tommy thought he heard an intake of breath, but, when he looked up, Brett just smiled at him, loose and nonchalant.

"Wanna shoot some stick?"

"Sure." Tommy grinned, relieved. Maybe it'd be all right and not matter as much as he thought. *Maybe.* "You're goin' down, though."

Brett laughed, fingers teasing the top of his Coke bottle. "Only if I lose."

Tommy blinked, then beamed widely. "You're on."

As it turned out, Brett happened to be pretty damn good at pool. They agreed on best of five, and by the third game, Tommy knew he'd be beaten. It hardly mattered. They had the kind of loose, casual fun, speckled with laughter and unimportant banter, that they'd not had in so long. It felt like getting to know him all over again or, Tommy supposed, for the first time. Crazy, he told himself, because they'd already shared so much. All those visits, those golden, dust-dry hours, had needed to be filled with something. They'd talked about almost everything, and Tommy had learned the twists and turns of Brett's mind—stories from his childhood, his views on everything from movies to politics, his innermost fears and his favorite memories—and yet, in the bleak chill of day-to-day life, perhaps they barely knew each other at all.

He wondered, sometimes, if that was true: if anyone ever knew anybody at all.

Time wore on, and the bar filled up. The music grew louder, and the room bore in on Tommy. Too many sweaty bodies and sounds from unexpected places, and he knew Brett saw him flinch a couple of times.

"Guess you wanna collect your winnings, huh?" Tommy said, because he wasn't about to admit he'd started finding it all a little too hard to deal with.

Brett grinned. "If you're ready to pay up."

Tommy nodded, and, once they left the bar, he started to relax again. The cold air, though a shock after the warmth inside, refreshed him. Snow crunched underfoot, and Brett walked close enough for their shoulders to touch, leaning in toward him.

Sliding into the Chevy felt like going back in time, though Brett kept it tidier than Tommy ever had. No photos tacked up behind the gearstick, no pervasive smell of weed.

Tommy let his head drop back and dozed as Brett drove.

"Will you stay?" Brett asked, pulling into the parking lot by his building. "Tonight?"

Tommy nodded sleepily. He didn't really want to get out of the truck. He did so nonetheless and followed Brett inside. He flopped down on the faded green couch while Brett shucked off coat and boots and put the coffeemaker on as if from some semiautomatic habit.

Tommy listened to him clattering about, wondering if he did that every time he got home from work. Did he always want something to drink, or was it just the noise, or maybe even the smell, that he liked? It was just something else he didn't know, he realized, feeling more isolated with every second.

"You hear back from that construction firm in Kremlin?" Brett called from the kitchen.

Tommy winced, recalling Mei's interest in his job hunt.

"Yeah. I didn't get it."

"Aw." Brett's head appeared around the door. "Shit."

"I know. Overqualified, apparently. Bull."

"You said it."

Tommy shrugged and looked at the natural flame gas fire ahead of him. As yet unlit, it was set against a faux cobbled hearth that must, at some point, have been intended to give the impression of cottagey charm. Exactly why, in the otherwise bland, anonymous setting of the apartment, remained unclear.

"I, uh, did talk to Karen, though."

"Yeah? How is she? I didn't speak to her yet this week."

Brett sounded so cheerful that it seemed wrong to bring this up. Tommy bit his lip.

"Oh, they're all fine," he said, keeping his voice carefully casual. "She has this uncle, got a little place... small-scale ranch. Might have somethin', if I go talk to him."

"Well, that's great!"

Brett emerged from the kitchen, looking encouraging and pleased. Tommy hated to puncture his mood.

"Uh-huh. Only it's over in Poplar."

"Poplar?" Brett's mouth curled in disdain. "But—"

"If he offers it, I gotta.... It's work," Tommy said, a little more brusquely than he meant to.

You don't understand that. You never have, have you?

Brett frowned, apparently giving it serious consideration.

"All right.... How far is it?"

Tommy swallowed heavily. He'd been dreading this.

"'Bout two thirty, two fifty."

"No!" Brett's head whipped around, his eyes wide and startled, clear hazel stained gray-brown with alarm. "You can't! Not... not that far."

Tommy dropped his gaze, staring at his feet.

"It's work," he repeated, a stubborn mumble.

"Two hundred and fifty miles?"

"If I clear it with the PO. And if Bill offers it. I guess I'd be away for the best part of the week, come back weekends. We could—"

"Fuck...."

Tommy looked up, surprised. Brett had never just turned away from him before. Not that he remembered. Only now he was stalking across the room, into the kitchen… angrily throwing open the refrigerator door, muttering as he rummaged inside it, retrieving two beers. Tommy peeled himself off the couch and reluctantly followed.

Brett cracked the top off of one bottle, tossed the opener down on the counter, and stood the other bottle beside it. He swigged the beer and glared at Tommy as he swallowed.

"Two hundred and fifty miles?" he repeated, as if daring Tommy to justify it.

Tommy shook his head. "I haven't even said I'll go speak to him yet."

And I won't, if you don't want me to. He almost said it, but a flash of irritation stopped him, abrupt and violent. *No. How dare you? Who the fuck are you to say what I can and can't do?*

Brett didn't understand. He'd never have understood. Not then, and definitely not now.

And you didn't have to care about me. I never asked you to. Never asked you to do any of it. I told you. No chains. It's not… it wasn't my fault. It wasn't.

He wanted to say it out loud, but his mouth wouldn't move, loath to frame the lie, the excuse. Tommy shrugged, moving to pick up the beer from the counter. He felt Brett's gaze on him, a heated, angry challenge. He didn't want to fight. He just wanted Brett to understand… though, at the same time, Tommy yearned to have the argument. That realization worried him. He knew it wouldn't help, that spewing gall and bile at each other wouldn't relieve anything, and that Brett had done nothing to deserve it in any case, but he still felt himself angling for it, pawing the ground in anticipation of that first tilt, that first blow.

Brett sighed, long and low.

"Well… whatever. I guess you have a point. It's work, right? If nothin' else comes up. I know it's getting to you, not finding anything."

Tommy inclined his head. *I should be grateful. I should say, yeah, you're right. And he is. I ought to be happy about that.* He flipped the top off the beer bottle, the opener clattering back down on the counter where he dropped it.

"Ah-huh."

Brett said nothing. Tommy risked a glance up at him and burned at the look of throttled fury on Brett's face. He knew what keeping it locked up like that did to a person's insides.

C'mon, darlin'. Yell at me. Let it out.

Brett took another mouthful of beer, apparently staring at a thin crack on the wall. Tommy searched for something to say. It wouldn't be forever. And it *was* a job. It was all hypothetical too, until he actually spoke to the guy. The words wouldn't come. He swigged his beer, watching the anger dance on Brett's face until, eventually, he sighed again—short and terse this time—and it all seemed to slide away.

"I'm gonna go take a shower," Brett said mildly. "Wanna come too?"

Tommy couldn't deny him that. He didn't even have to nod his assent. He just followed on, like always.

They didn't speak. The hot water pummeled out inequalities and tensions until only the taint of hostility remained. Brett backed him against the tiles, his touch possessive, mouth demanding. Tommy closed his eyes and let the spray erode his resistance, his worries... his self-respect. Brett still got him hard as a rock, even now he was within arm's reach almost all the time. No visiting orders, no waits... no need to patrol that twilit boundary between waking and sleeping any more, to pace lonely dreams, islanded and adrift. Even so, the sensation of being so easily played, so carelessly owned, scared Tommy almost as much as it enthralled him.

What he'd always wanted—belonging so completely, being loved so fully that he could be swallowed up by it, not have to carry everything alone—he still wanted that, didn't he?

Yes.

Brett pinned his wrists against the shower wall, and Tommy groaned, flexing into another hard, unyielding kiss. Brett pulled away roughly and stared at him with a strange, confused mix of lust, anger and... regret? The water plastered his hair down, darkened it, and clumped his eyelashes together. A single droplet clung to his upper lip, beading heavily before it splashed down to his chin.

It reminded Tommy of that Coke Brett had drunk at the bar; how he'd teased and tempted and not quite said what he really meant, or what he really wanted. How Tommy had wished he could give up, give in, give Brett everything he was asking for, every plan and hope and optimistic little dream… and found that he couldn't.

One day. Maybe, yeah, just… not yet. Oh God, not yet. Please.

He leaned forward. Warm water and another kiss. His tongue swept through Brett's mouth like a storm. Brett broke away and shut off the shower, his cheeks flushed. Tommy glanced down at the evidence of their arousal, the last traces of soap still slicking Brett's body, and licked his lips.

"I believe I still owe you a little somethin' from that pool game. Wanna collect?"

Wordlessly, Brett climbed out of the shower, tossed Tommy one towel and knotted another around his waist. He padded into the bedroom, and Tommy knew he'd follow. He didn't need to think about it, didn't even need to notice the coolness of the floor under his feet or the air raising gooseflesh on his wet skin. Total cruise control as he traipsed meekly after Brett… like maybe he always would.

CHAPTER SIX

THE room stank. The wallpaper, thick with nicotine stains and splashes of fat up behind the cooker, seemed to taint the air a kind of grimy brown. Tommy poked his tongue out of the corner of his mouth, concentrating hard on pouring the boiling water into the cups. He held the kettle with both hands, sloshed only a little bit, but left lakes of water and half-dissolved, spilled coffee granules behind him as he placed both cups—together with a plate of toast—onto the plastic tray.

Outside, somewhere between the hazy, pale gray-blue line of the horizon and the washing that flapped on the clothesline, a tractor crossed the lower fields in slow, dependable lines. Their house was a small concrete-block building, one of four that had once held farm workers but got rented out for extra income these days. Small agricultural towns like Chinook usually felt the pinch before everybody else.

Tommy picked up the tray and held his breath as he walked. He didn't want to spill or drop anything. He climbed the stairs sideways, like a crab, the heat of the coffee cups making the tray bow a little in the center. Scott appeared to be awake. Their bedroom door stood ajar, and the bleeps and pings of his Game Boy cut through the quiet. The distant sounds of the tractor drifted through the open window. Tommy frowned. Early start. Scott would probably manage to beat his high score on *Sonic*, and he'd crow about that all day.

Nuts.

Tommy pushed open the door to his parents' room with his elbow. The curtains, still tightly drawn, gave the light a cozy, pinkish glow. The blue bedspread had daisies embroidered on it, great big ones with white petals and bright yellow centers raised up, rough to the touch. He took the tray round to his father's side of the bed and rested it against the nightstand, trying to find somewhere to put it among the clutter. Glass of water, piece of string, keys and coins and a beer mat with a phone number scrawled on it.... Tommy pushed the tray a little further on, biting his lip as the mess looked set to fall to the carpet.

"Mnn?"

Martin stirred beneath the covers. He peered out blearily, face saggy and crinkled, as if not set into shape for the day yet, his eyes bloodshot and narrowed against the light.

"I brought you breakfast, Daddy."

Martin sat up, running his tongue over his teeth as if something had crawled between them and died. A black T-shirt clung to his sleep-stained body, and he pushed his fingers through his greasy hair. Beside him, Mei began to wake.

Tommy waited nervously. His father surveyed the tray. The toast was cold now, and a little on the limp side, and the coffee had slopped over the sides of the cups despite Tommy's best efforts. Martin grinned.

"That's nice. Thanks, Tommy. C'mon... get yourself up here!"

He reached down and, with a playful growl, hauled Tommy up onto the bed by the elbows. Wrapping him up in a bear hug that smelled of cigarettes and sweat, Martin bussed the top of his son's head. Tommy beamed, laughed... settled himself into the groove between his parents. Mei, though she complained about them rocking the mattress, stroked his hair and let him feel where the baby was kicking. He guessed Scott would be in any minute, but he didn't show. And, Tommy realized, something wasn't right.

For a start, his feet were bigger than they ought to be. Big, scuffed brown work boots rested on the blue cotton covers, against the daisies and the toast crumbs. The room changed around him, insidious as smoke, and he could hear Martin's voice, altered and echoing.

Get up! Get up, ya little faggot! What the fuck you gonna do, huh? Fuckin' shoot me? Y'come down here with a fuckin' gun, Tommy... what'cha gonna do? Huh?

Tommy frowned. He wasn't on the bed anymore, but the scene around him hadn't properly changed. Embroidered daisies clung to the walls of the alleyway. Nicotine, coffee, and stale beer assaulted his nostrils alongside the stink of piss and vomit, but he couldn't see clearly, or move. He'd just started to think how strangely dreams twisted things when the first blow landed, and something heavy skittered across the brickwork, knocked from hands that weren't really his. He shut his eyes, but he could still see. He saw the brick wall, the rain glittering on the sidewalk, and the hands that reached for him, the dark eyes wide in panic, shock… surprise.

Ain't never thought you had it in you, kid.

Blood looked black in the darkness. Everything warped, as if it was trying to change, but the dream kept sucking at it, pulling it all out of shape. He fought, like he'd fought his whole damn life, and the blows didn't hurt anymore…. Tears came. Snot, blood, and salt stained his face, and the breath gulped in his throat. The shadows wrapped around him, choking the air away, blanketing the images. They swaddled the panic close to his skin… and left nothing but soft whispers in the dark.

"Tommy?"

"TOMMY!"

Brett groped blindly for the light switch, clicking on the bedside lamp. He squinted, the light's sudden flare sending his eyes shrinking and his head spinning. His stomach lurched with the wrench from sleep to wakefulness, and Tommy flailed out, fighting any attempts to calm him.

"Baby… it's okay. It's a dream. It's just a dream. C'mon… wake up!"

Brett dodged the hand that swung dangerously close to his nose with practiced ease, and caught Tommy's wrist. Tommy yelped. The contact brought him out of his troubled sleep much faster than it would once have done. He jerked away as if burned, flinching across the bed and staring wildly around the room. He seemed to see monsters in every shadow. Brett wanted to touch him, wipe away that frightened look, but he knew he had to give Tommy time to calm down, to realize where he'd woken up.

"You okay?"

Dark brown eyes, glassy with fear, sought his. Tommy raised a hand to his head, pushing back his damp hair. He glanced at his palm as he lowered it, and Brett wondered what he expected to see.

"I-I'm all right. Did I wake you?"

Brett shook his head. "Doesn't matter." He looked critically at Tommy and bit his lip. "They're gettin' worse, aren't they?"

Tommy looked at him for a moment before letting his gaze fall, and Brett knew he was lying when he said, "No. I'm all right."

He moved to get out of the bed, but Brett reached for him, catching his arm.

"Don't bullshit me. I *know* you."

Tommy glared at him. Brett admitted it had been a low blow.

"D'you wanna talk about it?"

Tommy shook his head, but shivered a little. He swung his legs back under the covers and burrowed down, punching the pillow savagely back into shape. Brett watched him, said nothing, and moved to turn off the lamp.

"Nn-nn," Tommy murmured. "Leave it? F'r a minute."

Brett sighed. "Tommy, you need to talk to someone about this. If not me, then—"

"I don't wanna go to any more shrinks."

He didn't move, his voice small but obstinate, like a child. Brett could see nothing of him below the bridge of his nose, wrapped up tight in the covers. His chest ached for the kid Tommy must have been, the past he should have had.

"You don't have to," Brett said, sliding down the pillows to Tommy's level, gently peeling back the covers to expose a little more of his face. "But.... Look. If it's about *him*, he can't... I mean, that's all over. Y'know? It's all right to—"

Brett stopped abruptly as Tommy's hand shot out from under the covers and clamped over his mouth. His palm was salty, hot, the gesture suggesting he'd heard more than he could stand. Brett wasn't sure what he'd said wrong. Tommy wriggled closer, pulling out of the cocoon he'd buried himself in. He frowned, his face near enough for Brett to smell his skin.

"It's not that," he whispered hoarsely. "I…. Oh, shit… I miss him, Brett. You understand?"

Tommy's hand moved down Brett's face, fingertips grazing his chin as he seemed to search for absolution in his eyes.

"After everything," he said, his voice thick, "I still wake up sometimes and, y'know, I… I don't remember why he ain't here, and… then I do. And it hurts. All of it hurts, and I…. It's hard to get it back under control. D'you see?"

Brett said nothing. Tommy had fallen to staring at his chest, frowning as he traced the pattern of moles on the skin, and as those long, trembling fingers scribed lines over his flesh, Brett wondered if you could hear your own heart crack.

"Is that why?" he managed after a minute. "The nightmares?"

"Sometimes," Tommy said quietly.

"Really?"

"Yeah. Sometimes… other stuff."

Brett swallowed, his tongue feeling rough against the inside of his mouth. "Wh-what stuff?"

Tommy's breath rolled over Brett's body as he sighed. "Just—"

"Stuff?"

"Hm. Yeah."

Brett pressed his lips together. *Fine.* He didn't need to know. He tried to dredge up a smile for Tommy, but it came out as a grimace, an ugly curl of his mouth. He pushed it quickly away and combed his fingers through the ends of Tommy's hair where it lay against his chest, grateful for something to concentrate on.

"So, what are we gonna do? Tell me. How do we fix it?"

Tommy loosed a bitter chuckle. "You can't always fix shit, Brett."

Brett shook his head, bending the black strands into a loop. Occasional split ends popped up, and he rubbed a thumb across them.

"You can try."

Tommy sniffed, the sound of uncried tears pushed back into the night, and cleared his throat.

"Uh. I… I dunno. I've been thinkin' about going to see him."

Brett frowned, looking up at Tommy, annoyed by the way he purposely averted his gaze, pretending to study the wall above the bed.

"What?"

"The… thing, I mean," Tommy muttered. "Highland Park."

Brett's frown deepened, but he said nothing.

"I wanna go up there. Always said I wouldn't, but I gotta… I think I *need* to see it."

"Sure."

Brett felt Tommy's hand slip from his shoulder, roving down across his back, fingers crooked, the slight roughness of those short, blunt nails tickling against his skin. He wished it wasn't so distracting… or that Tommy didn't think he needed to be distracted in the first place.

"Does that sound stupid?" Tommy asked, burrowing closer.

Brett shook his head, any reply stifled by the kiss Tommy pressed on him, soft and questioning.

"No," he said, as they parted. "Want me to come with you?"

"Please."

The word felt like little more than the expulsion of a ragged breath on Brett's mouth, barely audible where Tommy pressed tighter to him. Brett knew what he wanted: to forget, to be made to feel alive again, brought out of the dark and loved. Brett wished he could oblige, and that sex wasn't one of the last things on his mind right now. Every damn day seemed to push them further apart somehow.

Tommy started to nuzzle at his jaw, murmuring formless nothings that buzzed against Brett's skin.

"So… when d'you want to go?" he asked. "Might be quieter midweek. I could take a day off and—"

Tommy's muffled response sounded like "Wednesday." His hand tracked south, caressing the curve of Brett's ass lightly enough to make him rock back against the touch before he even knew he'd done it.

"You wanna go Wednesday?" he pursued doggedly, determined not to let Tommy get away with this.

"Nuh-uh. Seein' Myers Wednesday I said. An' you don't have to take time off for me."

Brett relented a little, reaching out beneath the covers to pull Tommy closer. Tight together, legs intertwined and the heat and the solidity of him pressed up so near and so tender…. He cradled the point of Tommy's hip in his palm. Always just something about him. Something about the way they fitted together and how irrefutably right it felt. Part of him was almost annoyed enough to hate it.

"I'll keep my weekend free, in that case," he said, a touch sarcastically.

Tommy smiled, but the traces of that horrible disquiet still clouded his eyes. "All right. Thanks."

Brett said nothing. He wrapped his arms around Tommy, kissed him, and let them both concentrate on the swelling desire between them. Brett reached down, took hold of their twin shafts and, pressing them together, stroked slowly in that sweet, hot, intimate embrace. He sighed as Tommy's long fingers wrapped around his, the only touch he'd ever really wanted. He rocked against him, deepened the kiss, enjoying the laziness of it… though Tommy didn't let it stay that way for long. Brett moved with him until hands and kisses became imperfect messengers between them, spiked with a deeper want. Tommy's forehead pressed against his own, mouths clung breathlessly together, open but no longer furnished with kisses. Eventually, a soft keening sound passed Tommy's lips and he came, staring into Brett's eyes, so close that neither of them could have seen much of the other, rather felt the proximity and the heat of it.

After, Brett held him tight, guarding against whatever demons stalked the shadows. When he could be sure Tommy had fallen asleep, he'd turn off the light, and maybe sneak to the bathroom to bust that nut he'd not quite made. Tommy began to snore gently. Peacefully, Brett noted. Nestled there like that, gilt and sable in the lamplight, he didn't look like anything could shake him.

He looked… right.

If only more things seemed that way.

HIGHLAND Park Cemetery lay on the northern side of town. Not far, but they'd set aside the best part of the day to make the trip up there. More from Brett's concern over how Tommy would take it than the time it would actually eat up, but he'd tried his best not to show that.

Mei had expressed doubts—in her usual veiled manner—over whether Tommy really ought to go up there. She'd given him the plot number, drawn an *x* on a roughed-out map of the blocks, and quietly asked Brett if this was his idea. He'd shrugged, just said Tommy wanted to go. To see it. She had turned tight-lipped and given him that coal-eyed glare she'd used on him for the first eight months or so of Tommy's imprisonment. Brett guessed Mei blamed him for an awful lot of Tommy's ideas, but he said nothing.

So they tramped through the blank, anonymous plots, crossed the wind-scoured ground and, finally, found it. Brett stood a little way from Tommy as they looked down in silence at the granite tablet, nestled in the coarse, yellow grass and spotted with cold rain. A bunch of white lilies lay beside it, deep pink tongues to their petals. He thought of Katie, drawing her pictures for Daddy, and realized they must have been here recently. Odd that Mei hadn't mentioned it… or not, he supposed. Raindrops drummed on the cellophane wrapping, sliding softly down the velvet blooms. Their sweet, buttery fragrance seemed to grow stronger, and Brett glanced surreptitiously at Tommy.

He saw the muscle twitch in his jaw, and knew better than to speak. In the pine trees, back behind the desolate expanse of the blocks, birds called. The hoarse, throaty sound of a raven, maybe… the Secret Keeper.

"I-I think I just need a minute."

Tommy turned and walked briskly away over the spongy ground, his shoulders hunched into the hardening rain. Brett sighed. He could do nothing but let him go, and that sucked. He stared at the grave, the stone still so clean, so shiny. Scott had once said to him that, whatever else Martin had been, it hadn't stopped him being their father. Yet it seemed strange—sick, almost—that he should rest here, the plot tended, fresh flowers left, with that bald, mocking inscription so crisply carved.

Martin Timothy Hawks. At peace. Loved, mourned, remembered.

Just the dates that bracketed his life and those eight words that churned Brett's gut. He'd never met the man, but he'd seen his shadow. That whole summer, the way he'd been falling for Tommy had blinded Brett to his imperfections, but he couldn't have failed to see the scars. He remembered that very first night they'd been together, up at Beaver Creek Park... so caught up in the rush of it that he'd hardly even noticed the place on Tommy's side that marked those broken ribs. Worse, that he'd let him lie so obviously about it.

I was thirteen. I just fell.

He should have known he was being bullshitted even then. Maybe he had.

Brett glared one last time at the memorial. The wind whipped around his ankles, snaking low to the ground.

"Bastard," he muttered, leaving the graveside to head off back down the cinder track in search of Tommy.

He'd walked almost as far as the cemetery office. Brett found him by the pallid, slightly pathetic flowerbed that marked the midpoint between the west and east blocks. The paths had been arranged around the circular bed in a diagonal cross, probably someone's attempt at landscaping. It didn't work that well. The ground's gently rolling, windswept contours were far too bleak, and they sapped the colors from the flowers. Tommy stood on the far side, hunched in on himself, hands shoved deep in his pockets and his face that blank, expressionless mask that Brett had gotten so damn tired of seeing.

"You all right?" he asked.

Tommy glanced up, as if he really hadn't heard Brett's approach. His mouth twitched, somewhere between assent and denial. *Great. He's gonna be real fun for the rest of today.*

Brett caught the thought in midsneak. Well, what the hell else had he expected? He moved closer to Tommy, as nonchalant as he knew how to be, trying to catch a glimpse of something—anything—in his eyes.

"So... what? You wanna go back into town? Get somethin' to eat?"

"I'm not hungry."

At least Tommy had responded.

"Okay. Well, how about we—"

"You know, you don't have to run after me every five minutes to wipe my nose and hold my hand, Brett."

The words stung. Brett backed off, aware of the heat flushing his face.

"No," he said, determined to avoid rising to the bait. "I just...."

Tommy scowled at him, thick brows drawn low, eyes narrowed where the rain swiped at him. His hair, tucked into the collar of his coat, had started to frizz in the damp.

"Just what?"

Brett blinked rapidly. He hadn't heard Tommy get so bitchy since waiting for his parole hearing. But—like he always had—Brett swallowed the first angry response, resolving not to have the argument, because that's not what you did. You had to be supportive, patient... understanding.

"I worry about you," he said. "You know I do. I mean, this has all gotta be really difficul—"

"It don't mean you gotta treat me like a fucking kid."

Brett winced. "I didn't realize I had... I'm sorry," he said, though he heard himself sounding wooden, his voice without emphasis.

"Oh, for God's sake!" Tommy snapped. "Don't you dare start apologizing. Don't do that."

The wind started to get stronger, cruel gusts that ripped through the trees, rain eddying in their wake. Brett shifted uncomfortably, feeling stripped and vulnerable in the face of Tommy's sudden viciousness.

"You never fight back, do ya?" Tommy spat suddenly. It seemed impossible that his face, twisted now with something horribly like rage, could ever have looked blank.

"What?"

Brett shook his head, confused, which apparently only served to make Tommy angrier.

"You don't! You're so… *nice*. Always trying to make allowances for me, understand what I'm goin' through. Well, you could understand a guy to death, you know that?"

Brett stared. This wasn't Tommy. This creature—with blazing eyes, bitter mouth, and spiteful tongue—wasn't going to goad him into anything. Unfortunately, the blush of humiliation and anger already burned on his cheeks, and it threatened to carry him away on its tide.

"Yeah? Well, I'm sorry for tryin' to help you, then! I'm sorry for stickin' with you, and—"

"Oh, right… here it comes! 'Cause I gotta be reminded about all of that, huh? Can't possibly forget what you've done for me, can I, Brett? All your sacrifices and your fucking charity!"

Brett's fury rooted him to the spot when he knew he should have turned and walked away, left all this alone.

"You didn't have to damn well take it!" he yelled. "I only ever wanted to help you, but if you didn't want—"

"I didn't wanna be your damn project!"

Brett curled his lip. Surely nobody could be so stupid, so completely *blind*…. The rain needled his cheeks, and he tried to formulate some suitably brutal response, wanting to lash out and shock Tommy into shutting up. Nothing came.

"I didn't wanna be your lost cause," Tommy said, his voice dropping but still shrouded in the heat of that horrible anger.

"You never were!" Brett snapped, wanting to shake this ridiculous self-pity out of him. Tommy never used to reason this way, never used to think like this. "I'd'a done anything for you! You were... strong and... and amazing, Tommy, and I'd've moved the world for you." The blush deepened with words Brett never intended saying aloud. He saw the pained look on Tommy's face, and it only aggravated him further. "But you know what? You won't even move an inch. You've changed! You've changed so fuckin' much!"

He saw Tommy blanch as he said it, but the words couldn't be snatched back out of the air, spooled in like miscast fishing line. They weren't even completely true. Sure, Tommy *had* changed, but not in the ways that mattered. He was still the same person. He had the same strength, the same capacities for kindness, empathy, humor... *oh, God, I didn't mean it. I didn't....*

Tommy's mouth tightened, and he rallied bitterly, the wind blowing his hair across his face.

"I had reason, Brett! Not everybody lives in your world, y'know. Not everybody—"

"Oh, don't be such a fucking martyr!"

Tommy flicked his head, the hair whipping back from his forehead, and his eyes blazed with something not unlike the desire to land a punch on Brett.

Come on. Just you try it, sweetheart. Just you damn well try it....

He took a step forward. Less than two feet separated them, but Brett stood his ground.

"Yeah? What you gonna do, Tommy?"

Tommy stared at him, his mouth twisted and his eyes wide and so dark, as if something was trying to claw its way out from behind them. Brett met him inch for inch and wondered, in some flash of sick curiosity, what would happen if Tommy *did* hit him. Would he punch back? That day at Fresno Reservoir, when he'd found Tommy on the shore, battered, bewildered and terrified... they'd fought then. Blows and bloodied noses until Tommy had folded against him, shaking and sweating. Until he'd begged to be forgiven.

Tommy shook his head. "You know what?" he rasped, pushing back on his front foot, pushing away from the fight. "Sometimes it feels like I'm sleeping with fucking Gandhi!"

That did it. Brett pulled the Chevy's keys from his pocket and hurled them, too mad to aim straight. They collided with Tommy's chest more by luck than judgment, bounced, and jangled to the ground.

"Forget it, Tommy. Fix it your fucking self!"

He turned on his heel and stalked away, back toward the office and into the teeth of the wind, furious and ashamed. What had he wanted out of that? Blood? No…. He'd had enough of this, of biting down on every comeback, every complaint, and enough of putting up with Tommy's moods, tensions, and problems. Brett had never had to do any of this, and he didn't owe anybody a damn thing.

And… he would have to find some other way of getting home.

Aw, hell.

TOMMY stared at the keys lying on the gritty black path.

What the fuck did I just do?

Same as always, he supposed: wrecked it. If everybody could be born with one special gift, one innate ability, his would involve hurting people… he'd definitely got too damn good at hurting Brett. He'd never seen him look so mad. Only, a lot of it had been true. Brett's understanding—that terrible depth of heavy, cloying sympathy that felt like being buried alive—could be hard to take. Everywhere Tommy turned, he found new allowances being made for him, new excuses. Every time he opened a drawer at Brett's place, there would be new clothes in his size, still in their wrappers. Spare toothbrush and razorblades, soap and shampoo in the bathroom, packets of Stone Trapper Frybread Mix in the kitchen cupboard, and damn it, he never had to ask. Never had to say a word.

Things just appeared, and life went on, carrying him with it to uncharted, frightening places. And Brett still made it all okay, because being with him—when Tommy dropped all the baggage and just let

Brett hold him safe from the sharp edges of the night—was the only thing that mattered.

Ungrateful little bastard.

Tommy shook his head, pushing away the thought, the... voice. Only memories, nothing else. He fought the urge to turn and look back behind him. No more. He just wanted to leave this place. He seemed to flow back into himself, taut and awakened. He realized what he'd said as if he remembered it through some sleeping haze.

He'd have run after Brett, but he'd already passed out of sight. And in any case, however much it pissed Tommy off, he knew Brett would understand. Once he'd had time to calm down, he'd understand the spiteful words, the whole stupid fight, and, if Tommy knew him at all, he'd probably even forgive it.

That stopped Tommy from going after him.

He bent, scooping up his keys. He'd had the Chevy since his seventeenth birthday. His grandmother's last present to him: she'd passed away that winter. She'd made the little red dream catcher that dangled from the key ring too, woven with care and generations of tradition. He'd asked Brett to sell the truck when he knew he'd be taking the plea bargain... hadn't known, until he 'fessed up, that he'd sold his Bronco and bought the damn thing himself. He'd taken such good care of it, kept it running so sweet, and it had been such a beautiful gesture... like so much Brett did.

No wonder finding a way to ask him to stop seemed so damn hard.

Tommy exhaled tersely, tipped his head back, and let the rain run down his face. *Shit.* He'd been a complete asshole. He knew it, but he couldn't summon up the energy to feel guilty about it. Not yet. Let it keep him awake later.

He wiped a hand over his eyes, the rainwater stinging a little. He weighed the keys in his palm and started the walk back to the Chevy. Thunder began to rumble in the distance, maybe... what? Ten, fifteen miles away, probably. It would turn into a real rainstorm before long.

It annoyed him that his first thought concerned finding Brett and making sure he didn't get caught in it. Tommy swore under his breath. If only he could get the damn picture of his father's memorial out of his head, maybe he'd have a chance at staying mad. Everything was so… sliced up right now. Like there wasn't anything to him but a bundle of nerves someone had folded double and cut in half, leaving all the ends open, fraying in the elements. He wanted Brett—the way he held the world together—and that pissed him off, as if it represented every weakness, every failing he had.

Picking fights isn't gonna make you stop needing him.

Tommy had thought—hoped—he'd take it better than this. That seeing the stone, there in the grass, wouldn't be so bad. He'd had six years to get ready. Plenty of time to adjust, plenty of time to accept what had happened… what he'd done. He got through it with his mom by not talking about it; but then, hadn't that always been how she coped? Robbie and Lila had been—if not too young to understand—too young not to adapt. Tommy knew they'd had plenty of contact with the court-appointed therapist, the social workers, and they'd come out of it well, hadn't they? They'd seemed to, so maybe you couldn't ask for more than that.

He knew what Scott thought. Scott had never believed he didn't remember it—that he still didn't, not fully—and he'd always been convinced that Tommy had known exactly what he'd been doing that night, when he took the Western Field rifle from the unlocked gun cabinet and drove down to Deacon's Bar. Tommy could see it in his eyes, that sneaking distrust tinged with respect. With the wish, maybe, that Scott had found the balls to do it himself.

Tommy sniffed. Thunder broke against the sky again, louder now, lightning an almost instantaneous, metallic flash. He flinched, not knowing why… he'd never been scared of storms. Quite the opposite, in fact. Tommy shook himself and headed back toward the Chevy, mystified by the way his pace quickened, his breath heaved in his chest.

Brett stood by the truck, leaning against the dark brown paintwork, his arms crossed. Rain dripped off the end of his nose. He glanced impassively at Tommy.

"It's wet," he said, by way of explanation. "I need a ride."

"Yeah."

Tommy unlocked the Chevy, and they climbed in, shucking their coats. He turned on the heater, sneaking a look at Brett's stony expression. *Fuck, I'm an idiot*.... He cleared his throat.

"I shouldn't have said that shit. I'm sorry."

"Sure."

Tommy inhaled slowly. All right, he deserved that. He pulled out of the rapidly muddying lot and nosed the Chevy back onto the road, more than happy to leave the cemetery behind them. He just wished he could get it out of his head.

"Brett—"

"Forget it."

His words sounded stilted, and Tommy half expected them to descend into another argument. His pulse hammered at the thought that, if that happened, he wouldn't be able to stop himself... to stop all that hateful, bitter invective. It would have helped if he'd known where it came from. The sky split again, a rolling boom of thunder tolling through the sheeting rain. Tommy's breath caught in his throat, and he could have sworn he felt Brett's gaze on him, featherlight and warm on his skin.

Tommy glanced over at him, but Brett looked quickly away.

He said nothing and drove on.

CHAPTER SEVEN

TOMMY parked the Chevy at Brett's place. He waited after he shut the engine off, hands on the wheel, staring out the windshield. The rain started to ease; maybe there wouldn't be a storm after all.

Brett held out his hand, palm up.

"Can I have the keys?"

Tommy blinked. "Uh. Sure."

"Thanks. I was gonna say, soon as I get a new car, it'd only be right for you to have the Chevy back. I mean, it's always been yours, however you look at it."

Tommy wasn't sure how to respond. He glanced at Brett, but he seemed so impassive, so taut.

"I…. Thanks."

"Sure. Don't… don't come around for a while, though, huh?"

The world splintered silently around Tommy.

"Uh…?"

Brett sniffed, cleared his throat, and sounded so horribly, darkly stilted.

"You're probably right. I think we should take a break. Take some… time."

It hurt. A tearing, throbbing physical wound, right through the middle of his chest. Tommy wasn't sure what to say, or how to speak around the tightness in his throat, so he just nodded, and followed Brett's lead as they got out of the truck.

"Brett—"

"Just a while," he said flatly. "You need it. I need it. Just some space. Let us both clear our heads a little bit, yeah? That's all."

Tommy stood and stared at the asphalt. He didn't have anything to say to that. It didn't feel real. It was probably a good idea, but... it still felt like the world was slipping out from under him.

Brett locked the Chevy and—with one brief, weak smile flashed in Tommy's vague direction—he turned and crossed the lot, never once turning to look back. He'd almost reached the front door when Tommy saw him raise a hand, as if he was wiping the rainwater from his face.

Then he was gone.

Tommy hunched his shoulders and started to walk. There didn't seem to be much else worth doing. It should have been hard to believe he'd been so stupid, but somehow it just felt pretty standard. He headed north, cutting up by Rotary Park, oblivious to the whisking of cars on the wet road until a flatbed Ford sluiced to a standstill beside him, spraying muddy water over the patch of sidewalk that Tommy vacated just in time.

He looked up, still a little dislocated from the real world. The rain seemed to pull the sky down with it, crushing in on the buildings and the bare, gray street. A familiar face leered out of the Ford's window, and Tommy's heart sank. Lane Harding. Almost the last person he wanted to see right now. Just another reminder of the past, and all the things he couldn't leave behind.

It didn't help that the guy was an asshole either.

"Hey! You need a ride?"

Lane popped open the passenger door. Tommy groped uselessly for some believable refusal, but the rain pelted down ever harder, and he knew he couldn't back off without causing offense.

"C'mon! Where you headed?"

Tommy hesitated. He still kinda wanted to go back to Brett's and sit outside his door until they could talk all this awkward crap out, but he didn't know where to start, and anyway, Brett didn't... want him to.

Not for a while, apparently.

Words shouldn't carve holes in people. That wasn't how they were meant to work. Tommy wiped the rain off his face with the sleeve of his jacket and swung up into the Ford.

"Where you going?"

"Ha! I like your style, man…. I gotta go by West Havre, see this fucker owes me some money, and then I'm headed over to Sands. Party going on. You in?"

Tommy shrugged. "Sure."

"All right."

Lane kicked the Ford back into gear. He shot Tommy a quizzical look as the wipers squeaked their way across the windshield, smearing the view of the road ahead.

"So, what you doin' this end of town? Ohhh…. I know. You still make a habit of bangin' white tail, don't'cha, Chocolate?"

Tommy narrowed his eyes. He'd never appreciated that nickname—better than "fudge-packer," admittedly—but hearing it, and hearing Brett referred to like that, made his knuckles itch. Stupid, he realized, though he wasn't about to try and rationalize it.

"I get by," he said vaguely. "'Least I'm gettin' some."

Tommy would have liked to ignore him completely, but he knew better than to turn his back on a man—body or speech—unless he wanted to pick a fight. Lane laughed, and it sounded tight-wound and shallow.

"Yeah? Right…. I swear, when I first got out, my girl didn't walk straight for a week. And she's some fuckin' wildcat. You oughta get yourself a piece of pussy like that. Get you fixed right up."

"Uh-huh."

Tommy glanced out of the window. He should just have walked back to Mei's, found some excuse, some reason not to be here. Lane had been good to him inside—to a certain standard—because they shared tribal blood, but that didn't mean Tommy owed him anything now. He'd paid his debts, and he thought he'd made it clear back in Deer Lodge that he didn't intend to stay a part of that world. Somehow, he could smell the grit of the exercise yard and hear the shouts echoing in his ears.

The Ford rumbled along Old Post Road, the cornfields that planed away into the distance nothing but smudges of green and brown in the dampness of the spring rain.

"You know what?" Tommy said, taking a chance on Lane being in a good mood. "You could let me out here. I can walk. I oughta get… home. Y'know."

"In this mess?" Lane raised his eyebrows. "Nah. Anyways, I want you first."

Tommy blinked. That didn't sound good. He said nothing as Lane ramped the Ford off the main drag, into one of the little residential pockets that huddled away from Havre's heart. An early dusk slipped through the fingers of rain, and the wind howled in the distance, swallowing the echoes of the storm. Lane parked beneath a broken streetlight. Tommy glanced nervously out at the dusty, paling road, still grappling for something to say.

Lane grinned at him, turned up the collar of his jacket, and popped the truck's door. He hopped out, that curious fixed stare in his dark eyes and an unpleasant curl to his mouth. Lane reached under the driver's seat and pulled out a baseball bat with a red grip tape wrapped around the handle.

Oh, fuck.

"C'mon, Chocolate."

Tommy knew he should have stayed on the sidewalk and just got wet, major diss or no major diss. This *really* wasn't going to be a good idea.

"Uh, I don't—"

"Hey! Come on."

Tommy exhaled sharply. He'd seen the look in Lane's eyes before, the kind of look that led to fists under ribs and whispered threats in the darkness. People like him could be dangerous, unless you managed them right. He slid out of the Ford and followed Lane through the unlit street. Few houses lined it. Chain-link fences shone in the wet, and a derelict building that might once have been a small store stood on the corner.

Lane whistled cheerfully, the sound cutting through the grainy dusk, and swung the baseball bat in his hand. Tommy chewed his bottom lip, wondering how the hell to get out of this one. Prison society had its own rules, its special dispensations. Lane's boys had hung on the edges of the officially sanctioned groups that were there to support Indian inmates—the circle, and the lodge, all that stuff the tribal councils and welfare groups had fought so hard to get established—and they'd always been just the right side of really being called a gang. Lane himself had never claimed affiliation to any well-known crew, like a lot of would-be bangers, and Tommy had found that reassuring, at the time. He didn't puff up his reputation, or brag incessantly about what he'd done, or not done, or what he was carrying. Sure, he talked the talk, walked the walk, but he'd never seemed like a bad guy.

Tommy remembered the waking hell of his first weeks at Deer Lodge—albeit kinda patchily, because he'd gone pretty much without sleep—and how Lane and his boys had taken care of him. Made sure he wasn't left alone and vulnerable, dealt with the kinds of problems that could face new guys on the unit.

See? That's how we deal with fuckers like that. Your turn, man. One good fuckin' punch, right?

He pushed the thoughts away. No. Between Lane's boys and Roberto, one of the comparatively few other openly gay inmates who—at six five and 240 pounds—rarely got messed with, he'd been lucky. He'd had friends who had his back. The talking circle had been good to him too. He still had his copy of *The Sacred Tree*, that dumbass pamphlet that got handed around, and which a lot of the guys publicly dismissed as bull but sat up and read in their rooms, all the same. It talked about learning how to change things, how to focus your own will on making your life—and other people's—a little better.

It had helped Tommy believe there could be something clean and new at the end of everything. That maybe he could manage to come out of this and not be trapped. Not forever. He quickened his pace, catching up with Lane as he turned toward a small, low duplex with an overgrown tangle of weeds scrambling across the stoop. The sound of a

TV—the squealing tires and blazing gunfire of some action movie—trickled through an open first-floor window.

"So, uh, what's this about? Huh?"

"Told ya." Lane flashed him a look of irritation. "Fucker owes me money. Told me I could come by and collect it."

"Ah-huh." Tommy wondered how stupid Lane really thought him. "And the bat?"

Lane's expression hardened. Tommy knew he trod dangerous ground, pushing him like this, but he slipped between Lane and the duplex, keeping steady contact with those dark, fierce eyes. Lane curled his lip, and the chuckle that he loosed sounded almost friendly.

"Aw, Chocolate… c'mon, man. I ain't gonna *need* it. S'fate I came across you, right? I think we both know how useful you are with those hands of yours…."

Tommy said nothing. Lane pushed past him, buffeting his shoulder, and rapped on the front door with the head of the bat. Tommy closed his eyes. Not good. Very, very not good. All right, so there wasn't anybody around in the street, but who knew who'd seen them here? Roberto had always told him to stay the hell away from Lane. He'd said the guy was crazy. Tommy wished he'd listened.

"Lane?"

He turned, looking desperately up at that open window and then down at Lane. He'd begun humming under his breath, shifting his weight from foot to foot as he waited. From inside, more TV gunfire echoed. Tommy winced.

"Look, Lane…. I'm not down for this, okay?"

The bat swung around before Lane did, and it wavered under Tommy's nose.

"You wussin' out on me? You a warrior or not?"

"Not. And neither are you." Tommy winced, aware that wasn't the smartest thing he could have said. "This is—" He caught the bat as Lane opened for another swing. The wood smacked hard against his palm, jarring his wrist. "Shit! Listen, just leave me out of it, all right? I'm not your soldier."

He held the bat tight around the shaft, feeling the resistance of Lane's weight behind it. Tommy had an inch or so in height and maybe even a couple of pounds on him, but Lane had enough pent-up aggression and energy for it not to matter.

"Fuckin' thinblood fag," he muttered, jerking the bat roughly away.

Tommy clenched his fist and bit down on the pain in his hand and wrist. He backed slowly away and shook his head.

"Sorry, man."

Lane scowled but said nothing. Tommy kept moving, steady and without panic, and Lane stared after him, watching him right until he got far enough back down the street to turn and run. And Tommy ran as hard as he could, feet slipping on the damp sidewalk and cold sweat sliding down his back, until he wanted to stop and puke.

He hauled in somewhere around Rand Avenue, bent double, his chest heaving and his stomach tight, his pulse a staccato of panic. He shouldn't have done that. He'd made an enemy out of Lane Harding, for sure, and it would come back not only to bite him in the ass, but probably kick him in the head and steal his wallet. Not to mention Lane knew where Mei lived. All right, so he could have found out easily enough even if he didn't know, but the kids....

Oh, fuck. Fuck! What am I gonna tell 'em? How can I...?

Tommy fumbled for his cell phone. Not Brett. Brett didn't wanna see him, and Brett had an extremely good point. He was trouble. He attracted it like flies on shit, and he didn't deserve half the chances he got in life.

Pick up, pick up… pick up the fucking phone….

"Scott?"

"Tommy?"

His brother's voice sounded tinny against the background noise of the auto shop. Tommy wiped his nose on the back of his hand. The run had got him out of breath, sweating and streaming. His wrist throbbed dully, and he flexed his fingers as he tried to find the right words.

"Uh, I really need a ride. I-I'm stuck. Can you come get me?"

"What?" Scott sighed tersely. "Oh, for.... How old are you? Like, fifteen? Christ, Tommy...."

"Please. I, uh, I think I may have screwed up."

A pause on the line, then Scott swore under his breath.

"All right."

"Thank you. I'm, uh...." Tommy squinted up and down the road. "Can you pick me up at Sands Memorial Foundation?"

"What the fuck are you doin' there?"

"I told ya. I'm stuck."

"Can't Brett come get you?"

Tommy winced and stared up at the rumbling clouds.

"Like I said, I may have comprehensively fucked up."

RAIN flowed in seamless sheets down the glass. Brett linked his hands behind his neck and exhaled slowly.

I don't need this.

He stared gloomily at the wet, muted view. Summer would come soon. All this water had to be good for the plants. It was the deluge necessary to flush new life back into things. Only... sneaking thoughts came slithering, wheedling back, soothing and stroking at the worst parts of his brain. They sidled up to all the jealous, selfish impulses and curled around them.

I don't need this in my life.

Why should he keep making allowance, making apologies, excuses? Out of love? *Has that been what all these years have been about? Or have I just been scared?* Brett looked back and saw himself hiding behind every tie, every bond he'd made. The rain whipped against the glass, blurring his reflection. True, he'd loved Tommy—oh, still loved him, like he always damn well would—but maybe he wasn't prepared to keep on doing it at the expense of his own life.

No... that's not true.

Brett put a hand to the window frame. He couldn't even see the mountains now. It *wasn't* true. He'd had college, his own set of friends that had nothing to do with Tommy or his family. He had his work.

And even that I'm holding my breath on, waiting for him to make a decision.

Brett cursed under his breath and thumped the window frame, the dull ache it raised in his palm somehow satisfying. Tommy wormed his way into everything, whether he knew it or not, and maybe a love like that weakened what it touched, eroded even the strongest foundations. He should never have asked about Bozeman. He should've known then they weren't ready, that Tommy couldn't give him what he wanted.

That night at the bar, all Brett had hoped for was a word, an affirmation that yes, one day there'd be something sane and normal. *One day.* Tommy couldn't even do that.

Brett stuck his hand into his pocket and pulled out his— Tommy's—keys. He tossed them onto the counter, next to another, simpler fob. Just two keys on a steel ring. They should have been for Tommy: his own keys to the apartment, so he could come and go as he pleased and maybe even feel safe enough to not leave so often. But, given what had passed between them at the cemetery, Brett had felt in no mood to share.

It's like sleeping with fucking Gandhi.

It hadn't been Tommy talking. It had been the ugliness of the place, the day… the stress of it all. Brett *knew* there'd be tough weeks. He'd been ready for that. He wasn't afraid of it, or so he kept telling himself. All the same, old thoughts returned to plague him. Thoughts he'd managed to keep locked down, vanquished for the longest time, not counting the sweaty, sleepless nights before the parole hearing.

What if it's not enough? What if I've waited for this—waited and prayed and hoped—and it isn't enough?

Sure, he'd coped with Tommy being inside. Their relationship had slotted neatly into boxes, with calls, letters, and visits. Eternal waiting, endless banking on that perfect "one day" that he wasn't allowed to talk about. But what if he couldn't handle this new reality, the messy, uncontrolled explosion of it all? Love had never been easy from a distance, but what if, close up, it shriveled and died?

Brett shook himself and lurched to the bathroom, trying to peel his thoughts off along with his clothes. He couldn't go off the deep end like this every time they had a stupid fight. That stuff happened; people got mad and said things they didn't mean... everybody did. Things with a grain of truth in them, usually. Being close to someone meant being on the front line, and that couldn't be helped.

Part of him wanted to just call Tommy, get it over with and patch up the cracks again, but that was why Brett had sent him away. Patching up wasn't good enough. Not anymore. However much he wanted to help Tommy, to keep supporting and understanding and giving until he'd dug so deep inside himself he'd hollowed out his entire soul, Brett couldn't. And maybe Tommy had a point.

Maybe he'd been trying too hard.

SCOTT didn't look happy. His grease-smeared coveralls reeked of the auto shop—Tommy knew he'd been pulling weekend overtime fixing up a vintage Lincoln for his boss's mother—and the tiredness showed in his face.

"Christ, Tommy...."

"I know."

Tommy stared glumly at his hands. Scott had picked him up, albeit with a lack of grace, and headed without question back to his place rather than Mei's or Brett's. Glad of that, Tommy hadn't argued. He'd explained what had happened, leaving out the choicer parts of his fight with Brett at the cemetery and some elements of the encounter with Lane.

But Scott still knew him far too well.

"I didn't mean to get... involved," Tommy said. He sniffed and picked at his thumbnail. "I wasn't. Not really."

"And he went nutso on this guy with a baseball bat?"

Tommy looked up sharply at his brother. "I didn't see him do that. He prob'ly just went home."

Scott snorted incredulously.

"Well, he *coulda*," Tommy protested. "Nobody answered the door."

"And you left?"

Ran away, you pathetic little shit. That's what you did.

Tommy blinked. "Uh-huh. Told ya, I wasn't down for anything like that."

"Huh." Scott shook his head. "You're a fucking idiot. You know that?"

Tommy turned away and looked out of the window. Scott headed the beat-up Toyota he drove—rebuilt numerous times from the engine up and, he said, intended for Karen to use as a runabout when she finally got her license—on up toward the tiny house on the east side of town he shared with his wife and son. The buildings all looked lumpy and misshapen in the early dark.

Scott eased the Toyota into his roadside parking spot.

"You just better pray he didn't do anything stupid," he said shortly. "Broad fuckin' daylight, man! And I don't want you bringing this crap under my roof either. You understand?"

Tommy nodded. A light shone in the house, its low, gabled porch a bright, clean white that almost glowed in the dark, stark against the drab olive siding. Thick drapes hung at the front window. The light bled around them, oozing warmth into the street.

"You called me 'cause you were stuck. Fine. I asked if you wanted to come back to ours for dinner. You said yeah. You never told me where you'd been, what you'd been doin', or who you were with today. I don't know. And you're not gonna tell Karen."

It wasn't a request for complicity, but a statement. Conversations with Scott often ran that way. Tommy just nodded again.

"Sure."

"Good." Scott stared at the wheel for a moment, then exhaled. "All right. So, you hungry?"

"Yeah," Tommy said, without much emphasis.

He followed Scott inside. It wasn't that late—still before eight—and they found Karen sitting on the floor in the living room, playing

Hungry Hungry Hippos with Atian. He leapt up when he saw Scott, and flung himself on his father in a mess of plastic balls and gleeful shrieks. Karen got up slowly, her lips pressed together as she concentrated on balancing her short, dumpy frame—she'd never been svelte, but the excess weight she'd put on in pregnancy still hung from her midriff and thighs—and dusted her hands off against the knees of her pink sweatpants.

"Tommy." She nodded at him and frowned slightly. "Scott didn't say you were coming."

She kept the place nice, Tommy realized. The floors were spotless, everything tidy and neat. The black leather couch he knew to be her pride and joy, bought on credit in a Christmas sale, didn't have a scratch on it. Even Atian's toys all had plastic storage crates to live in. He dredged up a smile.

"Mm-nn. I kinda got stuck. If it's a problem…."

Karen shook her head. She crossed the room with her customary soft, shuffling gait and took him by the elbow. It surprised Tommy. Karen wasn't usually a touchy-feely person, least of all with him. Not that they disliked each other—rather that they nursed a cordial kind of mutual neutrality—yet she seemed genuinely concerned.

"You got caught out in all that rain," she observed, touching his jacket. "Why don't you take a shower? There's plenty of hot water. Dinner won't be long. You eat with us, yeah?"

"Uh… thanks, Karen."

Tommy glanced over at Scott. He'd knelt down on the floor with Atian. The boy was tracing his fingers over the appliquéd badge on Scott's coveralls, naming the letters.

Karen nodded again, apparently satisfied, and headed toward the kitchen. A thought appeared to strike her before she got there.

"You want to stay tonight?"

"Oh…. Well, I—"

"It's not a problem," Scott put in, from his crouched position. "You can, if you wanna."

The pressure of their kindness welled up on Tommy, thick and syrupy, like artificially flavored coffee.

"Thanks," he murmured.

He didn't understand why there should be all of this.

Why now? In the last few months before it all blew up, when things were at the worst they'd ever been, Tommy had needed help. With Mei in the hospital after a car accident, he'd been left solely responsible for the kids, and for Martin, so hazed with drink and painkillers that he'd barely known what day it was. Tommy had asked for help then and got nothing. Scott had left home that summer, throwing Karen's pregnancy at them like an excuse, a barrier, and Tommy was.... He frowned. Jealous?

He watched Karen shepherd Atian through to the bathroom for teeth cleaning, a quick bath, and pajamas, signaling to him it would be free in a few minutes, and it hit him hard. Yeah, jealous just about summed it up. And it still hurt.

This cozy, domestic warmth, isolated and protected. What he'd have given for that... to have chosen it like Scott had, to have fought for it and to have *won*. It left a bitter taste in Tommy's mouth. He realized Scott had spoken to him, and glanced round uneasily, sure he must have missed something important. The bathroom door shut behind Karen and Atian.

"You even listening?" Scott demanded, though not unkindly.

Tommy guessed he must have looked blank, because Scott gave a dry chuckle.

"See? That's what I mean. Even *I* can see it, Tommy."

"See what?"

Scott sighed and shook his head. "You're not really back, are you? I-I know it's gonna take time, it's gonna be tough, but.... I don't know. Forget it."

Atian's shriek of laughter from the bathroom pierced the silence. The look on Scott's face seemed guarded somehow, like he knew exactly what he wanted to say, but wasn't prepared to share. Tommy ran his palm along the back of Karen's beloved couch, and the leather whispered beneath his hand.

"Tell me." He looked up at his brother. "Scott? Wh—"

"This shit," Scott said sharply. "*You* know."

"I thought I wasn't s'posed to bring it under your roof," Tommy retorted, spikier than he'd meant to be but unwilling to put up with mixed signals and criticism. Not tonight. Not anymore.

"No, I...." Scott raised a hand, scrubbing at the back of his head in frustration. With a cursory glance toward the bathroom door, he lowered his voice. "I look at you sometimes, and you're... you're not there, Tommy. I just worry that, wherever you are, you're gonna bring somethin' back that you shouldn't."

Tommy stared at him. As if six years of prison life could be equated to a few bad habits picked up on vacation.

"Look," he said stiffly, "I'm tryin' to start right here, Scott. You don't know how hard that is. I still don't have work, I don't—"

"People like Lane Harding aren't the answer to that."

"You think I don't fuckin' *know*?"

"I didn't say...." Scott twisted his mouth, obviously uncomfortable. "Look. I just wanna know you're bein' careful. Don't.... I mean, I know how you get, that's all."

His words landed on Tommy like a slap in the face.

Uh-huh? How do I get, Scott?

He trod on the urge to ask, to blow it up into the fight that—just for a moment—it really felt like it would be worth having, and crumpled his mouth into a sneer. Scott didn't see; he was scowling down at the floor.

"I sat and waited for you, y'know," he mumbled.

"What?"

"That night. After... Dad... set on Lila for wettin' the bed, and you pulled him off." Scott cleared his throat. He looked up, and Tommy recoiled.

No. God, no. Anything but that.

His own brother... and Scott seemed afraid of him. Tommy leaned against the back of the couch. The upholstery was soft and yielding, and that felt wrong, somehow, for something that loomed between them, a great black bar that he couldn't climb. Scott shuffled, scowling again at the cherry-look laminate.

"She was so scared. She wouldn't stop cryin'. Kept saying he'd kill you. She really—fuck, y'know, *I* thought he would too. You remember how he.... Well, I took her in the other room, and we could hear you fighting.... I wanted to do somethin'. I really did."

Part of Tommy wanted to reassure his brother, tell him it didn't matter—it was all over, and there was no point dwelling on shit that couldn't be changed—but part of him was loath to interrupt. If Scott wanted to lay it out, Tommy wasn't prepared to stop him. He wasn't prepared to wash his soul with empty platitudes, either.

"So, how come ya didn't?"

Scott raised his head, eyes mournful and clouded.

"Scared," he murmured. "I didn't know what... and then he stormed off. Out. You were spittin' teeth in the kitchen sink, and the kids were so.... I wanted to call Karen, get some help settling them down. I mean, Mom was still in the hospital, and you were pacin' up and down, mutterin' to yourself. Look on your face...."

Sounds of Karen toweling Atian down after his bath came, muffled, through the door, and the gurgle of water pouring away echoed against their laughter. Oh, she kept the whole place so nice....

Tommy quirked an eyebrow. "Yeah?"

Scott shrugged, rubbing absently at the gold chain on his wrist.

"I ain't never seen that before. I... I always told the cops I never saw you take the Western. You know that, right? I mean, he never used'ta lock the cabinet. We all *knew* that, but—"

"We both know I took it," Tommy said wearily, disinclined to go through that night again.

"Yeah, and if I'd called out to you, Tommy—just said something before you went out that door...."

"Scott, it doesn't—"

"You looked just like him, man."

Tommy stared at his brother. In all the vast tracts of their lives spent mirroring each other—light to shadow and round to square in everything, each always butting against and struggling with the other— Scott had never so surprised him.

He swallowed heavily, that dark gaze burning into him, and yet he couldn't look away. Scott's voice dropped to a hoarse whisper.

"You did, Tommy. And I swear I knew what you were gonna do. And I was such a fuckin' coward, yeah? I just... sat there. Head in the fuckin' sand."

"Scott...."

"I'm sorry. Y'know?"

Scott shook his head, and, once more, Tommy saw the guilt written on him. The wish that he'd had the balls to do it himself, and the cold, cutting terror of that knowledge.

The bathroom door opened, and Atian pelted through in his Spider-Man pajamas, slinging imaginary webs. Karen tutted, muttered a little about how he'd hurt himself again if he tried to hang upside down off the doorframe, and trudged through to fix dinner. Tommy let it all pass by. They ebbed around him like ghosts, like they didn't really exist. The nice furniture and the clean floors and the happy families stuff... none of it seemed real. He couldn't break the eye contact he held with Scott, as if—so long as Tommy didn't look away—he would find something in his brother's face that forgave him. Scott blinked first. A muscle clenched in his jaw.

"Still, it's all, uh... all over now, huh?" he said, and stared levelly at Tommy.

"Yeah."

Tommy made himself smile. It felt foreign, like something he'd learned to do from a book. Scott nodded, and time flowed again. Tommy took Karen's goodwill and went to take a shower.

He turned it up to the high-power setting and closed his eyes while the water splintered off his skin... just more broken pieces he didn't know how to put back together.

CHAPTER EIGHT

IF BRETT regretted anything, it had to be his freedom. Nine times out of ten, when he put the question to himself, he didn't begrudge any of it: the changes to his life, his plans, his future, his self-image, and his reputation... whatever crap like that counted for in the first place. Tommy made it all worthwhile. Brett had never imagined he'd find anyone who'd have anything like the effect on him that Tommy did. He made the whole world pale away behind him, and what didn't vanish into insignificance took on the color of his love, echoes of him all the way through it. Tommy simply turned up in everything, for better or worse.

Brett had never prepared for those words, either.

In truth, he'd thought love was nothing more than the possibility of a continued state of attraction, tempered with friendship and a depth of feeling that, like all feelings, would change with time. He'd never held out for a fairytale, never believed in anything perfect or untouchable. He supposed—if he had—he might have been disappointed. After all, loving Tommy wasn't easy. It was more than he'd ever dreamed he'd find, but it wasn't easy.

Brett frowned at the clouds in his Long Island Tea. He really wasn't a cocktail person.

"He's not looking," he said, despite the fact he hadn't even bothered to glance across the bar.

The Shamrock Café, for all its plastic four-leafed greenery and other crimes of décor, occupied a site close to the hospital and, with an early happy hour and a wide-screen TV showing cable sports, found itself rewarded with a regular evening crowd of nurses and healthcare professionals.

The best place in the world to choke on a peanut.

"He *is*," insisted Laura, the petite mousy-brown intern who worked in the hospital pharmacy. "Ooh! He's looking at you again."

Brett winced. He and Laura didn't really know each other well—certainly not well enough for her to be playing the "gay best friend" game she seemed to want to—but she was nice enough, and he would have liked to make friends outside the circle of people he actually worked with, knew from prison visiting, or counted among either his own or Tommy's relatives. All the same, he wished she'd shut up. He wasn't interested in random bar hookups.

He raised his head and peered across the pub, to Laura's muttered protestations.

"No-oo! Don't look!"

Brett sighed inwardly—look, don't look… how the hell did women ever get any flirting done?—and almost dismissed her as a hysterical wannabe fag hag.

Only, the guy *was* staring.

Medium height, wiry build… a face that could have been chiseled out of slightly weathered sandstone, pitted and dry. Brett recognized him with a shred of cold alarm.

Lane Harding.

His hair looked a little longer than it had the last time Brett had seen him, at Tommy's place, and a voice snaked out of his memory: Karen, explaining what it meant to cut off your braids.

A mark of mourning. For somebody lost.

He'd never known that when Tommy cut his hair in the joint. Brett wished he had. He still wouldn't have understood, but…. Now, he wondered who it was Lane had been mourning, if anyone, and why he'd shown up here. A light shiver traced his spine, despite the heat of the room. Lane had seen him looking. He raised his beer to his lips and gave a slight nod in Brett's direction.

Brett stared. The rush of anger that washed through him came as a surprise, a sudden and irrational burst that, like an unexpected wave at the beach, left him breathless and unsteady.

He wanted nothing more than to wipe that smug look off Harding's face, though he couldn't have said why. His fingers flexed on the bar, almost itching to close into a fist, to feel the solid impact— the blissful release—of landing one good punch on that sneering mouth. Brett hadn't scrapped since grade school. He'd always been taught that violence wasn't the answer, and he'd believed it, even before seeing Tommy prove it so completely. Come to think of it, he supposed Harding had this effect on him because of Tommy, because of the way Brett had seen Lane treat him that day at Mei's.

He's just a jerk.

He shouldn't have the balls to show up here, grinning like that and just… just representing everything Brett wanted to pick up and choke the life out of until it turned cold in his hands. All the secrets, the hidden things, and the broken, used-up parts of life.

Gradually, Laura's voice filtered through his fugue.

"So, do you know him? D'you think he's hot?"

"He's a fr—a guy that Tommy knows," Brett muttered through gritted teeth.

"Ohhh…. Hey, you got a thing for Indian guys, huh? Do—"

"I don't have a thing." God, she'd never seemed this irritating at work. He regretted accepting her invitation. Harding was still staring. His gaze slipped to the door briefly, a silent question. "And… just no. Okay, Laura? No."

Brett pushed away from the bar and broke eye contact with Harding. He made for the door, aware of Laura bobbing at his elbow, her voice bright and incessant.

"Brett? Where you goin'? You didn't finish your drink…."

"Forget it, Laura… I'm just bad company tonight. Sorry."

He wished he could have lost her in the crowd. The night air hit, cool and unforgiving. Brett fumbled in his pocket for his keys— Tommy's keys—and longed to get home, to shut his door on the whole damn world.

"Hey! Batty boy... you ignoring me?"

Brett swore under his breath. Tommy wound his way into everything, sure enough. Not to mention all the crap he brought with him. The thoughts struck out, vicious and unwanted. Brett tried to ignore them; this wasn't Tommy's fault. Harding wasn't his fault, but here they'd be, clashing heads all the same. Brett extended his hand and caught hold of Laura's arm. He dragged her across the sidewalk, behind the potted dwarf conifers outside the pub, and pressed the keys into her hand.

"Go get into the truck, okay?"

She stared at him, wide-eyed, her sharp little face blotchy with uncertain excitement.

"I *said*—" Lane Harding's voice got louder, presaging his hand landing on Brett's shoulder. "—are you ignoring me? I know who you are, man."

"It's not a problem, Laura. Honest. Go on." He turned to face Harding. "Can I help you? You want something?"

Harding's mouth twisted in an ugly leer. "Yeah, I do.... Hey, Tommy know you're bangin' pussy on the side, white boy?"

From the corner of his eye, Brett saw Laura stumble as she moved to the Chevy. His whole body ached with the desire to rise to Lane's bait. *If only Tommy could see me now, about to get into a fight over him. Bastard would laugh so fucking hard....*

"I don't want any trouble," Brett lied, holding up his hands. He did, but he denied the itch, the temptation to let go control. The other man's anger filled up the night like cheap perfume. "Just goin' home, okay?"

Lane's easy, affable posture could have fooled some people. It might have been simple enough to miss the telltale bunching of muscles in his legs, the tension in his back and arms. Brett knew better, and sidestepped on the cusp of Lane's lunge forward, quick enough to pivot and grab him in a neck hold. His arm pressed close to the narrow, hard channel of Harding's throat, Brett pinned him and held down the fist that sprang up to clip the side of his head.

"Oh, very good," Harding said thickly. His Adam's apple bobbed, poking at the inside of Brett's elbow. "Not quite as handy as Tommy though, are ya?"

Despite himself, the words caught Brett's ear. "What?"

"Aw, c'mon." Harding loosed a stiff, dark laugh. His smell— cigarettes, cheap beer, and greasy denim—scratched at the side of Brett's face. "He'd'a had me on the floor'n kick seven kindsa crap out of me by now. Tough little bastard."

Brett pushed him away roughly, choked by the urge to squeeze that bit harder, twist that bit further, and cause some serious pain. He glared at Harding, aware of Laura watching from the Chevy, her finger probably already poised to dial the second one on her cell phone.

"I don't want trouble," he repeated, though this time he meant it a little bit more.

Harding just grinned. "Yeah. I mean... God, nobody *wants* trouble, do they?" he said with a sneer, brushing himself down. "So, y'know, you better be careful."

Those last words hung heavy in the cool air. Brett waited a beat, knowing he shouldn't respond. He should just walk away. *Just walk away.* Only, he always did that, didn't he?

"Threats?" He wrinkled his nose. "That make you feel like a big man, huh?"

Harding's grin got wider, but his lips narrowed. "Just advice, yeah? Just so you know."

Other figures had started to emerge from the bar, dim silhouettes unconnected and probably uncaring. Harding didn't seem to want to risk intervention, though. He glanced over his shoulder, then back at Brett.

"I'll see you around."

He left, footsteps sharp on the frosty sidewalk. Brett waited for a few moments, the knot of the Shamrock's patrons splitting to pass him. The smell of beer and the sound of laughter washed over him, staining the metallic taste of the air. Brett watched his breath coil sluggishly in front of him, pulse drumming angrily in his throat.

"Brett?"

Laura sounded cautious, worried... shrill. Reluctantly, he turned and went to her.

"It's all fine," Brett said, gluing a false smile to his face as he flopped against the Chevy's upholstery. "You want me to drop you off?"

She nodded. He knew this would be all over the hospital in the morning. She didn't talk much, just sat and looked at him as if he was a complete stranger. She had a point, he supposed.

Brett's palms grew moist on the wheel, all residual anger and bitterness. You could really fall out of love with a town like this.

PEOPLE didn't understand reservations, Tommy decided. He ramped his mother's red Taurus off the Old West Trail and onto one of the town of Poplar's many dusty avenues, the map Karen had drawn him rattling on the dash, next to a pack of gum and half a bar of chocolate. The gearbox protested, and he swore as he wrenched the stick, his wrist still throbbing from that little altercation with Lane. Tommy was reminded of how badly he missed the Chevy, but he had to bite down hard on the thought. Brett actually wanted to give it back to him. He didn't know what that meant, coming as it had in the mess of the awkward, painful thing that had happened, and that he didn't know how to fix.

Don't come around.

The words kept echoing, and they stung worse every time. He didn't know where Brett had left him, but he didn't like being there. Tommy shook himself and glanced out the car window as he peeled off the avenue and its low, eyeless, silent houses for a track that led southeast, away from the town. Fort Peck land looked a lot like the parts of Belknap rez he remembered from his childhood. Even the way the roads were laid out felt familiar. When he was a kid, going to see his grandparents in LP Town, so much of Fort Belknap had looked grim and desperate to Tommy. And it was easy, he supposed, for people to see only that, to think that these were places of desolation and despair, deserted and ugly reminders of past injustices and current inequalities. As a boy, he'd thought the same way. He hadn't understood why his grandmother had stayed in her rez house. It was all dark, pokey rooms, concrete blocks, and bleached-out siding, with the fire that spewed soot and always needing cleaning. Grandpa Tim could have bought them somewhere—some*thing*—much better in his native Canada, surely.

Tommy had asked Gramma once; he must have been around twelve. It would have been one of the endless winters when they'd visit for whole afternoons. His mother would have been busy with Robbie, only a toddler then, and Scott would have been off somewhere, getting into trouble. His... father would have disappeared like smoke, seeped off for a drink with some old buddy. Grandpa Tim had probably still been up north, driving the four-month season on the winter road, hauling mining equipment across the ice. Gramma worried, but she'd put all of it into her hands. Tommy remembered her sitting by the fire, busy at a piece of beadwork for the child of a friend or neighbor. Maybe a shawl. Come powwow season, it would grace the shoulders or dress of some beautiful dancer, and Gramma would crow with pleasure and clap in time to songs whose words Tommy didn't understand.

He'd loved his grandmother, but even as a boy, he'd seen the distance between them. She'd tried to explain things to him, how the rez wasn't about staying where you'd been put, but about the pride in who you were, where you came from and, just maybe, a little bit of fear when you thought about leaving. The same reason that, at powwows, even the most hardened spiritual warriors—the men who, at every opportunity, decried the outlaw, criminal US government and its treatment of First Nation peoples—would stand in silence for the Flag Song, perhaps with tears in their eyes.

Because nothing is ever simple, he supposed. The flag: symbol of both oppression and the struggle against it, the land that had always been their home and the country that grew up around it, and the belief that—despite everything—we are one people. The rez: barren land and dusty dogs, thrift marts and cheap construction... but laughter and community, terrible beauty and lasting determination. The strength of people bonded together, courage and optimism undimmed.

Tommy thought of Carla Nolan, one of the defense lawyers Brett had hired for him, a Blackfoot woman with a smart skirt suit and an expensive education. People like her changed things too.

He'd reached the ranch, shadowed by the sun hanging pale gold in a washed-out sky. Nerves fluttered lightly in his gut, and he told himself that was stupid, because it wasn't like this was the first job interview he'd had since he got out. It probably wasn't going to be any different to the others, either.

Tommy pulled the Taurus up beside the post-and-rail fence that opened on to a large paddock, screened with a windbreak of scrubby trees. A wide track ran next to the paddock, leading up to the house, and he could have driven further, gotten a little closer, but he didn't want to do that. He got out, left his mother's car where it was, and started to walk. Damned if he wasn't going to do one thing on his own two feet. A squirrel shot across the track in front of him, tail a bob of white as it vanished into the brush. The air smelled of pine sap after rain, with the warm, rich tang of horseshit beneath it.

Tommy took a big lungful. Better than bullshit, anyway. He'd had enough of that. And it was... good, wasn't it? To be out here, away from everything. No more demands and complications pressing in, all the people who wanted pieces of him just pushed back for a little while. He could get his head together, maybe. Think clearly for the first time since coming back. Was that even true? Probably not. He'd had moments of horrible clarity: standing on the scrubby grass at Highland Park, looking down at that fucking plaque, for one. Brett, spouting nonsense into the night about Bozeman, for another.

We could go somewhere else. It wouldn't be a problem.

What the fuck had he been thinking? What the fuck was there in Bozeman? A cowboy-boot economy and a lot of tarmac. Rents they wouldn't be able to afford and jobs Tommy wouldn't get... 'cause he'd still be an ex-con, wherever he went. Brett knew that. And Tommy wasn't about to let Brett throw away everything he had—everything he'd built—in Havre, just so he could set up to play house and look after them both. He couldn't be dependent on somebody like that. Not now. Only... he knew what Brett had meant. What he wanted.

Tommy had wanted to hold him tight, soothe away his worries and smooth over the entire can of worms, but somehow hadn't quite been able to make himself do it. The night had smothered him, the covers overly tight on the bed, Brett's skin too warm, and his love far too easy to take. It did sound good, though. A little place somewhere, just the two of them. Dog in the yard, view of the mountains. Fresh coffee bubbling.

Tommy shook the thought sharply, pushed it away, back into the cloaked recesses of his mind. He squinted up the track, toward the house. He'd screwed up, over and over, and now he just had to deal with it.

Place had been laid out well, he had to admit. To the right, Tommy could just see the stable blocks, rising against the sky, and a couple of horses—brood mares, by the look of their big, wide bellies—grazing the coarse ground. Further paddocks would stretch out on the other side of the yard, he supposed. Karen had said her uncle kept a very small concern, only a couple of full-time staff. He co-owned the place with an old Army buddy, apparently.

The house, cedar-shingled and heavily gabled, pierced the sky ahead of Tommy. A plate-glazed sunporch ran a quarter length of the first floor, and he guessed the property to be only fifteen years old or so, tops. He knocked on the door, stepped back, and waited. It swung open, and in a cloud of wet dog, fresh coffee, and furniture polish smells, Bill Standing Deer beamed cheerfully at him.

"Tommy, right? Hello! Come in, come in."

Bill looked to be around fifty years or so, iron gray hair bound in two braids that reached the middle of his broad, well-padded chest. A cream plaid shirt stretched taut across his belly, and his jeans— apparently blasted by years of plains grit and hard work—hung low on his body, capped with an ornate oval brass buckle.

His wide, toothy grin put Tommy at ease, his expression genial but definitely alert. He took Tommy's hand against his big, warm palm and shook it, clapped him on the shoulder, and ushered him inside.

"You make it down all right? Traffic on the highway can be a real bitch on the weekends. You come through… that's it. I got some coffee on. And don't mind the dog, okay? She don't want anything 'cept a pat on the head."

Tommy followed him into the kitchen, a long, open-plan affair with black granite work surfaces that shone with a dull, oily gleam. Despite the clean, modern look, a lot of work clearly happened in here. Bulletin boards hung on one wall, rotas and notes layered over each other like peeling paint, and the huge stainless steel range looked capable of cooking up to ten breakfasts at once. A scruffy crossbred dog, perhaps one-third Dalmatian, one-third some kind of pointer and one-third walking, overstuffed footstool shambled up to Tommy and sniffed him thoroughly. He scratched her behind the ears, and she thumped her plumy tail.

"Missy likes you," Bill observed with a grin.

They sat at the breakfast bar, and he poured out small, scalding hot cups of coffee, the kind strong enough to melt the end off the average spoon. Bill talked as he worked, and the easy pace of his words spooled through the room, filling up its empty and uncomfortable places.

"Karen used to come here a lotta times when she was a little girl. You know how girls are with horses, right? 'Course, that was before I bought in on the ownership. Place was just an old dude ranch.... We do a lot more bloodstock trade these days. Can't believe that kid's all grown up, got a baby of her own. So, she told me you're a sound worker, Tommy, and you're looking for a break."

Tommy swallowed hurriedly. The turn in Bill's speech had been unexpected, and the coffee burned his lip. Bill looked at him, eyes twinkling to some inner amusement over his own cup.

"Uh... yeah. I-I've been—"

"Away. I know." Bill nodded sagely. "They still got them badass Black Angus cattle at Deer Lodge? I always hated those things."

Tommy stared. He'd expected Bill to know about his problems and his record—Karen would have laid out any details the media hadn't—but he hadn't expected this.

"You were...?"

Bill shrugged. "Fourteen years."

"Oh. I-I didn't know."

Damn it, why did he have to make himself sound like even more of an idiot? Bill gave him another one of those wide, toothy grins and shook his head.

"No reason you should. Hell, not everybody does, y'know? They don't brand it on your forehead. Even if it feels like it."

"Uh." Tommy nodded slowly. "Right."

He blinked, aware that there were questions you didn't ask, even if it itched like hell to know the answer. Bill chuckled to himself.

"Armed robbery," he said gently. "Three of my buddies 'n' me decided to turn over a gas station on the highway, back in '82. We were all pretty wasted, but I guess I was worst gone, and I ran slowest when the cops showed up. Had the gun on me too. Never even fired the damn thing, but you know that don't matter. I got out in '98."

"Oh."

He slipped Tommy a sidelong glance and smiled again. It was infectious, and Tommy grinned disbelievingly. Damn Karen... he needed to stop underestimating that girl.

"So, you're a carpenter now?"

Back to business. Tommy twitched his lip.

"Kinda. I did a qualification on an ed program, but to be honest, I don't really have a lot of experience. Before, I worked with a company in Burnham, fittin' kitchen units, stone counters, and stuff... lot like this, actually," he added, nodding to the smooth expanses of granite. "Refits, mainly, an' we worked on those new builds up west of Havre. I work hard, and I don't mind tryin' my hand at anything."

"That's good." Bill nodded. "Work we got tends to vary a lot. I'd want you on fences, stalls... if you're happy to learn around the horses too, we can always use an extra hand."

"Sure." Tommy rubbed nervously at the rim of his cup. "I mean, I never—"

Bill waved dismissively. "Don't matter. We take in all kinds of extra help, time to time. You said you can learn, right?"

"Uh, well... yeah. I mean, yeah, I—"

"Then there you go." Bill gave him another wide, cheerful grin. "Let's talk details, huh?"

Tommy blinked. "Um... okay."

They did. Bill poured more coffee, and outlined a whole lot of things Tommy had never known about horses, and the breeding, rearing, and selling of them. Things hadn't been so good in recent years, and—rather than start putting prices on the animals per pound instead of per head—Bill and Herman, the old army buddy who was part owner of the ranch, had decided to scale back some of the operation. They diversified a little in the summer months, took in paying guests and students on the international BUNAC schemes who were prepared to accept a working vacation if it meant being able to sample somewhere new. They were usually pretty useless, Bill confided, but the program gave the ranch a small incentive for taking part. It was a slightly threadbare way of life, but for now, they were still getting by.

Bill said it like it wasn't much, like maybe it wasn't what Tommy was looking for, but there was a guarded kind of enthusiasm in his eyes. He drank his coffee and grinned periodically at Tommy over the cup, and Tommy was pretty sure he hadn't felt this much at home anywhere in a hell of a long time.

"So," Bill said eventually, raising his graying, unruly brows, "you think you'd be up for a trial run?"

"Yeah! I mean, yeah, I'd… I really appreciate that. Thanks."

Missy had been dozing on Tommy's foot for a while. She looked up sleepily and wagged her tail, giving him a soft doggy groan. Bill chuckled, but the smile faded in place as he fixed Tommy with a slightly harder look.

"We're a long way from Havre, though. How 'bout your, uh…?"

"Brett," Tommy supplemented automatically, suppressing his normal burst of irritation at the question.

Bill didn't have that look on his face that some people got, but still, it was the way he said it. Same way as everybody… every single damn time. Tommy had said something along those lines to Brett once, suggested they actually just give up and start introducing each other as "my uh….", but Brett thought it was funny. It wasn't fucking funny.

"Yeah," Bill said, eyeing him dubiously. "You got family an' all that, I know. I, uh, don't know if that'd be a problem."

Tommy shrugged. "Don't think so. It… well, it'll work out. I'm sure it will."

He smiled, meaning it as encouragement, but aware that the gesture stuck to him like a grimace. There was still something stiff and painful in the thoughts, like a wound yet to scab. He didn't even know whether Brett was going to be mad, or whether he just didn't care anymore, and that scared Tommy even worse than the idea of leaving the kids behind.

CHAPTER NINE

TOMMY'S phone kept going straight to voice mail. Brett couldn't work out why, but he wasn't about to leave some tentative, wimpy-sounding "please call me" message, like he had an apology to make or something. All the same, it worried him. Brett knew his persistent checking up pissed Tommy off, but it didn't mean he could stop doing it. Even if he *was* still mad. Only... no. Not mad, not exactly.

Just so fucking tired.

He kicked off his shoes, put his feet up on his scruffy green couch, and glared at his cell phone. After a while, he thumbed in another number entirely.

"Hello?"

Brett cleared his throat. "Hey, Nick."

"Oh, my God! Brett? How the hell are you?"

He stared at the ceiling. Nick always managed to sound precisely the same: bright and cheerful and full of life, just like he had when they were at college. There was a degree of phoniness to it, admittedly, but Brett still found it comforting. He admired the way Nick had been able to do it, to put on a disarming grin and brazen out virtually anything. Compartmentalize, maybe.

"I'm... good," Brett said, aware from the quality of Nick's silence that he understood. He had a talent for that.

You could understand a guy to death, you know that?

"How's it going?" Movement sounded on the line, like Nick had adjusted his position, perhaps pushed away from a computer… or whatever he'd been doing when the phone rang. "Is, uh, is he managing okay? How are *you*?"

Brett kept his gaze fixed on the ceiling, attention locked on something that either had to be a bug or a stain on the paint. How on earth a stain would have got up there he didn't like to imagine.

"Uh, yeah. I think… I think he's all right. He will be, anyway. It's, um, it's been a little hard to tell."

"And you?"

"Yeah." Brett blinked a few times, not sure whether he'd imagined the thing on the ceiling moving. He wasn't even sure whether he'd imagined the past six weeks.

"Brett?"

Silence for a beat. Brett heard the tightness in Nick's voice when he said his name, and pushed over it because he couldn't bear it. He used to sound the same way when they made l—when they fucked, Brett corrected. Guilt gnawed at him, the awareness of how he'd used Nick. A crutch, a bandage… a temporary measure. All the same reasons he'd gone with girls back in high school. Convenience and exploration. He wasn't proud of it.

He cleared his throat again. "So, uh… how are you?"

"Yeah." Nick took a breath. "Yeah…. I'm good too. World of pharmaceuticals continues fast-paced but boring. I'm going to San Francisco next month for a biz trip, though. First fun place this lousy company's sent me. Never been before."

Brett closed his eyes. Nick sounded breezy, chipper. He knew how hard that was to do. And, though the ardor of the strange, bounded relationship of theirs had cooled a long while back, Brett knew that—at least for Nick—it had mellowed out into a long-lasting affection. Maybe even love, of a kind. He felt bad about that, like he should have been able to give something more, something… honest. Nick had always known about Tommy, sure, but that didn't make it feel right to Brett. Nick deserved better. Moonlight and roses, if he wanted them. Trouble was, Brett had never wanted *him*… not anywhere near enough.

"That's great," he said, and for a little while, they talked about that, and how wonderful San Francisco would be.

"So, what's gone wrong?" Nick asked, jerking Brett sharply out of his attempt at normality. "Or is it all just kinda dark?"

Brett hitched one leg up and rubbed his palm across his knee, fidgeting on the couch.

"Well… yeah, a little. I mean, I… I sort of might have told him we were on a break."

"*What*? You broke up with Mr. Dreamy?"

"No." Brett winced at the nickname. "No, we didn't—I just told him… not to come by for a little while."

"Oh, Brett…."

"I just needed space."

"But you—"

"We're not on a *real* break," he said hurriedly. "Not… I mean, it's not… it's not like *that*. It's just…."

Nick sighed deeply, and there didn't even *have* to be words to it. Brett could practically see the look on his face: all "I told you so" and kindly resignation.

"I know." Brett picked at the seam of his jeans. "Yeah, I know. But it's been…. I took him to see his father's grave, all right? And… and I had to stand there and see him look at— It's tearing him up. More now than it ever did, and I just can't see what I'm s'posed to do. I don't think, as long as he's in this town…. I don't know."

He knew if he'd been there in person, Nick would have held him, and he'd have been able to cry, to have it soothed out of him like a kid with stomach flu. Brett squeezed his eyes shut again, blocked against the prickle of tears, and tried to recreate the feel of Nick's arms in his mind, to conjure up his presence. Pale brown hair and soft green eyes hidden behind lightweight glasses… a wide mouth with a sort of permanent upturn at the very corner of his lips, like he always had a smile in waiting. He gave great head. A similar kind of generosity in bed to Tommy, but Nick had never struck the same nerves, never opened up the same feelings in him, however hard Brett had tried to believe he could.

"I saw the picture you e-mailed." Nick sounded distant, like he didn't really want to mention it. "You both looked really happy. When was that taken?"

"Week or so ago. At his mom's."

"Mm. Well, what's changed? He's still the love of your life."

Awe tinged Brett's wash of embarrassment. If Nick was jealous, it barely showed.

"I—"

"Shut up. You know I'm right. You can see it on his face too. So just call him. Keep calling. And tell him you love him, for fuck's sake. You're still doing that, right?"

"Yeah, but—"

"Then you'll fix it. Listen… I'll be in Frisco for a week, starting the twelfth. If you want, you guys can use the apartment. Time out, change of scene? It's not much, but the view over the river's nice. Neutral territory, maybe."

Brett gazed damply at the ceiling. The bug—a small moth—unfurled its wings and flitted away to bump against the light shade. It wasn't really a practical idea, but it meant a lot to know that someone, somewhere, thought that he and Tommy might do normal things, like take short breaks together and make up after stupid fights.

He sniffed. One day, Nick would make some lucky guy so happy.

Life'd be hell of a lot easier if it'd been me.

"Thanks," he murmured.

"Don't mention it."

"No, really. I—"

"Don't. It's okay. Just… I don't know. If you do use the place, you can make a video for me or something."

Brett laughed. "What?"

"Yeah. Like I said, I got the pictures. He's fucking *hot*!"

Laughter helped. Brett was glad of it. It helped disguise the fact Nick had a point. However mad he stayed at Tommy, however sick he got of the difficulties that dogged loving him, it wasn't like Brett could just stop. It didn't make for a heartening choice: miserable without him or… with him? Not miserable, just waiting. Stuck in some windowless, heavy limbo.

By the time Brett let Nick get back to whatever he'd been doing, he felt better, like he wasn't alone. He felt kinda stupid too, for digging himself into a black mood when it wasn't his right, when there were worse things in the world than living through the fact his love life wasn't all raptures and roses. He sloped off to bed and burrowed under the covers, lonely for the warmth of another body beside him. He didn't sleep the night through anymore, half waking to listen for Tommy even when he wasn't there.

Brett got up again at about four, wishing he lived somewhere suitable for a dog. When he was a boy, Roscoe—the family German shepherd—used to sneak into his room and blunder up under the covers, with some innate canine sense for bad dreams or hurt pride. Roscoe had been gone a good few years now, and the void remained palpable. Even if Brett had tried hard not to admit it to himself, he'd thought about it: dog, career, home… life. All the parts of it that he'd somehow believed would fall into place around him. *Them.* Because Tommy would be there, right at the center, and they'd be okay.

Fuck… had he ever been so naïve?

Brett drank a glass of water and did some half-assed transverse abdominal reps on the living room floor, but they didn't much help. Later still, showered but unshaven, he watched the sun come up and wondered how the hell he was going to drag his sorry ass into work. He ended up calling Elaine as soon as he thought she'd be in and told her he'd come down with food poisoning. She told him to get better soon, said it wasn't a problem and they'd manage without him, and she even sounded like she meant it. Brett scowled disconsolately when he put the phone down and chewed the inside of his cheek. Laura would probably already be letting the whole hospital know about his encounter with Lane Harding. The sound of the rumor mill's cogs grinding into motion would echo all the way across town.

He dialed Tommy's number, not expecting to hear the phone ring, but it did, and the breath thickened in his chest.

"Brett?"

Tommy didn't sound all that pleased, and Brett winced.

"Yeah. Hey. Um… you got a minute?"

After a beat of silence, Tommy's voice softened against his ear. "'Course. Listen, I'm sorry. I—"

"Your phone was off," Brett snapped, surprising himself with his accusatory tone.

"Yeah. The battery died. Are you—?"

"You at Mei's?"

"Uh-huh."

Brett stared at the rumpled, unmade bed. Golden morning light sliced through the window, and dust motes waltzed gently in it. He wasn't prepared to do this anymore, he decided. He cleared his throat.

"Can I come over? Now?"

"Sure." Tommy sounded vaguely stunned. "What…?"

Brett broke the connection, already on his way down to the parking lot when he realized something. That certainly hadn't been a wimpy apology.

TOMMY had obviously heard him pull up. He opened the door in a dark blue T-shirt and ancient jeans stained with paint, his hair down and his feet bare. He didn't say anything at first, his silence a mirror to Brett's. The stair creaked under Brett's foot as he stepped up onto the porch, and it seemed loud against this awful, unyielding quiet.

Brett watched him carefully, looking for any traces of that blank, hateful mask. He'd seen enough of Tommy's jail face to last him a lifetime. He didn't look blank, though… his brows were drawn, his eyes guarded and narrow, and his mouth a little turned down at the corners. He wet his lips as he looked at Brett, and his toes curled on the rough doormat, every bit of him signaling uncertainty and apprehension.

Brett fiddled awkwardly with the Chevy's keys and cleared his throat. He glanced down at the little red dream catcher Tommy's grandmother had made, and then back up at those dark eyes.

He shrugged. "I… I'm sorry."

"Yeah." Tommy nodded. "Me too."

He raised his hand a little from where it hung loosely by his thigh, and his fingers flexed just a bit, like he wanted to reach out but didn't quite dare. Brett clenched the keys in his hand and—for once, not even thinking about it—made the step and crossed the distance between them.

Tommy didn't so much fall into his embrace as get claimed by it, his arms locking around Brett with equal force and hunger.

"I am sorry. Really sorry," he murmured, mouth hot on Brett's cheek, as if he really thought he had to repeat the words to make them real.

Brett hugged him tight and shook his head. He supposed he ought to pull away, make Tommy look him in the face and know that he understood it was all right, but he couldn't bear to break the embrace.

"Yeah," he mumbled instead, the words muffled against Tommy's neck. "I know. Same here. I love you."

Tommy let out a soft breath, his strong fingers rubbing a trail of apology up Brett's neck. Brett tilted his head, drawing him into a kiss… just the inflexible pressure of lips meeting and everything it represented.

Tommy groaned against his mouth, deepening the embrace. His tongue slid alongside Brett's, arms tightening around him. It was a long, slow, careful thing, like an oath of possession Tommy seemed to believe he needed to reaffirm.

Whatever it was, it turned Brett's knees weak and made his head feel light and shallow. Everything he'd meant to say, all the things that had seemed so important, just melted away. He knew, somewhere inside this great ray of hope and bliss, that fact ought to annoy him… that it probably would, later on. But it would be *much* later.

He pulled back, relieved to see the start of a fire lit in Tommy's eyes. Tommy tugged on his arm.

"C'mon."

Brett grinned and allowed himself to be dragged indoors, into the wax crayon, soy sauce, and air freshener smell of the house, with its shiny laminate floors and neutral walls. Tommy didn't look right against this, to Brett's mind. The place was far too empty to suit him, though empty had its advantages.

"They're all out?"

"Ah-huh." Tommy nodded. "Work and school. How come you're not at the hospital?"

Brett's grin widened self-consciously; he knew this would crack Tommy up. "I'm playing hooky."

"What? *You*…?"

Tommy's eyes widened, then narrowed to creases as a huge smile split his face. He started to laugh, bigger and broader than Brett had heard in a long time, and it was wonderful to hear. It made the world a little bit brighter, and he didn't do it halfway often enough. Brett found himself joining in, losing the shackles of all that serious, mundane stuff… even if just for a little while.

Eventually, Tommy got control of his splutters. He scrubbed a knuckle at the corner of his eye, mopping at the dampness there, and snorted as he looked incredulously at Brett.

"*Why?*"

Brett shrugged, allowing his gaze to drop to Tommy's chest and the blameless planes of his crewneck. He reached idly for his hand, just needing the warmth of that golden skin against his, palm to palm.

It made up for not being able to look him in the face.

"I missed you," he murmured. "I shouldn't'a got so… y'know. How I was. I know it's tough. You don't need me to make it worse."

Friendly, warm lies that coated his tongue like honey. Tommy squeezed his fingers.

"Ah, I don't know. Figure you've had enough of me dumping on you. I didn't need to say all the shit I did. Forgive me?"

Brett nodded. Tommy wouldn't say he hadn't meant what had poured out of him at the cemetery; they both knew he had. But he'd had a point. Brett tilted his head in a silent request, not quite breathing again until his lover's lips met his. Tommy tasted faintly of aniseed. Brett recalled the licorice root tea he'd taken to drinking—kind of nice, really—and pulled him closer. The kisses weren't conciliatory, though, but fast, shallow expressions of impatience.

"Wh' doin'?" Tommy mumbled as Brett squeezed him through his jeans.

"What d'you think?"

He chuckled, and Brett could feel him responding... he should have done this earlier. Just shown up and made it right, instead of sitting on his butt whining about how awful it was and waiting for things to change. He ground harder against Tommy, wanting his answering heat and the smell of his skin. Tommy's hands roamed his back, working hypnotic circles through his shirt until Brett wondered if the fabric could just melt away under his touch.

Brett kissed him hard and slow, until Tommy bumped impatiently against him, a needy little noise breaking from his throat.

"Hmm." Brett grinned triumphantly. "Wanna go upstairs?"

Tommy nodded, then frowned. "Uh-huh... oh. Wait. There isn't—"

Brett's grin widened. "Double bed in Mei's room, right?"

He loved the look of shocked surprise on Tommy's face. He could be so conventional, in the strangest ways.

TOMMY pulled Brett closer, aching with the desire to lose the rest of the day—the rest of eternity, ideally—in making love to him, on his mother's bed or, screw it, on the front lawn of the First Lutheran Church. He didn't care anymore. Brett's fingers were already working on his fly, tugging him toward the stairs like he could just be led by his cock, anywhere Brett wanted to go.

It was probably true, Tommy thought ruefully. He was vaguely aware that something didn't feel right, but there were too many things it could have been for him to pick just one out of the lineup. They needed to talk. Properly. Not simply trade a couple of words and fling themselves on the nearest mattress, but actually... talk. He needed to tell Brett about Poplar, and Bill, and all the goddamn paperwork he had to do for Myers, and the whole host of problems there was going to be with taking the job, even though he wasn't going to like hearing it.

They were probably going to fight again, Tommy reflected, as he stumbled up the first couple of stairs, still tangled up in Brett and feeling like it was the only thing that mattered. He couldn't wreck this. Couldn't mess it up… but he didn't want to give in and take all the sweetness Brett offered, not when there was this *thing* that he hadn't shared.

It was lying, wasn't it? Not telling him, staying quiet about it now, it was as good as hiding behind an untruth, pretending that things were okay. Only, they did a lot of that, didn't they? Pretending. Holding on. Maybe it wasn't so bad. Maybe it was a justifiable lie—or not a lie at all, because Tommy *would* tell him. Just, perhaps later. When the apologies had been forged into something warmer, something that felt really true and real, and he could hold Brett against him and know he wouldn't run.

Indecision hammered at him, leaving him almost as breathless as the kisses.

Negotiating the stairs was more difficult than it should have been, as if his legs didn't bend the right way, and there was a whole lot of nose bumping and teeth clashing. Brett laughed first, and Tommy couldn't stop himself following because, despite everything, that closeness was still there. Their soft chuckles, the lack of inhibition and pretense… he'd never needed to pretend with Brett.

If only he'd known that earlier, maybe life would have panned out differently.

Tommy didn't put stock in that kind of thinking. Things happened, and you lived with them, around them… *through* them. There wasn't any other choice, and wishes weren't real. You couldn't catch hold of them, and chasing dreams was pointless unless their tails reached the ground.

Brett popped open his fly as they hit the top stair, hand diving toward his goal with ruthless, eager efficiency. Tommy groaned into the deep kiss that united their mouths, and flexed his hips against the feel of those familiar fingers closing around him.

He needed to tell Brett about Poplar. They had to talk. Had to…
but… maybe it wasn't so bad for that to happen after the other stuff.

"I'll get a towel or somethin'," Brett murmured, breaking away
from him.

"Huh?"

He just grinned and disappeared into the bathroom, leaving
Tommy standing at the top of the stairs, jeans unbuttoned and thoughts
in disarray. It didn't seem possible that today had turned around so
much. Everything had hurt so badly, been so gray and misshapen, and
now it wasn't, it was… it was wide, and open, and it scared him a little,
the way so many things did these days.

"Brett…."

Tommy heard the note of uncertainty in his voice. It sounded
slightly like panic, as if he couldn't deal with Brett stepping out of his
line of sight, and he hated that, hated every whiff of insecurity and
neediness. Brett reemerged, a dark blue bath sheet folded in his hands.

"Go on." He nodded to the door of Mei's room. "I got it."

Tommy frowned. "Wait, I—"

Brett wasn't listening. He was smiling that impish, starry-eyed
smile that Tommy used to see on him sometimes when he'd walk into
the visitors' center. The first few times, he'd looked terrified to start
with, stumbling in at the back of a phalanx of wives and girlfriends,
brothers and bangers and who knew what else. He'd only calmed down
when he spotted Tommy, and then there'd be those few precious hours
that were never quite enough.

As they'd grown used to the routine, Brett had become more
confident in it. He'd walk in, talking to some of the other regular
visitors, and his gaze would find Tommy like he didn't even need to
try—like he already knew where to look, like something invisible
joined them together—and he'd smile that particular smile. It had been
the best thing to look forward to. Almost as good as the moment they
were allowed to touch, and Tommy could hug him, breathe in his scent
and take it right down into his lungs, as if he could hold onto the
memory until next time.

Tommy bit his lip. He couldn't do this. It wasn't fair, and it wasn't right.

He swallowed heavily as Brett took his hand, pulling him into Mei's room. The sweet, floral-scented air closed around them, and sunlight lanced through the pale curtains.

Brett had never been with another guy when they'd first met. It was the reason Tommy had taken everything so slowly… given Brett time to get comfortable with himself, and maybe ended up falling in love with him because of it, at least a little bit. Getting to know him, feeling like they mattered to each other—like *he* mattered to someone, someone bright and clean and wonderful who, for some improbable reason, actually cared about him. It had been amazing, and the first few times they were together, Brett had been such an eager little ball of nerves and insecurity.

Now he made Tommy feel like a virgin, clumsy and naïve, unable to say the things he wanted to or take control of the moments as they tumbled past him.

Odds and ends of years of therapy sessions filtered through his mind. He'd talked about so many fucking things… why should this be any different? All the violent offender stuff, it was all about resolution and articulation, and the talking circle was the same. You couldn't do anything in life until you took a hold of your own will and focused it in a clear, rational manner, and that meant truth and honesty and responsibility… and all that shit. Didn't it?

Tommy wasn't sure he knew anymore. The words felt hollow, and all those breathing exercises and visualization techniques were a long way off. Panic flickered somewhere at the back of his mind, an old and worn-out response that tasted of times gone by and memories he didn't want to dredge through.

He started to speak, but Brett was busy spreading the towel out on the bed, and then he turned and planted another kiss on Tommy, pulling him close and gazing at him with such clear, bright desire in those hazel eyes. Saying anything at all seemed wrong. It seemed… ungrateful.

Trouble was, *not* saying it was worse.

"IT'S better than the air bed, though, right?"

Brett chuckled, one hand pausing to toy a little with the ends of Tommy's hair while the other worked on starting to pull his shirt up. He dipped in for another kiss, fingers tracing a ticklish line along the warm skin above the waistband of his pants.

Tommy tasted good, and if Brett wanted to have him in his arms, that wasn't like admitting he'd failed, right? He'd come here to make up, and a bruised ego would soon mend. He wound the dry, smooth strands of hair around his fingertip and tugged lightly.

"This is getting really long again," he murmured against Tommy's mouth. "I like it."

"Uh... Brett?"

He frowned as Tommy pulled away, hanging back from him, hard and flushed.

"Babe...." Those dark brows knotted in alarmed uncertainty. "Can you just hold on? I need to—aw, crap. I-I need to tell you somethin'."

Brett's gut tightened. Nothing good ever started with words like those. He pulled back a little, one hand still resting on Tommy's hip, the fingers of the other braced against his chest.

"What?"

"Um." Tommy licked his lips. "I, uh, I.... I mean, this is nice. An' I *want* to, but... we need to talk. About that job. Y'know? The one Karen's uncle—"

"The job in Poplar?"

Suspicion tugged at Brett like a weighted line as Tommy looked down at the floor. He flexed his fingers, plucking the worn fabric of that familiar shirt.

"Tommy?"

"I-I'm taking it. Okay? Bill offered, and—and I'm gonna take it."

Brett stared, genuinely shocked. He wasn't sure he'd heard right; he couldn't have, could he? It didn't seem real, next to the thin sunlight coming through the curtains and the rumpled, undone parts of Tommy's clothes... and then, slowly, he realized it wasn't just the incongruity that had caught at him.

He had, Brett was appalled to discover, simply flat out assumed Tommy wouldn't get the job. He got passed over often enough. It hadn't crossed his mind for a moment that he'd actually—

"Poplar?"

He heard himself speak, choking out the word like a cough.

Well, there went the make-up sex. Tommy just folded his lower lip in, pinching it between his teeth, and he looked sorrowful and—in some infuriating, impossible way—relieved.

He couldn't do that. Brett, aware of his heart thudding harder and harder, felt Tommy's hand tighten on his wrist.

"It's... not permanent. I know you'll be mad, but—"

"No." Brett forced the word out and bit down on the curses that wanted to go with it. A sinking dread spooled within him, turning his limbs leaden and his mouth dry. "No, you can't...."

"I wanted to tell you all about it. Bill's a really nice guy. He was really... look, he's going out of his way to help me. I—"

All the apologies and the sorrowful regret in Tommy's face amounted to very little as far as Brett was concerned. He backed off, away from Tommy and his yielding warmth and the stolen comfort of his mother's bed.

It wasn't supposed to be like this. It was meant to be reconciliation. How had they managed to go from a little hot, illicit fooling around to... this... in less than a minute?

"No," Brett repeated, like it could actually change things.

Tommy reached out. "Baby, it's not—"

"Don't." Brett glared at him, his own hand raised defensively. "Don't. You just... you just come out with this now? I mean, you're just gonna.... Two-hundred-and-fifty-mile commute? Is that the plan?"

He hated the spite, the scorn in his voice, but it seeped out like a rotten, bleeding wound and he couldn't stop it. A bitter weight of angry tears boiled behind Brett's eyes, and he fought them down, the hurt giving way to invective.

"I'll probably be there during the week, come back for weekends." Tommy shrugged tightly. "Depends on what part of the season they want me for, or if…. There'll be times I'm off. It's a good chance, Brett. You have to see that. You—"

"I don't *have* to do anything! What about me, huh? What about what I want, what I need?"

There should have been something faintly ridiculous about them standing there, starting to have this fight in the middle of Mei's bright, sunlit, determinedly cheerful room. Maybe there was. Brett just didn't think he could find anything to laugh at… or anything at all beneath the swirling mass of rage and betrayal. Stupid, stupid things to feel, he knew, but he couldn't stop them.

Tommy just looked astounded, staring at him like he'd grown a second head and started speaking in tongues with it. Brett guessed he hadn't expected this kind of reaction, but he'd opened the floodgate, and there was no way to bite back now. The stupid, furious tears burned in his eyes and made his head throb, even as the last sane part of him sat back and screamed "stop."

"I need you *here*!" he whined, hating the sound that threaded through the words, and the thickness of a barely contained sob. "W-with me. I can't… I didn't really think you'd do it! You ca—fuck it, Tommy! Don't… don't."

The last words tumbled out, snotty and muffled, as Tommy gathered him into a hug. Brett sniffed, hating the awkwardness of his outburst, his selfishness, and the violent anger that still seethed in his blood. Tommy gripped him tight, two words rustling over and over again into his hair.

"I'm sorry."

Brett clung on. The tears wouldn't come. They just sat there, a dull ache on the bridge of his nose, taunting him.

"You got every right to be mad," Tommy murmured. "But don't be hurt. Please? I mean, this… it's for us, right? We both know I haven't—well, it's been tough. I know. I really think I need to do this, Brett. And… hey, it was you who said I oughta get out of this town, wasn't it?"

Brett grimaced. "I didn't mean—"

"I know. I know what you meant. But you see what I'm tryin' to do?"

Reluctantly, he nodded and let his arms slide around Tommy's broad shoulders, faces pressed close together.

Bastard. Why d'you always have to be right?

"I'm not ready to miss you again. I want you home."

"That's what I wanna make happen," Tommy whispered. "'K? If I can do this…."

"But—"

Brett fought it, fought the urge to yell, and the urge—a result of Tommy's palm working in slow circles over his back—to just give in and beg. He didn't know what he was supposed to say, or how Tommy had expected him to react.

Am I meant to be happy about this?

Tommy's free hand fitted perfectly into the hollow of Brett's lower back, burrowing under his shirt to caress warm skin.

"Hey," he said, against Brett's cheek. "I love you."

Brett accepted the reassurance of his lips, but sought it blindly, eyes tight shut and the breath hitched in his throat.

"Love you too," he muttered, like he'd said countless times before. The words weren't as big as they used to be, but they meant something tempered with time and so much else. Brett drifted back in Tommy's arms, leaving a little more space between them. Tommy looked at him like he hadn't in a long time; full of want, apology, and the vague suggestion that he was still searching for something. Brett wished he knew what. He traced the contours and tensions of Tommy's back, idly drawn into futile imaginings that he'd never said what he had, and they could just go to bed and let the rest of the world take care of itself.

"It's a long way," he said, not sure if it was an inability or unwillingness to let this go that colored his voice.

Tommy exhaled tightly and dropped his gaze. The corner of his mouth twitched. "I'd do four or five days a week, be back on weekends. Only part of the year."

He looked up from under his lashes, as if he was really worried about how Brett would take it. Brett sighed. However much he wanted to rant, kick and rail, shove Tommy in the chest and yell at him until his throat dried out, he couldn't. His body, leaden and useless, wasn't under his own control anymore, just lumpen clay, cold and unresponsive.

"Sure," he said.

Tommy's breath of relief grazed his cheek.

"Thank you." He tightened his grip on Brett's arm. "It's gonna be okay."

"Mm." Brett grunted.

That seemed like a pretty optimistic assessment. He'd thought the whole point of having Tommy home was building a life together, not watching him disappear again at the first available opportunity.

Tommy let go of him and took a step back. He frowned. "You're not all right with this, are you?"

Brett glanced at him, hating the anger he saw in Tommy's face.

You have no right to be pissed with me. No damn right at all.

"No." He shrugged. "No, I'm not. Not really."

"But—"

"Look, if you have to do it, if you think it's going to make things better—"

Tommy exhaled sharply, shaking his head in disbelief. "Fuck, Brett...."

"No, it's fine. Just do it, okay? Y'know, you're right. You *ought* to do it. You should."

He sounded numb, and angry, and bored. He was, he supposed. All of those things, and a whole lot more that would probably cut in later, when he'd had a chance to calm down.

Tommy's gaze flicked over his face, hard and agitated. "You're just gonna knuckle under and put up with it, huh?"

"Well, you're not giving me much choice."

"I could use some support here," he snapped.

It wasn't the best choice of words. Brett pushed back as if scalded, his mouth curled around a sneer. "What? What the fuck d'you think I'm trying to do? What have I been doing for six fucking years, Tommy? Huh? You do *not* make it fucking *easy!*"

Tommy glared at him. "Yeah, I know. I hear all about that, don't I? 'Cause fucking God forbid I oughta stop feeling guilty...."

"Bullshit!" Brett spat, Tommy's shirt crumpled in his fist before he really recognized he'd grabbed it. He shoved, hard, aware of Tommy taking hold of his arms and pushing him back, denying him the confrontation he wanted. "It's not about guilt! And it's not always about you, Tommy! I-I just.... Forget it, all right? Take the damn job! You need it. And... and time apart's prob'ly gonna do us good too. Okay?"

The look on Tommy's face cut him, sharp and deep. Such fear and terrible loss, somewhere under the mantle of his irritation.

"That's your answer again, huh? You came here, Brett. *You* wanted *me*. Just 'cause it don't all work out like you think you want—"

"You don't even *know* what I want!"

"Well, I'm not a fucking psychic!"

"Yeah? No kidding. I want this over. I wanna stop waiting for you."

He regretted the words even before they'd left his mouth. Tommy looked like he'd been kicked in the balls. If he hadn't been so angry, Brett would have wanted to hold him. Instead, he took a sick and twisted pleasure in sticking the knife in.

"I want you to stop letting me down."

Tommy's chest rose and fell tightly in the silence, his stiff breathing the only sound in the room. The enormity of what Brett had said dawned on him a little as Tommy's eyes filled, pain veiled in fury.

"Get out, then," he muttered through clenched teeth, seeming to look through Brett rather than at him. "Just... go, if it's that bad."

Brett stood his ground, in a moment that drew out, thick and wreathed with thorns. It would be so easy to go. He'd turn and run and spend days on end wavering around the place, like he'd done before he came here today, looking to make up.

Make up... huh. Yeah. Was that what this was? Maybe some things were too broken to fix. He saw himself taking Nick up on his offer, spending a week alone in his apartment: a different town, a different point of view. He could come back feeling better, put this behind him. Who knew, maybe there was even a future out there that didn't include Tommy.

Brett looked at him now, the blank expression he'd got so fond of adopting shot through with the jagged edges of hurt and anger... a little bit of hatred, even. His mouth was a grim line, his eyes wet and his body held somewhere between the desire to run and the urge to throw a punch. Some days, he barely seemed like the same man.

Brett wondered if he'd changed that much too, if he was still the same person Tommy thought he was... the same person Tommy had fallen in love with. He still wasn't sure how that had happened, all that time ago, but he'd learned not to question fate. Besides, he knew one thing for sure: he wasn't about to run out on any of it.

He shook his head. "No."

"I mean it. You can go, Brett, and—"

"Leave you? No."

"But if I'm only gonna let you down...." Tommy's voice seemed to echo in his throat, amplified by the threat of breaking.

Brett winced. "I shouldn't have—"

"No. Don't apologize for saying stuff you mean. I know. All this.... You wanted answers. The apartment. Bozeman... when you asked about that—"

"That was dumb. I didn't—"

"I'd do it!" Tommy snapped, voice rising a little in pitch. "Don't you know? I'd do it in a second. But I can't lose everything else. Family, and…. They're just… I dunno. There's… Mom. She pushes me out, and I'm like this outsider just tryin' to live here—fuck, y'know? If I give in and put it all on you, what happens then? I screw up, or I piss you off once too often and wreck things and…."

Tommy exhaled deeply, looking for all the world like a crumpled paper cup. Somewhere in Brett's chest, the last of his defenses crumbled. Tommy swiped at his eyes with the heel of his palm, scrubbing roughly, as if he could punish the tears into not falling.

"I'd have nothing. Less than nothin'."

"It won't happen. We're stronger than that. You know—"

"It's different now." Tommy backed away when Brett reached for him. "You see that, don't'cha?"

Brett sighed deeply. He did. Like a pale, ugly dawn, stained with red and the fat fingers of cloud, it all made sense. He saw what Tommy was afraid of, why he came second-best to it, and what, though it stuck in his throat, he had to do about it.

The hardest part of loving the stubborn bastard was going to be giving him the space he needed to build his own life.

Silence fell between them, awkward and heavy both with unsaid things and things that never should have been said. Tommy sniffed wetly and frowned at the floor.

Brett bit his lip and nodded slowly. After a moment, he let out a long, low sigh.

"All right."

Tommy glanced up, looking confused. "What?"

Brett shrugged. "We gotta start somewhere. You think you're gonna want the Chevy for this job?"

He was already reaching into his pocket as Tommy blinked, evidently perplexed. "Huh? Uh. Um, I guess. I… I don't have a start date, but…."

"There. Your old keys. I can carpool for work until I get something else fixed up. There's another one on there too."

"Oh?"

"My apartment," Brett said simply. "So, as and when."

"That's it?"

He looked wearily at Tommy. It wasn't exactly the grand romantic gesture he'd planned... but it was close enough.

"Yep. Do what you need to. I'll be here when you're done. I can't promise I won't be pissed, and I'm sure as hell getting my own back later, but... yeah. That's it."

Tommy clasped the keys tight in his hand, and his expression softened. His mouth moved, like he wanted to say something, but then he shook his head and just smiled, a small, shy thing, delicate and sad.

"When d'you think you'll start?" Brett asked, mainly to puncture the silence. "Roughly?"

"It'd be next month, I guess."

"Right." He pushed away that happy, sappy little dream he'd had, about going to Nick's place, spending a few days in some kind of make-believe world where they had a real life—beautiful, boring, mundane and wonderful—and talked about stuff like leaky faucets and newspapers over the breakfast table.

There would be more dark nights, lying awake to listen for the sounds of someone who wasn't there, waiting to be woken by a nightmare Tommy wouldn't talk about... living for the weekends, he supposed. And it wasn't fucking *fair*.

"Brett—"

"Look—"

They both started to speak at the same time, both stopped and exchanged looks of embarrassed apology. Tommy cracked a smile.

"You're the best, y'know? You are."

Brett said nothing, but frowned at his feet. He felt Tommy's hand on his arm, a comforting squeeze that shot through his body like softly radiating lightning—for no good reason at all—and he came very close to opening his mouth and telling Tommy about his encounter with Lane Harding outside the pub. He hadn't wanted to—he wasn't anybody's damsel in distress—but it was the only thing Brett could think of that would have stopped the inevitable erosion of his resistance. He didn't say anything. He wanted to believe it didn't matter, and anyway, it probably didn't.

After all, it seemed like, whatever happened, nothing really changed.

CHAPTER
TEN

MEI bubbled with excitement. Tommy couldn't remember ever seeing her like that before; he wasn't sure how he felt about it. The house sparkled, though. She'd lit scented candles and bought part-baked bread that now sent the most wonderful smell emanating from the oven. Dinner would be chicken, with salad and real butter on the bread. Baked Alaska too, she'd said. Sunlight ought to be streaming through the windows, yet the sky stayed obstinately gray and cloudy. Tommy finished clipping Katie's hair into a french braid and kissed the top of her head.

"You're all done, Starfish."

She grinned into the mirror, giggled, and reached up to touch the new hairstyle.

"You're clever!"

Tommy smiled. *Gay gene gotta come out someplace....*

"Don't keep puttin' your fingers all in it, or it'll come out before dinner time, okay?"

She nodded, and he watched her go, hoping she'd manage to keep it in place at least until Ron arrived. Tommy knew how important this seemed to be for Mei, and, despite his lingering sense of discomfort, he felt an obligation to at least try and make sure things went smoothly.

He kind of wished Brett could have been there, but they were still not-exactly-not-talking, which sucked. However, things could have been worse. He'd thought Brett would really lose it when he heard about Poplar, and Tommy supposed there had been a dozen better ways to break the news. No point thinking about that now, though. He'd already done it, and done it his same old stupid, clumsy way, and Brett had every right to be mad and hurt and whatever else he was.

That didn't make it any easier, of course.

They had managed to talk about things a little more, and without anybody actually yelling or slamming out of the apartment in a temper. Tommy guessed that was progress, despite the fact that Brett's disapproval was like an afternoon thunderstorm, roiling and grumbling on the horizon and throwing long, dark clouds over the rest of the day.

He was working overtime at the hospital… or so he said. Kept his phone switched off a lot of the time. Tommy had wanted to call him that afternoon, before all the intensity and chaos of preparation for this particular ritual got underway, but he hadn't had a chance to pick up a new battery for his cell, and, frankly, it seemed like the whole world was inexplicably set against him actually talking to his boyfriend.

He sighed and sloped through to the living room, just as Katie bounced past in the hallway, chanting "He's here!" over and over, at the top of her voice. It was probably going to be a very long evening.

Ron arrived in a shiny red Lexus, and wasn't at all as Tommy had pictured him.

Well, a little sweaty maybe, but that appeared to be nerves. He greeted Mei with a peck on the cheek and a bottle of dry white wine, and extended a hand to Tommy.

"Hi. It's, uh, it's nice to meet you, son."

Tommy saw the flicker of embarrassed terror on Ron's face. Obviously he hadn't meant that word to slip out. Not here, and not to him, of all people. Ron gulped heavily, and Tommy smiled, warming a little toward this thin, lanky man with his sandy hair, a high forehead, and pale blue, slightly runny eyes.

"Hi, Ron."

Ron's narrow mouth bowed into a smile, and he looked relieved. Mei slipped her arm through his. Tommy recognized the gesture: *We're a united front, honey. Don't panic.* Brett did the same thing sometimes. Now, Tommy wasn't sure whether it bothered him or not. Maybe it had always been hard to tell whose side his mother wanted to take.

Ron made a good impression on the kids, though. A ready smile, a kind but respectful manner with Robbie and Lila—no attempts at sticky compliments or misplaced humor—and it seemed to work. Katie stayed quiet at first, apparently reserving judgment. He won her over at dinner when he pulled out her chair for her and treated her like a grown-up.

Smart guy.

The meal went well, all things considered. Mei's manner—brittle cheerfulness and sparkling laughter—gave everything an unreal, ethereal air, and an uneasy mood hung over them. Ron fitted in well, nonetheless. He'd lived in Havre for more than twenty years, he said, moving originally from a little town in Saskatchewan—famed mainly for its proximity to the more entertainingly named locale of Climax— with his former wife, Judy. Tommy caught the break in his speech where he guessed, among other company, Ron might have alluded to the local joke about the towns' proximities. As drivers who were headed north across the border liked to say: *I can get to Havre, then Turner, but I never make it to Climax.* It led to a brief lull in the conversation, punctured by Katie's clear, confident tones.

"How come your wife's not here? Did she die too?"

Tommy saw the smile on his mother's face freeze, caramel lips curling horribly. Lila shushed her sister, seizing the bottle of strawberry sauce from the center of the table and squelching it onto Katie's Baked Alaska. The noise sucked at the silence, ripe and bubbling. Tommy prodded his spoon into his own dessert and frowned at the pattern on the china.

Eventually, Ron cleared his throat. "Well, uh, yes. Yes, she did. She got very sick with, uh, cancer... and she died. Five years ago now."

Tommy glanced up, attention divided between Ron, the mist descending over that mild, sandy face—Mei's hand on his wrist, frozen rictus replaced by a look of tender sympathy—and Katie, looking very intently at the pair of them. She nodded solemnly, and appeared to be sagely digesting the information.

For a moment, Tommy wanted to stand up and scream, throw plates at the wall... anything to break this moment into tiny pieces.

She was a child. She shouldn't be thinking like that. She should still be too young to see death everywhere, to attribute every absence to the sudden, unnatural ending of a life.

I did that to her.

No. He blinked the thoughts away, focused on all the techniques, all the crap he'd gone through in therapy. Management and rationalization. Not letting fear rule you. And that's all it was… fear. *She's fine. I'm fine. Everybody's… fine….*

The room suddenly seemed so hot, so small.

Lila had rallied magnificently and started talking about the new cancer care center at Montana Northern. She caught Tommy's gaze and raised her eyebrows.

"… right? Brett say anything about that?"

"Uh…." Tommy swallowed, a knot of ice cream and sponge cake as tough as leather in his throat. "Not really. I don't know how much the PT department has to do with, uh, oncology patients."

The talk veered away again, delicately navigated into calmer shallows, and for a while it wasn't too bad. Robbie was monosyllabic and sullen, Lila worked hard at keeping Katie quiet, and Mei chattered inconsequentially about some woman both she and Ron knew from the dry cleaner's.

Tommy missed Brett. He was so much better at all this shit, and him being here would have made the sideways glances Ron kept shooting at him more bearable.

After dessert, glad of the opportunity to get out of the room, Tommy volunteered to deal with the dishes and the coffee.

He'd barely got into the kitchen, dumped the plates and put the kettle on, before he heard the soft tread of Ron's sensible shoes on the linoleum. Tommy reached for the sugar and closed his eyes.

Aw, hell, no….

Ron cleared his throat. "So, uh, anythin' I can do there, Tommy?"

Tommy shook his head. "Nah, s'all good. Thank you."

"Hhmmn."

Tommy exhaled slowly through his teeth. He could pick out the language of Ron's movements without turning around. He heard the rustle of his poly-cotton shirt as he stretched his arms, the shift of his weight as he rocked gently on the balls of his feet.

I'm not going anywhere, it all said. *Let's talk.*

That had to be about as subtle as the yawning-with-the-arm-along-the-back-of-the-couch routine Scott used to try on girls in middle school. Not that Tommy wasn't grateful for Ron's desire to be… what? Accepted, or just acknowledged?

He turned and glanced at the kitchen door. Everybody else seemed occupied. Lila had taken Katie aside, and there wasn't a sign of Mei or Robbie. The strains of an old Mariah Carey album started to filter through to the kitchen, and—just for a second—a pained expression seemed to cross Ron's face. He masked it well, and Tommy couldn't help but like him a little better.

"So, uh, you're doin' all right, eh?"

Ron's diplomacy might be about as subtle as a half brick in a wet sock, but he meant well, Tommy decided, even if it was a little cringe-making. He shrugged.

"I'm gettin' along. It's… a process, apparently. Getting back to— Well, not to where I used to be, but… y'know. I'm doing good. Thanks."

Ron nodded and slipped his long hands into his pockets. "Hmm. That's—no, that's good. Your mom tells me you're starting a new job next month."

"Ah-huh. Got a couple more weeks to go, fill out more forms… then I'm set."

Tommy dumped spoonfuls of the cheap powdered coffee into four cups and moved to the fridge to get Katie's apple juice. He tried not to make eye contact, but Ron seemed to be everywhere at once, giving him that bland, genial smile.

Don't worry, Casanova. I'll be right outta your hair.

"It'll be, uh, difficult, I guess, won't it?" Ron offered, rocking gently on the balls of his feet. "Working away? Especially after—"

"Yeah. But I'll manage, thanks."

Tommy fumbled the spoon, metal clinking loudly on the rim of the cup, and reached for the kettle. He was mildly curious as to exactly what Mei had told Ron about their family, and how much he'd picked up along the way, but he didn't want to ask. He didn't want much, except to be rid of this strange, foreign interloper.

If his mother wanted a new life, fine. Great. If the kids liked him, good. For Tommy, it all just tasted bitter, like he was being pushed even further away.

That was stupid, he supposed. Ron was trying to be nice. And this whole thing… this wasn't about pushing anyone away. Hell, he did enough of that by himself without needing anybody else to do it for him.

Tommy frowned at the swirling eddies in the coffee cups.

Poor baby.

He was fucking sick of sympathy.

Ron cleared his throat, a rustle of poly-cotton and cheap slacks announcing the awkward shift of his stance, arms folded over his skinny chest. Tommy glanced up and watched him cock his head solicitously to the side.

"So, uh… about y-your mom and me—"

Tommy tossed the spoon to the worktop and turned around, leaning back against it. He wanted to laugh at the absurdity of all this, at the corniness, and at the stilted formality in Ron's face. And it *was* absurd. It should have been no more than that; just so silly it seemed funny. But that wasn't all there was to it.

What d'you think I'm gonna do if I don't like it, huh? Shoot ya?

The thought rustled darkly in Tommy's mind. He found it too easy to imagine the things people wondered, the things people whispered, and he could all too easily see the anxiety in Ron's pale, slightly bulbous eyes.

Are you scared? Really scared?

He sighed wearily, cradled one cup of coffee in his hand, and held out another to Ron. He could take the rest through in a minute. This needed to be dealt with first.

"Listen, Ron. First off, I think it's good. She deserves... somebody kind. Somethin' good. Second, I'm not the man of this house. You don't have to— I mean, it's not even my business. Y'know?"

Ron's wide, pallid brow furrowed, and he sipped his coffee, then swallowed and gave him a slow, faintly confused smile.

"Well, I don't know about that, Tommy. Seems to me, a family includes everybody. You all gotta live with people's choices, right? I, uh, I suppose what I'm saying is... life works when we all support each other, and, well, I'd like to help your mother in that regard. She's a special woman."

Tommy winced, then felt guilty about it. What, he disagreed with that statement? He blinked rapidly at his coffee and watched the bubbles spin lazily on its dark surface. It would just have been nice to know what Ron meant. Was he being offered a hand, or being pushed away?

"Yeah," he said. "I'm, um... I'm pleased for you. An' her. I... uh. Yeah."

"Well, that's good to know," Ron said, and he seemed pleasant enough, his tone warmer and more confident than it had been. "I'd, uh, I'd really like to think we can all get along well, you know? The kids... they could do with some stability, and your mom—"

"Yeah," Tommy said again, and the word cut through the air, short and blunt and tinged with an irate kind of steel.

He lifted his gaze, watched Ron smile blandly at him, holding his coffee cup in two long, thin hands, and he wondered just how long this whole mess of shit had been going on.

They took the coffee through. Tommy brought Katie her apple juice, and couldn't help noticing the way Mei glanced up at Ron, like there was some unspoken discussion there. She smiled that china doll smile, and Tommy looked away. He caught Lila's eye and pretended not to understand the lift of her eyebrows or the pursing of her pink-glossed mouth.

He sat on the couch, and Katie clambered up next to him, her piping voice a descant drill into his head as she contemplated aloud whether it was really true that cashew nuts came off of apples, and whether this new nugget of knowledge applied to all apples, or just special ones. Tommy squinted at her and gave a noncommittal grunt. Heaven only knew where she'd picked that one up. School, maybe, he supposed. Or the back of a packet of something in the kitchen... you couldn't tell with Katie.

"Don't know, Starfish. Does it matter?"

She looked solemnly at him, her glass of juice clutched in two small, stubby hands, a wet and sticky rime of it on her upper lip. "Well, *yeah*. If I don't know the answer, it does."

Tommy smiled wearily. Sometimes he was sure she'd go the furthest of any of them. He stroked her hair, where a few errant strands were already starting to escape from the french braid, and brushed her bangs aside with a fingertip.

"I don't think it's all apples. Just special ones. Okay?"

She looked thoughtful for a moment, then pursed her lips. "Oh. So... like, how things are different but the same?"

"Yeah." Tommy sipped his coffee. "I guess."

"Like how you're different?"

"Mm-nn." He swallowed heavily and forced the hot liquid down. "What d'you mean?"

Katie shrugged and swung her legs, heels rhythmically bashing into the front of the couch.

"Don't do that, honey," Mei said in passing, stepping delicately by with a box of chocolate mints in her hand.

She was wearing that same black skirt, Tommy noticed, and it flared and twirled against her pale skin as she picked her way across the floor. Ron had been making a valiant attempt at talking to Robbie, and was plowing his way through the monosyllabic responses while Lila cut in with vaguely related things about school and how it was totally unfair that Mei wouldn't let her get a part-time job until next year.

Katie's legs stilled, and she looked up at Tommy with a tiny frown creasing the triangle between her brows.

"*You* know. You're like us, but you're different. Because you were away... an' because you like boys. That's what Robbie says."

Tommy's chest tightened, a thin spiral of dread uncurling within him, even as he watched Katie's lips fold around the words. The air seemed to echo, and he opened his mouth, trying to get there before she said the inevitable.

"Robbie says that you like co—"

"Hey, you know what?" Tommy cut in quickly. "We should go fix your hair up."

She looked confused. "Wha…?"

"Come on," he insisted, taking the glass from her and setting it down on the coffee table, then raising her up by one small, splay-fingered hand, aware of the way the volume of all that polite conversation had increased. "I told you if you kept messin' with it, it'd all come undone, didn't I?"

Tommy led Katie out of the room with one brief glance back at his brother. Robbie just stared blankly at him, his face expressionless and his eyes flat and hard.

Every passing minute had felt heavy, like a choking weight of water or the greasiness in the air that comes before a storm. Now it all just seemed to pour over him, left him saturated and deaf, numb, and blind, and he didn't even care about the knot of anger in his stomach.

He took Katie through to the back of the house, to the bathroom, and sat her on the closed toilet seat, facing away from the mirror so she couldn't see her hair wasn't as badly messed up as he'd made out. Tommy gently unsnapped the pins, one by one, and reached for the brush that lay beside the sink.

"So, when did Robbie say that?" he asked, trying to keep his tone nonchalant… light. "'Bout me?"

Katie shrugged and swung her legs again, feet tapping out a rhythm on the pedestal of the toilet.

"He just says it. Sometimes."

"Ah-huh." Tommy dropped a handful of pins next to the sink. There didn't seem to be much point in redoing the braid. She'd be going to bed before long. "And what d'you think about that?"

His pulse thudded dully in the base of his throat. He'd never had *that* talk with any of the kids. Never seemed to need to. He remembered

Lila—just after he got out, the night he came back here for the first time—peeping from the doorway as he kissed Brett good-bye.

If you two were any sweeter, you'd melt in the rain.

She didn't care. And anyway, if people *did* care, that was their own fucking problem, right? It wasn't his problem. He didn't need anyone's approval. Not Robbie's, or Ron's, or even his mother's, sitting down there next to her new squeeze, eating chocolates and smiling like she'd just won the fucking lottery.

Tommy stopped himself, aware that he was holding his breath, and sweat had begun to prickle on his palms. He exhaled slowly, switched the hairbrush to the other hand, and scrubbed his right palm against his jeans.

Katie's heels drummed against the toilet with a thin, regular, tinny *clunk*.

"I don't know," she said, eventually. "Boys are okay. Except when they're gross. Or mean. I like some boys."

"Ah-huh," Tommy murmured.

Did she really understand? He wasn't sure, and he didn't feel ready to ask any further questions, though he knew somebody had to probe this issue, and Mei sure as hell wasn't likely to do it. Katie fixed him with those dark eyes that so often seemed way more serious than they should, set into that small, round-cheeked face.

"But… uh." He cleared his throat and unwound a section of her hair, ready to brush out. "You know how it's different, right? Like, um, like with me and Brett."

Katie's brow furrowed, and her mouth screwed up. "It's just kissing," she said disapprovingly. "And all *that* stuff."

Tommy took a breath, frowned, and decided he wasn't sure how to counter that one.

"Uh… yeah." He gave a nervous cough. "We, um, we kiss. And stuff."

"I saw Mommy kissing Ron," Katie said conspiratorially.

Tommy bit his lip, feeling mildly deflated. "Yeah?"

She had a point. There was no damn difference at all. Whoever was doing it, it was just kissing… and all *that* stuff. The thought made him want to smile, and he brushed her hair out carefully, laying the smooth strands forward across her shoulder.

"So, d'you like Ron?"

Her heels thunked some more against the toilet. "Mm-hm. He's okay, I guess. I like Brett," she added, after a moment's apparent thought.

"Me too," Tommy admitted. He wasn't sure if the comparison she seemed to be drawing should worry him, or if there was other stuff he ought to say or not. "Uh… so, um…."

"Robbie says you're going away again," Katie announced, frowning up at him. "Why? Did you do something?"

He flinched. "Wh—? No, I… no, Katie. I got a job. I have to go to Poplar, to work. For Karen's uncle."

"Oh."

The distant strains of new background music filtered from the living room, faint and with a full, rounded bass line. Katie's mouth turned down into a very defined pout.

"Why?"

Tommy sighed and set to work on the other side of her hair. "Because I have to get a job somewhere. Hey… Bill's got horses. You know that? I'm gonna be working with horses."

"Really?"

She brightened at that, and he smiled. "Ah-huh. Maybe you'll be able to come down and see 'em. Maybe even ride one. Wouldn't that be cool?"

Katie grinned and nodded, but the distraction wasn't as complete as Tommy had hoped. Her grin faded, and she frowned again.

"Tommy?"

"Mm-hm?"

She chewed the inside of her lip thoughtfully, and thwacked her heels against the toilet one last time.

"I'll miss you."

Tommy swallowed and tried to ignore the pull in his chest. He laid the brush down and smoothed out her hair. "I'm gonna miss you too, Starfish."

She wrinkled her nose a bit at the nickname, but smiled anyway. He guessed maybe he had another year before she started complaining about it, and he bussed the top of her head.

"C'mon."

Katie slipped off the seat, sniffed, and wiped her hand across her nose. Tommy opened his mouth to tell her to use a tissue, but decided not to bother. It probably wouldn't have done much good.

Instead, he smiled, even when she slipped her slightly sticky hand into his, and took her back through to the living room. It was finally over... or almost. Ron left not long after, and there were cheerful smiles and warm good-byes, and Tommy knew it wasn't the last they'd be seeing of him, though he wasn't completely sure how he felt about it.

He busied himself collecting cups and glasses and taking them out to the kitchen. Robbie had already left the room, and Tommy hadn't seen where he went.

The click of his mother's high heels on the linoleum alerted him to her presence, though Mei said nothing. He turned the faucet off and stood the cup he'd been rinsing upside down on the draining board before shaking the water from his hands.

"Okay?"

"Mm." Her footsteps seemed loud against the buzz of music in the other room, the chatter of Katie and Lila bickering about something, and the weight of every single passing second. "Thank you, honey."

Tommy flexed one shoulder into a casual, indifferent shrug. He ought to turn and look at her, he supposed. He wasn't sure why he didn't want to.

"Ron's nice," he said, hearing how dull and threadbare his voice sounded.

"Mm-hm. I'm glad you think so."

"Yeah." He sniffed philosophically. "He, uh... made a good impression, I think. With everybody."

The sound of one heel scuffed against the floor. "Yes. I'm glad about that."

The back of Tommy's neck prickled, and he resisted the urge to rub at it, instead scrubbing the hand he'd already half raised against the leg of his jeans.

"So," Mei said sweetly, "are you going to Brett's for the weekend?"

The question surprised him a little. He'd mentioned the idea in passing—all the time they could take together before work started was precious, and more so given the things Tommy knew needed patching up—but he hadn't expected her to remember.

"Um, maybe." He glanced over his shoulder. "I don't know... he's been really busy at work."

Mei gave him a tight, delicate little smile. "Well, all the more reason, right?"

"Guess so."

She tilted her head to the side, regarding him coolly. "Is everything okay, sweetie?"

Tommy shrugged again. "Ah-huh."

"Really?"

There was a note of something in her voice he couldn't quite identify. A little tiny whiff of "I told you so," maybe, or some trace of self-righteous suspicion. He frowned and let his gaze drop to the pale linoleum, following the subtle pattern of lines and scuffs on it.

"Brett's still kinda pissed about Poplar. I get why, but... it's not easy."

"Oh."

She stepped forward, and Tommy caught himself flinching. He turned, and she was closer than he expected, reaching out to him with that small, gentle smile on her face. She rubbed his arm, and then her slim, hard fingers moved to his cheek, her touch cool and gentle.

"Don't get me wrong, honey. I like Brett. I really do. It's just that... you ought to give yourself time, you know? Really think about things. Because you may not even know what you want right now."

Confusion screwed Tommy's eyes into slits. "What?"

Mei's hand fell to her side, and she crossed her other arm over her body, catching hold of her right wrist with her left hand and twisting a little on her feet. It was an incongruous, girlish gesture, and he didn't care for it.

"Well, you know… I just think you ought to go, see how this thing in Poplar works out. It's for the best, and if he can't see that—"

"He sees it, Mom," Tommy snapped. "Doesn't make it easier, that's all."

Her lips twisted into a dismissive pout. "Maybe. Just, all I'm saying… sometimes everyone needs a new start, right? And you have to think about what you want from that. What you're planning for, in—"

In the long term.

"—the long term," she finished, just as Tommy had absolutely *known* she would.

He couldn't quite believe he was hearing this. A dozen different invectives boiled on his tongue, but he choked them all down.

She's still your mother. Remember that.

"I know what I want," he said quietly. "I wanna be with Brett. I want us to have a normal life."

"Oh, I know, honey. I know."

Tommy pretended not to see the curl of her lip, and not to hear her delicately bitter chuckle.

He pretended she didn't make his fingers itch.

CHAPTER ELEVEN

BRETT slept in on Saturday morning, glad of the opportunity to do so. Work had been crazy, and didn't promise to calm down any time soon. In addition to everything else, Elaine kept giving him recommendations for books and website reading, and while it was all very interesting and well worth pursuing, he knew he was pushing himself a little harder than he ought to be.

He knew why too.

So Brett shuffled around the apartment in boxers and a sleep-warmed, slightly stale T-shirt, nursing a cup of coffee and idly wondering if Tommy was going to come by. In a perfect world, they'd have found somewhere to go on Friday nights by now, a place they could knock back a few drinks, get a little stupid together... have *fun*, like any other couple. Only Tommy didn't usually want to go out that much, and, when he did, he got irritable if Brett ended up paying, so they were pretty much limited to the kind of night out that cost less than ten bucks a head.

Mostly, they just stayed in. Brett had no real problem with that—the whole Tommy being home thing was still new enough, even now, to be wonderful in its own right—and they did have a lot of catching up to do. It felt weird, getting to know him all over again; learning how to be with him, instead of being there for him. Brett wasn't sure on that point. It was possible, he acknowledged, that he was trying to do both.

He let his mind drift as he allowed himself to wake up slowly, the coffee prodding him toward alertness and the absence of the weekday rush soothing his lingering tension.

Tommy probably would be by later. They'd had a kind of loose plan: spend some time together, maybe grab a bite, get a beer, then come back here, watch a movie and go to bed… then stay there and let the whole of Sunday just slip by without them. Brett had to admit, it sounded like a *good* plan. It was enough, anyway. For now.

When the first knock on the door sounded, he was standing in front of the refrigerator, peering into it and inwardly lamenting the lack of visible bacon. Brett scratched sleepily at his head, kicked the fridge shut, and wandered over to see who wanted what. Tommy couldn't possibly have lost his keys already, could he?

"Yeah, yeah," he muttered, as the banging intensified.

A brief glimpse through the peephole scuppered all of Brett's assumptions, and he slipped the chain off the door, suddenly both a great deal more awake and a great deal more panicky.

"Where is he?" Scott demanded, filling up the doorway with a cloud of anger and overpowering aftershave.

A gold chain glinted at the neck of his worn Grizzlies sweatshirt, but his lowriders bore grease and paint stains, and the laces of his sneakers were loose. He scowled and stabbed an accusatory finger at Brett.

"Is he here? Because I'm gonna fuckin'—"

"What the—"

Scott pushed the door open, stalking into the apartment and glaring around the room.

"—fuck?" Brett managed, peering out in the hallway beyond.

His neighbors weren't exactly a hands-on, communicative bunch, but somebody was probably going to be pissed about the noise. It was still comparatively early. He shut the door and frowned at Scott, lip curled in confusion.

"Tommy," Scott demanded, turning to face him. "Fuck is he?"

"Not here. Wh—"

"We had fuckin' cops at our house, Brett. I *told* him… I am not having that shit under my roof. You sure he's not here? Because when I find him…."

"Wait, what?" Brett winced, struggling to catch up past the sudden lurch of cold dread. "Scott… what cops? Why would…?"

A dozen possibilities—parole violations, stop-and-searches gone bad, accidents or something worse—whirled behind his eyes, and the world pitched beneath him. Brett strafed his fingers through his hair, half of him already sinking into panic, and the half of him used to years of dealing with medical crises and penitential routines already manning up and wondering if he needed to pack an overnight bag.

"They were looking for Tommy," Scott growled, although he appeared to have settled to the fact his brother wasn't hiding anywhere in the apartment. "Something about an assault or shit, I don't know. I told them I hadn't seen him since Tuesday. I don't know what he's done, but I *told* him…. It's that fucker he was hanging with, I'll bet. Fuckin' stupid…."

Brett stared, his mouth dry and the threads of horrible suspicion weaving through every breath. He blinked, forcing himself to focus on the words, not the possibilities.

"What guy? Hold on… why were they at your place? Why would—"

"I gave him a ride that day he got stuck, didn't I?" Scott grumbled. "Last time I do my goddamn brother a fucking favor! Next thing I know, fuckin' cops rollin' up, said they got a witness saw an Indian guy runnin' down Rich Street, getting picked up on Post Road, got *my* license plate—" He struck his chest with two fingers, then flung the hand out wide, encompassing the whole room in a gesture of defiant fury. "—and they're at *my* door, because my stupid fuckin' brother gets his fucking fingerprints all over whatever the shit happened when Lane *fucking* Harding decides to beat the crap out of somebody, and Tommy hasn't even got the goddamn sense to… what?"

"Lane Harding?" Brett could hear the bitter ice in his voice. The pulse hummed in his forehead, the room dimming a little at the edges. *Goddammit, Tommy….*

Scott glared irritably at him, like he was either an idiot or being purposely obtuse. After a moment, his scowl slackened a little, and those dark eyes that were both so like and so unlike Tommy's softened as he realized Brett truly didn't understand.

"He didn't tell you about any of this?"

"No," Brett said, his tone cold and distant. "No, he didn't."

"Fuck," Scott said flatly. "Y'know, I really thought he'd be here. S'why I came here first. I didn't wanna worry Mom, if... I mean, they accepted what I said, about just givin' him a ride. They didn't push it, but—aw, shit."

He pulled his phone from the pocket of his jeans and started dialing, already muttering again. Brett's anger finally started catching up through the anxiety and fear.

"Scott, you could at least tell me what the hell—"

Scott held up a hand as whoever he was calling apparently answered. "Mom? Yeah, it's me. Wh— Really? He was? They did? What? No, I thought he'd be at Brett's. Nah, I'm there n— Did she? No, I told Karen *not* to call you. I was gonna—aw, fuck it...."

He muted the phone against his shoulder and glanced at Brett.

"Yeah, cops were at her place half an hour ago. Pulled him in for questioning. You might wanna get pants on, bro."

Brett opened his mouth, then took a deep breath and headed wordlessly to the bedroom. There would be time to lose his temper later.

TOMMY wasn't familiar with the inside of the city police department, although he wasn't surprised to find that the room in which he was interviewed had the same scratchily upholstered beige chairs as the sheriff's office, and the same faint odor of industrial disinfectant and air freshener. It almost smelled like the scent of baking cookies drifting in from somewhere. Beyond that, however, everything was different. There was no kaleidoscopic buzz of activity, nobody taking his prints or his clothes, or powdering his hands for gunshot residue.

There were just so many questions, and stupid ones at that.

He turned off, mainly. Looked at the table and answered yes, no, or "I don't know, sir." They didn't believe him, of course. His prints were on the baseball bat, and on the inside of Lane Harding's truck, and that bastard had dropped him straight into the shit, hadn't he? Tommy just slumped into the scratchy beige chair, shook his head, and stuck stubbornly to the same four sentences. He didn't know the guy, he'd accepted a ride from Harding and nothing more, no, they didn't socialize, and no, he'd never been inside the house, much less laid a finger on whoever the poor bastard was who'd landed himself on Lane's bad side.

They showed him pictures of the guy's injuries. He was a mass of bloody, swollen flesh, propped up in a hospital bed. Black eye, lip puffed out and stitched, and the shiny, greasy-looking blooms of fresh red bruises crawled all over his face. Tommy wasn't really surprised.

They went back over old ground too. Time in the joint, Lane's various infractions… not to mention the stuff that had gone down while they were inside that never made it onto the COs' radar. They wanted to talk about a lot of things, and Tommy didn't have a whole lot of choice in the matter. Seemed like Lane had been saying an awful lot for a man who made out he had a warrior's tight-lipped integrity.

The only evidence against Tommy was circumstantial. He clung to that, and to saying he wanted to speak to a lawyer and to his parole officer, and, beyond that, he tried to be as cooperative and honest as he could… though there were some things it would have just been dumb to mention.

Yeah, so prison had taught him where to land a punch. He'd known a lot of that already. It had made sure he stood up for himself when he needed to, but he'd never pushed it past that need. He hadn't wanted to be a big man. He'd just wanted to be left alone. All right, he'd run with Lane's boys, but not the way the cops were trying to make it sound. One of them seriously asked him if he felt like a tough guy, if he got respect out there for the time he'd served.

Tommy kept his gaze fixed on the scarred surface of the interrogation room table. He didn't look up at the clean, neutral walls or the clean, neutral officer questioning him, and he just shook his head.

"No, sir."

It wasn't respect. The talking circle had taught him that. He'd never wanted the kind of acceptance that came from Lane and the guys like him. Sure, there'd been a time when he'd needed it, but that was over now. Tommy didn't say so. People didn't understand. His whole damn life, people hadn't understood.

When he was a kid, he'd thought everybody lived like they did. He thought it was normal. As he grew and realized it wasn't—that not everybody walked on eggshells at home, waiting for the monster to come out—he tried to ask for help, but all the people who were meant to be there to do that, the teachers and the grown-ups you were supposed to go to, they didn't seem to care. He got ignored, or brushed aside and told things would be fine, and he thought maybe they would. He pulled everything inside, and he toughened himself up around it, until he found he'd become protective of the difference, jealously guarding all the things that were private and separate.

Us and them.

It had been that way for a long while. Too long.

It wasn't ever meant to be like that again.

Eventually, the cops decided they weren't going to formally arrest him. Maybe they believed him, maybe they didn't. Maybe they'd actually seen some goddamn sense and realized they didn't have a grain of proof that he'd done what they said he had, or that he'd known that Lane was going to do what he'd so obviously done.

No, sir. I had no idea. I wasn't aware of any of it.

That wasn't strictly true, Tommy supposed, but he didn't plan on digging into that whole mess. He was going to have enough shit from his PO to deal with, and he wasn't about to get into anything worse.

He was pretty sure it didn't really count as proper lying.

It was past midday by the time he got out. He was tired, his head hurt, and he wasn't sure whether the shame, anger, or flat-out indignation stung more. He was too damn tired to care, though.

So far, it had been a fucking awful day: cop car in front of the house, his mother going nuts, then being bundled down here and sat there like an idiot while they talked and fucking *talked....*

He knew it wasn't going to get much better when he walked out to the front desk and saw the welcome committee waiting for him.

Scott slouched against the wall, wearing his I'm-worried-about-you-which-pisses-me-off-and-I'm-gonna-take-that-out-on-you   scowl, and chewing on what Tommy guessed was a sizable chunk of nicotine gum. Beside him, Brett sat on one of the hard plastic chairs, unshaven and hard-eyed, his mouth drawn into a tight, anxious line and his hand resting on Lila's wrist.

A tangled pull of gratitude and regret tugged at Tommy's chest as he looked at his sister. He couldn't have expected for a moment that she'd be there, but there she was, a dark gray parka tossed on over a short skirt and cami, her hair pulled back too tight and her eyeliner smudged. She looked like she'd been crying.

She was the first to look up and see him, and she rose awkwardly to her feet, a damp tissue balled in one hand.

"Tommy!"

He reached up and tucked his hair behind his ear, trying to marshal a comforting smile that said everything was fine. It didn't work all that well. She crossed the room in tentative, uneven strides, then flung her arms around him. He hugged her tight, aware of every crinkle and rustle of her coat, the damp expulsion of her breath, and the fruity scent of her shampoo when she buried her head in his shirt.

"Hey," he murmured, rubbing her back. "What…?"

"What'd you think I was going to do?" Lila snapped reproachfully, tipping her chin so she could glare at him without pulling away. "Wait nicely at home with Mom?"

Tommy said nothing. He didn't have words for this, so he just hugged her tighter and tried not to make eye contact with Scott. He glanced nervously at Brett, expecting the full weight of his anger—and why wouldn't he be angry?—and was alarmed to find his face almost expressionless.

Lila sniffed, and Tommy gave her a last squeeze before she broke away.

"It's okay," he murmured, but the bruised, pouty look she shot him showed she didn't believe *that* for a second.

Brett stood up as he got there, but he didn't move toward Tommy, or even smile.

"You all right?"

He sounded tired. Really, really tired. Tommy nodded.

"Ah-huh. They didn't…. I, uh, y'know. Misunderstanding, that's all."

Brett shoved his hands deep in the pockets of his jeans. "Yeah."

"Right." Scott cracked his gum irritably and nodded to the door. "Can we get out of here, then? Huh?"

There was a muttered chorus of assent, and Tommy trailed after him out to the parking lot. The sunlight seemed bright, and it made him squint. He couldn't help thinking of Lane and the poor bastard with the busted-up face and the broken ribs.

Tommy had no idea if the guy really had owed him money, or if there had been some other reason for the beating. In his experience, that kind of smackdown usually came *with* a reason, and it was worth knowing what it was so you could avoid the provocation.

Maybe Roberto had been right all along, and Lane was just crazy. Tommy guessed he wouldn't have been surprised.

Still, the guy wasn't dead. He'd recover. Lane was probably going to get, what, three to five? No… most likely more, Tommy thought, given his record and the fact the crazy asshole couldn't seem to keep his mouth shut. Plus, they could always bump it up to aggravated assault. Did a bat count as a weapon? Yeah, of course it did. Maybe as much as fifteen then, unless he got some great lawyer to whittle everything down to the reasons it hadn't been his fault. He wondered what the chances of that would be, and was barely aware of the other realization settling around his shoulders like smoke.

Fifteen years. That coulda been you, dipshit.

Tommy didn't understand why it only felt real now, why it hadn't sunk in for one minute of the time he'd been sitting in there, faithfully repeating the same mostly true story. He slumped in the back of Scott's car, and the smell of warm upholstery and too-strong aftershave washed over him. He glanced up, but Brett was in the front seat, and though Lila was sitting beside him, she stared out of the window and didn't talk much.

They went to Dairy Queen. It was only a few blocks down from the police department, and it was a welcome bridge between everything that had happened and all the stuff that was going to hit later. Scott called Mei, then Karen, and went through the same set of short, codified responses. No, he was out. Yes, he was fine. No, they hadn't brought any charges.

Tommy sat behind a chicken sandwich and a side of onion rings and wondered if Scott was going to say that he hadn't done anything.

He didn't. He didn't ask if Tommy wanted to speak to their mother either, and *she* obviously hadn't asked to speak to him. Tommy wasn't sure if that was a bad thing or just meant everything was normal. Things didn't feel normal.

Once Scott was done, he tossed his phone onto the table with a sigh and rubbed a hand over his forehead before grabbing his half-pound burger and tackling it like a man who hadn't eaten in a week. Lila rolled her eyes.

"Ugh. You're such a pig."

Scott grunted and flicked a piece of lettuce at her. She wrinkled her nose, but it was a familiar, companionable kind of disgust. Under the table, Tommy felt Brett's knee nudge against his, and he glanced up, surprised.

They were sitting near the window, looking out onto the wide, gray sweep of the street beyond. Weekend traffic sluiced by, blurs of color and movement between the tarmac and the narrow band of pale blue sky. Brett had been depressingly healthy and ordered a chicken wrap and an orange juice, but he reached across and stole one of Tommy's onion rings.

"You sure you're okay?" he asked quietly, just before he bit into it.

Tommy nodded. "Mm-hm. I... I'm gonna have to go back to Mom's and let her yell at me for a while, but later, can I...?"

"Yeah." Brett's gaze tracked his face, those clear, wide eyes stained with fatigue and a dark, tight kind of resignation. He knee nudged Tommy's again, and he smiled thinly. "But if you scare me like that again—and I mean *ever*—then, hand to God, I am going to cut your balls off."

His expression softened a little, and Tommy knew he wasn't really angry. He didn't know why, because Brett should have been so mad that they should have practically gutted each other in the PD parking lot. He'd expected that. He'd expected the disappointment and the wounded betrayal and the sheer blind fury that he was so sure he deserved, and he wanted to know why it wasn't there. Had Brett gone past caring? The thought frightened him, and he frowned, wishing Scott and Lila weren't there, and everything else wasn't there, and they were just somewhere quiet, like they used to be when they got in the Chevy and drove out to Beaver Creek or Fresno… and nothing else mattered.

Things had been so much simpler then, in a lot of ways.

Brett picked up his juice and took a sip. The way his lips tightened as he swallowed made Tommy want to follow him back to the apartment right now, and just sit down on that faded green couch and not move a muscle until they'd talked through every last little thing, however awkward and difficult it was, and no matter how scared and vulnerable it made him feel or how much he hated the idea.

Prison had taught him that too, he supposed. All the time he'd done, the circle and the therapy and everything else…. Respect didn't come from other people. It wasn't what they thought or how they treated you; it was how you faced yourself.

Tommy figured it was probably time he lived up to that.

BRETT stood under the shower spray, waiting for the day to wash away. It seemed to be taking a long time to do so.

Scott had dropped him off a good few hours ago before driving over to Mei's, but Brett had struggled to settle to anything since he'd gotten in. He wasn't exactly unwelcome over at the house this afternoon, but it seemed better if he stayed out of it. That much had been obvious that morning, when they'd swung by on the way to going to find Tommy at the PD. Scott had wanted to see his mother, maybe try and calm her down a bit, but they'd ended up with Lila demanding to come too, despite Mei's furious protests, and the look she'd given Brett as her daughter clambered into the Toyota was enough to make his balls shrivel.

He didn't envy Tommy having to deal with her, and he was a little disgruntled at being so summarily pushed out and left on the sidelines, but he guessed it was one of those things Tommy had to fix on his own. She wasn't going to be happy, but then police cars and mothers were rarely a good combination. Brett shuddered and turned up the water heat as he recalled Monica's reaction, the day she and his father had come to pick him up from the sheriff's office.

This, though… this was different. He'd got Tommy's side of the story out of Scott—or at least the version of it Tommy had given to his brother—and it was enough to piece certain things together. Why Tommy hadn't called *him* that day, for example. It stung, though he supposed he shouldn't have been surprised.

Still, he was uneasy. That night outside the pub, Harding had seemed vindictive, spiteful… like he was planning something. Was this it? Or had it just been a vague and rootless anger, frustration at Tommy not fitting into whatever role Lane may or may not have intended for him?

Brett rinsed the shampoo from his hair and tried to rub the ugly suspicions out from behind his eyes. He'd been right—gossip was all over the hospital about what had happened with him and Harding, and Lane's arrest was hardly going to improve anything on *that* score—but Brett kept catching himself thinking other, stupid things. Without even trying, he could picture a dozen separate ways those oppressive, claustrophobic bonds of obligation and community could have snared themselves around Tommy's throat.

He'd never been involved in the multifaceted shards of gang culture when he was inside. Or at least he'd said he hadn't, and Brett believed him. However, he'd worried when Tommy first started with the lodge and the talking circle, because from the outside all kinds of groups looked the same. Besides, Brett was aware that, when life was so closed up, it intensified every tiny pressure and detail, and even the noblest causes fell prey to factions and divisions. It didn't even need to involve the word "gang."

Hell, there'd been a time one year that he'd driven all the way down for a visit, only to find Tommy's unit was on lockdown because an inmate had been beaten up by seven other guys in reprisal for appropriating somebody else's cup of pudding. It was easy for a man to lose perspective in that world, Tommy said.

Brett suspected it was probably just as dangerous a pitfall out here too.

After all, here he was, using up all the hot water and twisting himself into knots of confused and jealous insecurity over things that might never even have crossed anyone's mind, let alone actually *happened.*

Lane Harding scared him. He admitted it, in the privacy of his own head. And not just that; he represented too many possibilities, too many maybes… and the maybes were the thing that had almost killed Brett every day for the best part of six years.

Tommy had been so young when he'd started his term. And pretty. Very pretty. He'd always said prison wasn't like people thought, and that he knew how to take care of himself, and Harding had said that too, hadn't he?

Tough little bastard.

Brett stepped out of the shower, snatched a towel from the rack, and tried not to think of the things that were bothering him the most. Tommy might not have done *this*, but what else had he done? All those years of clear conduct—not counting that damn tattoo, which still made Brett mad every time he thought about it—but what had really happened when the lights went out?

That thought—that sneaking, awful thought that Brett didn't want to have, because it felt like a breach of trust—led to other places. He wanted to believe he'd dealt with viewing Tommy as a violent offender, but had he? Brett had always held that what he'd done had been a mistake, an aberration… that it had been self-defense, or as good as. Tommy wasn't a violent man. He *knew* that. He believed it wholeheartedly.

So why, this morning, had it been so easy to imagine the worst?

Brett growled out a frustrated sigh and wrapped the towel around his waist. He padded through to the bedroom, and catching the little glimpses of Tommy's stuff—a comb, a packet of aspirin, a discarded sock—just lying around the place, carelessly forgotten, made him smile.

Tommy wouldn't ever be like Harding, Brett told himself. And he wouldn't ever throw away all the things he was working so hard to put right.

And if he did?

Would I still be here?

Brett blinked the thoughts away and crossed to his dresser, rifling through the drawers and leaving trails of messed-up, turned-over clothes in his wake. He pulled on sweats and a worn-out, over-washed, and yet very comfortable T-shirt, and glanced at the window.

Outside, a low grumble that might have been distant thunder seemed to echo against the concrete. Brett tugged at the hem of his shirt and frowned as he contemplated the prospect of dinner. It would be easier if he knew whether Tommy was coming by or not. His stomach grumbled, and he sighed.

At that moment, the heavens opened. Thick trails of rain beat against the glass, every drop a wide, glossy splash as the darkness of a sudden cloudburst rolled over everything, blotting out the sunshine and leaving the clear blue sky muddied with a palette of grays and dirty whites.

It must mean it was nearly summer, Brett supposed.

CHAPTER
TWELVE

THERE wasn't much about it on the local news. It probably didn't warrant a lot of interest, Tommy guessed, though he kept half an eye on the bulletin while he waited for his order. The small TV bracketed to the wall didn't provide a lot of information; "local man arrested" was all they really said. He wondered whether the charge would end up being aggravated assault or not, and decided Lane was his own worst enemy… not that it was his problem anymore.

Whatever the guy thought he was, whatever rights to a rep he believed he had, they'd ended the second he'd tried to drop another man in the shit.

Tommy paid, took the bag the girl behind the counter gave him, smiled and thanked her, and headed back out to the Chevy, with the tantalizing aromas of the takeout rising to tug at his nose. He grinned to himself as he climbed into the truck. It felt good, being back in his own wheels.

He fiddled with the radio until he found a station playing some pretty sweet drum music and, in passing, tapped a finger against the empty spaces behind the gearstick, where the pattern of faded lines showed there had once been photographs. Memories pinned up and held, secure and perfect, where nothing could touch them. He needed some new ones for when he left for Poplar, Tommy decided. Pictures on his phone were one thing, but there weren't as good to touch as real photos.

With that plan in mind, he'd bought a disposable camera. They were all long overdue for new family pictures anyway, and he wanted a good one of Brett. He *had* suggested shirtless, or possibly pantless as well, but his honey hadn't looked all that impressed. A shame, Tommy reflected, but not much of a surprise.

It had been a long day. Mei had been just as mad as he'd expected, yet a lot of the yelling had seemed to roll right off his back. The beauty of anticipation, Tommy supposed, or maybe he was still a little numb. It didn't really matter. She hadn't come up with anything innovative, and, when she got teary-eyed and hugged him to her in a moment of intense, angry relief, he hadn't really known what to do.

The rain hit just as he got to Brett's place. Tommy jogged across the parking lot as great waves of it seemed to break from the sky in an uncontrolled deluge. He wanted to laugh, he realized. Take off his boots and run in it, barefoot and soaked to the skin.

He didn't, because dinner would have gotten wet. But all the same, it was a nice thought to have, and nice to think that he *could*.

There was something equally incredible about putting his own key into the lock, and turning it, and hearing the mechanism click. Something beautiful about pushing the door open—he still had to jiggle it a bit, and he still found himself knocking on the wood as he did so, just to announce his presence—and knowing that he was welcome.

Honey, I'm home!

Tommy stifled a chuckle, resisting the urge to call out the words. Brett would probably have thought it funny, but it would maybe have been a little too close to the mark. This *felt* like home, and that was enough.

Brett stood by the bookcase, thumbing through some medical textbook or something. He glanced up and grinned.

"Hey."

Tommy took a breath and let a smug smile leak across his face. It was a smile that—if he really thought about what had happened today—he knew he had no right to, but he didn't care. Brett was obviously not long out of the shower, his skin pink and clean-scrubbed and his hair darkened to deep brown, damp and ruffled. Barefoot, he was clad in gray sweats and an old college T-shirt, threadbare with years of wear, that pulled very slightly across his chest, shoulders, and biceps, and rode up just a bit when he moved, exposing a tiny sliver of belly or back.

It drove Tommy nuts, which he suspected Brett was not only aware of, but probably using to personal advantage. He could be sneaky like that... even if he never seemed to know how good he really looked.

"Hey," he echoed, hefting the bag. "You didn't already eat dinner, did you?"

Brett shook his head, eyeing the takeout suspiciously. "No. What—?"

"Mu shu pork with hoisin and pancakes, special fried rice, extra mushrooms, and spring rolls." Tommy's smile widened as he reeled off the menu. "That's right, isn't it? Did I get it right?"

Brett nodded, his expression a mix of grateful tenderness and mild disbelief as he arched an eyebrow. "Yeah, I love mu shu, but... you went all the way up to Peking Kitchen?"

It was a fairly redundant question. Havre wasn't exactly overburdened with Chinese restaurants.

"Ah-huh." Tommy frowned and peered at the bag. "It may need warmin' up a little. I, uh, figured we might as well talk on full stomachs."

He held out the peace offering, if that was what it was, and looked hopefully at Brett. The moment seemed to stretch out into a long, aching thread of a thing, and, for the first time since getting out of the Chevy, Tommy started to worry.

Brett smiled tightly, the textbook drooping in his hands. He tossed it down onto the coffee table and crossed the room, smelling faintly of soap, shampoo, and citrus. Tommy breathed in, wanting to anchor them both there in those few seconds, before anything had a chance to blow up in his face.

"I didn't do it, y'know," he said, as Brett took the bag from him. "Whatever shit Lane had planned, I didn't—"

"I know." Brett looked evenly at him, his eyes clear and free from any hint of anger... though anger would probably have been preferable to that faint look of guarded suspicion. "Scott filled me in on a lot of it."

He took the food through to the kitchen, and Tommy followed, self-justification bursting out of him even when he meant it not to.

"You think I should've called the cops, right? Look, he just rolls up at this guy's place, suddenly gets this bat out... the guy never answered the door. Lane coulda left. He—y'know, I *thought* he...."

Tommy sighed and slumped against the door frame, watching Brett work quietly and gracefully through the motions of microwave, plates, and forks. A collection of unwashed plates, mugs, and cutlery bobbed in the sink—a couple of days' worth, by the look of it—and Tommy guessed work really had been cutting into him.

He crossed behind Brett, turned the faucet on and, once the water started running to hot, began to do the dishes.

"Cops arrested him?" Brett asked, with the barest glance at what Tommy was doing.

"Yeah. I don't know what the charge is gonna be. I don't wanna know."

"I thought you guys—"

"We weren't friends," Tommy said shortly, flicking the suds from his hand before reaching for another grubby plate. "It was just the Four Winds thing, and... you know. We were just in the same place, same time. It—"

"Was convenient?"

There wasn't exactly anything in Brett's tone that was really, truly argumentative or accusatory. He didn't even sound cold, but Tommy knew him well enough to catch the things he was afraid of, hiding beneath the surface of the words.

"It was never like that." He rested his palms on the edge of the sink and frowned at the soapy dishes. "It was just... you don't go against a guy like that when he's got people behind him. It'd be stupid. And he was good to me. Okay, for his own fucked-up reasons, but... it wasn't like that."

He shook his head. Lane Harding was a homophobic asshole with anger-management issues and a tendency toward enjoying casual violence almost as much as the attention that violence got him. Not that the homophobic part necessarily mattered, under certain circumstances, and Tommy was aware that Brett understood that, even if they never, ever talked about it.

Funny, really, he thought. There wasn't much they hadn't talked about in six years, but that was the one thing that they never broached, the one thing he thought Brett *couldn't* talk about.

It was ironic, in a way. Tommy had seen the fear in him on those first few visits to Deer Lodge, though the words never got voiced. And even after he tried his best to put Brett at ease, Tommy knew he still worried. He always did. But it wasn't *like* that. Tommy didn't expect him to understand... and he was glad, really, that he didn't. It meant Brett was untouched by it—all the ugliness and the politics and the insidious, dangerous ways it clawed at you.

Depending on how you defined it, sex could be a lot of things: currency, power, obligation... friendship. Maybe just something to take the edge off of life. Sometimes it was okay, sometimes it wasn't. Sometimes—according to at least one participant—it had never even happened at all.

The microwave beeped, and the smell of the pork and mushrooms permeated the tiny kitchen in heady, appetizing wafts. Tommy bit his lip. It was tough trying to explain how much you missed normal human contact once it was taken away. Just a touch, a hug, a hand on your arm... or even a lover's smile. It was no wonder a lot of guys closed off, drew in on themselves and got a little crazy.

Maybe not all as crazy as Lane, but still....

"I never screwed him," Tommy heard himself say, and his voice sounded strained, desperate, like he had something to prove. "I never touched him, I swear. It was just the lodge, and the—"

"It doesn't matter."

Brett always said that. He'd always said he didn't want to know if Tommy had played in the joint, or who with, so long as it had been safe... or at least as safe as possible. And yet he'd been so painfully honest about that guy from college, and Tommy had never had any damn choice but to say it was okay, because he knew chaining Brett up to some set of stupid ideals he couldn't possibly meet would only have meant losing him. He couldn't have stuck that—couldn't stick it now and, if he was honest, probably wouldn't ever be able to—so he'd had to live with knowing there was some other bastard out there with his grabby little hands on the guy Tommy loved.

It *did* matter.

A lot of things mattered… but they didn't all need dragging out into the open.

Brett touched the small of his back as he reached over to get the food out of the microwave, and Tommy felt the brush of that one tiny contact run up the whole length of his spine. He thought suddenly of Roberto—six five and two forty, with practically an entire flash book inked onto his arms, neck, and back—sobbing disconsolately after his partner, Javier, wrote to break things off.

Four out of six years, they'd been on the same floor, him and Roberto. And, yes, they'd been friends. Javier used to come all the way from California to visit. Brett had met him. Tommy had seen them walk in together a couple of times. It had been good, not being the only ones… and it had scared him, watching a big guy like Roberto shatter into such little pieces.

Tommy turned his head, following Brett's movements as he spooned rice onto two plates and divided up pancakes and the little Styrofoam cups of hoisin. Every action was one of cool economy, and it left him apprehensive, holding his breath for the moment the anger finally burst out.

"Nothing like this is gonna happen again," he said, turning his attention back to the last few dishes in Brett's sink. "I promise."

"I know," Brett said quietly, tapping the spoon against the side of the rice container.

Tommy looked up sharply, and met the determination in those clear, honest, tired eyes. "Wh—?"

"It's not," Brett said. "Because you're not going to put yourself in that position again. Not after everything. You're just… not."

He wasn't mad. He said it as if it was already a fact, like he'd read it in the newspaper and was simply passing the information on. Yet there was a current in his voice Tommy recognized. It wasn't hope. It was the thing that hope becomes after you've hung onto it for so long it's lost its shape… that formless, defiant breath of belief, which you need to keep clinging to if you're not going to go completely crazy.

They'd never talked about "one day," never built up dreams and made little worlds between them. It was too much like planning for the long term and banking on things that might never happen.

A lot of the stuff in the lodge and the circle had involved the future. You were meant to be able to visualize who you wanted to be—the next cycle of your growth, your potential—and picture that place. The vision was meant to pull you toward it like a magnet, the power of your volition, your will to live up to what you *could* be dragging you on, even when there were obstacles to overcome.

It was *meant* to work like that, anyway.

Tommy cleared his throat. "You're, uh… you're not yelling at me," he said uncertainly, hoping it might pass as a weak attempt at humor. "I, uh, kinda thought I deserved yelling at."

"No." Brett shook his head, and his face was solemn, so serious that Tommy felt it, deep in his chest. "I was scared, baby. Not angry. Scott told me about the day he picked you up 'cause you were stuck. That guy…."

"Brett—"

"I had my own run-in, y'know. You were right. Crazy bastard."

Tommy frowned. "Huh? You…?"

"Came at me outside a bar in town." Brett folded his arms, spoon still in his hand, and shrugged, like it wasn't important. His eyes darkened a little. "Same kind of shit he gave you. I don't know if it was meant to scare me, piss me off, or what, but he didn't stick around."

Lane had…? And Brett hadn't said anything. A combination of territorial anger and fear flared in Tommy, and his frown deepened.

"You didn't tell me that," he said reproachfully, regretting it almost instantly.

He hardly had the high ground there.

The corner of Brett's mouth twitched. "Nah. You didn't tell me everything either."

"Hmm. No, I guess not."

To his surprise, Brett just twisted a little, swinging his upper body and bumping an arm against Tommy's chest.

"I think," he said, with his brow wrinkled and his mouth caught around a bitter half smile, "that we oughta do that from now on. Don't you? Talk about stuff a little bit more?"

Tommy nodded slowly, feeling small and humbled.

"Yeah," he murmured. "It's a plan."

THEY ate the takeout on the couch, with the radio playing softly in the background and their legs intertwined. Brett rested his feet in Tommy's lap, and sucked hoisin thoughtfully off his thumb as he considered the possible fallout from today.

"So, it's not going to affect Poplar, is it? You speak to your PO yet?"

"Yeah." Tommy grimaced at him over his last forkful of mu shu. "Myers is not a happy camper. They didn't charge me, though, so... I think it's okay, technically. Turns out Bill's pretty damn good at filling out those change of residence request things. Did a whole statement on why it'd be beneficial for me or whatever."

Brett nodded slowly and let his toes idly caress Tommy's thigh. It was too good to sit here, warm and comfortable and safe, and know that the world was shut out for the night. He just wished there could be more times like this to look forward to, instead of the looming specter of separation.

"So, uh... about that," Brett began, slipping Tommy a sidelong look. "Do you, uh, know how long it's going to be for yet? I guess not, right? I mean, it's work, and—"

"Yeah."

"Mm." He nodded ruefully. "Okay. That's... that's fine."

It wasn't fine. There was precious little time left before Tommy would be going, and, at that moment, every day he'd be away looked like an insurmountable challenge.

Tommy frowned and leaned across to set his cleared plate on the coffee table. He rubbed Brett's foot as he straightened up and fixed him with a soft, apologetic stare.

"Babe...."

"I'm gonna miss you," Brett blurted. "That's all. I just... I hoped we were gonna have more time together, the longer you were out. Not less."

Tommy's fingers circled his ankle, his touch light and soothing. "I know. Let's just see how this works out, huh? It might be a step to something closer, right? Or... well, we'll work it out. Won't we?"

He stretched forward, took Brett's empty plate, and set it on top of his on the table. The clink of china seemed loud against the quietness of the room and the music's low buzz.

"Yeah," Brett said reluctantly.

"Mm."

Tommy's expression was shadowed with concern and apology, and he wanted to grab hold of him and shake the look right off of his face. He shouldn't be sorry. He needed this opportunity, Brett knew. He *needed* the time, and the space, and the chance to have something that was his. A chance to be independent, and to learn how to be himself again, how to adjust to a completely new life.

If only giving him that chance wasn't so damn hard.

The texture of the air seemed to shift between them as Brett stared at him, willing him to understand, to be the one to say it was all right... to say that feeling this messed up was okay.

Tommy frowned again, dropped his gaze to his lap, and pinched Brett's toe affectionately.

"Y'know… you're the best," he murmured. "You know that, right?"

Brett wriggled his toes. "Yeah?"

"Mm-hm. And… and it will get better. It will."

Those dark eyes held such impassioned promise, such sincerity. Brett nodded awkwardly.

"I know." He held out a hand. "C'mere."

Tommy grinned as he laced his fingers into Brett's and let himself be tugged gently forward. There was a clumsy shuffle, a ballet of banged knees and elbows, and Brett smiled as he wrapped his arms around his lover.

He kissed Tommy gently, just a peck on the lips, and waited for his response, mouth still cleaving close to his. Tommy's soft laughter enveloped him—he felt rather than heard it whisper across his skin—and he traced his fingertips along Brett's jaw, pulling back just enough to look him in the eye before kissing him again, gently and insistently. Brett slipped slowly into the warmth of him, eroding under his quiet rhythm and the feel of that dark hair hanging down, brushing against his face. It finished too soon, leaving him breathless, hard, and happy.

"Want you," Tommy murmured, tracing Brett's chest through his cotton crewneck. "Want all of you."

Brett had to agree. Tommy filled his arms, his warmth and his scent all mixed up with the taste of the takeout and his kisses, and the overwhelming fact that he was home. The couch wasn't the most comfortable place in the world for this, but it didn't matter as much as he thought it would. Brett squeezed Tommy's ass through his jeans, delighted by the eager little growl that rumbled against his throat.

"Bed?" he asked, a little muffled by the fact he still had his mouth crushed to Tommy's jaw.

Part of Brett cried out in angry complaint at how easy it was to let go of everything else and fall into him, despite all the things that had happened today—and all the things that *could* have happened—but he knew that was next to pointless. There had always been could-haves and maybes looming above them, painting the sky black and daubing hopelessness across the horizon. What mattered was that they took this intimacy, this affection, and held onto it, knowing that things were imperfect, and yet not caring.

Tommy's fingers ran through his hair, then over the back of his head and down to the nape of his neck, his caress light and gently teasing.

"Mmm. Hair's still damp," he murmured. "Did you take a shower?"

Brett squirmed eagerly under his weight. Tommy smelled of pine and cotton and cinnamon, overlaid with the slight tang of nervous sweat.

"Uh-huh."

Tommy nipped his earlobe, his voice a low, seductive purr. "Was it a really *good* shower?"

Brett hesitated. Tommy taunted the flesh lightly with his tongue, then traced a hot, wet line around the rim of Brett's ear, a subtle promise that made his meaning perfectly clear.

Yes. Oh, God... yes, please....

It wasn't something Tommy did for him often, and Brett wasn't about to squander the opportunity on wondering what had made him offer.

"Uh...." Brett swallowed heavily. "Uh, just give me a minute. 'K?"

Dragging himself out of Tommy's arms proved hard—achingly hard—but he sped through the bathroom in record time before stumbling back into the bedroom, a towel wrapped around his waist for the second time that evening. Eagerness and nervous lust beat an impatient tattoo in his stomach, but at least he had confidence in his scrupulous, and intimate, cleanliness.

Tommy hadn't undressed. He stood by the window, slouched up against the wall, staring at the risen moon. Warm light from the bedside lamp he'd switched on bathed him. He looked over at Brett and smiled when he let the towel drop from his hips.

"Wow." Tommy folded his arms and tilted his head to the side, feigning critical curiosity. "Y'know, it's almost like the little guy wants something...."

Brett pulled a face.

"Shithead," he muttered, crossing the room.

He'd never felt this at ease with anyone before, confident despite—no, *because* of—his nakedness, comfortable with the way Tommy's gaze roved over his body, and the reaction that attention elicited. Brett reached out and deftly unfastened Tommy's fly, fingers slipping inside as Tommy pulled off his shirt. He smelled incredible, and touching him was heat and warmth and everything that felt good about another man's body. Brett traced the packed solidity of Tommy's chest with his free hand, ran his fingers down the uneven ripples of his ribs. He'd never been really ripped, but he had put a little muscle on in the joint. Working out had its benefits and provided all the addictive potential of endorphins, Brett supposed, even if the guys weren't allowed to get too pumped. He squeezed Tommy through the flimsy confines of his underwear, dragging a rough moan deep from his throat.

When things got like this, it was tough to tell which of them needed it more.

Tommy dropped the crewneck to the floor and helped Brett edge the jeans and briefs down over his hard-on, bottom lip snared between his teeth. He grinned, balancing on one foot at a time to remove them completely.

"Lie down for me," he said, peeling off his socks.

Brett stretched out on the covers, hands behind his head. He couldn't help but smile at the silliness of Tommy hopping up and down on one leg, loving him even more for that awkwardness, tender and unplanned. Yet, as Tommy clambered onto the bed, there wasn't anything awkward about the unquenchable enthusiasm of his touch.

Tommy worked so slowly down his body. He knelt across Brett, teasing and tasting, but avoiding all of his hottest spots until he was arching against the mattress, his breaths short and hard. Tommy rubbed Brett's hip and looked up at him in feigned innocence, grinning as he pressed a kiss to his navel.

Brett gasped, his stomach cinching in from the contact. He pushed himself up on his elbows, wanting to reach for Tommy, wanting to reciprocate every glimmer of pleasure, even as his cock begged for attention. It wavered between them, jutting up insistently next to Tommy's mouth, and he just smiled. Brett started to stifle a small moan, but then supposed he didn't need to, and let it out. Tommy's smile widened appreciatively. It felt the way being with him always did: natural, beautiful, and right... just like the laughter did, when Tommy pressed a kiss to the end of his dick that had Brett alternately gasping with pleasure and giggling with warm glee.

He raised a hand and tucked Tommy's hair behind his ear, mirroring that gesture of his, that little tic that Brett remembered noticing about him from the very first time they'd met. Tommy's gaze softened, and a smile curled at the corner of his mouth, half hidden and wholly delectable.

"Turn over," he said, patting Brett's thigh companionably. "Before I get distracted."

Brett complied, though not without a crack about how distraction might be fun. Tommy swatted him lightly on the ass before kneeling over him, the weight and the heat of his body a potent, calming, wonderful thing.

He closed his eyes at the feel of Tommy's hands on his back, then the warmth of his thighs as he straddled Brett's legs, his hair tickling as he bent his head.... The gentle pressure of kisses peppered his spine, and Brett sighed appreciatively, spreading his legs a little on instinct as Tommy's hands worked down across his lower back and ass. His hair pooled against Brett's back as he kissed his way over the skin, fingers kneading and tracing ever more complicated patterns. It was easy to relax under his touch, despite the way the need was building.

The warm, wet trail of Tommy's tongue on his last vertebra nearly had Brett whimpering aloud, and then.... *Oh, God....* He gathered the covers into a knot under his elbows and gave vent to a low moan.

Tommy's lack of inhibition in bed had always impressed Brett. Oh, there had been plenty of things they hadn't done, but he seemed to find trying anything easy. He never shrank from being watched or touched, or from touching Brett or himself. He made love as easily as other people made toast, and his enthusiasm was infectious.

Brett gasped as Tommy spread his thighs and cheeks and dived into his tenderest spot. Pleasure burst through him in waves, chased like it always was with a slight sense of unnerving exposure. No matter how much porn he watched, Brett could never quite feel as blasé about rimming as those guys, and he was afraid it showed. Tommy never made him feel clumsy or stupid, though, not even when he was moaning like a prom queen, his back tense and his legs shaking.

Caught between Tommy's incredible mouth, his restless hands—fingers and tongue working in tandem now, stroking and teasing every intimate, secret place—and the yielding friction of the bedclothes, Brett bucked and arched, desperate for the release being so expertly drawn out. He barely heard his own litany of curses and cries, aware he'd begun to beg and not caring.

When Tommy pulled away, it was an awful moment of emptiness and terrible desolation. Brett moaned in disappointment, though he was aware of Tommy's hands on his ass, spreading him, then a warm palm on his hip, urging him to turn over.

"Lemme see your face, huh?"

He did it—did anything Tommy wanted, however he wanted it—and was rewarded with that hot, wet mouth engulfing his shaft, accompanied by first one and then two fingers in his ass, crooked just so, perfectly balanced and devastatingly accurate. Brett hooked one leg over Tommy's shoulders and screwed his eyes tight shut, letting the blood rush in his ears and the intensity of the sensation fill him up.

He panted and flexed to Tommy's touch, his mouth working silently, chewing on empty sounds before he relented, slammed his head back against the pillow, and whimpered.

"Want you," he murmured, a cracked gasp of a sound, as Tommy pulled off and planted an open-mouthed kiss on his thigh. "Wanna feel it...."

Tommy chuckled happily as he crawled up the bed, reaching to the drawer of the nightstand for the lube and condoms. The warm light touched the long, lean lines of his body softly, and the shadows blurred around the dragon on his shoulder. Things in the drawer rattled as Tommy groped around, and Brett guessed by the glint of amusement in his eyes that he'd bumped against the toys that lived in there.

He squirmed, as much due to the mild tug of embarrassment as impatient arousal, and reached out to rub a hand along the crest of Tommy's thigh. Tommy smiled and, necessities retrieved from the drawer, leaned over him once more, pausing to tweak his nipple.

"You turned into a total bottom while I was away, didn't you?"

"Did not!" Brett protested weakly.

He heard a trace of genuine indignation in his voice, and Tommy looked at him carefully, as if assessing how pissed off he actually was. Brett flexed his shoulder against the mattress in what he hoped looked like an unconcerned shrug.

"Maybe a little." He brushed his fingertips up Tommy's arm, hating the way the words were so hard to say. "I just… this is our thing, y'know? You're—you're my guy. If I can… y'know… I know you're here. This is *us*."

"Oh." All traces of that lopsided smile were gone from Tommy's face, and he looked oddly, darkly vulnerable. "Right."

Brett bit the inside of his lip. "Leave the… uh… leave it off?"

His gaze dropped to the small square wrapper in Tommy's hand. Tommy looked down, frowned, and opened his mouth to speak.

"Please?" Brett squeezed his wrist gently. "I mean, I know we're both… you know. So, it'd be okay, right? I mean, how many more tests d'you wanna do?"

Tommy's frown twisted in a moment of unbearable uncertainty. Brett knew how careful he'd been, and how worried, given the rates of infection among the inmate population. Hepatitis, HIV, and a whole lot of other nasties lurked, waiting to spring on the unwary or careless—just one of the reasons they'd fought so bitterly about that damn tattoo of his—and despite all the clean bills of health he'd had since his release, Tommy had retained some hang-ups.

He raised his gaze, gave Brett a small smile, and tossed the unopened rubber aside.

Brett grinned.

It definitely felt different without it... even more so for Tommy, he guessed. They were closer, warmer, like they were two halves of the same thing, the same flesh, and Tommy was unstoppable, unshakeable, moving against him like a tide.

"Can I kiss you?" he murmured, his voice an urgent, hot whisper.

Legs locked around him, Brett squeezed and tugged on the curtain of dark hair falling between them.

"You damn well better," he growled.

Tommy obliged, and the bed, the walls, and the oxygen all seemed to vanish from the room. Nothing remained but the way Tommy made him feel and the way Tommy seemed to feel, abandoning himself so completely, so utterly, until he hit his peak with his mouth against Brett's neck, crying out his release like he used to do... as if there had never been any reticence between them.

"Whoa," Tommy murmured as he stilled, the word tailing off into a small, sated chuckle. "Nearly there?"

"Mm." Brett grunted as Tommy's hand reached between them and covered his. "Baby, please...."

Tommy pushed the hand away as he began to slide down the bed, and tutted in mock reproach. "God. It's just want, want, want with you, isn't it?"

Brett smiled breathlessly. "Uh-huh. Get to work, boy."

Tommy laughed, and Brett wanted to think of something else funny to say, but it was hard to think at all when that incredible mouth touched him again, and he knew he wouldn't last.

The white, searing comet of his climax burned a line down his body. It was Tommy's name on his lips, he thought, as that loud, foreign cry exploded from him, ending in a series of needy, choked whimpers.

"Good?" Tommy asked softly, and his breath scraped Brett's over-sensitized cock, sending aftershocks quivering through his flesh.

Brett lifted his head from the tangle of pillows and covers and squinted blearily at him. "Fuck, yes."

Tommy smiled and gingerly levered himself up the bed, on his side to avoid brushing Brett's more delicate parts. He flopped against the pillows, and Brett stroked the comfortingly familiar planes of Tommy's face with his thumb.

"Love you so fucking much," he murmured.

Tommy arched an eyebrow. "Love fucking," he corrected.

"Shut up," Brett said affectionately, though he couldn't hide his grin.

CHAPTER
THIRTEEN

BILL was outside when Tommy rattled up the track to the ranch house. The Chevy hadn't responded well to the journey, but he'd made it in one piece... just.

"Holy shit," Bill said as he got out, greeting him with a wide, disbelieving grin and a shake of his head. "You came all the way in that thing? How come the engine didn't drop out?"

Missy had padded out on her pudgy little legs to investigate the newcomer, her plumy tail wagging. Tommy shrugged and leaned down to scratch her behind the ear.

"Ah, Scott's gone over pretty much everything on her and screwed with it, one time or another. I don't think there's much left that's original."

The drive had taken the best of the day, and thin late afternoon sun lanced off the ranch house, turning the glazed sunporch to molten gold, painting the fields that pooled around it in muted pastel tones, and picking at the mica in the dirt.

"Huh." Bill shook his head again. "Well, glad you got here, anyhow. Let's get you settled. You hungry?"

"Uh, yeah." Tommy heaved his grip bag out of the truck and locked up, rubbing his thumb absently over the little red dream catcher fob as he tucked it into his pocket. "Thanks."

Missy nosed him in the back of the leg and followed on behind as he trailed after Bill, the aches and stiffnesses of the journey pinching his muscles. Birds cawed in the scrubby little stand of trees, and the sound of horses calling to each other drifted down on the air. Tommy couldn't deny he was a little nervous, but, as Bill led him into the kitchen, the cloud of mixed-up air freshener, wet dog, and coffee scent rolled over him and felt more familiar than he guessed it should have.

He drank coffee while Bill fried off a couple of eggs, and Tommy realized his stomach was actually rumbling. He took the plate gratefully and slipped Missy a corner of toast while Bill ran down what needed doing over the next few days, and asked after Karen and Atian.

"They're good." Tommy nodded, swallowing a forkful of eggs. "She an' Scott took him to go see the Wahkpa Chu'gn buffalo jump thing last week. Said he really enjoyed it. Got him doing swimming and, uh, soccer. Seems to really give him some focus."

Bill pulled out the chair opposite him and sat down at the table with a sigh, setting his own mug of coffee on the bleached wooden surface.

"Yeah? That's good. See 'em at the Milk River powwow come end of July, I bet. Huh… seems like only yesterday she was yea high, y'know?" He shook his head and laughed softly. "Anyway, we'll get you fixed, give you a chance to settle in. Bunkhouse isn't much… well, we *call* it the bunkhouse… been meanin' to fit a lot of the outbuildings up for a long while. You'll see."

Tommy shot him an apprehensive look, but Bill had already taken off on another tangent, and begun running through the names of the permanent and semipermanent staff, including the couple of other guys who came in, and Tina, the woman who did twice-weekly visits to take care of most of the secretarial and financial stuff. Apparently, as Bill took great delight in relaying, Tina had once had a thing with Herman, the other part-owner of the ranch, and it had ended badly.

"Served him his balls on a plate," Bill confided, grinning broadly. "He don't come in on the days she's here, not that he'd ever admit he's terrified of her."

Tommy chuckled and, fed and watered, began his full orientation of the place, with Missy padding along behind like a slightly arthritic honor guard.

It felt faintly surreal, he decided, as Bill showed him to the loosely termed bunkhouse. Tommy couldn't help thinking of the last time he'd been given this kind of introduction to a new life—those first few hours, choked up with dreamlike disbelief, as if maybe none of it was actually happening—before the practical mechanics of prison cut in, and it had seemed like there'd never been anything to his world except not making eye contact in the dayroom and waiting patiently for chicken day.

Of course, *this* looked pretty damn palatial in comparison to a cell.

The bunkhouse was a short, low construction, consisting of four rooms, bathroom, and a tiny kitchenette with a kettle, microwave, and gas burner. Mostly all the interiors were lapped pine, and two of the rooms stood empty, with dust sheets and old paint splatters indicating renovations started but never quite finished. Bill said that, when they had part-timers or kids on the BUNAC programs come to do a couple of months' work, they usually slept here, but there was only one booking this year, and that wasn't until August. So, one room was being kept back for Nathan, one of the local part-time guys, and the other—which overlooked the back end of the yard and away to the north paddock, and smelled very faintly of stale carpet and newly washed linens—would be Tommy's for as long as he needed it.

"You wanna fix any of this stuff up, by the way," Bill said, gesturing expansively at the pine-clad walls, "you go right ahead."

Tommy peered at the narrow bed with the crooked shelf over it, the rickety curtain pole, and battered, slightly lopsided nightstand and dresser.

Definitely palatial, he decided, aware of the grin spreading across his face.

"Sure," he said. "Thanks, Bill."

HE TOOK the afternoon to settle in, though unpacking clothes and filling up drawers still seemed strange. Tommy tacked his photos up on the patch of wall between the bed and the crooked shelf: an old one of him, back when he still had braces, with Gramma and Grandpa Tim, the picture Brett had sent him of Scott and Karen just after Atian was born, and a newer one of all three of them. Atian had his mouth open and his hands up, roaring at the camera, and Karen was smiling down at him instead of looking at the lens, her hand on the top of his head. Then there was his mom with Robbie, Lila, and Katie… and one of Lila, one hand on her hip and the other behind her head, making duck lips at the camera while her face was coated with some kind of mud pack thing. Tommy smiled to himself as he recalled how loud she'd yelled when she realized he actually *had* taken the photograph. He'd been lucky to get away with himself intact.

The smile widened and softened a little as he stuck the last picture in place. He hadn't taken it; Lila had, after she'd cleaned the mud pack off and stopped threatening to permanently injure him. It was just him and Brett, standing in the living room at Mei's place, and looking… happy. Brett had his arms around Tommy's waist, chin propped on his shoulder, and that big goofy grin on his face. Tommy remembered the moment Lila had taken it, and how he'd started to turn his head and been caught, just in that moment of change, some word or start of a sentence on his lips, cutting through the smile. He was looking at Brett anyway, and Brett was just turning to look at him.

Tommy remembered kissing him a couple of seconds later, and Brett laughing, and Lila making exaggerated gagging noises and telling them to get a room.

He let his finger rub against the corner of the photo, feeling the thick, glossy edge on his skin, like that made it somehow more real: a testament, a record of a minute caught in time. And time mattered. It really did, because of how easy it was to let it get away from you.

A small nudge of guilt tugged at Tommy's chest. Two hundred and fifty miles wasn't a lot, considering things like the railroad, or the size of the world in general, but it felt like more… especially after the drive. He wasn't sure whether he wanted it to be easy to fall back into missing Brett again or whether he wanted to feel every single mile. Either way, he didn't have time to dwell on it. He finished unpacking, took a rather tepid and leaky shower, and walked down to see the brood mares before dinner.

There were two grazing not far from the fence, one a paint with a feathery, creamy mane and tail, and one a dark blood bay, both with big, wide bellies. Bill had said three of his girls were due in the next four weeks, and so they were kept close to the house and checked up on regularly. The paint looked up at Tommy, pretty little ears pricked and a scruff of grass dangling from her soft pink muzzle. She swished her tail, snorted, and evidently dismissed him as less interesting than grazing, which she promptly went back to. He grinned.

It had been years since he'd been around horses. Not since they'd lived in Chinook, and... well, everything had been different then. They'd all been different.

Tommy didn't really want to think about it, so he balanced one foot on the first bar of the fence, swung his other leg over the top of it, and perched awkwardly on the top rail, resting his weight on his hands. The wood still held the traces of the day's warmth, its surface grained and ridged, yet fairly smooth. Tommy flexed his fingers against it, feeling the air stir his hair as the last gold-hued rays of light leached from the deepening, blue-smudged gray of the sky.

The horses snorted, and the bay lowered her head and shook it, ruffling her thick, black mane. She gave Tommy a suspicious look, and he held out one hand, just gently lifted from the fence and extended, slightly curled. He clicked his tongue, and, slowly, the mare took a couple of tentative steps forward. He grinned and reached his other hand to the pocket of his jeans, finding the tube of Life Savers he'd filched from Brett's apartment the night before. Tommy thumbed out one of the mints and offered it, flat in his palm, to the bay.

She edged closer, tail switching and ears twitching, each in separate directions, as she seemed to weigh up who this new human was, and whether the promise of candy was worth investigating further. She must have thought so because, foot by foot, she edged up to the fence and lipped the treat out of Tommy's palm, crunching it while she allowed him to pet her velvet-soft muzzle.

She seemed pretty happy to make friends after that. He scratched her forehead, the heavy, coarse lock of hair there spilling over his hand, and rubbed his thumb over the little white star between her eyes, just a little left of center. She whickered and, after a few minutes' bonding, decided she'd had enough, turned, and without ceremony, ambled off to join her companion again.

Tommy smiled to himself as he watched the gradually encroaching dusk outline the horses, the air dotted with the black specks of flies and midges. He wiped his hand absently on his jeans and glanced down at the amount of shed hair on the denim. The smell of the horses—their warmth, the weight of their presence—was comforting, and his smile widened as he sat on the fence, just letting the dusk cool around him.

WHEN he slipped into the kitchen, he found Bill already cooking, the room wreathed with steam and the smell of boiled greens, onions, and chicken. Missy lay sprawled on the tiles beside the table. She looked up as Tommy entered, wagged her tail, and gave one short, hoarse bark. He smiled down at her, but the smile stiffened as he glanced around at the other figures in the room. Two Indian guys sat at the table, each probably no more than twenty-five, both short-haired and wearing well-used shirts and jeans. An older man, heavy and with a black T-shirt and close-cropped graying hair, stood by the door, arms folded. They were a relatively surly-looking bunch, and Tommy was definitely the whitest guy in the room, which always felt a little weird.

"Hey, Tommy." Bill glanced over his shoulder and nodded. "Guys, this is Tommy. Tommy… guys."

He grinned, laughed to himself, and set back to work at the stove. Tommy raised a hand in awkward greeting.

"Uh… hi."

His new colleagues stared at him as one, then the older guy's mouth twitched into the small, slight approximation of a smile.

"Hey. I'm Herman. This is Nathan and Joe. Sit down, huh?"

Tommy smiled his thanks and sat, a little awkwardly, at the far end of the table. Places were already laid, and he hoped he wasn't late. Still, the introductions were stilted but friendly enough. Herman didn't look a whole lot like Tommy had expected, though he noticed the service tattoo a few inches above his left wrist, and wondered if Bill had one like it.

Of the two younger guys, Joe was tighter-lipped, at least until the chicken was in front of him. He identified himself as Wahpeton Sioux, like Herman, and Tommy suspected there was a degree of cruelty in his eagerness to use the language. He had to admit to being limited to English, and it was an embarrassment that he felt sure was received with more than a little glee.

They ate, complimented Bill's cooking—which seemed to be something of a hobby with him, Tommy decided—and he nodded and listened carefully to all the stuff about fencing and when the vet was expected next. Bill dug a huge tub of pistachio ice cream out of the deep-bellied freezer, made more coffee, and wouldn't let anyone else get up to clear the table.

The evening drew in, and the kitchen was a dim, warm pool of convivial light, and even a little laughter in the darkness. Tommy struggled at first, fitting in with that, but then Joe made a crack about the beater of a truck parked out front, and talking about the Chevy was easy because it touched so many other things: Scott, and their grandmother, and all the little threads that wove through the past and tied the present to something real.

It helped.

Herman left at about ten, and Joe went with him, catching a lift back into town and telling Tommy he'd see him the day after tomorrow. His manner had the still quietness of pine trees—banked in steady, jagged ranks, impenetrable and dark—but he nodded and even smiled briefly.

Overall, Tommy was pretty damn glad to put an end to the evening. He was tired—bone-achingly tired—and, however welcome he'd been made to feel, the promise of the bunkhouse's relative privacy and peace still called loudly.

Nathan walked with him, hands in his pockets and boots scuffing halfheartedly at the ground. He glanced up at Tommy as they got past the bend in the track.

"So, uh…." He cleared his throat. "It's true, is it?"

Tommy lifted a shoulder in a resigned kind of semishrug. He knew exactly what Nathan meant, but he wasn't going to admit it. "What?"

"*You* know. That you were at—"

"Yeah."

"Oh. And did you really…?"

"Yes," Tommy said shortly. "I did."

"Oh."

He said nothing else. Tommy shrugged and stayed quiet.

BRETT'S apartment felt empty, which was stupid, he supposed. It wasn't as if Tommy had actually been around every evening… but knowing he *wouldn't* be, that it wasn't going to happen, was what made it tough. That, and the day he'd had at work.

Braden Solberg's therapy hadn't gone well. Brett had noticed a marked decline over the boy's last couple of appointments, and today he'd barely managed to walk a couple of steps. There was more talk of wheelchairs. Braden had cried. After the family left, Brett had sat despondently on the break room couch and asked Elaine what they could do to help him. She'd simply shrugged, sipped her coffee, and smiled sadly at him.

Not much. He'll probably be in the chair full-time by next year.

And she was so horribly practical about it. That was what Brett hated. It didn't seem fair. Well, it wasn't fair… and he knew that. He still wanted to rage and rant and complain about it, and believe it could be changed, but, realistically, he knew it couldn't. Braden would keep declining, and eventually Duchenne's would claim him, and there was nothing they could do to alter that.

Brett just wished there was someone at home he could lay it all out for, who would make the right sympathetic noises at the right times, and understand why he got so damn angry.

Tommy had texted him a couple of times, just to let him know he'd got to the ranch safely. Brett messaged back that he was glad, and yes, everything was fine with him. Saying otherwise wouldn't really have helped, and he wasn't in the habit of it, he supposed. The only time he ever used to say anything negative about work was during longer visits, when his little burst of self-indulgent whining could be sandwiched between things that would buoy Tommy up. That was what you did, even if it meant closing off all the parts of yourself that needed people to complain to, to be angry with, or to just mope in front of.

Not for the first time, Brett regretted how many friends he'd lost over the past few years. Fine, so he'd never been crazy popular, and he'd always figured on a few people having a difficult time accepting him for who he was... although that had been seriously intensified by the rather overdramatic way he'd outed himself.

Things hadn't really improved, though. The friends he'd lost from high school—all those guys who were still in Havre, still working the same jobs they'd had after graduation—didn't really want to know him. The people he'd met at college were scattered all over the place, too far away to commiserate over a beer with, and work colleagues and acquaintances kept looking at him oddly ever since the business with Lane Harding had popped up on the local news.

Brett cracked open a beer and stared sullenly at the computer screen. He didn't notice at first when the chat window popped up and announced Nick's familiar greeting with a chirpy jingle.

—*Hey, handsome!*

Brett blinked, then winced. He took a swig of his beer and typed back a recalcitrant:

—*Hi.*

After a moment, Nick responded... just like Brett had known he would.

—*Everything OK?*

He wrinkled his nose and sighed.

—*Yeah. Long day. T started new job.*

—*Ahh... all alone, huh?*

Brett muttered a cuss under his breath, grateful for the fact there was no audio or visual on the chat.

—*Kinda*

It was true, he supposed. Pretty much. Despite the things he'd said, Tommy wouldn't be coming back on the weekend, instead electing to stay and get the hang of life on the ranch. Apparently, Bill and a couple of the guys wanted to replace an old stock fence, and he intended to help. He'd sounded oddly enthusiastic about the whole thing, Brett thought. He swiped his tongue over his lower lip and typed hurriedly, eager to change the subject.

—*How about you?*

He knew Nick had been a little chary about him declining the offer of the apartment while he was away for work. Brett had tried to explain about things like Tommy needing his PO's approval to travel in that kind of way, and how they wanted life to be small, normal, and quiet, just for a little while... but he doubted his friend really understood.

—*Yeah,* Nick came back. *Good. Met someone on the weekend....*

Brett quirked an eyebrow.

—*Oh?*

—*Yep. Soooo f'in cute. Party at Kelsey's—he was dancing like Jean-Claude Van Damme....*

Brett sniggered. He'd met Nick's sister, Kelsey, once when she came up to Washington. Nick had obviously explained the limits of their relationship to her, and she hadn't made much secret of the fact she thought Brett wasn't good enough for him.

He hadn't blamed her.

—*Wait, that's a* good *thing?*

—*Oh, shut up. He's nice. Blond, big blue eyes, and a smile that could melt your... well, you know. Seeing him again tomorrow.*

Brett grinned and pretended he hadn't felt a brief, unpleasant flush of absurd jealousy. His fingers flexed against the keys, and he grabbed his beer for a quick swig.

—*Cool.*

—*So, how's things with Mr. Dreamy?*

He swallowed a little fast, and the bubbles burned at the back of his nose.

—*Good. We're getting there.*

—*Getting there?* Nick's familiar indignation was almost palpable. *What, while he's two hundred miles away?*

—*Yes,* Brett responded, perhaps a little sullenly.

—*Ur not getting any, though… amirite?*

The well-worn argument was accompanied by a winking smiley face, and Brett scoffed as he typed:

—*He needs this.*

—*And what abt u?* Nick countered, with barely a pause.

Brett shook his head, more frustrated than really annoyed.

—*It's fine.*

They'd gone over this more times than he cared to admit. Sometimes, he'd drifted close to thinking Nick was right. Other times, it had been good to have someone to take his anger out on by disagreeing, and he'd almost suspected that was what Nick was trying to do.

—*So, how long's it for?*

Brett stared at the words for a moment, then frowned as he took a sip of his beer.

Tommy hadn't wanted to talk about that. He'd just skirted the issue, like he was so damn good at doing. Who knew? Maybe it was just until he could find something closer to home. Maybe a few months, simply to get himself back on his feet.

Or maybe it would be longer.

That thought had occurred to Brett, though he'd been pretty good about stamping it down and not dwelling on it. His fingers paused above the keyboard, hesitation and uncertainty weaving an awkward duet across his mind.

—*I don't know.*

—*Why not? What, it's a long term thing?*

For a moment, Brett seriously considered faking having to go and deal with the doorbell or a phone call, if it meant avoiding the question. It wouldn't be *that* long, though… probably. Would it? Maybe it would. And what would he do then? Just settle into a truncated routine of snatched happinesses and voids of lonely time?

—Don't know yet, he repeated. *We'll see.*

There was a pause, and Brett guessed Nick was restraining the urge to say something they might both have regretted.

—Well, maybe it's romantic.

Brett frowned, about to demand an explanation when Nick's next message popped through.

—Can just see you following him out to some pissant town on the prairie. Homesteading and saloons and all that country shit. Is he really a cowboy now?

Brett grinned and shook his head incredulously.

—Tommy's not a cowboy.

—He is! Nick retorted. *Isn't he? Oh! Oh my God....*

Brett was halfway through typing a protest when a music video link popped up. He clicked it, and burst out laughing when the bouncy, insistent rhythms of Buffy Sainte-Marie's "Indian Cowboy in the Rodeo" started playing. Not only did it give him an unsettling and somewhat distracting mental image of Tommy in chaps and a Stetson, but the damn song was going to be stuck in his head for days. He shook his head again and took another swallow of his beer.

—I fucking hate you, asshole.

Nick's only contribution was another grinning smiley face.

CHAPTER FOURTEEN

TOMMY shivered violently in his sleep. Despite the comparative warmth—muggy summer air and slow-moving plains breezes that seemed to grow sluggish in the darkness, preferring to cling to the ground like shadows instead of racing against the clouds—he felt cold, and he felt the needling, chilly sting of rain against his skin.

Just a few shreds of dirty light illuminated the alley, and the brickwork smelled of secondhand beer.

He waited in the truck and watched the other people leave. A shrieking woman with bleached blonde hair held a newspaper over her head and urged her boyfriend to hurry up and unlock the damn car. Somewhere, a dog barked. Tires skidded in the far-off night, and there might have been a train going someplace.

The Western's slim barrel lay across Tommy's knee, cool and perfect. Rain spotted the windshield. The pattern of it—stippled pools of neon-tinged light, pale and shadow, blotched with uneven edges—danced against the Chevy's upholstery and the pictures behind the gear stick, and on the rifle's dully gleaming surface. His tongue probed the torn, bloody places in his mouth, butting against his split lip as if pain could nudge him toward thinking, feeling… understanding. His head hurt, and the vision had yet to clear properly in one eye. Everything was just that little bit off, the way it had been for years and years.

He got out of the truck, turned his face to the deep, starless sky, streaked with the torpid bellies of clouds painted gray against the darkness, and let the rain run down his face. He didn't feel it. He should have, he supposed.

The door opened. That familiar figure stumbled, lurched, laughed…. Just a regular guy, old buddies sharing one last smoke, one last laugh, one last slap on the back for the road. An unlit cigarette wagging between his lips, he smiled as he bade farewell to the friend who habitually greased him up with drink and sent him home again, and he managed one foot in front of the other as he stepped out into the brick tomb.

Tommy saw him clearly in the dream. No moment of half sight, no clouded picture of a broken man, a monster, or a messed-up memory never quite properly recalled. He saw the greasy hair clinging to those wide cheekbones, the dark eyes narrowed in angry, confused recognition, and the sneer that twisted his father's face.

Fuck do you want?

The rain pattered softly against the bricks. Everything was wet, but his mouth was dry, and the gun felt slippery in his hand. He flexed his fingers against the stock, rough textures on roughed-up skin, and his mouth bent awkwardly around the words he didn't know how to say.

I… I don't think you should come home, Dad. Not tonight.

He remembered the laughter, a hoarse cough of it wound through with tight, ugly threads of disbelief.

What?

The gun felt lighter than it should, he was sure, so light he almost dropped it.

His father's smile split wide, the unlit cigarette sticking to his lower lip and his tongue pressed up, fat and thick, to the yellow rank of his teeth.

Fuck is that? What…? You bring a fucking gun *down here? What are you going to do, ya fuckin' faggot? Shoot me?*

Tommy remembered the first blow. He saw it coming, but he didn't move, and he didn't know why. He just took it, and the world tasted of stars and blood, and the Western scudded to the ground.

He remembered fighting back, eventually. He remembered the yielding crunch of knee to groin and the hard, bone-thudding aches of punches and elbows in ribs and jaws. He remembered yelling, screaming at the broken, shackled-up monster that he wasn't going to do it anymore. Not to the kids. No more hitting, no more crying, no more fear.

Not after what he'd done... what he *could* do.

He remembered falling, cracking the back of his head against the door of the Chevy, his bruised and throbbing hands scrabbling on the rough, wet ground. The solid outline of a work boot clipped his shin, and he pulled back as if scalded.

Get up! Get up, ya little faggot! Come on, pussy....

If there were still people around, they weren't coming out to see what the noise was. They didn't care, because people never did. People minded their own damn business, and they didn't get involved. They never, ever got involved, and that was okay, because it wasn't anything to do with them.

This was private.

The roaring, swinging thing ahead of him lunged, and he pushed himself up, the ground scything away beneath him and the bricks spinning in shadow-smeared streaks. The Western's barrel trembled like the last leaf on the hard curve of a winter bough, and his voice was a high, tight yelp of panic as he whimpered out a plea, a warning... maybe both.

Martin spread his hands out wide, laughing. He swayed jerkily from side to side, a grinning marionette with his head cocked and his eyes too sharp, too open.

What you gonna do, huh? Y'come down here with a fuckin' gun, Tommy... what'cha gonna do? Huh?

One hand, fingers splayed, slapped the barrel. Tommy moved away, because they were always circling each other, weren't they? Always on each other like dogs, tasting the air and getting ready to snap at one another's throats. There was a dark, thick moment, and his back was no longer against the truck, but pressed up to the side of the alley, wet with rain and filth.

He raised the Western and closed one eye. The gun jerked and jumped in his hands; the recoil was more than he'd expected, violent and jagged. The shot echoed, the smell of powder cutting sharply through the stink, and it disoriented him. Silence roared in the space the sound left behind it. His father's hands, reaching out, or perhaps trying to push him away... everything was dark and muddled, wrought with confusion and the interlocked shapes of chaos.

He fired again. His fingers shook and slipped, but blood was hard to tell from sweat. Martin had never looked so surprised. Tommy's pocket rattled when he put his hand to it and drew out the cool, smooth cylinders. A small, sweet cord of calm coiled right at the center of the panic. His chest hurt with every breath, the dull thud of falling flesh still pummeling his ears, and he wheezed as he reloaded the rifle.

Just because he was down didn't mean he wouldn't get up. He always got up.

And the bastard always came up swinging.

Only... not this time.

This time, he stayed down. He stayed still, even at the third shot, and the smell of it all started to cut through the reek of piss and puke and beer. It was a smell that was almost a taste, like the sharp tang of green copper—the metallic staleness of old coins clutched in a sweaty palm—and the pallid greasiness of uncooked meat, hanging thickly in air tainted with the burn of powder.

He ran.

It was unclear in the dream, that running. There was the moment the Western slipped from his fingers and the slickness of hands on the Chevy's wheel, and then the world disappeared in a smeared mess of concrete and rain and panic.

Tommy knew where he'd gone. Fresno Reservoir, where the light hit the dark, gritty, gray earth in pale, slanted beams, like it was afraid of what it might find there, or like it was just daring to scrape the foreign soil of some alien shore. He remembered the pine trees and the rain, and the cold wetness that clung to everything and seeped right through to the skin. It seeped in now, like he could feel it all over again, and he shook and twisted beneath the clammy covers.

The water gnawed at the shore. An old, bleached, worn piece of wood rested in the dirt, and the wind worked at it, over and over, until Tommy was sure the little twigs that marked the terminals of the branches would have to break, have to snap, and yet they didn't. He wondered why that was, and why it had to hurt so much to cry when the tears fought their way out of sore, swollen eyes and mixed with the blood on his face.

He woke with a sudden, pitching lurch, as dislocating as the sense of falling, and he wasn't sure where he was. He wanted to leap up, to move, to pace, to do anything at all... but Tommy lay still, chained by the sense of unfamiliarity. He waited, and willed his breathing to slow and his eyes to grow used to the dark. Shapes danced in the air above him, and his pulse thudded in the heavy, close confines of his head, every beat echoing heavier and heavier.

Tommy kicked off the covers and jackknifed into a sitting position, wondering at the coolness of the air on his skin. He held his breath for a little while, just tracing the outlines of fuzzy, dim shapes in the room. Dresser, shelf, pictures, door... he knew this place. He knew himself. There was no panic, no stomach-dropping moment of fear or loss of control.

Everything was... well, everything *was*, and maybe that was the best he could expect just now. It was good enough, anyway.

He swung his legs out of the bed and padded across the darkened room, making for the window and the thin, grayish threads of light that worked their way through the curtains. Tommy twitched them aside and peered out at the rough, blurry shapes of the world.

Things made more sense like this, in a strange way. They weren't clear-cut. There were no expectations, no sharp lines, no bright, intimidating colors... just quiet. This was time not beaten into the molds of assumptions or shackled to things that should happen, that *might* happen.

He could just pick out the shapes of the stock fence, and the house, and the trees in the near paddock. Tommy looked out at the darkness, and, for the first time in a long while, it felt like he could breathe.

"HEY, Brett?"

He blinked guiltily, aware he'd not been paying attention. Lila kicked his ankle, and the sharp jolt of pain dragged him back to the present.

"Oh, sorry. Uh… what?"

She snickered and shook her head. They were sitting at one of the tables in Julie Red Dog's taco place, watching Karen talk animatedly to a large woman in a dark blouse on the other side of the room. It wasn't awfully busy, and the whole place smelled of the golden, slightly greasy rime of fry bread, beef, and onions.

"I bet I know who you're thinking about," Lila said slyly, leaning forward and fluttering her eyelashes at him. Today, her eyes were outlined in thick black cat strokes, with a little too much silver-blue shadow.

Brett wrinkled his nose, and she laughed, pinching the straw in her Coke between her thumb and forefinger before she drank. Her short, blunt nails were painted dark red, but the polish was already chipped and scarred.

Tommy had been gone for nearly two weeks. Phone calls sucked. He said he was going to get e-mail or instant messaging fixed up or something, but Brett doubted it. Besides, it didn't sound like he got all that much privacy. Hushed "I love yous" on the phone were better without the thirty-minute cutout from the penitential facility's automated service, but they still weren't as good as him actually being there.

"Did you just wanna tease me?" he asked, fixing Lila with his best puppy-dog eyes. "That's cruel."

"No." She slurped at the last inch of her Coke and rattled the ice in the bottom of the cup with the straw. "Well, not *just* that. I wanted to ask you something."

He raised an eyebrow. Over by the counter, Karen and her friend laughed uproariously at something. Brett glanced at his watch. When he'd volunteered to play taxi service while Mei was sick with the flu and Scott was working late, he hadn't actually intended to get lumbered with quite so many errands.

"We need to pick the kids up in twenty minutes," he said doubtfully.

The black nylon tote housing Lila's ballet stuff sat at her feet, next to the groceries Karen had wanted to stop off for. Then it would be Katie and Atian, fresh out of swim club and smelling of chlorine and strawberry shampoo. Brett wondered how Tommy had managed it all, back when this used to be his life, and he felt a little uncomfortable with the sensation of somehow appropriating it.

Lila looked studiously at him over her Coke.

"What's it like, working at the hospital? I mean, I know you're not a doctor, but you're helping people, right? That feels good, yeah?"

Brett blinked. "Uh, yeah... but what—"

"Because I was thinking," she went on blithely, stirring the straw around in the half-melted ice, "y'know, there might be worse things I could do."

He stared as she peered up at him from under her lashes, smiling shyly.

Holy crap, am I good example of something?

It wasn't a familiar experience. Brett cleared his throat. "Well, uh, yeah. Yeah, physical therapy is rewarding. There are plenty of different things you could do within that, or you could look at taking a premed, be a doctor, or a nurse, or—"

"Anything I want to be," Lila said, her voice oozing with sarcasm. "Yeah. I know."

He shrugged. "Well? You could."

She scoffed, and Brett bit the inside of his lip, not sure whether to push the encouragement or sit back and let her make her own decisions. He glanced at his watch again.

"We, uh, we should maybe get going."

Lila sighed laboriously and, pressing her palms to the table, slipped off the bench and stood aside.

"Come on, then," she chided, bouncing impatiently on the balls of her feet, as if she'd been waiting for him for hours.

Brett said nothing, but the look on his face obviously spoke for him. Lila laughed and elbowed him in the ribs as she snagged her ballet stuff. Karen bade her friend good-bye and joined them as they headed for the door, and the warm, wide rays of summer sunshine lanced through the windows, golden flares dancing across the floor.

It was funny, Brett thought, how these little skeins of time wound out into things that felt both insurmountable and so horribly fleeting. Like there'd never been anything else to life but this, and yet that there never would be again.

He'd settle to it, he supposed. It was probably just because it was too much like missing Tommy, and too much like the kind of time they'd just got out of. That wasn't meant to happen again—no more stale days filled up with waiting, no more chunks of life squeezed into boxes—and Brett was certain he wasn't meant to accept this new separation so easily.

He had, though. He knew that.

Brett had found it horribly easy to fall into the rhythms, into the patterns of life, to just let it lap at the edges and fill up the spaces. He hadn't expected that. Oh, the core of it was still there: the anger and the bitterness and the flat-out misery of being without Tommy, especially after those precious, beautiful months of almost having a normal life... but this was normal too.

Funny, he guessed, how strange "normal" could come to be, with time.

BRETT spent the weekend at his parents' house, mostly at his mother's suggestion. Monica made a vague attempt at a cover story concerning his father's inability to put a shelving unit together properly, but he suspected she knew he wasn't really buying it. She knew Tommy was, once again, staying down in Poplar, and she knew that—whatever Brett said—he did mind.

The offer was kind, he supposed. So he allowed her to distract him. He allowed his father to make obviously stupid mistakes with the shelving unit, and they negotiated some tender moments of male bonding over ball-peen hammers, plywood, dowelling, and little sachets of glue that leaked everywhere when you tried to apply them to the correct surface.

He spent most of the time in grubby jeans and a paint-spattered T-shirt, and Monica cooked mustard-glazed pork chops for Sunday's dinner, with creamed potatoes and fluffy little whirls of applesauce.

Later, Brett sat out on the deck, his legs dangling through the rails, and slowly sipped a beer as he watched the sky deepen out into darkness. He heard Stephen's footsteps on the boards behind him, and the first twinges of uncertainty fluttered in his chest. He remembered all the times he'd come and sat out here in the past, during Tommy's imprisonment and even long before that, when there were other things that made life seem dark and bleak, and the only perspective he could find on anything was in the fragmented shapes of the shrubs and trees against the sky.

It was usually his mother who did these talks… if that was what this was going to be. Brett wasn't sure, and he didn't know quite how to respond when his father leaned on the railing beside him and glanced down, the curve of a half smile loitering awkwardly on his lips.

"So, uh… back to work tomorrow, huh?" Stephen said, lifting his own beer to his mouth.

It was getting properly dark now, and the porch light spilled a warm glow out behind them. When he turned his head, Brett could see it reflect in his father's glasses, like little blocks of yellow daubed on by an inexpert hand.

"Yeah," he said. "Well, kinda. Partially a training day. Got another one of those seminars… y'know. Just keeping on top of things."

"Oh." Stephen nodded. "Yes. They, uh, they work you hard, huh?"

Brett shrugged. "Elaine's a *proactive* manager."

He grinned, the buzzword a reference to an old in-joke about medical jargon, and he filled with warmth when his father got the gag, and chuckled. There was comfort here... a kind of familiarity and security he'd never find anywhere else, Brett supposed.

Well, probably not.

"So, um...." The toe of Stephen's shoe tapped idly against the deck. "Have you, uh, heard from Tommy?"

Brett smiled tightly. "Yeah. It's going well, apparently. Busy, but... good."

"That's good," Stephen echoed, staring out into the yard. "That's really good. How, um, how long does the season last? I mean, it's a seasonal thing, right? Or...?"

Brett took another mouthful of his beer and let the bubbles burst slowly on his tongue before he swallowed. Part of him wanted to admit that he and Tommy weren't talking about this the way they should be, but that would have meant, well, *admitting* it. He wasn't sure he could do that, especially to his father.

Better him than Mom.

He swallowed and cleared his throat awkwardly. "I, uh, I don't really know. I guess it's... I don't know. I haven't asked him too many questions about it. Just that, y'know, it's work, and he's happy with it, and Karen's uncle is a good guy. I assume it pretty much dries up come winter, but...."

He shrugged again, a little more defensive this time, although he tried not to be.

Stephen just nodded, his mouth pursed like it was when he had a client's spreadsheet up on the computer or the sports pages were yielding particularly bad news.

"Uh-huh?"

Brett hated that little noise. His mother did it too: a tiny, undeniable prompt, which was almost impossible to ignore. He could already feel the urge to respond, to fill in all the gaps in the silence, welling up in him, irresistible and irrepressible. Years of conditioned upbringing had drilled it into him, and he wasn't thinking when he spoke, just letting the words slip out, as ill-considered as excuses.

"I don't know what he's gonna do. I don't think *he* knows either. I... I don't even know if there is anything he could get that's closer, or if anyone would—y'know. I mean, no matter how much he does for Bill, or whatever qualifications...."

Brett frowned down at the beer bottle, his thumb worrying at the corner of the label. Stephen shifted his weight, leaning more heavily on the rail as he seemed to search for the appropriate words.

"And you're, uh, you're fine with that, are you?"

A pit of awkward discomfort opened up in Brett's gut. He shrugged and swung his feet idly, heels scuffing the tops of the shrubs beneath the deck. Given everything they'd had to work through, he wasn't surprised conversations like this were still uncomfortable as all hell with his parents, even though the intentions might have been good.

"Not really."

"Uh-huh?"

And there it was again. Not an outright demand for information, not a statement of disbelief, or criticism... or anything at all, really. Just a nudge, a hint toward a small, yet powerful connection whose strength Brett couldn't deny.

"I don't know how long it's gonna be for," he said, returning to picking at the label on his beer. "That's what— I mean, Poplar has a hospital. I checked. It's small, but maybe I could—"

"What?"

The shift was abrupt but not unkind. He could feel Stephen's gaze on him, the surprise and the inquisitiveness—perhaps even the trepidation—etched into that small, single word. Brett bit his lip. It was true; he had looked into it. For all of about six minutes. He shook his head.

"It doesn't matter. I don't have the qualifications, and I'm not exactly easily transferable. Huh, you know what's ironic? If I'd stuck with the plan of the premed, or if I'd just—"

"There's a lot of mileage in 'maybe,' Brett."

His mouth snapped closed in response to the hardening of his father's tone, and he frowned at the darkening shapes of the yard. The last cerulean bands of the day's light had all but disappeared under the shadowed weight of clouds, the few remaining streaks of sun gilding their bellies and smudging the boundaries of the dusk. A brief glance at Stephen confirmed he didn't seem truly angry, but this was a sore, tense point, a wound that had healed into a rough, unsightly scar.

"I'd'a been better off qualifying as a nurse, that's all," Brett said quietly. "I could… well. You know."

Stephen knocked back the rest of his beer and shook his head. A sound a little like a small, disparaging scoff escaped him.

"You're planning to move down there now?"

"No," Brett snapped, sounding terser than he'd intended. "I mean, no… well, I don't know. I haven't thought about it."

That wasn't entirely a lie. He *had*, but they were all stupid thoughts, quickly dismissed. Silly, romanticized pipe dreams… like Bozeman, or Billings, or that clean, neat rancher that Tommy wanted, in sight of Bear Paw and with a door they could close on the whole damn world.

"You sound as if you might have," Stephen pressed. "Is that what you want?"

"No, Dad." Brett shook his head hurriedly. "Well, not… aw, hell… I don't know."

He strafed his fingers through his hair and sighed. What he *wanted* was an end to the waiting, and he might even have wanted it enough to change everything, all over again. It wouldn't have been the first time Brett had given up all the choices he'd made for Tommy, and part of him desperately wished that, thinking about it now, the decision seemed as easy as it had once before.

Back then—that chain of awful days, brimming with terrible, frightening clarity—there had been no choice at all, no moment of indecision. Brett had known exactly what he wanted to do. College, his premed… all those carefully planned things meant nothing next to what Tommy had been facing. He'd known what he was doing, and he'd never truly regretted spending the money. The lost opportunities, the altered career path, the deeply hidden anger and humiliation in his mother's eyes every time she looked at him for the next three years... all of that, maybe. But not the act itself.

"I've inspired someone," Brett said with a wry smile, hoping it might be enough to change the subject just a little.

"Hmm?"

"Lila. She wants to look into nursing or physical therapy."

"Oh?"

His father's raised eyebrow annoyed Brett very slightly.

"Yeah. She was talking to me about it the other day. I think she could do worse. She's a smart girl."

Stephen made a noncommittal noise in the back of his throat and held his hand down for Brett's empty beer bottle.

"She is," Brett repeated, passing the bottle up before he hauled himself to his feet and dusted his palms against his jeans. "And she's doing well in school. I'm going to help her look at some different study programs and stuff, show her what kind of thing might be available."

"That's... no, that's good." The bottles clinked gently in Stephen's hand, their slim brown necks chinking together. He glanced at Brett from behind his glasses, the porch light reflecting once more across the lenses. "And next weekend, Tommy's...?"

"Yeah, he's back then. I, uh... I guess I ought to try and weasel some information outta him." Brett smiled thinly, though his father didn't return the gesture. "Just find out how things... are."

Stephen nodded slowly and glanced toward the kitchen door.

"Mm. Best not mention it to your mother, right? If you are— I mean, if you do think about...."

He gesticulated loosely in the air with the empty bottles, and Brett winced.

"Yeah. I won't say a word. And, anyway, it's not even... I mean, for all I know, Tommy could be home by September, right?"

"Right."

The word that left Stephen's mouth might have been an agreement, but it didn't seem to reach as far as his eyes. Brett smiled again and watched him turn and start to head inside, pausing only to toss the beer bottles into the recycling bin that sat by the back door. For a moment, he was haloed by the golden light of the kitchen, and the smell of pork chops and potatoes lingered on the air.

Just as quickly, it dissipated, and Brett shivered a little at the cool breeze skimming his arms. He followed, making his way back into the house as, overhead, the first glimmers of stars began to pierce the night.

CHAPTER FIFTEEN

THE wheat had grown high and ripe, all those vast stretches of muddy brown and green turned to gold under the shimmering disc of a pale, glistening sun. The Chevy kicked up dust on the back roads like a bitch, and Tommy was glad to get onto asphalt. Thin trails of cloud leached across the sky, barely making a single fissure in the wide expanse of blue, and it really did almost feel like flying as he pointed the truck toward the distant outline of Bear Paw and home.

Tommy didn't bother to head to Mei's first. There was really only one place he wanted to go, and it struck him as ridiculously odd that his hands were slick and sweaty on the wheel when he got there.

He'd texted Brett from his last break on the highway to give him a rough ETA, and the anticipation had been building ever since. By the time he was standing at Brett's door, key in hand and still not completely, totally sure he actually had the freedom to just walk in, like he had a right to it, Tommy was practically buzzing with excitement.

He didn't get to use the key. The door opened, revealing a ruffled and tired-looking Brett, still in orthopedic clogs and white smock. He flung his arms around Tommy and clung on, like he'd never been held before.

Tommy hugged him tight, digging his fingers into Brett's broad, firm back and reveling in the warm solidity of his body. Tommy kissed his cheek, breathing in that scent of citrus and musk and hospital disinfectant that he never knew just how much he missed until it was too late. His mouth found Brett's neck, found the ticklish spot just under his ear and the hard, stubble-shaded line of his jaw, and then

Brett was pulling him in, dragging him into the apartment and toeing the door shut after them.

"Mm... hey," he murmured, pulling back from Tommy's embrace and grinning fuzzily at him. "Good journey?"

"All right." Tommy squeezed his hand. "Not been in long, huh?"

"'Bout ten minutes. You made good time."

He smiled. "Floored it all the way for ya, babe."

Brett chuckled and peeled himself away, making for the kitchen. He tossed another grin over his shoulder at Tommy.

"Yeah? Well, I'd rather have you late than scraped off the highway."

Tommy scoffed and padded after him. "I'm a great driver. You know I am."

"And modest with it," Brett called over the familiar, comforting bubbling of the coffeemaker. "Sometimes I don't know what I did to deserve you."

Tommy lolled against the doorframe and watched him putter about, doing the same thing he always did with spoons, mugs, and milk—and even the little bag of licorice root tea that he'd started keeping in the cupboard—and it was the most perfect, wonderful piece of domesticity.

"You were prob'ly Genghis Khan in a previous life," he said sagely, smiling when the joke made Brett snigger. "So, how was your day?"

Brett shrugged. "All right. Nothing special."

"Huh." Tommy nodded slowly, weighing the brush-off against the slight tension in his body and the tightness in his voice. "So... nothin' wrong?"

Brett looked up sharply. "No. Well... no. Not really. Just... a long one, that's all."

"Ah-huh?"

"Yeah." He shrugged again and shot Tommy his best semblance of an innocent smile. "Another one of our elderly patients passed yesterday. His wife called in this morning... outta everything, and the thing she was most twisted up about was him not makin' his appointment."

Tommy watched him set the milk carton down a little too firmly.

"You take the call?"

"Yeah... I said it wasn't a problem and she shouldn't worry, and she just kept thanking me. And crying. It was...."

He shrugged, suppressing a small shudder, and Tommy crossed the floor to him, looping his arms around Brett's waist. He slid his hands across the taut plane of his stomach and rested his chin on the tense curve between neck and shoulder.

"Horrible?"

Brett let his breath catch in his throat a little before he answered, unguarded and undisguised, and he tipped his head back, giving himself over to the embrace.

"Yeah. But it could have been worse."

Tommy gave him a gentle squeeze. "Hey," he murmured, though he wasn't quite sure why, or what better words there might have been. Maybe the words themselves didn't matter. He frowned as he considered it, but then Brett smiled and laid his hand over Tommy's.

"Thanks."

They stayed like that for a few moments, and Tommy reveled in the feel of Brett's warmth against him. Holding him like this, feeling his yielding solidity, it seemed a silent admission that he wasn't perfect, and that he needed this closeness... that he needed Tommy's strength, just once.

Tommy pressed a soft kiss to the base of Brett's neck before releasing him. He leaned against the cabinet and watched him pour the coffee and the tea to steep, the silence that had settled between them strangely comforting.

"You going over to your mom's place?" Brett asked, shooting him a sidelong glance.

Tommy frowned. "Uh... why? Are you tryin' to get rid of me?"

He grinned. "No, I just—I think she's out tonight, that's all. Thought maybe we oughta call Lila, see if she needs a hand."

"Oh." Tommy seriously considered pouting but suspected it wouldn't have got him far. "I was, uh, kinda thinking—"

Brett's grin widened as he stirred his coffee. "Yeah, I bet I know what you were thinking. I was thinking it too, believe me, but…."

Tommy sighed and looked at his feet. He'd spoken to his mother not two days ago, and she hadn't mentioned any plans. There probably wasn't any reason she should have, he supposed. Still… it smarted a little.

"Ron?" he queried, raising his eyebrows at Brett.

"Yeah."

"Oh." Tommy nodded. It made sense. His shoulders slumped, all the same. "Yeah. We should call… probably. You're right. I'll do it."

Brett smiled. "'K. Thanks, babe."

Tommy mumbled something nondescript and noncommittal and ambled back into the other room as he dialed the number. Lila answered with her customary brittle chirpiness, and he couldn't resist harking back to one piece of old times that had never been all that bad.

"Hey, Bear Bait."

"Tommy!" she squeaked, and it sounded just as much like the glee of recognition as it did annoyance at the ancient nickname. "Are you at Brett's?"

"Ah-huh. You holdin' down the fort?"

"Yeah. It's all right. I *can* actually cope, you know."

Tommy grinned. All that teenage bombast and arrogance… and yet she probably could. He wasn't remotely surprised.

"I know. Mom's out?"

"Dinner and a movie. I don't think she's coming home," Lila confided in a harsh and faintly appalled whisper.

Tommy wrinkled his nose. That wasn't really a prospect he wanted to dwell on.

"So… you got Katie and Robbie to manage, huh?"

Lila sighed dramatically, and the sound of her breath crackled on the line. "I can cope. Really. It's not—"

"Well, if you wanted me to bring some food in, or—"

"It's *fine*," she said through gritted teeth. "Seriously. Lindsay's coming over. We have a math thing to study for. Why don't you and Brett just... you know, kick back? Relax. He misses you when you're away. Real bad."

It was kind of a low blow, and it struck Tommy right in the center of the chest, hard. He glanced toward the kitchen, glad that Brett was still messing around out there, and cleared his throat, but it didn't stop his voice coming out as a hoarse, dry croak.

"Yeah. I... I know. But—"

"Tomm-eeee...."

He grinned, the momentary poignancy of Lila's words withering in the face of how much she sounded like the child she'd been. He bit his lip.

"Lindsay, huh?"

"Just a girl from school," she said crisply.

Yeah, right.

He didn't argue. Tommy had spun more than his fair share of useful little lies in the past, and he could hardly stand in judgment now.

"Oh," he said instead. "So...?"

Lila gave a sharp, frustrated growl, the universal noise of teenage girls who've grown tired of questions. "It's *fine!*"

"All right, all right.... Um. Have fun."

"It's algebra," she said laconically. "It's not fun."

Tommy chuckled. "Mm. Sure. Everybody else okay?"

She sighed. He could almost hear her looking toward the door, waiting for the arrival of whatever guy she'd invited under the guise of an apparently innocuous school friend. Given a different time, a different place, he'd probably have done the same. Still, thinking about it—about *her* in that role, entering that phase of life—was more than a little uncomfortable, and he suddenly wanted very much to get off the phone.

"Yes," Lila said. "They're fine. Katie's got a sleepover, and Robbie's upstairs, blowing stuff up on the computer. Happy?"

He grinned. "Sure. I'll come by tomorrow, huh?"

"Yeah. Yeah, that'd be great."

She sounded distracted. Tommy wondered if whoever the guy was had already arrived.

"All right," he said gently. "See you, then."

"Bye."

"Mm. Bye."

She'd already hung up. He frowned as he blipped the phone off, and glanced at the kitchen doorway. Brett filled it, coffee mugs in his hands and an inquiring expression on his face.

"I, uh, I think she's fixed for company."

"Oh?"

Tommy pocketed his phone and rubbed a hand over his face. "Yeah. I don't wanna think about it."

THEY settled on a night in and a movie instead of going out. Coffee, tea, and the tentative comforts of conversation—swapping details of the week, the odds and ends of lives uncomfortably lived by separation—faded into companionable silence, and Brett sent Tommy for a shower while he threw dinner together. It wasn't much, just a few things from the freezer and a small carton of store-bought tiramisu for dessert.

They ate, and Tommy talked a little more about the ranch. He opened up a bit, Brett thought, all wet hair and wide smiles when he spoke about the horses or retold a couple of Bill's choicer anecdotes. It was good to see, though unease lingered at the back of his mind. Two days was all they had, and then Tommy would be gone again, for the week, at least.

However much Brett wanted to ask his questions, and however determined he was not to stumble back into those old habits of staying quiet for the sake of preserving Tommy's optimism, he still hesitated. This was precious time, and he really didn't want to screw it up. He decanted the tiramisu into two bowls and brought it in, taking care to wipe the thoughtful frown from his face as he sat down.

"I'm glad it's working out," he said carefully, watching his spoon break the soft, cocoa-dusted dome. He glanced up at Tommy across the little table. "It's... well, it's pretty steady, right?"

Tommy shrugged, spoon already in his mouth and a happy little grunt escaping him. Brett smiled at the fleeting look of bliss on his face. He had such a sweet tooth.

"Kinda," Tommy conceded, frowning as his spoon hovered over his dish. "This is really good, y'know."

"Yeah. But... I mean, would you maybe look for something in that line, for the whole year? Somewhere—"

"I don't know."

"—closer?" Brett murmured, already regretting the words.

He'd seen the look that crossed Tommy's face—irritation and blank, closed-off denial—and, though it was only fleeting, he didn't want to push his luck.

"Doesn't have to be closer to here," he muttered, digging down to the boozy sponge layer, the clink of metal on bowl filling up the space between them. "I just wondered if—"

"I know," Tommy said shortly. His bare foot nudged Brett's ankle. "I'll... well, I'm not sure. All depends, right? You know that."

"Yeah," Brett said uncertainly. "I know."

Tommy gave him a small, worried smile, his mouth a little folded in on itself and his eyes shaded with apprehension. He turned back to eating for a few moments and then glanced up at Brett again, suddenly laying the spoon against the edge of the dish.

"It's not like I could just get part-time in a shoe store or somethin'."

His tone seemed flat, lacking the argumentative edge that Brett might usually have expected, and his expression was pleading, not defensive. Brett sighed, wanting nothing more than to stop picking at this particular scab, but Tommy was looking at him like he wanted to hear an affirmation, and he could hardly deny him that.

"I know," Brett murmured again: his mantra, his perpetual assurance of acceptance and understanding. He wondered if he really thought about the words anymore. "I know, but—"

"Way I see it, I'm there for as long as they want me there. After that... I got no idea. I... I don't know."

Brett reached across the little round table and squeezed his hand.

"That doesn't matter. You know that, right? All that's important is that you're—"

"Yeah." Tommy's brow tightened, like he wanted to disagree, but he threaded his fingers through Brett's, thumb rubbing small, insistent circles on the underside of his wrist. "Yeah, I know. It's just—"

"It's all right." Brett flexed one shoulder into a diffident shrug. "We'll work it out." He gave Tommy a thin, slightly sickly smile. "We always do, don't we?"

Tommy tightened his grip on Brett's hand. "That's not really the point."

Brett winced. Maybe it wasn't, but what choice was there? Tommy needed the time and the independence. Anything else could get patched up later.

Reluctantly, he extricated himself from Tommy's grasp and collected the dishes. He glanced at the clock.

"I'll do these. Movie's starting in ten. Want popcorn?"

Tommy was studying the tabletop. He blinked and looked up guiltily, as if he'd been caught napping.

"Hm? Yeah. Thanks, babe."

Brett nodded and took the dishes out to the kitchen. After a moment, he heard Tommy's chair scrape, then the sound of him pad over to the couch and flop down. The TV clicked on, and, out of habit, Brett flipped the coffeemaker on again before he started to rifle through the cupboard for a pack of popcorn.

TOMMY muted the commercials, leaned his head against the back of the couch, and let his eyelids start to droop. He was full, comfortable... safe, even, and yet his body still threw out weird curveball cravings for nicotine or weed from time to time. It was mostly habit, he guessed. Times like this, once, with everybody who ought to be in bed tucked up safely and the house quiet, he'd have smoked something to take the edge off, just to put a barrier between himself and the night. It seemed strange to welcome the stillness now.

He listened to Brett moving about in the kitchen, mildly annoyed with himself for backing out of things like he had. All the same, there wasn't much else he could have said. Brett deserved more than empty promises and vague possibilities, even if Tommy had no idea how he was meant to bring it all about.

There used to be a lot of talk about that. Embracing your future and deciding to become the person you wanted to be. The process of adjustment and the importance of not letting your past define you. All the words seemed to spool back to him as if through a fog, and Tommy remembered sitting through a lot of the sessions with his gaze fixed firmly on the floor. Wanting to believe it was one thing, but making it happen—truly, really thinking it could—was something completely different.

He let himself turn away from the thoughts, idly wondering if Mei was having a good time, wherever she was. Tommy tried not to dwell on the inevitable places the mental images led, like sex and the image of Ron as a permanent fixture. Marriage? Probably. She was maybe even still young enough for another baby, he figured, if... damn. Would she want that? Would Ron?

That'd be so weird.

He cracked open one eye and watched Brett pass in front of him, then stand two steaming mugs on the coffee table. In the kitchen, the microwave hummed to itself, its low buzz interspersed with the soft bangs and pops of the corn. Brett arched an eyebrow and cocked his head to the side.

"What?"

"Hm?" Tommy glanced up at him. "Oh. Nothing. Just thinkin'."

"Yeah?" He smirked. "You're doin' it loudly."

Tommy scoffed. "I think loud?"

"Yep." Brett flopped down on the couch next to him. "Cogs whirring like jet engines. Wanna talk about it?"

"Not really."

"Okay."

And that was why Brett was wonderful, Tommy decided, reaching out and laying a companionable hand on his thigh. After a little while, Brett's fingers brushed the backs of his knuckles.

"What's he like? Ron, I mean."

Tommy shrugged. "'K. All right, I guess. He's… nice."

"That's good."

"Hmmn."

That wasn't fair, he decided, listening to the indecision in his own voice. Ron *was* nice. And that *was* good. Mei deserved that much, and so did the kids.

It was—well… *nice*.

Brett squeezed his hand gently, moving it aside as he stood to go and get the popcorn. The microwave must have pinged, and Tommy realized he hadn't heard it. Was that good? He frowned at the TV as the soundless commercials ran into each other, and the smell of synthetic butter and sweetener filled the air.

"Scoot," Brett ordered, reappearing laden with two bowls of popcorn: one large and sweet, one small and salty.

Tommy obediently shunted along the couch, and balanced the bigger bowl in his lap as Brett settled beside him, feet tucked up beneath him and the heinous salt-soaked popcorn on his knee.

"You think they're gonna get married?" Tommy asked before selecting a puffy, sticky, buttery kernel and rolling it between his thumb and forefinger.

There was a news bulletin running before the movie. He didn't bother to thumb the volume up.

Brett reached over and snagged a handful of the sweet popcorn, dumping it into the bowl of salty and indulging what Tommy considered a deeply peculiar taste for mixed flavors. He watched from the corner of his eye as Brett stirred the whole lot around with his index finger and then sucked the digit clean.

"What?" he asked thoughtfully, fingertip still locked between his lips. "Your mom and Ron?"

"Mm-hm."

It was gross, Tommy decided. The salt-and-sweet thing, not the image of his mother *in flagrante delicto*, though that definitely had its unsettling properties. Still, his gaze followed the finger and the curve of Brett's lips as they molded around a small smile.

"I don't know." Brett shrugged. "You know, Lila asked me the same thing. I asked what she thought, and she said it was a distinct possibility." He tossed a piece of popcorn at Tommy and grinned when it bounced off his chest. "Why? What do *you* think?"

Tommy picked the salty morsel off his shirt and threw it back. Brett almost caught it in his mouth, but he missed, grinned, and settled back against the arm of the couch. Tommy sniggered.

"Don't know. Maybe. I think she wants to." His smile faded as he considered the prospect. "Gives her a sense of security, I guess. Makes her feel safer."

"Maybe she just loves him," Brett said reproachfully. "Isn't she allowed a little romance?"

Tommy pulled a face. "Aw, c'mon... she's my *mother*! That's... weird. And gross."

Brett snorted, so Tommy threw another piece of popcorn at him. It didn't stop the giggles. Brett tossed another one back, and the air soon filled with tiny greasy projectiles. Tommy considered cheating and leaping on him, but busting out the power of tickles seemed a little unfair, however tempting it was. Anyway, it would have sent the popcorn flying.

"Lila asked me somethin' else, actually," Brett said after a few moments, holding up a hand and drawing a truce in the burgeoning snack projectile war.

Tommy ate the bit of popcorn he was about to use as ammunition. "Ah-huh?"

"Mm." Brett lazily unfolded his legs and prodded Tommy with one foot. "She, uh, asked me if *we* were... y'know. Gonna do that."

Tommy swallowed heavily, then gave a strangled cough, the popcorn catching in his throat and mixing with the disbelief. On the

TV, the weather lady smiled cheerfully and waved her hand at a swath of low pressure and possible rainstorms.

"Uh, what? What, you 'n' me, get…?"

"If we could," Brett said evenly with a small shrug.

Tommy stared at him. They'd never dipped into this side of things much before. There had always been so much else that seemed more immediate and more important than talking about politics and legalities. He blinked, suddenly unable to shake the visions of tuxedos and carnations.

"What'd you say to her?"

Brett dipped into his popcorn. "Oh, y'know… I didn't know. Not in the foreseeable future, that what matters more than your legal status is that you're actually happy… that kinda stuff."

"Oh."

Tommy nodded slowly, and for a moment they fell silent. The movie's opening sequence started to roll, and Tommy switched up the volume. He kind of wished he'd taken more note of what the story was meant to be about. There was a city, and it was raining. Probably, within the next ten minutes, someone was going to manifest mutant superpowers or aliens would land. Brett was pretty big on sci-fi.

There seemed to be a lot of concrete and a lot more rain. They made inroads into the rest of the popcorn, and Tommy frowned.

"Brett?"

"Mm?"

Tommy shot a sidelong glance at him, his gaze resting on the ruffled red-brown hair and the dark smudges of fatigue swiped under those hazel eyes. It really had been a long week, he reflected. Brett arched his brows inquisitively. On the TV, a girl blew up a car with her newly discovered telekinetic powers. Tommy cleared his throat and tried to make the words sound casual.

"W-would you… want to?"

There were people running and screaming, and a giant fireball coursed along the center of a built-up city street.

"What, get hitched?" Brett smiled amiably and nudged Tommy's thigh with his sock-clad foot. "Do we need to?"

Tommy shrugged. "I'm curious."

The movie cut to commercial just as the fireball threatened to swallow the camera, and Brett's smile widened a little.

"All right." He leaned forward, setting the now empty popcorn bowl on the coffee table, and dusted his hands together slowly, like he was counting off points on his fingers. "Well, I believe everybody deserves the *right* to do it, but I don't think it affects you and me. I mean, we already bicker about things that don't matter, and you already leave your underwear all over my floor, so—"

"Hey!"

"—it's not like a nice, legal piece of paper could make us any more tied together."

"Guess not," Tommy admitted, unsure whether it was relief or regret that was sluicing through him like iced water. "But...."

"Why?" Brett looked at him in surprise. "You wanna?"

He shrugged. "N—well, I don't know. It'd be... weird."

Brett snorted. "Great, thanks. Weird, huh?"

"I don't mean—" Tommy stopped, aware he was being teased, and wrinkled his nose. "You know what I mean. It'd be... well, you're right, anyway. We don't need it."

He cleared his throat and leaned over to set the other popcorn bowl down. They mirrored each other, near enough, standing there amid the clutter of bits of paper and discarded rubber bands, keys, and the white-petaled coffee plant in its little zinc planter. Suddenly, it was hard to think beyond the vision of what something like that might mean, and how all those strange, nebulous ideas of futures and long term plans might somehow coalesce into a real life. A good life, maybe.

Sure, it didn't need a piece of paper. But it needed something.

"Um." Tommy swallowed heavily. "But... if we did do it...?"

Brett laughed, and tenderness flooded his face as Tommy sat back, his hair still clinging damply to the nape of his neck. He felt oddly exposed, he realized—even here in this soft, sacred space—

although the feeling started to go away when he looked into Brett's eyes and found what felt like understanding there.

"That was the worst proposal ever," Brett said dryly.

"It wasn't a— Look, I'm being hypothetical here."

Brett caught his lower lip between his teeth, impish and tempting.

"Hypothetical?" he echoed, arching his brows. "Oh, okay. Hypothetically, then… yeah. I mean, it's a good excuse for an open bar and a two-week vacation, right?

Tommy narrowed his eyes, struggling to hold down the grin. "See? This is why I'm not getting down to propose on one knee. There's no point with you."

The angelic, wide-eyed look Brett gave him was one of heartfelt innocence, albeit shot through with giggles.

"No? Awww. Still," he added with a cheerful grin, "I guess it doesn't matter. I mean, I can get you on your knees if I *really* want to."

Tommy snorted. "Mm. You usually do."

"And you love it," Brett drawled, prodding him again with that sock-clad foot.

The toes were faintly grubby, and the foot itself definitely bore a distinct odor of orthopedic clog. Tommy's smile widened. There was no point denying it. He did. He loved all of it. He grabbed the foot, slipped his middle finger down to the center of the sole, and hit the potently ticklish spot that made Brett yelp with combined protest and laughter.

"Argh! Fuck off!"

Somewhere amid the bursts of uncontrolled laughter, tickling, and profanity, Tommy completely lost what little thread he'd had of the movie. It didn't really matter.

They watched the rest of it tangled up in each other, Brett resting against him with his head on Tommy's stomach and his legs draped over the end of the couch. Tommy played idly with his hair from time to time, enjoying the feel of it beneath his fingers. Eventually, Brett's breathing deepened out and he started to snore softly. Tommy held his breath and eased one leg out from under him, gingerly touching his foot to the floor and waiting for the pins and needles to wear off. He kept an eye on the movie so he could fill in the "what'd I miss?" blanks when Brett woke up, and wondered what the best superpower would be.

He was debating between flight and superspeed when the credits began to roll. Brett grunted, snorted, and mumbled something about being awake, and Tommy prodded his shoulder.

"Yeah, yeah. Sure y'are. C'mon. Bed."

Brett rubbed the heel of his palm across his eyes and yawned sleepily. "You… ungh… you're always tryin' to get me… thing."

"Yep," Tommy agreed, manhandling him to his feet and propelling him toward the bedroom. "There's nothin' sexier than an exhausted physical therapist. Now get that tight little ass into bed."

He swatted the butt in question for emphasis, and Brett flipped him off in a halfhearted, dozy kind of way before stumbling through the process of undressing. Tommy grinned to himself and breezed through shutting the apartment down for the night, flicking off lights and letting the shadows pool in the thickening quiet.

The toilet flushed as he rinsed up the last few things next to the sink, and he wiped his hands on the seat of his pants. By the time he got into the bedroom, Brett was already flaked out under the covers. He barely stirred when Tommy stripped down and slid in next to him, though he yielded to the arm that snaked across his chest and made a small happy noise at the back of his throat.

Tommy held him close and pressed a kiss to the burnished crown of his head.

"Night, boo," he murmured.

CHAPTER SIXTEEN

TIME passed in its usual way, lulling with a sense of gradual change, yet never quite closing the gaps on the days. Weeks plodded by with monotonous regularity, the sharp edges of wanting and waiting dulled to a blunt, oily ache by repetition. Routines formed; the back and forth of Tommy's weekly or sometimes biweekly commute and the predictable patterns of snatched time snuck their tendrils into life.

It wasn't quite the way it had been, but it wasn't the way Brett had imagined either, and it wasn't what he wanted. He wondered, from time to time, why he wasn't more bothered by it, when Tommy showed every sign of just settling more deeply into life at Bill's place instead of motivating himself to use it as a springboard up to something new.

Of course, things never would have been the way he'd pictured them. He knew that. Besides, Tommy was doing well at the ranch. Every time he came back, he seemed to have something to say about this idea or that piece of news... like he was becoming a part of the working life of the place, contributing more to it than just the odd mended fence. One weekend, he came back in paint-speckled jeans and an old T-shirt stained with mastic and the smell of sweat. They were fixing up the rest of the bunkhouse, he said. Brett didn't understand the implications of that, but Tommy just grinned widely and talked about diversification and the possibility of branching out into taking in double the number of paying guests next year. Then he got onto acreage and arable quality, and what Bob Hendricks—who apparently owned the cattle ranch that bordered one side of Bill's land—had been saying about potentially selling off a parcel of grazing.

He was starting to sound like he belonged... and Brett was glad of that, he supposed. It seemed, in a lot of ways, only natural that it should be Tommy's right to find his own place, to slide into a little corner of the world that was his. He deserved it, and, against the thought of that, Brett guessed the potential of a few small sacrifices wasn't all that much to get himself tied into knots over.

At the end of July, the whole family—extended and protracted in all its messy glory—was meant to meet up for the Milk River Indian Days event, marking the birth of high summer.

Brett had gone before, trailing along after Karen when Tommy was away, making the most of one of her many gestures of kindness. Then, he'd felt so very cultured, attending for the first time as something slightly more than a white guy with a camera. It was going to be different, going with Tommy and Mei and the kids, and Ron, and Scott and Karen, and even his own parents tagging along behind, uncertain and faintly uncomfortable.

Tommy had said the brother—or brother-in-law, or cousin, or something—of one of the part-time guys was dancing, though he didn't offer any further details when Brett asked. It was the weekend before the event, and thick slabs of golden sunlight lay lazily across the bed, highlighting the crests and planes their bodies made beneath the covers, like some kind of cotton-sheathed mountain range. Tommy's foot prodded Brett's shin, disrupting the vista and causing a minor landslide somewhere around the lower peaks.

"Hell, no," he said with a grin. "I never wanted to do that."

Brett smiled, enjoying the ease with which he could pull Tommy over and into an embrace, and the sheer luxury of being here at nine thirty in the morning, wrapped up in each other. Two mugs steamed gently on the nightstand, and pretty much everything seemed more or less right with the world as his fingers traced curves and swirls over Tommy's back.

"Not even a bit?" he teased, as Tommy filled his arms, knee slipping between Brett's legs and mouth fastening onto his neck. "You're sure you never wanted to—?"

"Nope," Tommy said, somewhat muffled. "I'm not a dancer. Never was. Anyway, it's… y'know, it's s'posed to be more of a calling than a choice, and that's not really my thing."

He pulled away, hair mussed up and hanging down between them like a curtain, and Brett frowned. He reached out and touched Tommy's jaw lightly, half wanting to let the topic slide away in favor of a little quality time, and half too curious to resist.

"I thought you were getting pretty into that side of, uh, stuff," he tried, hoping ambiguity would protect him from causing offense. "I mean, you did all of that with the talking circle and—"

"That was different," Tommy said shortly, though the traces of a smile still wreathed his mouth and softened the words a little.

He rolled off Brett's lap, making the mattress bounce as he settled back on his own side of the bed, and he flipped his hair from his shoulders before he reached past Brett to get the coffee and his licorice root tea.

Brett's frown deepened a little. He'd thought they were all different aspects of the same culture—a culture that he had been under the impression Tommy wanted to embrace—but it was perfectly possible he was wrong. It would hardly have been the first time. He took the mug Tommy gave him and peered at the bubbles eddying on the coffee's surface. The tea's aniseed fragrance lingered in the air.

"How is it different?"

He shouldn't have asked, he supposed. It would probably have been easier to let everything stay at the level of jokes and playing. After all, they'd gone a long time with too little laughter.

"It just is." Tommy shrugged, and he looked away when Brett glanced at him, suddenly turning serious. "I don't know. It's… well, that whole side of things. I didn't grow up with it, and I don't… it's just not me. Not all the way through, you know? And, as for what I believe, that's between me and whatever—I mean, it's personal. It doesn't need airing in front of everybody."

"Right." Brett nodded slowly. "Okay."

Tommy sipped his tea, and the summer sunlight that streamed through the bedroom window brought out every golden tone in his skin as he sat there, bare-chested and beautiful. There were times, even now, that Brett couldn't help staring at him... or staring at the blurry blue-inked tattoo at the top of his arm.

"Sorry," he murmured. "I didn't mean to—"

"You didn't," Tommy said quickly, glancing at him with the swift, soft curve of a smile. "S'all right. I just... I'm not... I don't wanna be all that involved with it. Not like Joe and those other guys. That, uh, isn't really me. You understand?"

Brett smiled weakly. "Mm-hm."

He didn't. Not fully, although he saw the root of this new defiance. Sometimes, he could read Tommy clearer than block print on white paper, and it made up for every mixed signal and hidden feeling. He felt inferior, Brett guessed, like he didn't belong, and that almost came as a surprise.

Brett thought back to all the letters Tommy had sent from prison, and all the slightly scary enthusiasm he'd had for the sweat lodge and the talking circle, and how his commitment to it—his first steps walking the Red Road, as he'd insisted on writing more than once—had really seemed to help him. It had given him identity, motivation... something of his own to hold onto.

It felt different out here, Brett imagined. Tribal enrollment was one thing; truly belonging could well have been another. He supposed he wouldn't know. Ultimately, however frustrating it was to admit, Brett knew he could read all the books and pamphlets he wanted about spirituality and tradition, and never get much closer to really understanding... but then he'd come to terms with that a long time ago. He'd never needed to understand everything, so long as there was common ground to meet on.

Gradually, he grew aware of Tommy looking suspiciously at him, and he arched an eyebrow. "What?"

Tommy shot him a teasing look across the rim of his mug. "Aren't you gonna ask me if I believe in God?"

Brett shook his head and nudged Tommy's foot with his own. "Nope. Not unless you wanna talk religion. Do you?"

Tommy knocked back the rest of his tea, swallowed, and grinned as he leaned across to replace the mug on the nightstand.

"Not really," he murmured, straddling Brett's lap once more and dropping a kiss to the hollow of his collarbone. He trailed his fingers up and down the lines of Brett's arms, his voice a low buzz against Brett's skin. "'Cause, when you come down to it, I don't even think it matters, y'know? I mean, *you* matter. This matters. Us… and the people we care about. And if there is more than that, that's where it is."

He nuzzled Brett's neck, the combination of heady words, warm skin, and hot, spiced breath almost enough to make him pour the rest of his coffee down himself. Brett swallowed heavily and stroked his fingers through Tommy's hair.

"That's… an interesting philosophy," he managed, reaching out to push his mug back onto the nightstand.

It was tough to do without looking, but Brett managed not to knock anything flying, and it suddenly seemed very important to have both hands free for holding Tommy, touching him… feeling what he said he believed in. He leaned in, and the kisses tasted of licorice root and the faint hint of toothpaste, laced with a leisurely sense of closeness and security that left Brett completely wrapped in the moment.

He'd never been particularly religious, although he had yearned for the comfort of it sometimes. Right now, he decided, he could believe in a clean, pure humanism, where life was nothing more than perfect coincidence: a spark in the void and a flare of hope to be clutched and nurtured. Maybe there didn't need to be anything more than that, any great hope or neat plan. If that was the case, it made everything that little bit more urgent, and that little bit more important.

It meant there weren't any second chances.

TOMMY wriggled eagerly in Brett's lap, soft laughter breaking through his grin as they parted. He rubbed his thumb over Brett's chin, relishing the unshaven prickles and the fullness of his lips, dampened and ever so slightly reddened with kisses. Weekends were great, because they felt like they were made of all the time in the world, and there was nothing to do on them except live. Funny thing was, he could hardly remember feeling this impatient.

"Fuck me?" he suggested nonchalantly, loving the little stab of hungry lust that sparked in those clear hazel eyes.

Brett smiled, his face maybe even tinged with a tiny bit of surprise, like that kind of request really came out of left field. Tommy chuckled, catching his lower lip between his teeth and squirming against the hardening weight beneath him.

"You're not gonna make me beg, are you? It's not pretty when I beg."

"Oh, it is." Brett smoothed a palm over his thigh, raising little threads of warmth all through the flesh. "It's really pretty. But I'm too good to you."

Tommy's grin widened. "Hmm. Yep."

He rolled off and bounced playfully on the bed, sending the springs thunking, the frame creaking, and Brett bursting into joyous laughter… just before he surged forward, tackled Tommy around the middle, and bore him to the sheets.

Tommy yelped in glee as they wrestled, kissed, tickled, and fought, every touch a movement in a familiar dance. He knew the steps. He remembered every rise and fall, every touch and intimacy, and it was beautiful. His fingers traced well-worn patterns over Brett's body, skimming the moles that scattered his arms and chest and chaining them together like stars.

The warm expulsion of breath on his neck hinted at Brett's growing need, and Tommy was only too ready for him, only too eager to pull him close and marvel at the solemn intensity of his expression. It was as if, at that moment, every doubt took wing and nothing could ever have been too big, or too difficult, to be more than a whisper between them. The teasing yielded to open, unashamed passion, and he loved the way Brett bloomed, taking charge and owning that sense of authority that clung to him like a second skin. As he hooked his knees over his lover's shoulders, Tommy reflected that Brett was probably one of the strongest people he'd ever known.

He smiled and wrapped himself up in the thought, his fingers tugging at that messy red-brown bed-head as he pulled Brett in for one wet, hot crush of a kiss before lying back against the pillows and letting him take control.

"Fuck," he murmured again, as Brett slid home. "Oh… fuck, I want you, baby."

"You want this?" Brett purred, filling him up with voice and touch and love.

Tommy nodded, his mouth slackly curved around a slight, shapeless sound. Brett knew what he wanted, what he liked, what he needed… and it seemed to last forever. The bed groaned and creaked, the rhythm building until it broke the last boundaries between them and he was just clinging on, hollering and panting as the dirty-sweet words Brett had learned from him all that time ago echoed back on gasping lips. Sweat slicked their bodies, and the world disappeared into a white-hot nimbus, leaving nothing but the pleasure-heat of flesh, and Brett pounding into him like a jackhammer.

Yeah, weekends were definitely great.

After it was all over, they basked in the warmth of sunlight and satiation. Tommy lay on his front, nested in a muddle of tangled covers with Brett beside him, hands behind his head as he stared up at the ceiling.

"Hmm," he said thoughtfully, rolling over onto his side and blowing through pursed lips.

The breath skimmed the back of Tommy's heel, and he twitched his foot idly, as if he was trying to shoo a fly.

"What?"

"Oh, nothin' much." Brett reached out and trailed two fingers up the back of his calf, pausing to dip in and plant a soft kiss on the flesh. "Just thinking."

Tommy smiled and stretched luxuriously against the bed, taking personal inventory of everything that ached, felt scraped or bruised, or would probably be sore later on. The warmth of Brett's palm smoothed the back of his thigh, and his smile widened lazily.

"'Bout what?"

"One of these days," Brett said nonchalantly, giving him a small, gentle pinch, "you and I might actually have a conversation that doesn't end with you tryin' to distract me with sex."

Tommy chuckled. There was sufficient steel beneath the words for him to know Brett wasn't entirely kidding, but there was also warmth enough for it not to scare him. At least, not right now. Not in this comfortable, sleepy, beautiful little haven of time.

"Maybe," he murmured. "Not that I thought you were complaining."

Brett snorted quietly and got up to go for a shower.

WHEN Monday morning came, the early start and the long drive reminded Tommy pretty emphatically of his previous exertions. At first, it felt like a dirty little secret, which was kind of exciting... but then he hit the potholes and the dirt roads, and by the time he got to the ranch, he wanted nothing more than a long, hot shower.

The work on the bunkhouse was almost done, and that was where Bill met him, waving a clipboard with a spreadsheet tacked to it, a pencil tucked behind his ear.

"Hey, Tommy! You wanna take a look at this?"

Tommy lifted a hand in greeting, backpack slung over his shoulder, and ambled up the path. The air smelled of cut grass and sawdust, and the distant whine of a table saw seemed to be drifting out from somewhere.

"Uh... sure."

"We got the quote on the extension through. It's not that bad. Better than I expected, and I figure Herman can knock the guy down a little if he tries. Come on, come in and take a look."

Bill clapped him on the shoulder and thrust the clipboard in front of him, still talking cheerfully. Tommy winced and peered at the rows of numbers and, beneath the top sheet of paper, the printed letter and estimate concerning the work Bill had been thinking about having done to the house. Sunlight dappled the whiteness of the paper, making everything jump around a little, and yet, when he glanced up at the building, with its glazed porch and clean lines, it was easy to see it exactly the way Bill wanted.

It would be a sizable job, Tommy thought, but doable: a set of long-held plans and ideas finally grinding into life, worked on piece by piece until they came together. He wasn't sure where Bill's sudden wave of fervor stemmed from, but he guessed, if the combination of available cash and skills worked, it'd be good news for the ranch.

"Lemme just dump my stuff," he said, nodding toward the bunkhouse.

"Sure." Bill smiled, accompanying him along the path. "Good drive?"

"Not so bad," Tommy conceded as they entered the bunkhouse, ducking into the dimness, scented with fresh paint and newly stripped and varnished wood.

He couldn't help the grin that spilled over his face as he surveyed the small, plain room. Bill lingered in the doorway while he set his gear down, and for once it didn't seem quite so important to have everything lined up exactly straight. The room felt enough like home for it not to matter so much, and Tommy's smile widened even further as he glanced across at the photos pinned up beneath the shelf by the bed. None of the furniture was so rickety now—a couple of hours with a hammer, tacks, and wood glue had seen to that—and even the smell of pine cladding and the tang of new paint seemed comfortingly familiar.

They walked back up to the house together, talking about the plans and the possibilities. Bill had so many ideas, and his enthusiasm was infectious. From the way he talked—his words laced with big, open-palmed gestures that swung out to encompass the trees, the sky, and even the brief black shapes of birds that hung against it—Tommy figured he must have had these plans for years. First, he wanted to extend the ranch house itself. Then, eventually, there would be another two cabins looking out toward the pastures that ran right down to the pond, below the slight dip in the land that, in this flat terrain, passed for a hill. They'd buy up a bigger parcel of land, lay in some proper trails along the boundaries, really look at improving the structure of the place... it was all mapped out in his head, or so it seemed.

Herman wasn't so much of a forward thinker, Bill said. He'd have been happy simply getting by with the way things were, but that just wasn't practical.

Tommy frowned doubtfully. "You really think you'd get more people payin'?"

"Why not?" Bill shrugged and stuck his thumbs in his belt loops. "Look at all this space, huh? If we market it right, they'll be queuing up. Big Sky Country, y'know?"

"Yeah… I guess."

Tommy wasn't all that familiar with the business dynamics of dude ranching, but he had to agree there was probably more money in it than cattle farming or bloodstock, with the way things appeared to have been going. If the cash could be raised, it was probably a sensible option, and Tommy had to admit he understood about grasping those with both hands.

"You know what I'm talking about, though, right?" Bill asked, looking at him with uncharacteristic solemnity as they neared the kitchen door. "Things don't stay the same. You got to move with them, change with them. You know?"

Tommy nodded. "Yeah. Yeah, I know."

"Exactly." Bill grinned again and clapped him on the shoulder. "Now, I wanna talk to you about joinery…."

MOST of the week got swallowed up that way. The renovations on the bunkhouse were just about done, which meant Bill was already knee-deep in plans for the extension—including numerous ways to slice down the already meager budget and undercut pretty much every single quote he'd been given—and making calls to Bob Hendricks about that land deal. Tommy had no idea what had brought it all on, or what the financial background to the whole thing was. Given the slight tension that seemed to echo around the place every time Herman showed up, he wasn't sure he wanted to know.

Tina just tutted and rolled her eyes at Bill's wave of enthusiasm.

"He gets this way every year," she confided to Tommy over the payroll, pursing pink-painted lips and narrowing her eyes. "Just before the first BUNAC kids show up. Last year, it was two Swedish girls. He was like a peacock the whole damn summer."

Tommy grinned, but he was privately relieved they didn't have many bookings of that kind this year. He rather liked the fact there were so few people to deal with here. Like solitude, but not so complete, not so frightening. He could be alone, yet not entirely so, and that was good.

As the weekend loomed, talk of the building plans and the new foals—all three strong and healthy, and one likely to be carrying all the markers of his father's much-coveted Appaloosa coat—gave way increasingly to the Milk River Days gossip. Joe's cousin Trey would be dancing, as he never seemed to shut up about, and his pride was fierce as noon sun. Tommy got a little lost in all the talking about it. Most of his memories concerning the powwows he'd been to with Gramma were just snatches of hot summer days, with bright colors against dusty arenas and bellyaches from eating too much.

He nodded and smiled when the others jawed about some guy who was apparently a legendary grass dancer, and Herman strung more words together on that subject than Tommy had ever heard him say all at once. It was high praise, though, because then they were into a technical discussion about Joe's cousin's footwork, and how it reminded him of this guy, and this one time at Crow Fair.... Tommy tuned out a little, and suppressed a grin when he caught Nathan's eye across the table. He had the same glassy look on his face, and he blinked hurriedly and stared at his plate, as if ashamed at being caught in his ignorance.

Tommy watched those long, slim, knotted fingers clutch a little too eagerly at his fork, that dark head bent diligently to the task of eating, and decided Nathan was maybe a little younger than he'd first thought. All that wide-eyed, awkward innocence and faintly naïve awe... he remembered feeling like that once. Hell, he remembered seeing it in other people, when everything was a little newer, a little fresher.

It was cute, really. As a matter of fact, Nathan was kind of cute. Not that Tommy had any intention of pursuing that thought, but there was something refreshing in being able to think it, even if it didn't matter.

Once he got back to the bunkhouse, door closed against the world and nothing but the soft sound of horses' calls drifting down on the thick, deep blue night, Tommy sent Brett his routine good night text message. They'd somehow fallen out of the ritual of phone calls over these long weeks. He couldn't remember quite how, or when the slackening off had begun, but Brett didn't seem to mind. Neither did he, really. Tommy guessed things stopped seeming so painfully important once you didn't have a reason to need them.

As he slipped under the covers, reveling in being able to stretch out, lengthening every tired and taut muscle after a day of shit-shoveling and gophering, his phone beeped. He picked it up and peered at the screen in the gray-blue dimness of his small, comfortable room.

Night, baby. I love you too. x

Tommy smiled and set the phone carefully on the nightstand. He glanced at the shadow-blurred photos on the wall and let a long, low breath slide from his lungs as he wriggled his shoulders into the pillow.

CHAPTER
SEVENTEEN

IT WAS a long drive to the powwow grounds, and the whole day had a slight air of a complexly planned military operation. Brett was glad he'd opted to get a ride with his parents, leaving Scott and Karen to take Atian, while Ron would apparently be driving Mei, Katie, Lila, and Robbie. They were supposed to meet Bill, Karen's parents, and Tommy there, and the thought of seeing him sustained Brett through the stupidly early start, the weekend traffic, and the endless hours of his father's terrible singing along to the radio.

By the time they arrived, the sun had already begun thumping down on the sea of parked cars and trucks, and the air smelled of hot metal and dry grass. The thin, tinny, semidistant sound of a Tannoy announcer echoed over the thrum of activity, and the whole place seemed to be buzzing. The huge arbor that housed the central circle was hedged by lights, ready for the dance competitions that would last into the evening while, beyond it, the white tents and marquees of the vendors' booths glimmered beneath the sky's sharp, raw blues. People came from all over for events like this, and many of them were thronging the grounds, the chatter of excited voices mingling on the warm air. Beyond the stalls selling crafts, regalia supplies, food, drink, and all manner of other bits and pieces, further gaggles and groups of people—singers, costumed dancers, and proud friends and relatives identifiable by their broad smiles—hung around laughing and talking, while plenty of other visitors had brought chairs and coolers and were clearly camped out for the duration.

"Whew!" Monica passed one freckled hand over her forehead, swiping the soft red bangs from her eyes. "Busy, isn't it?"

Brett murmured an agreement, already scanning the crowds for familiar faces.

As they drew closer to the main approach of the arena, a guy in full traditional regalia—a huge porcupine hair roach on his head, his apron and gauntlets heavily beaded, his knee bands fringed, and a wide feather bustle spreading out behind him—headed by on his way to the Porta-Pottys. He nodded and smiled in passing, and the three of them grinned back admiringly. As he moved toward the rank of green plastic bathrooms, Stephen squinted after him, the sunlight catching on the lenses of his glasses, then turned to Brett and Monica.

"How do you think he—?"

Brett's eyes widened in reproach. "Dad!"

"What?" Stephen shrugged. "Really. I mean, look at the size of that thing. How would you even…?"

"It's sacred," Brett hissed with a shake of his head, though he couldn't completely stifle his snigger.

"Oh, I know." Stephen sighed. "All the same…."

Brett drew breath to respond, but was interrupted by a shout from across the grounds.

"Hey!"

He glanced in the direction the sound had come from and saw Lila with Mei, Ron, Robbie, and Katie, almost halfway across the field. She bounced on the balls of her feet as she waved to him, and Brett waved back enthusiastically, grinning as he started toward them.

"Hey, you!"

Lila greeted him with a big smile and a hug he hadn't really expected, and Brett patted her bare shoulder tentatively as she broke away to say hi to his parents. Brett did the usual semiawkward round of smiles and hellos, privately amused by Ron's ever-so-slightly starchy politeness. Though they'd met once or twice since Tommy had been working in Poplar, Brett got the feeling the guy really wasn't at ease with him. He didn't know exactly why, but it failed to bother him as much as he'd thought it would, and he supposed he ought to find that strange.

Still, Brett had spent plenty of years refusing to let people's assumptions affect him, and he wasn't about to start now. He turned to Lila, wincing for a moment as the light caught on the glitter sunburst picked out on the front of her cami. The stridently bright, floral scent of her perfume caught at his nose.

"You guys seen Scott and Karen?"

"Not yet." Lila screwed up her face and glanced over her shoulder. "I don't know if they're here. Lemme check my phone...."

Mei muttered something about wanting to take a look at the food booths, and Katie tugged at her hand, apparently eager to get the pocket money she'd been promised for shopping. Mei sighed and unclasped her purse, fishing out a small, brightly colored woven wallet.

"There you go. Remember what I said. Stay with your sister, and don't go anywhere until we've met up with—"

"Mo-om...." Thumb dancing over her cell's keypad, Lila rolled her eyes theatrically. "Do I really have to—?"

"Yes! Yes, you have to keep an eye on her. We talked about this in the car...."

The familiar rhythms of a family that wasn't quite his—but which had lapped at the edges of his life long enough for the distinction not to matter—washed over Brett. He glanced at Ron, taking in the studied blankness of that pale, runny-eyed face, and the way the light summer breeze ruffled his thinning, sandy hair. Robbie slumped beside him, hands deep in the pockets of his baggy jeans, apparently already scanning the horizon for potential escape routes.

A piercing whistle cut across the air, disrupting the creaking tensions of another brewing mother-daughter argument, and Brett turned to see Scott and Karen bearing down on them. Atian ran ahead, arms flailing and hair wind-tousled, while Karen's parents, plus her sister and her kids, were following on behind, accompanied by another older, heavyset man and, right at the back, one last familiar figure.

Brett's chest clenched around a sudden and ridiculous spear of delight, and he couldn't do a single damn thing about the grin on his face.

As the group drew nearer, he knew he was staring, but he didn't care. Tommy looked... different. And amazing. And....

Wow.

Low-slung but immaculate jeans hung from his hips, teamed with a dark blue T-shirt and a red plaid shirt tied around his waist. He wore his hair loose, and the sunlight caught at the two shiny black falls that trailed against his chest. It was the hat that caught Brett's attention, though. An actual, honest-to-god cowboy hat. Fawn, with a short brim and a dark band around the crown. It shaded his face, but couldn't disguise the big, white, delighted smile that burst from him as Katie ran across the field toward him. Tommy crouched, hugged his little sister, and, in one smooth movement, swiped the hat off his head and dropped it onto hers.

She laughed, clutching at it with both hands, then Atian shrieked something, Katie wriggled free of Tommy, and the kids were both running again, splintering off into a pack of cousins, oblivious to various parental shouts... but Brett wasn't really watching. The dry grass crunched under his feet, the sea of greetings parted around him, and still the distance between them meant nothing.

"Hey," Tommy said, grinning at him.

"Hey."

Brett let himself be pulled into a rough, tight, wonderful hug, and he clung on for everything he was worth. Tommy's shirt smelled of sun-warmed cotton and horses, and when he pulled back, he was beaming goofily, his eyes shining and the dry, rough streaks of just a little touch of sunburn bridging his nose and cheekbones.

Tommy stayed close to Brett as they parted, the bright rattle of introductions and greetings washing all around them. He kissed Monica's cheek, got a manly kind of half hug from Stephen, and nodded to Ron. Brett was wondering whether he might have been imagining the coolness between Tommy and Mei when he found himself being introduced to the widely beaming, warm-palmed figure of Bill, who grinned at him from underneath a short-brimmed hat much like the one Tommy was currently wresting back from Katie.

"Uh... hi," Brett managed, weakening a little in the face of so much enthusiasm.

Tommy had said a lot of positive things about Bill—about his optimism and his determination, his friendliness and his generosity—but he hadn't mentioned the disarming quality of those twinkling eyes, or the grip of steel.

"Nice meetin' you, Brett," Bill assured him then, with a grin at Tommy. "Hey, don't forget, better be there to catch Trey, right? We miss him, we ain't never goin' to live that one down."

"Ah-huh." Tommy nodded. "You got it."

Bill chuckled and, gradually, their broad and sprawling group started to splinter off a little. Brett made to follow, but Tommy caught his wrist.

"It's good to see you," he murmured, hanging back a little, his voice buzzing close to Brett's ear. "You okay?"

Brett turned to him, breathing in deeply, as if he could catch all the scents of sunlight, new-mown grass, cinnamon, and pine, and lock them into one perfect memory. He nodded, hardly noticing the way he reached out—an automatic, unthinking gesture—fingers already half-curled, to take Tommy's hand in his.

"Yeah. It's just... well, it's a little hard to believe."

One thick brow arched as Tommy looked incredulously at him. "What?"

"Oh, come on.... *You* know." Brett fixed him with his best expression of solemnity and leaned in just a little, so he could impart the words in a conspiratorial hush. "You're a goddamn cowboy."

Tommy laughed then, wide and open and beautiful, and shook his head.

"What? Oh, come *on*... I'm not a—"

"You looked at yourself?" Brett teased, unable to stop himself grinning like a loon. "Really looked? With the hat and everything? You are. You're an Indian cowboy."

Tommy guffawed. "I am *not* a cowboy. I… just… fix things."

Their laughter thinned as the words took on a slightly different hue. The crowds passed on by around them, and Brett looked at Tommy carefully, reaching out for the meaning that what he'd said might hold.

"You do, huh?"

Tommy nodded, his gaze steady and brave. "Ah-huh. Well, I think so, maybe."

His voice was rich with a beautiful, warm optimism, timid but so very clear. Brett shrugged and tipped his head to the side.

"Well, whatever you're gonna call it, it's hot. You look good. And I missed you."

Tommy's smile widened, and that breath of tension—that moment of meaning, hard-wrought and full of possibilities—seemed to recede. Not as if dismissed, but as if carefully tucked away, put aside for later like something precious.

"I missed you too," he murmured, then dipped in and pressed a brief kiss to Brett's cheek, a soft and chaste gesture that surprised him a little. "Come on. We should get going. You have a good journey?"

"Not so bad," Brett admitted.

Tommy bumped him playfully with his elbow as he reached up to drop the short-brimmed hat back on his head. Brett grinned. It was a beautiful day, he decided. So full of color and life, the air touched with a heat shimmer that rose just a little from the dry ground, and the smell of fry bread, tacos, and hot earth on the sultry breeze. It made it easy to fall into step beside Tommy, to walk with him beneath that sky of such clear, acidic blue, cloudless and wide as ages.

THEY made it to the main arena before Grand Entry started, the MC's announcements a tinny drawl over the loudspeaker, and Brett found himself perched on a folding chair wedged in next to Tommy, with Bill on the other side of him and Karen's father standing behind them. Just like a family Christmas, there were never enough chairs to go around. The arbor was packed, and even before the Eagle Staff and the flags started to come in, a sense of expectation hung over the whole space. It was a sacred thing, this procession, a path between old and new, tradition and history, a river along which culture and honor flowed. As the great, soulful cry of the host drum's opening song went up, honored elders, veterans, and dancers all passed, presenting at the MC's table.

Katie climbed up onto Brett's knee, her nose wrinkled as she tried to get a better view of what was going on. He held her steady and, quietly intent, she watched. Eventually, a small, tight-lipped smile curled her mouth.

Over the course of the event, there was a whole lot more to be experienced than the singing and dancing alone, but Tommy was adamant Katie should see at least some of it. As the program wore on, Brett realized they'd managed to acquire her as a semipermanent appendage. Lila had apparently borrowed a trick from Robbie and disappeared when no one was paying attention, while Mei had wandered off with Ron, and Scott was apparently being goose-stepped across the arbor to go and make nice with his in-laws' family.

Tommy leaned across Brett's shoulder, explaining the different dance styles they were going to see to Katie, and Brett caught sight of Monica giving him an odd, slightly lopsided smile. He grinned at her, and she and his father edged a little closer through the straggling crowd. A youth drum group from North Dakota had struck up, and though Brett didn't feel confident enough to judge their skill—he'd learned a lot over the couple of years Karen had been bringing him along, but still got completely and utterly lost more often than he was happy with—they sounded good.

"We're going to go take a look around," Monica said, bending slightly so Brett could hear her. "You... uh, you look comfortable."

Katie wriggled on his knee, craning to see what Tommy was pointing out to her, and Brett's smile stiffened a little as he watched the subtle shift in his mother's face. Stephen squeezed her shoulder and nodded at him.

"We'll see you in a bit, then."

"Sure, Dad." Brett inclined his head, watching them go.

Tommy glanced at him enquiringly, and he smiled, just before Katie piped up with a question about feathers. She was drumming her heels thoughtfully, so that with every second beat they either hit the chair or Brett's shin, and the air beneath the arbor grew ever hotter and thicker.

THE dances themselves could get pretty competitive, especially given the prize money, though it was about much more than that. By the time the men's grass dance started, everything seemed to throb to the pulse of drums, and the whole circle filled with the rising rhythms of song and the wildly flashing waves of color. As the dancers began, Katie wriggled, turning to give Brett an eager, bright-eyed smile.

"It's loud," she confided, wrinkling her nose up again. "I like it!"

Brett grinned, glad she was keyed up by the noise instead of unsettled. He wouldn't have dreamed of admitting it, but the first seeds of a headache were already germinating behind his sinuses.

As ever, he was aware of how little he knew of the technicalities of the style, and Brett was thankful for Tommy leaning down to point things out to Katie, and thankful for the presence of a firm yet gentle hand on his shoulder as he did so. Tommy glanced at him as he spoke, and the flicker of a smile curled his lips. Brett felt a warmth not entirely to do with the heat of the day or the press of people rise in his cheeks, and smiled back.

The dance apparently derived from the old practice of stamping down the grass to make an area for the dancing. The long, pale fringes on the men's regalia symbolized the dried grass that the dancers used to tie to their belts, while their whole outlines were sleeker and slicker than the full traditional costumes... and they looked incredible. It was all incredible—a blend of power and elegance that rose from the ground and vibrated in the very air—and Brett got breathless just watching.

Tommy pointed out Trey, the guy who he said was the cousin of Joe, from the ranch. He said it like he thought Brett ought to know who he was talking about, and finally, with a tiny huff of frustration, pointed across the circle to where Bill was standing with a knot of other guys— mostly over fifty and mostly all favoring well-buffed work boots and sharply pressed shirts—and a slim, serious-looking young man.

Brett nodded and pretended he remembered, though he was frankly starting to get a little lost in the reams of names that went unattached to introductions or faces. There wasn't time to dwell on it, though, because the drums were picking up, and the energy of the dance spilled out across the circle, the splashes of color and movement flying like paint on canvas, the strokes of some bold, impressionistic passion pounding against the packed dirt to the beat of beaded moccasins.

Trey certainly seemed popular, clad all in light tones of fawn and yellow, with beaded belt and side tabs over his shirt and pants, and a beaded harness that hung to his knees. Bright geometric patterns burst over it, the fringes and ribbons of the outfit flashing and spinning as he danced, hard and powerful, every whip of movement like a burst of flame across the hot, gravid air.

Halfway around the circle, Atian, like a few of the other kids watching, was out of his seat by the midpoint of the first song, trying to mimic the dance steps and losing himself in the music. Brett caught sight of Karen smiling indulgently and snagging the back of her son's T-shirt, reining him in when he got too carried away.

The songs didn't always have words. Tommy had been explaining it to Katie: there were sounds, and patterns, and maybe words in between the shapes, but most of the time the singers sang the way they did so that tribal language didn't matter. This was something shared, something bigger than any one dialect, any single people, and that was why it mattered. She nodded sagely and pulled in her lower lip, like she did when she was drawing, and her heels tapped dully against Brett's leg.

Words or not, the songs he didn't understand rose higher and higher, singers and drummers craning for the sky with great, raw, shimmering notes and cascades of rhythm that burst beneath the burning golden disc of the sun. The crowd erupted as the drums finished in almost as much of a flourish as the dancers—Brett made out Trey at the far side of the circle, panting heavily, the screen pipe he carried in one hand brandished aloft—and the MC's announcement threaded through it all in a metallic whine that didn't even seem real.

Brett couldn't help wondering at that. He'd come to this event before—watched the dancing before—and yet today felt so different.

He glanced up at Tommy, catching the grin on his face and the light in his eyes, and a pull of desire tugged insistently at him. Not lust, he noted. Not here, not now… just the ache for closeness, the bittersweet bite of sharing this, yet not sharing, and the acknowledgment of every intimacy and every separation.

They watched hour after hour of the dancing, its highly competitive appeal winning out over even the eating and the shopping. Katie was—as Tommy had predicted she would be—enthralled by the spiraling, swirling shawls and glittering fabrics of the girls' fancy and jingle dances, and the graceful elegance of the women's traditional. They moved around a little bit, and she sat between them on the folding chair, her eyes wide and her hands locked onto the edge of the seat as the drums pounded, the songs rose and twisted into the heat-heavy air, and the dancers moved and circled through their rhythms.

Brett couldn't help snatching the odd glance at Tommy, taking in how happy and comfortable he looked, and the way—every time he bent his head to say something to his sister—he smiled a little wider and tucked his hair behind his ear.

Eventually, Katie started wriggling again, and confessed the need to pee. Brett nodded and looked around for Lila, but she'd long since disappeared again, probably to the vendors' booths, along with Mei and Ron, Robbie, and Brett's parents. No one else seemed to have stayed for as long as they had, he noticed. Scott and Karen were still there, though they were deep in conversation with another couple who had a cooler and a picnic blanket, so Brett cast one more look around for Lila, never more grateful than when he caught sight of her wandering back over, sucking the last illicit traces of a taco off her fingers.

"What?" She arched her thin brows, her expression a mix of resignation and heavily affected teenage apathy that couldn't quite disguise the fun she'd evidently been having. "Oh. Yeah, I can take her. Come on, Squirt," she added, holding out a hand to Katie.

"You hungry?" Tommy asked, as Brett watched them go.

He'd put that damn hat back on, and Brett couldn't help the tempting pictures that stalked behind his eyes: memories of long grass and warm afternoons not unlike this one, when they'd lain together on a plaid blanket tossed over stony, uneven ground, and he'd unpicked the slow secrets of Tommy's body through layers of dusty denim and worn cotton. The smell of fry bread still tugged at the air, and now it prodded his stomach into a halfhearted growl.

"Could be. You wanna get somethin' to eat?"

"Maybe." Tommy took a step backward, his weight on his rear foot and his hands deep in his pockets, gazing at Brett consideringly, like he wanted him to follow.

A lazy grin spread over Brett's face, and he squinted out at the smudged, pale band of the horizon, pricked by the black stalks of trees. Sunlight thickened out like syrup, heavy bands of it dripping through the clouds that had pulled across that wide, flawless sky. The afternoon had passed so quickly, and Brett couldn't deny a sudden burst of fear. The powwow would last three days, but they hadn't intended to stay past tonight. All too soon, he'd be getting a ride back with his parents, and staying at their place, probably... alone. He wasn't sure what Tommy was planning to do. That depended on Bill, he guessed.

Brett shrugged. "All right."

Tommy smiled. "C'mon, then."

Things were still pretty busy, the day's warmth clinging to everything like a veneer of protective lacquer, though it was easy enough to pick out familiar faces in the crowds. A little way past the vendors' booths selling regalia supplies, they caught sight of Mei and Ron, lip-locked like teenagers. Tommy winced and, taking Brett's hand wordlessly, turned away.

Brett let himself be led, biting down on the comment he'd been about to make—just some stupid, throwaway line—because it didn't matter. Tommy let go of his hand and strode across the grass, and Brett knew he'd follow. It wasn't even a question. He simply went, footstep for footstep, and let it feel as natural as it always did.

Tommy bought two tacos and smiled shyly at Brett when he handed one over, fingers brushing his beneath the greasy paper plate. Brett stifled a grin and followed on again when they started to walk once more, away from the throng and heading toward the tree line. They ate in companionable silence, and, after a little while, the noise and bustle was behind them, but not too far, and the smells of food cooking, warm crowds, and hot canvas still marked the air.

They sat on the dry prickles of baked grass, close enough for their knees to touch, and Brett picked thoughtfully at the stodgy edges of his fry bread.

"So, uh...." He cleared his throat. "Are you happy there? At the ranch?"

He snatched a sidelong glance at Tommy, watching the light gild his profile, his eyes dark and hooded as he chewed thoughtfully.

"I like it," Tommy said eventually. "There are fences... but you don't hear the wind whistle through 'em. Y'know? I don't ever wanna hear wind on razor wire again."

Brett felt his chest clench around a small knot of bitter compassion. He wanted to reach out, lean closer, do *something*... but he knew better than that. He just nodded and sneaked a look at Tommy, taking in the hard lines of his face—shaded by that hat that it was still so very difficult to adjust to seeing—and watching the gentle breeze stir his hair from his shoulders.

"Hey," Brett said at last, hearing how odd his voice seemed against the quiet. "I, uh... I've been thinkin' about something."

Tommy glanced at him like he'd been pulled from some tainted thought Brett didn't really want to know about. He blinked, and the darkness left his face, replaced with a soft smile as he licked salsa off his thumb and forefinger, quick and catlike.

"Hm?"

"Well...." Brett scuffed the edge of his sneaker against the dry, ridged ground, bending back the crisp stalks of grass. "I mean, you're at Bill's for... well, for as long as, right?"

"As long as what?"

"*You* know." He shrugged, stuffing another mouthful of taco and grateful for the fact it was heavy enough to make him concentrate on chewing for a couple of moments. "Long term."

Brett glanced at Tommy, just catching the tail end of the wince before he looked away. Tommy really seemed to hate those words, but he nodded all the same.

"Guess so."

"So… there's a hospital in Poplar," Brett said quietly. "It's pretty different to where I am now, but—"

He broke off as Tommy turned to face him, brow furrowed and eyes shaded with incomprehension.

"Brett, what—?"

A guy in grass dance regalia wandered past a little way behind them, apparently trying to locate a patch of ground with better cell phone service. Tommy broke off, took a breath, then lowered his voice.

"What are you—?"

"Just listen. It's smaller, but they do need nursing staff. I've been making some inquiries, asking a few people for opinions, and… it, uh, it might be a possibility."

Tommy's frown deepened. "You're not a nurse," he said flatly.

"No." Brett couldn't hold his gaze, so he fell to scuffing his feet against the grass again. "But I've been thinking I could retrain. Did… did you know I could pick up an LPN at community college in as little as a year?" He glanced up, wishing he could see approval in Tommy's face instead of that awful, uncertain blankness. "I could do that. Find something in Poplar, or-or maybe Wolf Point. Be, like, twenty or thirty miles away instead of two hundred. Maybe. W-would… would that be…?"

The air shimmered a little with the late gold of afternoon sun, the day's dirt-baked heat condensed and folded across itself like a blanket. Sweat prickled at the small of Brett's back, and the seconds seemed to slide out into endless spools of silence.

"Retrain?" Tommy echoed, cutting through all the tentative questions that hung on the air. "I thought you wanted to—"

"It's still medical," Brett said, perhaps a little too hurriedly. "It's still what I wanna… I mean, it *is* what I want to do. Just… I want to be with you too. Qualification like this, I could be more flexible, maybe. Go anywhere."

Tommy was still frowning. It was hard to be sure whether that reflected disapproval or confusion, and Brett was nervous of saying anything more. Still, he supposed he couldn't dig himself into a much deeper hole.

"I thought," Tommy said slowly, folding his empty paper plate in half with calm efficiency, "that was the point of your whole sports therapy idea."

"Set up my own practice?" Brett chuckled, surprised he'd even remembered the possibility being mentioned.

"Ah-huh. In… Bozeman, or Billings, or wherever you—"

"I can't afford that. Not yet." Brett swallowed heavily, then cleared his throat, like he was struggling to admit some stupid mistake, some humiliating defeat. "Anyway, what do we wanna go there for, huh?"

"Brett…."

"It's okay. I've been thinking it through. Really thinking."

It was true, Brett had to admit: one way or another, he'd been thinking about little else. Even before talking with Stephen had made him admit it, he had already started nibbling at the edges of the idea… and it *was* an idea now, more than just a possibility or a pipe dream.

Tommy scowled at the ground, his whole manner laced with a curt, unsure stiffness.

"I don't know. I thought you wanted—"

"I told you what I want," Brett said quickly. "And what about you, huh? What do *you* want, Tommy?"

That uncertain frown deepened even further, but Tommy's body inclined to him as he turned, raising his gaze from the grass. The sound of drums and voices drifted on the air, and the sunlight had begun to thin. Cautious, hungry optimism seemed to frame his face, his eyes wreathed with dark folds of hope. He wet his lips tentatively.

"So… you'd be a registered nurse?"

"Nursing assistant," Brett corrected. "If I did the LPN. Full registered nursing course would take two years. Either way, it'd still depend on qualifying, then actually *getting* the job, but—"

"It's a long-term plan," Tommy said with a soft smile.

Brett grinned. "Yeah? Yeah, it is. And…?"

"So, you'd be workin' locally, right? Like, right there in Poplar?"

He was already sounding more positive. Brett bit his lip. "Uh-huh. I mean, you'd still have a hike when you were goin' home to see the kids, but... but *we*—"

"We could get a place together," Tommy murmured, a hazy look slipping over his face. "Couldn't we? You and me. It wouldn't be much, and I guess I'd still have to be on-site for Bill, at least part of the week, but... we could, couldn't we?"

The words dropped from him in an awe-tinged whisper, his mouth curled around a small, tentative breath of hope. Brett nodded slowly. He hadn't known the thought meant quite that much to Tommy.

"Yeah. Would—?"

"Fuck, yes." Tommy's words were almost swallowed in a short cough of laughter. "Yes, I want that. I want... I want that so much. But, babe, it's a total change for you. Again." Another frown tugged at his brow, uncertainty beginning to taint his longing. "You already... I mean, I-I don't wanna be the reason you give up everything that—"

"You're not," Brett said gently. "You won't be. It's my decision. Nobody else's."

"And you wanna do it? You really want to?"

Tommy looked at him, face drawn tight with doubt. The urge to lie tugged at Brett, willing him to say the choice was easy, and that this was what he should have done all along. He *could* have, he knew. He'd had this argument more than once with his mother, back before he started training for the physical therapy qualification. "Just do your RN," she'd said. "Complete the training later... you can still be a doctor."

He remembered what he'd said, almost word for word. It had been the arrogant impulsiveness of youth. How, after all that time working in a nursing home, he'd been scared of getting trapped in a never-ending future of bedpans and geriatrics. He'd wanted a change, he said, and oh, how she'd rolled her eyes at that one.

Brett suspected Monica would enjoy this.

"It would be a change," he said slowly, "and it would be difficult. But I think it's a good idea. I don't mind moving my plans around. You know that. You know—"

"I don't want you to keep doing things for me," Tommy said with a trace of sullenness. "You should be doing what *you* wanna do, not—"

"I would be. Really. This... this could be a great opportunity."

Tommy's mouth twitched, though he said nothing. He took the other paper plate from Brett and folded it crisply, just as he had his own. His fingers worked deftly against the grease-smeared paper, and he seemed totally focused on that one small task. Brett knew better than to say anything, though the desire to demand a response burned in him almost irresistibly. He wanted to beg, plead, or even start getting irritable, because sometimes it felt like yelling at each other was at least communication of a kind, and damn it if Tommy didn't know how to be one of the most frustrating people on the planet... but it wouldn't help.

So he waited.

Eventually, Tommy glanced up and smiled sadly at him, the deepening shadows of a long, hot afternoon thrown in muted bars across his face.

"Can you afford it?"

Brett shrugged. "I don't know. It's a commitment; a good couple of years before I even know if I'm qualified, probably, but—"

"And you want to?" Tommy winced, like the words were heavy weights. "It's not just because of me?"

"No. I want to."

It was true. Brett was sure. He was... well, yeah. He was almost entirely sure. The plan made sense at practically every level. Maybe he could even talk to his parents about working out some kind of loan for school, and, hell, it was a qualification worth having, wasn't it?

Tommy was looking at him with a guarded kind of optimism, midway between the careful blankness of the jail face Brett had always hated so much, and the raw, completely open desperation that he'd seen on him in other, sharper times. Only his eyes betrayed how much he wanted to sink into this beautiful dream, and, when he blinked and looked away, frowning at the dry grass, Brett knew he'd won.

Up until that moment, he hadn't even realized it had been a battle.

"That's where we start, then, right?" Tommy murmured, like he was familiarizing himself with a new set of rules.

Perhaps he was, Brett thought. Maybe they both were. He swallowed, his mouth dry and his tongue feeling rough behind his teeth.

"I guess. I mean, there are details to—"

"Oh, yeah. Yeah. I know. But… I don't know." Tommy peered at him from beneath the brim of his hat, the hint of a seductive smile touching his lips. "As a *plan*, I like it. I really like it."

"Really?" Brett grinned. "Good. So, uh, what do we…?"

Tommy stretched out his legs and, with a sigh, got to his feet.

"Right now," he said, holding out a hand to pull Brett up after him, "we oughta go help Mom load the kids up. S'getting late."

Brett blinked, distracted for a moment by the skin-to-skin warmth and the sudden change of topic. "Huh?"

"You heard." Tommy hadn't let go of his hand. He molded his lips around a half-blown kiss and squeezed Brett's fingers. "Then, later, you and me talk details. Properly. Next weekend sound good?"

"Uh, yeah. Yeah, I guess so." A stab of despondency picked at Brett. The knowledge that he had to go home without Tommy had somehow slipped away amid all the sunbaked warmth and relaxation. "Wh-what are you…?"

Tommy shot him a self-deprecating grin. "Me? Probably slummin' it in the back of Bill's truck tonight. I don't think we're goin' back until tomorrow at the earliest. But, y'know, I got sweet dreams to have now, don't I?"

Brett laughed incredulously. They'd always worked so hard at steering away from "one day," that mythical, make-believe thing that was so impractical, so impossible to achieve, and so painful to sustain. He'd never made demands on Tommy, tried never to tie him to a future he might not be able to fit into… but they couldn't live day to day forever.

Even as Tommy's hand brushed lightly against the side of his neck, and he felt himself drawn close for one sweet, long, subtle kiss, Brett wondered whether he should have said anything. It wasn't hypocrisy, was it? To need something more, to open his hands and let go all the things he'd built, all the things he'd worked for.... It wasn't, he told himself. It was fine. A change of direction, a natural curve in the road. Someone had to make a sacrifice, anyway, and why not him? Why not this?

In the protective shade of the tree line, Brett pressed into the kiss and silently promised that—just this once—things were going to work out right, and sane, and practical.

They deserved that much.

CHAPTER EIGHTEEN

OF COURSE, the decision was the comparatively easy part. Once Brett knuckled down and started looking at the details, every single piece of the impossible puzzle seemed to loom more and more darkly. There was the matter of funding, of his current employment… and talking to Elaine, for starters.

She took it well, he thought, nodding solemnly and agreeing that it was "a sensible string to add to his bow," especially given economic concerns, employment, and "the importance of transferable skills." Then she hugged him, and Brett didn't know what to do with himself or where to look. Nevertheless, knowing he still had a job—and at least a degree of moral support—helped, and it made talking to his parents just that little bit easier… or it should have.

Seeing as Tommy was pulling another weekend at Bill's, Brett stayed at their place Friday through Sunday. He didn't really have anywhere else to be, and the relentless quiet of time spent on his own—while wonderful to begin with—soon grew empty. He'd long since given up dwelling on his lack of social life too… especially considering that Nick was the only friend he habitually bitched to about it, and *he* was now officially head over heels for Eric, the blue-eyed blond with the terrible dance moves. Not that Brett wasn't happy for him—he *was*, but it kind of curtailed the amount of whining he could do without Nick drifting off into something funny Eric had said or somewhere great that they'd gone recently.

So, it was a Saturday morning that was peculiarly like a lot of Saturday mornings from Brett's childhood. Sunlight poured through the window, the house smelled of toast and air freshener, and dust motes danced in the thick, lazy light. Brett was even addressing a boiled egg, which sat nestled in the green-and-yellow striped eggcup he used to use, just like old times, and he found he was glad of those small snatches of tradition.

Monica sighed deeply, her elbows propped on the kitchen table. Brett dipped his toast into the golden stream of egg yolk and, eyeing his mother carefully, took a tentative bite. He chewed, swallowed, and waited for the volcano to erupt.

Monica steepled her fingers in front of her mouth, looking oddly worn and resigned. Behind her, Stephen was making coffee, and he glanced at Brett over his shoulder, giving him a brief, small smile.

"Well, I think it *is* sensible," he offered, bringing the jug over to the table. "Don't you, honey?"

"Maybe." Monica pursed her lips and stared straight ahead. She blinked as her husband poured her some fresh coffee, and flicked him a brief, tight smile.

"Thanks, Dad." The corner of Brett's mouth curled as Stephen topped off his mug, but he broke eye contact and stared down at the tiny bubbles twirling on the dark surface.

"I just… oh, never mind." Monica sighed again, curving her fingers around her mug. "If that's what you're going to do, I hope it works out."

Brett blinked at her incredulously. He'd expected more of a fight, or at least an "I told you so" or three. The third chair squealed against the floor as Stephen sat down.

"What are you going to do for money?" he asked shortly, with all the briskness of a career accountant. "I assume you've looked at the cost of the courses…."

"Uh, yeah." Brett swallowed heavily. "I, well, I *think* I can—"

"If you need a loan, son, we can work something out."

Brett's mouth worked soundlessly around a couple of shapes as he tried to assimilate that. He hadn't expected it, hadn't imagined it would be offered so easily, so openly. Stephen took a piece of toast from the plate in the center of the table and set about buttering it economically. Brett gaped at his father, then glanced at Monica, who appeared to be staring into space. She pulled herself upright in her chair suddenly, blinked, and looked at Brett with a strange, sad sort of half smile.

"Of course we will, sweetheart. If you need it. Now, eat up. Your egg's getting cold."

It was, in a weird kind of way, so much easier than he'd thought it would be.

Oh, they didn't *like* it. Brett could tell that—it was effectively etched in neon letters on each of their foreheads—but they were prepared to overcome whatever misgivings they might have had, if it helped him.

That knowledge made him feel very small.

All the same, it took planning. He and Tommy talked things over—over and over again—until the bottom seemed to wear out of the words, and there was no other end to it except knowing the plan was a gamble… but a gamble worth trying. Brett half expected them to fight about it, with all the endless talking around in circles, but they didn't. Not very much, anyway. There were a few snaps, a couple of heated debates, but nothing melodramatic. Things just didn't go that way anymore. Tommy seemed so much more relaxed, more confident, and Brett didn't find himself butting up against that old core of frustration either.

He wasn't entirely sure whether they'd just flown past it, or whether they were both trying too hard to be sensible. Either way, he wasn't about to complain, because it seemed to be working.

SUMMER turned to fall, and as the temperatures dropped and the sun thinned, the low grumbles of warm-waisted, thick-clouded storms gave way to cold rain and the chill foreshadowing of ice. Tommy had been rolled back to three days a week at the ranch for the last couple of months, while the BUNAC part-timers were there—a British girl and a guy from Finland, apparently, both pretty useless at anything except shit-shoveling and taking endless photos of sunsets—which made him a little edgy, but he tried not to take it out on anyone.

It wouldn't be all that long before the ski season started up, and he'd been thinking about the possibility of trying for something along those lines. The thought made him smile, riven with memories of the sports store he'd been working in when he and Brett met, and the recollection of the moment Brett had first walked through the door, wrapped up in all that ski gear and with a bloody cut on his chin.

Of course, Mr. Klass had sold up and retired a good few years ago. Tommy remembered him as a cheerful, round-faced man with a bone-dry sense of humor, and assumed he now probably spent his time between fishing and his grandkids. He wasn't sure what was in the store's place now—either a cheap sports chain or possibly a bakery. Like most of the parts of town he used to be familiar with, Tommy hadn't really wanted to explore that area.

Life moved on. It always seemed to, anyway. You just had to work out a way of not letting yourself get completely left behind… a way of grabbing on as it all slipped by and making the most of what you had in your hands, no matter how hard it was to hold on.

Lila seemed very excited about Brett's nursing plan. She was going to do it too, she said. Study really hard, go to college, and help people like Brett did. She talked about it over dinner one night, waving a forkful of mashed potatoes like a laser pointer as she detailed all the things she wanted to do and the things she wanted to learn.

Pride welled up in Tommy, though the edges of it were a little dog-eared and crinkled, stained with the doubts and nervousness of experience. She'd seen more—lived through more—than a lot of girls her age, and he wasn't sure if that made her tougher or more vulnerable, likelier to succeed or… well, he didn't really want to think about it.

"It's a noble thing to want to do," Ron said helpfully, beaming genially from the end of the table.

Lila preened, and Mei passed the cream-colored dish of potatoes around, her mouth studiously tight and her gaze fixed on the serving spoon as it made pass after pass over plate after plate. Tommy watched his mother and wondered—as he had so many times in the past—just what she was thinking.

Scott called it her "I'm not scared" face. She'd go blank as a plaster mask, as if she could just ignore any part of life she didn't like, didn't understand, or just didn't want to deal with, and pretend that was enough to make it go away. It used to make him so mad, and it did now… a little bit, anyway.

Tommy guessed he'd just grown used to it, the same way he'd grown used to these family dinners. They were still a little weird, but nice, in their way. And that was worth holding onto, the niceness, wasn't it? It had to be, he supposed, because that was how things were meant to change. Slowly, gently, easily, not in those great, violent rushes that ripped you apart and left you reeling.

Whatever else happened, Tommy knew he didn't want that. Never again.

So he let the burgeoning discussion—the complexities of a medical career, the length of study, and the differentiations between being a doctor and being a nurse—wash over him, just lapping at the distant shore of a place to which he was only slightly connected.

"I'm gonna be a fireman," Katie announced.

"Firefighter," Robbie corrected sullenly, his voice currently phasing through one of its deeper swings.

"Whatever. I wanna put out fires. With a hose and a big truck."

"Yeah, good luck with *that*."

She pouted indignantly. "If I wanna be a—"

"You can be a firefighter if you want to," Mei cut in, soothing with a tired kind of automatic-pilot resignation. "Robbie, don't tell your sister she can't—"

"And what are you thinking of, huh?" Ron asked brightly, his voice flowing effortlessly over hers and seeping into the cracks she left. "Got anything you're really interested in doing?"

Tommy blinked, quietly surprised… but evidently not as surprised as Robbie. He watched as his brother shrugged, his face adopting that familiar pulled-in, vacant look, but then Robbie frowned.

"Computers," he said shortly, and shoveled a forkful of green beans into his mouth.

Ron looked fleetingly smug and smiled encouragingly. "Yeah? Well, that's interesting. And you know a lot about hardware already, right?"

That was probably true. The components and bits of things strewn all over the room whose floor Tommy still occasionally shared were testament to that, and he was a little ashamed to admit he had no idea what most of them were for, or even where Robbie's interests with technology lay. As far as Tommy knew, he played video games, probably watched way too much porn, and interacted mainly through the machine as a substitute for dealing with people. It seemed normal enough for a kid his age.

Mei snorted. "He wants to make computer games. I don't know, does that even pay money? It's like I told your brother: you need to have a trade, yes? Something you can depend on."

"Well, it *is* a trade, isn't it?" Ron's encouraging smile broadened into a flat-out grin. "I think that's a really neat thing to do. I guess there's a lot you need to know, huh? You, uh, you looking at programming and development? More the writing side, or design? You know, my nephew worked on this project...."

Clever, really, Tommy thought. The guy made enough of an effort to make himself indispensable, and yet held onto enough otherness to never quite fit in. Or did he? Tommy was starting to wonder whether it was him, and not Ron, who didn't fit anymore. It could well have been, he supposed.

After dinner, he and Lila split doing the dishes. She was still in talking-about-college mode, chatting animatedly about the things she was going to do, the stuff she was interested in... maybe just a little about the guy she might or might not have been seeing.

Tommy quirked an eyebrow. "Oh, yeah?"

"Shut up!" She flicked him with the dishcloth. "It's not—I'm not talking about it with you!"

Tommy flicked the water off his hands at her, and she squeaked. He grinned.

"Aw, come on, Bear Bait… is he cute?"

Lila wrinkled her nose, but her eyes shone as she nodded. "Mm-hm."

"Are you dating?"

He recognized at once the glimmer of guilty glee that passed over her face as she shrugged, and his grin widened, despite the void of mixed horror and panic that opened up inside him. The edges of a whole different conversation seemed to be pressing in on them, and Tommy wasn't sure he wanted to know any of the details. Part of him—despite all the evidence to the contrary—wanted to believe Lila was still seven years old.

"Maybe," she said as she folded the dishcloth and stacked the last of the plates away. "I mean, yeah, we… well, we're…."

She shrugged again as the words trailed away, full of self-conscious vacillation.

Aw, hell, there's stuff I'm supposed to say, isn't there? Oh, shit….

Tommy winced and cleared his throat awkwardly. "You, uh… you guys are being safe and everything, right?"

Lila's eyes bugged, and a squeak of indignant embarrassment escaped her. "What? Oh, God. God…. We're… we're not doing *that*."

"No?"

"No! I'm not a—" Her mouth snapped shut, a look of exquisite mortification cutting across her face. "It's not like that."

He raised his eyebrows, unsure whether he was more surprised or impressed.

"Okay. So, what *is* it like? 'Cause you can still have a lot of fun, even if—"

"Tommy!"

Lila's wide-eyed reproach made him laugh, and that felt good, though he sure as hell wasn't getting any further details out of her on the boyfriend thing. Not tonight, at least. Tommy didn't mind. He hadn't expected them, and he wasn't totally sure he wanted to know.

He was proud of her, though, proud of her maturity and her determination and how damn levelheaded she'd managed to be, despite everything. Sometimes, he wished he could be more like her.

Eventually, he got the hint that it was time to leave. Not that he was exactly unwelcome to stay the night except, as Mei put it, the kids had school in the morning, and Brett would probably want to see him anyway. Fair enough, he supposed. She had a point... like she always did. All the same, as he nosed the Chevy down toward Rotary Park, Tommy felt the familiar pangs of regret and emptiness claw at him.

He wasn't sure, but they seemed to taste just a little less bitter.

MEI and Ron announced their engagement in December. No one was really surprised.

It was the day before Brett's birthday, and Tommy lay in bed, listening to the buzz of his electric toothbrush as he screwed around in the bathroom. Not exactly the most intensely exciting way to spend a Friday night, but Brett had been working late, and there hadn't been much time for anything except dinner and a DVD. The apartment— *their* apartment, in all honesty, because it housed just as much of Tommy's detritus as Brett's these days—was clean and tidy, Tommy having blitzed it by way of a favor before Brett got in. He liked having his own key, he'd found. He liked belonging. Decorating for Christmas together was pretty fucking awesome too.

In the other room, a small artificial Christmas tree, swathed with lights and red and gold baubles, stood beside the bookcase, and paper stars dangled from the ceiling. On the coffee table, a small bag with a brightly wrapped gift inside it awaited Brett, along with a suitably cheesy card and strict instructions that he wasn't to open, prod, shake, squeeze, or otherwise attempt to guess at the contents before his birthday. He'd never get it, anyway, Tommy thought with a brief flush of glee. Once Brett unwrapped it, the first thing he'd see would be the gaudy pack of edible underpants. Only once he'd finished laughing about that would he find the jeweler's box beneath, and the new watch with the simple, honest message engraved on the back. Tommy's lips curled in soft, secret anticipation at the thought.

Hands linked behind his head, he stared up at the paper star closest to him, wafting gently from side to side in the lazy convection of the draft from the open door. A warm pool of electric light spilled onto the carpet, and soon Brett would pad in, slip off his boxers, and slide under the covers. Tommy let his eyes close, waiting until that blissfully familiar presence filled up the doorway.

"They set a date yet?"

Tommy cranked one eye half open. "Huh?"

Brett stood in the doorway, minty fresh and nearly naked, all pink-scrubbed and delectable. It made it momentarily difficult to focus on what he was saying.

"The wedding. Your mom. Date?"

"Oh." Tommy frowned. "Nah. Well… I don't know. Not that anyone told me."

Brett shucked off his underwear, and Tommy opened the other eye, gazing appreciatively at him as he crossed the floor and hopped into bed.

"Cold tonight, huh?" he observed with a wicked grin.

Brett snorted. "Fuck you."

For emphasis, he wriggled closer, pressing his toes to Tommy's shin like little blocks of ice.

"Argh! Fu—all right, all right." Tommy grimaced and wrinkled his nose as Brett chuckled gleefully and seized slightly more than his portion of the covers. "You know, you could always wear something warmer to bed."

Brett reached out from his cocoon and switched the lamp off, letting the shadowed dimness envelop them. Moonlight filtered through the shrouded window and pitted the far wall.

"Yeah? Like what?"

Tommy rolled over and snaked an arm around his waist, pulling him close and enjoying the solidity of Brett's body tucked into his, tangled up in the smell of his skin and the security of their little cotton cavern.

"I don't know. Tube socks and flannel jammies? I could peel you like a furry banana."

Brett laughed as Tommy hooked a leg over his, thigh to thigh, all crisp hair and cool flesh growing warm, and popped a kiss at the base of his ear.

"Furry banana? Seriously? Huh. You're a kinky bastard really, aren't you?"

"Yup," Tommy agreed, smiling happily as he ran his lips over Brett's nape.

It wasn't true, he reflected. Frankly, they were both as vanilla as each other, but it had never mattered. He'd always been too absorbed in the fact it was Brett in his arms to pay much attention to the plethora of things they'd never tried... and, he had to admit, they'd never had much chance.

An old wound lingered beneath that thought—the fear that he'd held Brett back somehow, that the chains Tommy had always sworn never to lay on him had weighed him down—but it was touched with something new now. They had all this time stretching out ahead of them, filled with possibilities and opportunities.

There were no more excuses, and there was no more waiting... and they could do so much more of what they wanted.

He was just starting to consider that when Brett twisted beneath the covers, turning until he could reach Tommy's mouth. His kiss was a blend of light affection and deep need, and Tommy doubted he even knew how completely devastating it was.

It had terrified him once, the way just a word, just a look from Brett could raise him up or break him in two. Like a casual, unconsidered kind of ownership... like he wasn't even aware he was doing it. After a while, Tommy had realized he probably *wasn't*, and that was even scarier.

"Hey." Brett broke the kiss just as he was starting to get light-headed, and squirmed impatiently against him. "Hey?"

"Hmm?"

"When do I get my birthday present?"

He didn't mean the gift on the coffee table. Tommy grinned and squeezed his ass affectionately. "Well, I guess it depends on how nicely you ask."

"Huh." Brett pouted. "Pwetty pwease widda cherry on top?"

The whole wide-eyed cutesy thing was too much for Tommy to bear, and he spluttered, lost as much in the laughter as the silliness that intimacy brought.

"Aw, hell… that was horrible!" He shook his head incredulously as Brett sniggered, and traced the line of his jaw with gentle fingers. It wasn't like he could possibly refuse him this, anyway, even if he'd wanted to. "All right, fine."

Tommy started his descent down the bed, wrapped up in the softness of the covers and the impatient tensing of Brett's body, tautening at every place he paused to drop a kiss. Chest, belly, thighs… he didn't need to look, didn't need the lamp or even the dappled light from the uncovered window to guide him, not when there were those whispers of soft encouragement and the hungry flinching of warm, soap-scrubbed, spice-scented skin.

Brett was half-ready to meet him. He thickened lazily, his shaft pressing against the fullness of Tommy's lip like a lover's long-awaited kiss or a promise finally fulfilled. His fingers sought the weight of Tommy's hair, fumbling a little as he pushed it to the side, sweeping it away from his face. Brett's thumb brushed his cheekbone, and Tommy growled softly, deep in his throat, drawing another shiver from his lover.

He took his time, spun every second of it out like threads of burnt sugar, fragile and delicate and perfectly controlled. After a while, Brett managed to kick the covers off, and the pale swaths of moonlight painted the walls and their bodies alike: blurred lines of bluish gray, between which the boundaries seemed to fade, lost in the deceitful melding of shadows and half-light.

Tommy didn't stop. He looked up, relishing the sight of Brett splayed out just for him, his stomach taut as he panted. His weight rested on his arms, the curves of bunched muscles and the fluid cup of his waist both beautiful contrasts to the planes and hard angles of his body. Tommy wanted to tell him that—tell him how good he looked, how good he tasted, how fucking wonderful he was—but there wasn't time. No time to be selfish, or to do anything but give him this… give him everything. Brett's head dropped back as Tommy engulfed him completely, lost in how good it was to be full of him, full of his heat and his taste.

He pulled back, breathless and dizzy, with his pulse thudding behind his eyes, his jaw aching, and his chest tight. All the same, he'd timed it well, matching Brett's peak effortlessly and with indulgent enthusiasm. Those sweet, hoarse gasps and cries lifted to a crescendo as Tommy coaxed him through it, not letting him go, not letting him miss out on a single needle-sharp second of pleasure.

"Fuck," Brett murmured plaintively as Tommy nestled between his legs, arm wrapped around his thigh and cheek resting delicately against his groin. Brett raised his head and peered blearily down at him. "Huh. Are you…?"

"No rush," Tommy soothed, giving him an affectionate pat. "Happy birthday, baby."

Brett chuckled sleepily and combed his fingers through Tommy's hair. "Thanks. C'mon… get up here."

Tommy grinned and obliged. Every nerve seemed to sing when Brett touched him, and, wound as tight as he was, it didn't take long to put him over the edge. Brett kissed him softly, smiled as he tasted himself, and then let his head rest on Tommy's shoulder. A quiet sigh of contentment left him, and Tommy grinned drowsily into the moon-smeared dimness.

"April," he said, his voice a little thick and fuzzy.

"Hmm?"

"April. I think they might pick April."

Brett frowned. "Wh— Oh. The wedding? Why April?"

Tommy tilted his head, turning his face just enough to breathe in the scent of that tousled red-brown hair—shampoo and sex and citrus—and wrinkled his nose.

"Mom's birthday is in July. Before that, you got Christmas… if they pick April, it's pretty much in the middle, or close as it can be, right? Gives people time to save up for a decent anniversary present." He sniffed philosophically. "S'what *I'd* do."

Brett scoffed. "That's cold. That's… that's mercenary!"

Tommy grinned. "I think it's sensible. Now shut up and go to sleep. I'm gonna make you pancakes in the morning."

"Really?"

"Ah-huh. With syrup. And because it's your birthday," Tommy added, levering his arm out from under Brett before it went completely numb, "you get to decide where the syrup goes."

That got another smutty, sleepy chuckle, and he leaned over to rearrange the covers and pull them up before Brett had a chance to hog the entirety of them. Tommy glanced at the window, watching the shadow-spattered gloom shift around patterns of telltale dancing spirals.

"It's snowing again," he observed as he snuggled down.

Brett grunted indistinctly and hooked his ankle over Tommy's shin.

CHAPTER NINETEEN

IT WAS a hell of an event, when it finally came. Ron booked a package at a hotel about an hour outside of town—far enough from the view of the railway and all Havre's industrial, square practicality to make it look like they were really nestled in the middle of wide open country, and there was nothing for miles but cornfields and sky. It catered to a lot of people who came from out of state, Brett supposed. Weekend weddings and people who wanted to buy into that whole Western pioneer thing. The kind of people who thought of dude ranches when they thought of Montana, and associated those dreamy visions with big sunsets and bourbon on the porch instead of their boyfriend pulling long weekends and coming home smelling like motor oil and horse shit, with splinters in his palm that they had to sit and pick out with a magnifying glass and a pair of thin-nosed tweezers.

Still, it looked pretty in the pictures he'd seen: a big ranch house with fields all around, spilling out with wildflowers and sculpted, still ponds. The ceremony itself would be in a purpose-built part of the resort, like a little chapel, and the reception would take place in the large, lavishly decorated former barn. According to Tommy, there was meant to be an open bar too, which should at least go some way toward oiling things along. It promised to be a good day, Brett thought, with a great evening to follow, even if he wouldn't be staying for the Sunday morning. The weather was even lifting, the last rimes of ice and slush all but gone, and the sky had turned that clear, acidic blue, laced with clouds so white and sharp they looked as if they could have been starched.

As Brett dressed that morning—slightly regretting that he was at home, while Tommy had spent the night at Mei's, lost to that whirlwind of preparations and chaos—he thought back to the last thaw. So much had changed in a year... and so much more was going to change. After all those years of stagnancy, that dry, arid time that passed in stale, pressed pages, he couldn't wait for the hope of something fresh and new.

He rode over with his parents, Stephen all crisply presented in a charcoal gray suit, and Monica swathed in a dress with tiny green flowers on it. The text messages Brett had been swapping with Tommy all of Friday had contained several references to smart shirts, ties, and all the other sartorial stuff that Tommy was getting tied up with, including bribing Katie over the lacy pink frock she didn't want to wear. Brett smiled to himself as Stephen drove, sneakingly glad, in a way, that he *hadn't* had to be all that involved.

Quite a few of Ron's relatives were coming down, apparently, which made up for the lack of family on Mei's side. Tommy said both his maternal grandparents had passed on when he was small, though he thought Mei had some cousins in Seattle. She hadn't invited them, and Brett got the feeling there was possibly some kind of dark and lowering family history there. As the fields slipped by the car windows and the sky got wider, he wondered whether, if she hadn't been as adrift from her relations as she seemed to be, Mei would ever have found herself in such an unhealthy marriage to Martin... but those were thoughts he tried never to dwell on, because of the places they led.

Today wasn't a day for that. No guilt, no what ifs, no futile mental recriminations, and no room for old memories. Today was for making new ones.

"WELL," Monica observed as they pulled up, "looks busy."

"Yeah." Brett nodded, thumb punching the final word on his "we're here" text to Tommy. "Doesn't it?"

Her slingbacks crunched on the wide sweep of gravel driveway, and Brett eyed the parked cars and occasional knots of people. The hotel was selling itself on still looking like an old-fashioned homestead, and it rose darkly against the sky, heavy weatherboard a little at odds with the big glazed windows and the white painted trim on all the sills. It was too early in the year for wildflowers like in the pictures, but someone had diligently filled a huge number of troughs and window boxes with straggly, wind-whipped bedding plants, and they patched that dark frontage like smeared dabs of watercolor paint.

It was nice, though the illusion of clean, crisp organization was broken within a few seconds, when Katie came pelting out of the doors, bare-legged and in a pink, lace-trimmed dress—coupled, for some reason, with a pair of men's black woolen socks that were flapping off the ends of her feet—shrieking with laughter and followed by a slightly frazzled-looking Tommy. He caught her around the middle as she stopped to wave to Brett and, with a grin, hoisted her up to hip height. Katie wriggled and laughed, and didn't resist when he put her down and, taking her hand, crossed the lot to them in long, easy strides. His hair was tied back, and the suit he'd complained so much about— whatever he said—drew Brett's attention to every line, plane, and broad angle of his body. Ironic, he supposed, that Tommy hated formalwear with a passion, when it made him look so good.

"Goodness me!" Monica exclaimed, staring at Katie in exaggerated surprise. "What on earth happened to you?"

Katie beamed, her face a mix of sly triumph and sudden shyness, and twisted the sock-clad toes of one foot into the ground. Tommy sighed.

"They have a slate pond out back. *Somebody* thought the rehearsal was boring, and it would be more fun to go paddle in the water." He lifted the right leg of his pants fractionally, exposing one bare ankle, and grinned sheepishly. "The white pantyhose bought it, and pink satin pumps'll never be the same."

Monica winced. "Ooh."

"Yeah." Tommy shrugged. "Well, let's get you guys settled before everything gets crazy. More crazy… whatever."

He squeezed Katie's hand and, as they turned to head into the hotel, allowed her to run ahead. Monica and Stephen followed, with Monica already making observations about the architecture and décor, and Tommy dropped back a little to slip Brett a small smile.

"Hey."

"You look great," Brett murmured, glancing ahead at his parents, and the great rise of flowers and weatherboard that loomed before them.

Tommy's smile widened, and he dipped a hand into his pocket. "Got somethin' for you."

"Oh?"

Brett craned to see what it was, his mouth framing a soft, low sound of surprise as Tommy drew out a small boutonniere, exactly like the one pinned to his lapel: just a white carnation, bound with florist's tape and a sprig of gypsophila. It was a little crushed, but not too much the worse for wear, and as Tommy held it out, his smile softened, his lips pinched together in that uncertain way of his, a bite of hope and want.

"Here."

Brett looked at the flower nestled in his palm and felt a stupid, lopsided grin spread over his face.

"You got me a corsage?"

Tommy snorted and—with a faintly proprietary air that sent spirals of affection flowing warmly through him—reached over to fix it to the lapel of Brett's suit jacket. His touch was gentle but assured, and, once he was done, his fingers rested against Brett's chest for a few moments. Brett held his breath, watching the unspoken depths swirl in those dark eyes. Tommy's mouth twisted into a wry curl as he gave Brett a mock-critical once over and brushed his shirtfront down, the warmth of his fingers a comforting caress through the thin cotton.

"I think you'll do. Prom date."

Brett sniggered. "Thanks. When does this thing start, then?"

Tommy bit his lip and glanced over his shoulder. Monica and Stephen were already heading into the hotel, with Katie bouncing around them, explaining in a stream of high, excited, officious chatter what kind of food there was going to be at the sit-down dinner, and how the whole barn was full up with Christmas lights.

Tommy looked at Brett wearily and shook his head. "There's plenty of time yet… but we gotta get all the people who're staying the weekend settled. Lila's doing her maid of honor stuff, and I'm just tryin' to keep Katie from any more swimming lessons. You sure you still wanna volunteer to hold the fort tonight?"

Brett took his hand and squeezed it gently. "Sure."

There were limited places for guests to stay the whole weekend, so priority for rooms and seats at Sunday morning's wedding breakfast had gone to Ron's relatives. Brett didn't mind that. In truth, he was kind of looking forward to spending the Saturday night at Mei's, cooped up with Tommy in that strange, wonderful kind of domestic chaos that always seemed to fit him so well.

Tommy's face softened, his lips parting just a little as he started to lean in for a kiss, and Brett smiled as he heard Katie's piping tones drift across the parking lot.

"… and she was so nervous, she threw up *everywhere*, so the whole band practice had to move outside, but you could still smell it…."

Tommy winced and groaned softly, and Brett's smile became a grin.

"C'mon. I think you gotta go put your sister on a leash."

"Huh. Maybe we could gag her. Think that'd work?"

Brett snorted. "Nah, but it's a thought. Five bucks says someone sets her up to say something during the objections part."

Tommy groaned again. "Don't. That's not funny. I already warned Robbie about that."

Brett gave his hand one last squeeze as they parted and started to head in.

"You're a mean old man," he said, over his shoulder. "Did you confiscate his hip flask too?"

Tommy stuck out his tongue, and Brett's laughter drifted up past the flowers and the white-trimmed windows. Monica glanced back at them from the glazed double doors that led into the foyer, and smiled.

THE service itself was simple, small, and plain… and went off pretty much without a hitch. Brett sat with his parents, near the front, and watched Tommy sweating lightly as he tried to keep Katie, Atian, and a bunch of small kids from Ron's side of the family, in three piece suits and frilly dresses, all under control. He seemed to go through two pockets' worth of hard candy, but he managed it, and, Brett observed, it kept him occupied to the extent that the sore, hollow hardness in his face when Mei and Ron exchanged their vows was barely noticeable.

She looked happy, with her ivory jacquard skirt suit, misty eyes, bouquet of pink and cream carnations, and vague sense of triumphal accomplishment. Ron spent most of the proceedings wearing that faintly stunned expression of his, although, when he smiled, it was huge and wide and honest. Brett sat, and smiled in all the right places, and found he truly did wish them both well. Lila appeared to be enjoying herself, soaking up as much of the attention and responsibility as she could get away with, and Ron's best man—an electrician called Alex, apparently—did a lot of grinning and nodding, and seemed like a pretty nice guy, if a little out of his depth.

Brett was aware of his mother sniffling delicately into a handkerchief at one point, and tried to pretend he hadn't heard.

All in all it was… nice, as weddings went. He could feel all the things that lay behind it, though, however much he told himself he couldn't. Part of him suspected they were the reason Mei had asked Tommy to watch the kids that night. Obviously, she couldn't have *not* had him there, but Brett wondered if maybe they weren't both being pushed behind the scenes a little. Or if Tommy was, at least. The whole thing, he reminded himself, was really nothing to do with him. It sucked, but it was a fact the entire family had never completely let him forget.

He was a lot of things to them, but not blood… and not a legal spouse.

He smiled, nonetheless, when Mei and Ron kissed, and she threw her arms around her new husband's neck, those slim, hose-encased legs kicking up in delight as she held on, more animated and delighted than Brett had ever seen her. She was a totally different person to the small, hunched, pale woman he'd met all those years ago, with the bitterness wrapped around her like paper wings.

Brett shot a glance at Tommy, taking in the shaded, closed-in look around his eyes. He was smiling, sure, but it wasn't reaching as far as up his face as it ought. Brett stifled a sigh. He'd tried getting him to talk about it, but Tommy just shut him out every time he tried, and then they argued, and there was no point pushing it after that. All the same, he was sick of seeing those last few lingering traces of a jail face on Tommy, and sick of thinking he ought to find ways around them.

Tommy glanced up at him then, and he caught his breath. It was like some sudden omen, some hidden sign, and the way his smile broadened—grew more genuine, somehow—made Brett's throat tighten a little and brought warmth to his cheeks.

IF THE service had been simple, the reception got a little more complex.

The old barn, as the brochure described it, didn't so much resemble a barn as a huge, open-plan grotto, with every beam and column wrapped in strands of tiny lights, just like Katie had said. They twinkled, little points of warm white light in among all the woodwork, fake greenery, and ebullient chatter. There *was* an open bar, and sets of white chiffon curtains marked it off from the seating and dance floor areas.

The photos were taken both inside and outside, some framed by the lights, and some by the barn's wide, wooden doors. Brett was pretty sure nobody needed that many pictures, but the photographer was the son of some friend of Ron's and seemed terribly eager to please. He snapped the bride and groom, the bride and her smallest bridesmaid— Katie, still wearing Tommy's black socks and an oversized grin—and a bunch of Mei, looking over her shoulder, holding her bouquet and smiling while the Christmas lights twinkled around her like fireflies.

There was a photo op with the great, teetering cake, its tiers wreathed in flouncy ruffles of frosting, and there were pictures that all the close family got dragged into. Tommy grabbed Brett by the elbow and practically frog-marched him into the group, and he felt like an interloper as he stood on the very edge of the frame, unsure of what to do with his hands and trying not to look like an idiot. He could see his mother in the crowd, smiling genially—and probably at his expense.

Once it was over, Mei got up onto the small dais at one end of the barn, where the DJ booth was set up, and threw her bouquet into the sea of bouncing, squealing females, to a chorus of giggles and more flash photography.

Brett applauded along with everyone else and wondered where the hell Tommy had got to. Kid patrol, he supposed, and he realized he hadn't even known how much he was missing him.

A few moments later, Brett started, catching his breath as Tommy emerged stealthily from the throng behind him and pinched the back of his waist. He turned his head, drinking in the smell of half-worn-out aftershave, and the delicious, comforting warmth of that familiar presence.

"Hey."

"Hey, yourself." Tommy's grip on his waist tightened as he leaned closer to Brett's ear, making himself heard above the chatter. "Drink? I just handed the kids back. Mainly."

"Mainly?" Brett echoed, arching a brow.

"Pretty much." Tommy winced as Atian charged past with his tie on his head, Rambo-style, yelling and windmilling his arms. "Told Scott he shoulda got him a clip-on."

Brett smirked. "C'mon."

They wound their way through the knots of people and, once furnished with some slightly acidic glasses of champagne, came back to settle Monica and Stephen at the right point in the seating order.

"You're table three," Tommy said, taking a large gulp of his drink. "Two left of the top. Me too."

Brett eyed him circumspectly over his champagne and said nothing.

They sat two tables down from Mei and Ron for the meal, with a Canadian couple who introduced themselves as Carol and Dean, and made polite small talk over poached salmon and creamed potatoes. Brett kept a smile plastered to his face and latched onto talking about work—Carol turned out to be a registered nurse, which gave them enough in common to keep the conversation going—instead of giving into his irritated, protective frustration. Tommy shouldn't have been relegated like it seemed he had… even if *he* didn't appear to mind. He was knocking back the champagne a little too readily, maybe, and Brett got closer and closer to wanting to say something, only then Scott appeared at his elbow and coughed awkwardly, asking if Tommy could come give him a hand with the kids.

In the natural progression of weddings, with the sit-down dinner almost over, the first of the smallest relatives had already eaten too much and been taken queasy, and the excitement and stimulation of the day was cranking the others up like pure sugar.

Tommy grinned, making his excuses as he got to his feet. Dean and Carol and Monica and Stephen all smiled those glassy, accommodating smiles, and Tommy's hand brushed Brett's shoulder as he stood, fingers curling for a moment against the smooth fabric of his jacket.

Brett's gaze followed him, drawn like always just to the way he filled up the space around him, and he smiled softly at him as he left. Tommy didn't look back, of course, busy heading after his brother. Brett tilted his chin down, just catching a glimpse of the carnation in his lapel—and a hint of its tired, thin-worn fragrance. His smile deepened a little before it faded, and, as the music and the chatter in the room swelled, he reached for his glass and nodded politely at something Carol had just said about healthcare reform.

BRETT was getting sick of making nice by the time Tommy wove his way back through the crowds. The dancing had started. They'd all dutifully applauded Mei and Ron's awkward first shuffle around the floor, and now other couples were following them and the terse echo of overloud movie ballads had begun to claw at Brett's temples.

Monica and Stephen went first, basely abandoning him to the mercies of the banal Canadian couple, and Brett had the smile stapled so firmly to his face his cheeks were starting to hurt.

He didn't see Tommy at first, only alerted to his presence by that little tug in the air that happened just before he emerged out of the throng… that way Brett's body seemed to have of acknowledging Tommy, even when *he* didn't realize it.

"Hey," he said, glancing up at the unexpectedly giddy, grinning face.

Is he drunk?

Tommy kind of looked it. He looked flushed, warm, and really rather beautiful.

"Wanna dance?"

His breath smelled of champagne, and a blindly cheerful sort of haziness shrouded his eyes. He'd pulled that much-hated tie loose—as loose as his hair, which was about halfway to completely falling out of its ponytail—and his whole deliciously disheveled air had Brett stifling the urge to laugh.

"Scott let you off kid patrol?"

Tommy wrinkled his nose. "I've cleaned up, mopped up, and refereed. We got maybe an hour before we're gonna have to take Katie home, anyway, so... one more time: you wanna dance?"

Brett scoffed incredulously as the fuzzy resonance of a syrupy eighties movie theme rolled over the dance floor and lapped around all those shiny-faced, smiling couples like a sea of gooey nostalgia.

"Tommy...."

His lover placed one strong golden-brown hand on the tablecloth, and leaned over Brett as his fingers flexed against the cream linen.

"It's my mother's wedding," Tommy said, his complete solemnity belied by the glimmer in those dark eyes. "Get off your ass and come and have one goddamn dance with me."

"All right." Brett grinned. "All right... if it makes you happy."

He turned to make his excuses to Carol and Dean, and found them awkwardly getting up from the table, all shy smiles and dropped napkins.

Brett got to his feet and let Tommy take his hand and lead him out into the crush of people. Gaudy spotlights twirled through the dimness, star-shaped beams in shades of jaundiced yellow and bilious green, contrasting against the ropes of little lights that wrapped every column and beam. It felt unreal, like some twinkling, shifting dreamworld. Tommy slipped his arms around Brett's waist and pulled him close, swaying to the song's slow rhythm in that awkward kind of middle-school dancing that didn't really do much except rock them gently to and fro in one place. Brett didn't care. He crossed his wrists behind Tommy's head and pressed close to him, breathing in the scent of cheap champagne and overcooked salmon and letting go all of the long, tremulous tensions of the day. Tommy's warmth, the smell of his skin, and the scent of his hair all wound up in Brett, teasing and tempting him as he lost himself in those dark eyes and the goofy charm of that slightly crooked, tipsy grin.

"Love you," he murmured.

Tommy unhooked one hand and stroked the back of Brett's head lazily.

"Love you too," he said, the callused tip of his thumb just grazing the outline of his ear. "Love you so much, baby."

He leaned in, closing the whisper of a gap between them with a soft kiss. Brett hugged him tighter, lost to the rhythm of the music and the embrace. It was sweet and slow, and yet, with Tommy's body swaying against his, an undeniable heat burned between them. His lips parted in gentle encouragement, laughter and tenderness coiling in the breath they shared.

They broke at the sound of a throat being strenuously cleared somewhere not far from Brett's right shoulder. It was barely audible above the music, but definitely a determined gesture. Tommy pulled back a little, though his gaze didn't waver.

"Go 'way, Scott," he said, still smiling blurrily at Brett.

Brett grinned and glanced over his shoulder. Scott was dancing with Karen… or at least she was partially draped across him, reaching about the middle of his chest in a vivid montage of peach satin and hairspray. Scott shot Brett an uncomfortable grimace.

"Uh…."

"Hey." Brett slid his hand down the side of Tommy's neck, skating his lapel and resting against his chest. "Wanna go get another drink?"

Scott's look of embarrassment sprouted tendrils of relief. "Yeah, that's a plan, huh?"

Karen was tugging at him impatiently, eager to get back to the dancing. Brett felt Tommy tense up a bit, though his expression remained genial.

"What?" He looked levelly at Scott, and his eyes narrowed just a little. "I'm not allowed a li'l public display of affection?"

"I didn't say that," Scott protested, and Brett noticed for the first time the number of glances they'd been getting.

They were still getting them. The nice, respectable people he didn't know—the Canucks and the accountants and Ron's work friends—were looking at them, and then looking away with that particular kind of studied nonchalance.

He didn't know whether Tommy was aware of it or not. It didn't seem to matter very much. It was the easiest thing in the world to put his hand to Tommy's cheek and turn him away from the argument, away from all of it, bringing him back to center and then—despite Scott's small noise of appalled embarrassment—to lean in once more and plant a long, slow, sweet kiss on his lips.

Just for once, Brett decided, they were going to do things in their own damn time.

CHAPTER TWENTY

LIFE took a while to settle after the wedding. Tommy wasn't surprised, although in some small, stupid way he supposed he'd been hoping it would all work out like magic. Obviously, the kids already knew Ron—liked him, even—but making it official changed things, just as he'd known it would.

It took Robbie the most time to adjust. For a couple of months, there were letters from the school and arguments at home, full of the kinds of slammed doors and strained, sharp-edged silences that stalked Tommy's memories. He wanted to help, but he had no idea what he was meant to say.

Lila was easier. She worried him too, in her own way, being so independent all of a sudden, with all that self-important teenage confidence, and so determined that she was going to follow through on those plans of hers. College, nursing... all the stuff she and Brett had talked about. He was helping her understand the choices out there, and every time Tommy saw them together, he couldn't help but think of the way Brett had been back then, when he was just a few years older than she was now, so full of optimism and with the whole world cracked wide open, groaning with possibilities.

Tommy wanted that for Lila. Wanted it really, really badly, and hated that it wasn't something in his power to give her. He couldn't even talk it out with her the way Brett could. He had to resign himself to just nodding and saying "ah-huh" in all the right places, and he fervently hoped that would be enough.

Katie, he could manage. She was still young enough to have no more pressing problems in life than the boy in her class who kept calling her "Cootie Face" and the perennially thorny matters of learning how to spell and how to stop periodically falling off of her bike.

Somehow, Tommy found grazed knees a hell of a lot easier to deal with than a person's entire future.

He still thought about *his*, of course, from time to time. It was unlikely he'd spend the rest of his life working for Bill, though some days it seemed like not only would he do just that, but it would all be spent shoveling the exact same pile of shit. No... it was possible, he guessed, if the ranch continued to hold its head above water. He had a place there. Bill and Herman had both said as much. There was always a need for someone who could fix things and didn't mind working, and that was fine. He was happy there, or as near it as he'd ever been. The guys were good people, and the only thing wrong with the whole deal was it being so far away, which he and Brett were working on.

Waiting for Brett to get his course at the college underway sucked, but they were good at waiting, and it was leavened with more fun than it ever had been before. Tommy found a whole new level of joy in sitting up in bed together on lazy Saturday mornings, drinking coffee and tea and thumbing through real estate listings on Brett's laptop. All right, it mainly served to confirm the kind of thing they wouldn't be able to afford, but there was still a possibility of something, somewhere... some tiny corner of a place that would be marked out as theirs. A shared space, together: that was enough, even if, one time, Tommy was almost certain one of the pictures showed the decomposition outline of a body on the floor.

It would mean not seeing so much of Mei, Ron, and the kids. That was the other thing that tugged insistently at his mind, though Brett said it didn't have to be like that.

Tommy wasn't so sure. As it was, he rarely stayed over at his mother's anymore, despite what his PO's paperwork said. Myers had lectured him pretty hard about the importance of regulations and details after he'd been stupid enough to get himself caught up in Lane Harding's assault case. It hadn't caused any real problems, though, for which Tommy was grateful. Nothing had stuck and—technically speaking—he hadn't really done anything wrong... apart from not being quite as completely truthful as he could have been, he supposed, but what nobody knew did no harm, right?

Not that it mattered, anyway, whatever Myers said. The ranch was duly noted as his approved residence during the working week, and Tommy had kept himself squeaky clean. He had been nothing but the model of rehabilitation and earnest good conduct, which was harder work than he'd expected.

Well... *almost* nothing but.

IT TOOK just under eight months, all told, for Lane Harding to come to trial. He'd spent the whole of it at the county detention center, and Tommy kind of wanted to feel for the guy, because he remembered what that was like.

He didn't visit, though the last few dogged cobwebs of old loyalties said he should. There had been a time Lane had been good to him—all those guys had, when he needed it the most—and he couldn't lose the feeling that he owed something back. However, Tommy also figured, after everything Lane had done, loyalty could take a running jump and the guy could go fuck himself... plus, he was terrified of being asked to testify.

Tommy wanted nothing to do with any of it. Trouble was, he knew he was unlikely to have a choice—and he was proven right.

The prosecutor's office called him while he was at Bill's, which was good in a way, because he'd been hoping that nobody would have to know. It was a stupid thought, Tommy realized, but Brett was all caught up with preparing to start his LPN, and Mei would just have gone nuts, and he didn't really want to have to look any of the kids in the face if he had to say he was going to court.

He responded to pretty much everything the woman said in monosyllables and, when he'd turned his phone off and finished up with the electric fence he'd been repairing, sloped back up to the house to find Bill.

Tommy found him in the office, sitting behind a sea of paperwork and comparing contractors' quotes on the computer, while Missy dozed in her basket. He knocked gently on the open door and cleared his throat, glancing down at the holes in the toes of his socks—his muddy boots having been left by the kitchen door, as usual—and how incongruous they seemed against the soft beige carpet.

Bill peered at him across his in tray and smiled. "Hey, Tommy. Problem?"

"No." Tommy shook his head and then frowned. "Uh, well...."

Bill's smile folded into a kinder, warmer expression of careful neutrality. "Why don't you close the door and come sit down, huh?"

He did what the older man said and sat for a moment, holding his breath, before he spoke. When he finally let it out, the words came in a rush, and he knew he didn't make all that much sense, but Bill just nodded solidly and let him take his time, and Tommy loved the guy for that.

He talked, and talked, and the world didn't end.

Bill understood. Tommy had known he would. He understood in a way that other people didn't, in a way that nobody did unless they'd been there. He didn't pass comment, didn't make a huge thing out of it, just crumpled his lips together, nodded slowly, and said "oh." He didn't say Tommy ought to tell anyone, or mention things like paperwork or dressing smart, or ask if he was all right with doing it. He just asked Tommy if he knew when they'd call him and if he wanted someone to go to court with him. Tommy nodded fervently and frowned at the floor.

Someone, yeah. Just not Brett.

HE GOT through the best part of two weeks without telling Brett about the call. He realized he was going to have to when they started falling back into those old, ugly habits of sniping and snapping at each other, and that wasn't fair, because Brett was tired and worried about money anyway. Tommy knew how much he hated taking the loan from his parents to pay for the college course, no matter how they'd phrased the offer, and the last thing he wanted was to make anything worse.

Tommy told him on one stilted, silent Sunday night, when they were both still stewing in low-grade irritation. He didn't mean to. He meant the first words out of his mouth to be an apology for acting like a dick that weekend, and he stared blankly at his knees as he sprawled on Brett's couch, wondering how it was that—after all this time—he could still be such an idiot. Canned laughter spilled from the TV, though Tommy hadn't been paying much attention to the show and had no idea what might have been funny.

"What?"

He glanced at Brett, painfully aware of the terseness in his voice and the tightness around his eyes.

"Uh... y'know. Lane's coming up for trial, and—"

"So what?"

"Well, I gave a statement, remember?" Tommy's frown deepened. This hadn't exactly been a point of great equanimity between them the first time around. "Like it or not, I'm—"

"You're going to court?"

Brett's tone was dull and hollow, but Tommy recognized the dark, hard well of anger underlying it. He bit the inside of his lip, holding down the urge to argue. Brett didn't get it, and he couldn't expect him to, so there wasn't much point in bitching or getting annoyed.

"We'll see," he said vaguely. "I don't know yet."

Next to most things, it was only a little lie. He frowned and picked at the seam on his jeans as Brett glared at the TV. The space between them on the couch—though it wasn't much, given how they tended to spill out like this, all shoulders and elbows and feet slung over the furniture—seemed wide and insurmountable.

Tommy breathed in, deep but silent. Brett's proximity filled up the air, filled up everything with the sense of a life that was here, and real, and more complete than pretty much anything he'd ever had before. He wasn't scared, he realized. He'd thought he was—thought he *would* be, and that there might yet be some real danger he'd somehow lose Brett inside all of this crap—but it didn't matter. It didn't matter in the slightest if they argued, or if Brett didn't understand, because there would be a time when it was over. It might seem like a long way off, but it would come. He felt safer in that knowledge than he had in just about anything. And they were going to have their own place and their own life, and people like Lane—and, fuck it, even Tommy's father, who was still there, right at the back of every breath, every heartbeat—couldn't tear that down.

He cleared his throat. "I'm gonna get a drink. You want anything?"

Brett shook his head, the TV's reflection dancing over his face in muted blue patterns. He seemed to change his mind as Tommy laboriously scrambled up, and frowned.

"Uh, there's hot chocolate in the cupboard over the toaster. Can I...?"

There was something about the look on his face—his head tilted at just that angle, his eyes just that little bit widened, and his lips slightly parted—that made Tommy smile fondly. Brett watched him for a second, apparently curious, and then his expression softened, he shrugged, and the last dregs of that whole air of tension and guardedness between them seemed to crack.

"Sure," Tommy said, his smile widening out as he sloped into the kitchen.

It didn't matter. It didn't matter at all.

He just hoped Brett felt the same.

LANE'S trial didn't generate much in the way of publicity, not that Tommy went out of his way to read up on it. There was a sentence on a local news bulletin and one article he spotted in the paper, and he wasn't sure whether he ought to feel angry at that, like somehow Lane deserved more attention... even if he was an asshole.

Bill didn't make a fuss over it, though. All the arrangements and the stifled exposure—even the court date looming up like a black cloud—he just took completely in stride. He came into the ranch house's kitchen while Tommy was reading the paper, peered over his shoulder, and made a small "huh" in the back of his throat.

"Remind me I gotta stop by the post office when we're in town, will ya? My nephew's grandkid has a birthday coming up."

He clapped Tommy on the back in passing and headed off to make the coffee, as if there was nothing out of the ordinary about any of it. Tommy supposed that was just the way some people were, the way they coped. And that was fine.

It didn't stop him worrying, but it helped.

The night before Bill was going to drive him to the courthouse, he sat up in bed and flipped through the very creased, very dog-eared copy of *The Sacred Tree* he'd had since the talking circle. The thick, heavily shaded line drawings that punctuated the pages—and the blocks of text about understanding the different gifts of wisdom, and growing from them—were familiar to him after all this time, but he still didn't really identify with the words.

Tommy missed the circle, sometimes. He'd got really into it at first, and he smiled to himself as he remembered the bug-eyed look Brett used to get on visiting days when, to hear him talk, it had probably sounded like he'd had some kind of evangelical conversion. It wasn't like that, though. It was hard to explain, especially to a guy like Brett, but it had nothing to do with fire and drums and squeezing himself into a new identity. It was about owning who he was... and everything that had happened.

Tommy knew it had been important to do that. He wasn't finished doing it yet either, but he was pretty sure he'd got a little further down the road.

The book said the North was the final lesson: balance, and the wisdom to understand how the connections in life worked, how all of the people fitted together, and maybe how all the parts of yourself did too. That was what justice meant, apparently. It was about being able to stand in one place and look over to all the other places you'd been and all the other things you'd learned, and that were yet to be learned... because life never stopped. There was never an ending, never a place you got to where you sat back and said that was it, you were finished, and everything was neatly, tidily packaged away.

You had to live with who you were, what you were, and where you'd been.

TOMMY called Brett before they left for the court date. It wasn't much of a call—just a few words, a way of talking without naming anything, and Tommy supposed that shouldn't really have surprised him.

"We're going," he said, as he stood on the graveled driveway, squinting a little in the sunlight and watching Bill back the truck out.

"Right." Brett sounded tired and maybe a little worried. "Okay."

"I'll see you, uh… well—"

"When you're back. It's all right."

He nodded, and although the phone was warm against his ear, it really wasn't a lot like having Brett actually there. Tommy kind of liked the shorthand that had grown up between them, nonetheless, and he smiled softly, flattering himself that—out of all the things it would be nice to say and nice to hear—they didn't really *need* them.

"Okay."

"Right." Brett exhaled, and his breath grazed the line in a way that, even now, made the hair stand up on the back of Tommy's neck. "Take care, baby."

He smiled. "Yeah. Love you."

"Love you too."

And there it was: their sign-off, that little code that sounded like nothing and meant everything, and had kept him sane on so many long days. Tommy's smile widened as he cut the connection, and high above in the vast, sharp blue of the sky, the black shape of a bird wheeled between the thin wisps of cloud.

He loped over to Bill's truck, climbed in, and, as they rattled off toward the road, things really did seem a little brighter.

Bill glanced at him as the sunlight flared off the rearview mirror.

"Nervous?"

Tommy shook his head. "Nah. Well… yeah. Maybe a little."

He grinned and tugged at the cuff of the smart shirt he was wearing. It wasn't as bad as the full-suit-and-hair-tied-back deal he remembered being decked out in for his allocution, but it was still court clothes, and that meant everything itched like hell.

He wrinkled his nose. "Guess it's gonna be weird. And, y'know, it's hard to feel I don't kinda owe him something, even a little bit. Like, doing this is—"

"Doing this is the right thing to do," Bill said, his tone calm and mild as he steered the truck past a tractor that had hauled up to load hay bales.

"Ah-huh."

"Plus," Bill added philosophically, "if you didn't, you'd get your ass burned by your PO and get yourself dragged back into the whole mess, right?"

He grinned when Tommy gave a short cough of incredulous laughter.

"Hey, don't forget. I've been there, you know?" Bill shook his head as, outside, the flat expanse of pasture and cornfields started to sprout more crops of low, pale houses. "And you don't owe that guy nothing. None of it. No, because you know what, Tommy? It's guys like him that need the help. They don't make it long on the outs. They can't deal with it, so they go back in. And you don't have to do that. You don't have to be like that. *They* don't have to... but they're not always that strong, hmm?"

He'd cracked the windows down, and Tommy stared as the breeze picked at the couple of loose gray hairs pulled from Bill's braids. The sunlight sliced across his broad, genial face, and he shot Tommy the briefest of smiles before turning his attention back to the road.

THE day passed in that strange, elided time where hours could have been minutes, and yet the seconds felt like years. Tommy pushed dully through rooms that smelled of linoleum and disinfectant, and answered when he was spoken to, and said the things he had promised to say. He didn't look at Lane, sitting there in the orange shirt and pants the county lockup gave you, that were made in one generic size and didn't fit anybody at all, and itched and had that kind of waxy soap smell on them. He didn't need to look, to feel the hatred burning in the other man's eyes, like it could actually scald into his flesh from right across the room.

In any case, it was over eventually, and Bill was waiting for him outside, and he didn't say anything except to ask if Tommy wanted to go and get a cup of coffee.

"Yeah," Tommy said dully, the word a small whitecap bobbing atop waves of gratitude that surged inside him.

They stopped at a small chain: a narrow building with tall plate glass windows and an all-permeating, bitter-roasted smell of coffee beans and flavoring syrups. Tommy slumped awkwardly in a tubular steel chair and tried to will the weight of the day to lift off of him. Outside, the sky was still that same sharp, bright blue, and he supposed that meant that the world was still spinning, and everything was still okay. When he turned his phone back on, he found a text message from Brett. It was just three small words, but they meant a lot, and Tommy sat and stared at them as Bill set his coffee down in front of him.

Proud of you.

He smiled and let himself relax into the uncomfortably shaped chair.

CHAPTER TWENTY-ONE

TIME moved on, and for once there didn't seem to be anything that felt wrong or strange about that. There were no frustrations, except for the ordinary, boring, day-to-day ones, and no huge dramas. Mei and Ron were settling happily into married life—or apparently so, anyway—and Tommy spent more time than ever at Brett's. The summer rolled by a little like it had once before, a long time ago, when the time they spent together was what felt more real than anything else, and the days all seemed to have that smell of long grass and warm cotton.

House hunting picked up the pace in early October, and they took a trip to Poplar to view an apartment Brett had found online. Finding somewhere in their budget had been much harder than either of them had anticipated—let alone how damn difficult Tommy's conviction made things—and Tommy had suggested just taking the place on principle, slamming the money down and having done with the whole thing.

Brett being Brett, of course, he disagreed. So they looked it over, and looked past the faint damp stains on the walls, and the carpets and bathroom fixtures that needed replacing, and the strange, tense kind of smile the woman from the realtor's office had when she showed them into the apartment's solitary, small bedroom.

"We could get a double in here no problem," Brett observed as he crossed to check out the storage space.

One thing Tommy had learned about his partner on this particular adventure was the fact that the guy was apparently obsessed with cupboards. He suppressed a grin as Brett half disappeared into the short rank of fitted closets on the far wall, still complete with their original 1980s louver doors, in tatty white vinyl.

"Plenty of space," Brett said, slightly muffled, and Tommy's mirth spilled out into a stifled chuckle.

He skirted around behind Brett, sorely tempted to grab the denim-clad ass that was sticking so provocatively out of the wardrobe, and wondered if there was some kind of kinky tally they could work out over how many times storage got mentioned in the course of the afternoon.

Four times or under, and I get a blowjob in front of the TV tonight. Five to eight, we play with blindfolds, and if it hits ten, it's fluffy handcuffs and tickling until you scream for mercy....

He was just idly contemplating the possibilities of syrup and ice cubes when Brett backed out of the closet, so to speak, and nearly collided with him. Tommy grinned, and that grin widened at the sweet, tentative smile Brett shot him, so attractively laden with affection and slight embarrassment.

It started to feel real after that. Their own place: their first place together, and that first true, honest, demonstrable thing that carried with it so many big, scary responsibilities and commitments that, somehow, were so much less scary just by the fact of sharing them with *him*.

It was pretty much a done deal that they were going to take the place... or that Brett was, in technical terms. Bill had already signed a letter, as Tommy's employer and guarantor, to say he wasn't a ravening psychopath who scrawled on the walls in his own blood, and the realtor had accepted that, and accepted him as a tenant, but it would be Brett's name on the books. It didn't really matter, Tommy supposed. He'd pay his half of everything, and they would probably argue about money from time to time, all the same, but then, they were good at arguing about stupid things. Anyway, what mattered was that this place—this crappy little place, with its outdated fittings and its patchy walls and the dents on the carpet from where the old tenants' couch had been—this was going to be *theirs*.

Brett told the realtor they were going to think about it, and they went to forage in town for something to call lunch. It ended up being burgers, and they sat opposite each other in plastic seats, looking across a plastic table while, through the plate glass window, they watched the sun creep out from behind the clouds and lightly gild the empty road.

"Hey." Brett nudged Tommy's foot with his and looked meaningfully at him over a french fry. The sleeve of his sweater had slipped back a little, exposing the watch he still wore every day: the one Tommy had bought him for his last birthday, which caught the light with surprising brilliance for a cheap timepiece.

"What?"

"You sure about it?" Brett asked, raising his eyebrows inquiringly. "The—"

"Yeah. Yes," Tommy repeated, nodding. "We said. It's the best we're gonna get for the money. It's central, it's clean… ish. I think it's a good idea."

Brett's mouth crumpled into a folded line, an expression that wasn't so much agreement as acknowledgment of all the stuff that lay ahead of them.

"And you're sure that it's what you wanna…?"

Oh, he's not seriously asking that. He's not… is he?

Tommy scoffed. "I am very, very sure," he said, leaning forward and breaking the words right down into nice, slow, simple syllables, so there was no way in hell Brett could possibly misunderstand him. "I want to. I wanna hole up with you and spend every single minute we got together. Love you, remember?"

Brett's solemn, solicitous expression slipped into a lopsided smile. "Uh-huh. Love you too," he murmured, and the words they'd said so many times warmed the air with well-worn comfort.

Tommy dunked a fry in Brett's ketchup and chewed on it thoughtfully. "How many boxes you think you're gonna need? I mean, you got your books, and the couch, and… what?"

"We're getting a new couch," Brett said decisively. "And a new bed."

Tommy frowned. "That sounds expensive."

"Not really. Anyway, we won't have to pay for a moving company. Dad said he can fix that up. He and Mom'll bring my stuff down. Figure it's only a couple of carloads, so if we both drive, it's only going to take one trip. Unless you've got much to go?"

Tommy shook his head. He didn't. Pretty much everything he owned was at Bill's, maybe with one or two bits and pieces left at his mother's house... virtually nothing that wouldn't fit into a few suitcases, with maybe a couple extra for all the damn clothes Brett kept buying him. Not a lot for a life, he realized, thinking briefly of the running away case he'd stowed under the bed at Gramma's house when he was a kid. Funny what you thought was important sometimes.

Brett was talking again, whirling off into that enthusiastic spin of ideas and plans that almost disguised how nervous he was about throwing everything into the LPN, especially when there was no complete guarantee of a job at the end of it. His foot was still resting between Tommy's, somewhere beneath the blank block of the plastic table, on the bland, shiny linoleum that wasn't quite the same pattern as the flooring he remembered back in the visitors' center. Tommy prodded the toe of his work boot into Brett's ankle and watched the faintly inquisitive look creep across those hazel eyes as the tumult of words finally slowed.

"... and so, probably, that'd be all we need to do. I guess."

"Mm-hm." Tommy smiled encouragingly and tried not to think about the whole weltering pile of details that was going to emerge as soon as the move got underway.

He felt fairly sure it was going to be hell, but he didn't say anything.

After all, he was equally sure it would be worth it.

LANE HARDING'S trial concluded a little over a week after Brett signed the tenancy agreement. Fifteen years, with a minimum of eight to be served. There was a short piece about it on the local news, and, for one horrible moment, Brett thought they were going to mention Tommy's name. It had popped up once during the trial coverage, in a rather vitriolic newspaper column that had tossed around mean-spirited, spiteful words about parolees giving evidence, its more personal attack only thinly veiled. He didn't think Tommy had seen it. He hoped not, anyway.

They didn't talk about Harding either, though Tommy got withdrawn and moody after his PO called to tell him about the sentencing. The guy didn't have to do that, and Brett made the mistake of saying it was nice of him to have made the gesture, which earned him an irritable retort and very nearly cycled them back into another of those stupid, wearing, pointless arguments. Tommy having to leave for the ranch derailed it, and Brett wondered whether that would still work when they were in the new place. Would they still avoid the fights because they'd outgrown them, or was it going to make things worse again? He didn't want to think so, especially when, by and large, everything had been so good, and he didn't want to pollute all the stuff they were looking forward to about the move with overanalysis, but it was hard to avoid.

He started packing during the week, and Monica came around to help, which Brett suspected was a lame disguise for taking the opportunity to poke at the doubts he didn't want to admit to having. He couldn't blame her, though, and he wasn't about to refuse the assistance, so he gritted his teeth and nodded his way through her probing questions, however much subtlety they lacked.

"So, honey," she ventured when they took a coffee break from wrapping Brett's mismatched kitchen china, "is everything okay?"

Plates and bowls sat carefully swaddled in newspaper and stacked up in a cardboard box on the counter, and Brett leaned back against the sink as he waited for the coffeemaker to finish. Its quiet, steady drip and hiss filled the air. Monica tilted her head, looking dubiously at him when he smiled.

"Yeah. No, it… it is, Mom. Really."

She nodded slowly, like she didn't believe him. "Nervous?"

He folded his arms, the shrug he gave her perhaps a little defensive. "Maybe a bit. It's all gonna be new, but… not new, y'know? That feels kinda weird. But I'm looking forward to it. I think we both are."

Her freckled cheeks dimpled slightly as she smiled: a big, wide smile with a faint hint of sadness behind it. The look in her eyes told

Brett he probably shouldn't seem too enthusiastic about moving away, however hard she was pretending it didn't hurt her, and he wished it was easier to explain things.

"Well, it wouldn't be natural if you weren't worried," Monica said matter-of-factly, reaching past him to pour the coffee.

Brett blinked. He'd been going to do that. She mothered him at every possible moment, even now… and he realized just how much he was going to miss it.

"I didn't say I was—"

"It's a big move," she continued blithely. "And I know you two have been pretty much living together here, but it *will* be different. You know, your own place, and he'll be there more, and—"

"Getting under my feet," Brett supplemented, grinning to try and leaven the awkwardness.

Monica chuckled. "Mm-hm, and getting in the way. You know, I say the same thing about your dad."

"Mom…."

She shook her head. "I know. I know, you already *know* everything, and I'm not telling you anything new. But you remember what I said before, right? Any time you need anything—*anything*—you can call your dad and me, okay?"

Brett already had his mouth open to frame some casual assurance, but something in her face stopped him. Her hair was pulled back into a rough ponytail, disheveled by the afternoon's work, and gray roots peeked from beneath the soft red color. Laughter lines edged her mouth and eyes, and they seemed to hold a kind of sad hopefulness as she looked at him, half smiling and half just staring, as if there was something about this moment that she wanted to drink in, to pull close and savor.

"I will," he said quietly.

Monica nodded briskly, then turned her head to focus on the coffee.

"All right," she said, apparently addressing the sugar packet. "So I can stop fussing now, can I?"

Brett laughed softly, his arms still folded but his shoulders loosening.

"I don't know." He slipped her a sly, sideways glance. "You could do it a little bit. If you really wanted."

She shook her head incredulously, and the sound of her laughter rippled through the apartment, grazing the collection of boxes and drifts of packing paper.

THE move went surprisingly well, all things considered. It was fragmentary, chaotic, and full of frazzled nerves and ridiculous coincidences, but, as Brett kept saying with the determined repetition of a mantra, it could have been worse.

They'd had everything planned out... or, rather, *he'd* had it all planned, because he always did. Monica and Stephen were meant to be driving down from Havre with Brett, laden with his stuff, less the bags and boxes that Tommy had already packed into the Chevy and, with Bill's permission, been stacking up in the bunkhouse for the past two weeks. Of course, they got stuck in virtual gridlock trying to get out of the city, and were running three hours later than planned by the time they called. That turned out to be more than a minor inconvenience, seeing as the realtor wouldn't let Tommy sign for the keys and insisted on waiting for the named tenant.

"I know it's stupid," Tommy said, cupping his phone to his ear as he waited in the Chevy at the end of the block, the clatter of the heater almost drowning out the radio. It was cold outside, the first week of December, and the roads were gray with slush and ice. "But there's not a lot we can do about it. I can wait. It's okay. How long d'you think you'll be?"

Brett sighed irritably. "No idea. Three hours, maybe?"

Tommy winced and tried to inject some nonchalance into his voice. "That's cool. Don't rush."

"'Don't rush?'" Brett echoed incredulously, the words crackling in Tommy's ear and eliciting another wince. "What about the furniture people?"

Tommy eyed the road ahead of him doubtfully. It was, like a lot of Poplar, sparse and kind of flat. There wasn't much to it, just like there wasn't much to most of the town. The buildings were generally made of flat planes, shallow roofs, and bleak, sharp corners, and their new home wasn't much different. A small, scrubby collection of shrubs had been planted near the steps that rose from the sidewalk, and although they were evergreens of some kind, they looked pale and stringy, like they were clinging onto survival out of sheer grim determination.

He exhaled slowly, warming the fingers of his free hand in the heater's slow belch of air. "Baby, they said any time between seven in the morning and six in the evening. They could show up whenever. If they're here before you, I'll get 'em to leave the stuff on the curb or something."

"Oh, great." Brett groaned in frustration. "So now we gotta move a couch, a bed, and a table plus chairs up three flights of stairs?"

Tommy suppressed a small smile. He started to point out that they'd only have to move anything if the delivery actually *happened*, but Brett was muffling the phone while he relayed the information to whichever one of his parents it was who'd just asked what was going on. Tommy shut up and waited for him to finish, quietly amused by the rising pitch of the fuzzy voice he could hear.

As long as he wasn't actually in the same room as him at the time, he found Brett's aggravation mildly adorable.

The realtor had long since gone back to her office, so he settled down to wait and listened to the weather bulletin on the radio. More snow, apparently, though it didn't seem like this winter would be as cold as last year's.

A lot had changed in a year, Tommy reflected. Twelve months ago, more or less, his mother had announced her engagement, and he and Brett had just been edging up to the practicalities of this thing that was now finally real… this whole new world of theirs. Changes all around, he supposed, and that was good. That was right. It was what was supposed to happen, and he welcomed it the way he welcomed the whole turning of the wheel and all the rest of that shit. You couldn't really do much else, could you?

Nevertheless, a soft smile curled his lips as he looked at the pictures tacked up behind the gearstick: Lila, preparing to go to some party or other, wearing a huge smile and a pink sheath dress that made her look way older than it ought to, with her hand on her boyfriend's arm. His name was Paul, and he'd been to the house once. In retrospect, Tommy kind of felt sorry for the guy, because he really hadn't expected the surprise interrogation by two brothers, one stepfather, and whatever the hell kind of surrogate cousin or brother-in-practically-law Brett had become. He'd coped with it pretty well, though, and Tommy had rather liked him, as long as he didn't allow his imagination to fill in too many of the probable details. There was a shot of Karen and Scott with Atian, taken at Bill's place, when Bill had put the boy up on one of the horses for a little while. He'd loved it, and the whole afternoon had been one of those beautiful, blissful fall days that felt like they were drops of time outside of everything.

Tommy's fingers skimmed the edges of the pictures, and his smile stalled for a few moments. Funny how so much changed and yet remained the same... and how some things changed so much, so quickly, that it seemed impossible to believe they had ever been different at all, even when you knew they had, because you remembered every tiny detail.

He rubbed his thumb along the bottom edge of the photo of Brett, wearing the watch Tommy had bought him this time last year, with his hand on Katie's shoulder as she straddled her new bike. She didn't fall off so much now, and Ron had bought bikes for him and Mei too, instigating weekend rides and nature trails and all manner of other crap Tommy would never have believed his mother would do. She seemed happy, though, happier than he'd ever seen her, and he was almost reconciled to the weird way that made him feel.

He sighed and settled back against the seat as the radio started churning out bland chart pop. Tommy wrinkled his nose and reached for the dial, smirking to himself as he ended up on one of the local stations that played the kind of eighties garbage he and Brett used to make out to, back when they'd park up at Beaver Creek or somewhere and snatch at the little oasis of bliss this truck gave them.

Tommy left the dial where it was and huddled up in his coat, humming along to Foreigner as fat flakes of snow began to spiral gently down to pat against the windshield.

"IT NEVER rains, but it pours," Monica said helpfully, pulling the apartment door back as far as it would go and trying to avoid being hit by the double mattress edging its way through the aperture.

"Snows, Mom," Brett grunted, shoving his end of the mattress past the doorjamb with a grimace. "*Snows*."

Monica pursed her lips. "Fair point."

They had arrived, eventually, five hours later than intended. Brett had been fidgety to start with, his mood not improved by then having to wait another hour for the realtor to come out with the keys... the wrong keys, in fact, as quickly emerged when they broke in the lock. The truck delivering the new furniture showed up while they were waiting for the locksmith, resulting in everything being deposited on the sidewalk, in the snow, because the driver said he wasn't able to hold off on the rest of his route on their account. By that point, Brett had been virtually incandescent, and Monica was impressed by the way Tommy had managed to calm him down. She and Stephen had offered to go in search of food, which left the boys a little time alone and gave everyone a much-needed breather. All they'd managed to turn up was soggy drive-thru burgers with too much relish and plastic cheese, which hadn't really helped matters, but at least it was food of a kind.

Now, Tommy and Brett were hefting boxes and furniture into the apartment, and the mattress that was passing perilously close to Monica's nose was—due to torn plastic wrappings—both damp and dusted with snow.

A clatter from the handkerchief-sized kitchen heralded Stephen unpacking saucepans and hopefully the emergency kettle, and Monica winced as she heard him swear.

"It's fine!" he called, as Brett and Tommy edged the mattress toward the apartment's tiny bedroom, where the bed frame was already resting in plastic-wrapped pieces, promising "easy home assembly."

The boys exchanged knowing looks, and Brett groaned as his father's voice echoed once more:

"Brett? Do you have any spare plugs? And a screwdriver?"

Monica sighed and shut the door. Someone was going to have to work out how to operate the antiquated heating system too... and, next to the heavy boxes and whatever chaos Stephen was causing, that seemed like a job she'd be happiest doing.

She slid the chain on the door and went to investigate the thermostat.

Despite the disorder, and the fact that most of Brett's things had been brought down piecemeal—in secondhand boxes and spare duffel bags instead of by a proper moving company—she couldn't help noticing that there wasn't much stuff of his.

Monica didn't understand how a person could get through life amassing so little clutter. Brett had moved out more than five years ago, and yet the family home was still full of things she and Stephen hadn't even known he'd left there. They had box upon box of things in the attic, from old report cards and school projects to broken-but-never-mended childhood toys and the half-finished fossil collection that he'd lost interest in at the age of eight. The garage held apparently endless quantities of things Monica didn't even remember acquiring, and some things she distinctly recalled telling her husband to throw out. There was still a beaten-up kayak in there somewhere, despite the fact he hadn't used it in years.

She shook her head and focused on programming the timer. If she and Stephen were staying the night before driving home, it would be better not to freeze to death, and she did feel a little better once she'd checked out things like the radiators, water heater, and smoke and carbon monoxide detectors. Monica was dubious enough about the apartment's sparse plainness without worrying about its safety standards.

By the time she'd finished, Tommy had disappeared to go and put the bed frame together, while Stephen and Brett had fixed the kettle, slit the plastic off the couch, and were struggling with a self-assembly shelving unit, much like the one he'd helped put up at home. Cheap and cheerful, she thought, like this whole arrangement. She watched the way Brett lined up the pieces of chipboard—so neat, so precise, because he was always so careful about everything. Well, almost everything. Had been since he was a little boy. Monica remembered him sitting on the kitchen counter in their old house, aged maybe six, being stoically tight-lipped and quiet while she patched up a bumped, grazed knee. She'd called him brave, but it wasn't just that. He'd watched everything she did, every part of the process of cleaning and healing, because he wanted to know how things worked... how you went about mending people.

He always had. He'd have been a wonderful doctor, she felt sure. Even a wonderful physical therapist. And yet, here he was, giving everything up again.

She wasn't crazy about watching him move away. It had hardly come as a surprise, and perhaps it wouldn't be indefinite, but it still stung. The fact it wasn't the first time had helped—as Stephen had pointed out, Brett had been much further away at college than he was in Poplar—but this was different, and they all knew it.

Monica wished she'd been able to talk to him about it more. She wished they hadn't argued so often, rubbing each other the wrong way until the sparks inevitably burst like static, and she wasn't even sure why that had happened. She and Stephen had always thought they were raising their son to believe he could talk to them about anything. They'd always *said* that, hadn't they? That there was no need to be embarrassed, no need to feel he had to hide anything. They'd tried so hard to be open about everything, to give Brett the kind of personal, emotional freedom neither of them had ever had as children or teenagers, and somehow it just hadn't worked.

Somehow, beneath the façade of honesty—the way he'd joke and smile with them, and let them both think they knew how his mind worked—it had all gone wrong. He'd never told them he was gay, for one thing. And he should have been able to, shouldn't he? If they'd done their job properly, he should have, and yet Monica wasn't even sure he'd *wanted* to. At first, she'd thought he was ashamed—either of the thing itself, or the way they'd found out, both about him and about Tommy—but it hadn't been that. It was as if, in some way she didn't fully understand, he'd wanted to wait. He'd said that once; he'd expected it to be at college, when he had room to spread his wings.

He'd fumbled so clumsily around the words, trying to express his meaning, and she'd grasped it slowly: a first boyfriend, a validation... a reason to tell his parents who he was.

Why did you ever think you needed a reason, honey?

They'd adjusted, though. She had to admit that, however unreal it had all seemed once. The police cars and interviews, TV reporters and prison visits... it had been like falling headfirst into someone else's life, and she hadn't known where to even look for a foothold. Then, somewhere along the way, it had all just been absorbed, and grown to be part of how things were. Maybe none of it ever sat quite right—maybe Monica was always wondering exactly how things might have been different—but it all stopped spinning, and life seeped back into the edges of things, filling up the cracks with new realities, new equilibriums that, gradually, became normal.

He'd done that. Her boy. She supposed it was a mark of the strength he really had.

THEY got most of the heavy lifting over with early, and once the furniture was put together, it was just a case of starting to unpack. Brett didn't really want to do too much of that while his parents were there. He wanted it to be something he and Tommy did together... that long, drawn-out ballet of finding places for things, compromising and tweaking and, yeah, probably arguing about stupid, unimportant details. But it would be wonderful.

Bill dropped by very briefly, with the welcome moving-in present of a bucket of chicken and a six-pack of beer, plus a few groceries "so they could survive," as he put it, at least until they'd found their way to the local store. Brett grinned when he saw the packets of Tommy's preferred brand of fry bread mix—a running joke that had obviously spread further than just the two of them. Sometimes on weekends, when they spent long hours being lazy together, he made it from scratch. They'd eat it, still warm and drizzled with honey, and get pleasantly sticky, and Tommy would make that well-worn crack about fry bread being like sex: great when it was good and, when it was bad... still pretty damn good.

There were smiles and tired laughter, and Brett was just a little glad that Bill declined the offer of staying to eat. He shook Brett's hand warmly, shook Stephen's, kissed Monica's cheek, and gave Tommy a rough, loose hug before he left, taking some of the chaos with him back out into the night and leaving Tommy smiling long after the door had closed.

Brett kept stealing looks at him while they ate. Hair dull and ruffled on his shoulders, eyes bright but baggy, his old clothes were a mess and his hands were scuffed in numerous places from all the messing around with screwdrivers, Allen wrenches, and hammers. They probably both looked as worn-out as each other, Brett decided, and yet Tommy seemed alight with a free, golden kind of happiness he hadn't shown in a while, and that more than made up for the string of complications the day had thrown at them.

The conversation floated over their rickety little dining table—a gate-fold affair in beech veneer, with four folding chairs and one leg that remained resiliently wobbly, even after Stephen had taken it apart and put it back together twice—in a happy kind of fug, and Brett couldn't get over how familiar all the new things felt.

"You don't get a lot of noise from the road, though, huh?" Stephen observed, as Monica added the chicken bones and cartons to the trash they'd accumulated from all the packaging.

Brett blinked and glanced at the dark glass of the window that faced the street. The dim glow of streetlights and the lit windows of other buildings pricked the blackness, and his own face looked back at him, this whole domestic little scene mirrored: a moment caught in time. A car swished by, the damp sound of snow and grit barely audible from inside and its engine only a faint purr.

"No," he said thoughtfully. "Better than I thought, really."

And it was. Everything was. Brett supposed this was what people called a honeymoon glow, and the thought made him smile even more widely.

Tommy was in the kitchen—*their* kitchen—helping Monica put away stacks of newly unpacked plates and glasses. He was probably putting them in all the wrong cupboards, going by some bizarre inner logic that only he would ever understand, and Brett was sure he'd spend the next six months trying to remember which drawer the forks lived in, but it didn't matter. Or, he reflected, it did, but it mattered because it was a part of their life, this new life they would have, full of its own idiosyncrasies and stupidities, each one like the facet on some delicately cut stone, just waiting for the light to touch it and bring out its fire.

When the time came to call it quits and hit the hay, Monica and Stephen seemed very slightly uneasy about taking the bed, but Brett insisted, even though part of him wanted to let himself be swayed by their protests. There *was* a certain tempting quality to the thought of collapsing on the new mattress with Tommy, after all. However, the snow had begun to fall again, and it had grown late while no one was looking, so he and Tommy unrolled sleeping bags on the living room floor, and Monica smiled as she lingered by the door that led off to the bedroom.

"Hmm. You can fight for the couch, I guess."

"Tickle fight," Tommy said unthinkingly, shaking his sleeping bag out and smirking very slightly as he looked up. "I'll win, so don't even try it, sweetheart."

Brett sniggered and glanced reflexively at his mother, his laughter broadening out when she tutted and shook her head.

"As long as the screaming doesn't keep me awake. It's been a long day."

Monica and Tommy grinned at each other, and Brett pulled a face at it being at his expense, though he couldn't really bring himself to mind much. Besides, the day *had* been a long one, and he was looking forward to even the small comfort of the floor.

The apartment didn't offer much in the way of privacy, but finally the toilet flushed for the second time, and his parents secreted themselves away in the bedroom. Brett glanced at Tommy, already pulling his T-shirt off and revealing the smooth, golden-brown expanse of his back.

"After you, if you want," he said, as Tommy tossed the shirt on top of his boots, which stood at the foot of his sleeping bag, their tongues sagging and laces spilling out like unspooled yarn.

Tommy tucked his hair behind his ear and nodded. "Okay."

Brett watched him cross the small, square room, and slowly exhaled the breath he hadn't quite realized he'd been holding. He smiled to himself when the bathroom door clicked shut. It had taken a good couple of years, but Tommy had started closing doors again, without even thinking about it. That was good. Even better, Brett was pretty sure that most of them were going to stay shut.

He waited his turn, then took care of business himself and, when he got back, smiled all over again at the sight of Tommy bundled up in the sleeping bag, just one shoulder and part of his head visible. He squinted up at Brett.

"Turn the light off?"

"Sure." Brett obliged and picked his way across the floor in the amber-tainted dark, starting to learn the fuzzy outlines of their new furniture—this whole new landscape—with every step. "You okay?"

Tommy nodded sleepily as Brett slid under the slippery folds of the bedroll. "Mm-hm. Though, I admit it's not quite how I pictured our first night."

He said it with a trace of mirth instead of resentment, and Brett rolled over, propping himself on one elbow so he could regard his partner quizzically. The darkness smoothed Tommy's face, all except for the wide, pale crease of his smile and the suggestion of light from the window catching in his eyes. The combination of mischievous grin and swaddled-up, half-hidden features had Brett washed with affection for him, unable to think that he looked like anything but some impish kid… and that was right, he supposed. They were kids again tonight: sleeping bags and fast food, and whispering so as not to wake the parents. Once you took away the sore muscles and the lingering irritation with the realtor, this was basically a slumber party.

Best slumber party ever.

Brett grinned at the thought and stifled a soft laugh, his grin widening as a new thought struck him.

"Well, we could always zip 'em together," he offered, batting at the underside of his sleeping bag suggestively. "What d'you think?"

Tommy wrinkled his nose. "Your parents are in the next room."

"So? We'll be quiet."

One pen-stroke brow arched in the dimness. "You're never *that* quiet," Tommy whispered dryly. "Anyway, it'd feel... weird. They'll be going tomorrow, though. Early, right?"

"Early," Brett agreed. "So—"

"We get the whole day," Tommy murmured. "Just you and me. Do whatever we want, whenever."

"Mm." Brett stretched, luxuriating in the softness and warmth of the fabric surrounding him. "That sounds good. Better than good."

"*Really* good," Tommy agreed, his voice a low, warm ripple among the shadows that sent a shiver skittering down Brett's spine. "Hey...."

One long, lean hand worked its way out of Tommy's sleeping bag and crept across the faded carpet to tug at the zipper on Brett's bedroll. Brett chuckled and reached out, catching at the warm, familiar grasp of his fingers.

Outside, the night clouds shifted, allowing a few pale strands of moonlight to lance the window. Slivers of it picked at Tommy's bare skin as he squeezed Brett's hand, then withdrew for a moment, stifling more soft laughter as he wriggled his sleeping bag across the floor. Brett snorted at the sight of him, like some shiny-backed bug squirming its way over the carpet, hair falling over his eyes and the moon limning his broad shoulders... and the blurred smudge of the dragon on his arm.

The sleeping bags crinkled, the smooth susurration of nylon whispering in the dark, and then Brett had Tommy spooned against him, fidgeting about until he was finally comfortable.

"Mm. That's better."

Brett smiled. "Cuddle-slut," he muttered affectionately as he brushed the hair off Tommy's neck, allowing him to spoon closer and press a kiss to the warm, soft skin that smelled of sweat and spice and all those wonderful, familiar things.

A small noise of approval rumbled in Tommy's throat, and Brett snaked an arm around his waist, resting his cheek against the back of his lover's shoulder. Funny, he supposed, how even sheathed in separate sleeping bags, they felt this close.

"Night, baby," Tommy murmured sleepily, his hand moving to cover Brett's, long fingers flexing slightly over his knuckles. "Love you."

"Love you too," Brett echoed, the words a whisper against his skin. "Night."

He felt Tommy's breathing start to lengthen out as sleep crept up on them both, and then he stirred a little, smiling again.

"What?" Brett asked idly, just in case he wasn't already asleep.

"Hmm." Tommy shifted against him, the long, solid lines of his body plain beneath the nylon padding. His fingers tightened over Brett's hand. "Welcome home. I meant to say that too."

"Oh." Brett blinked in the darkness, a wide, warm grin spreading slowly over his face. "Yeah. You too. Welcome… uh, welcome home."

He was aware of the burr in his voice at the edge of those words, but he couldn't bring himself to be ashamed of the way he held tighter to Tommy, smiling into the darkness as sleep came. It softened the bounds of his thoughts, until the great well of love and peace and, hell, yeah, even contentment filled him completely, and Brett felt himself fall into it, safer and happier than he remembered being in years. Because some shadows pass by, but some are always with us. They become part of who we are, and we have to live with them—accept them—acknowledging that they grow and change with us.

Only then do they start to fade, and pale into the night.

M. KING resides in a damp, verdant corner of Southwest England, where she may usually be found behind a keyboard and a vat of coffee. A former Arvon Foundation Award winner, she is an inveterate scribbler and teller of tales and has never yet met a genre she didn't like.

Her work features flawed and fascinating characters, vibrant storytelling, and worlds to lose yourself in time and again, with titles ranging from horror to fantasy, humor to romance, erotica to tear-jerking drama… and more.

On the very rare occasions she isn't writing, M. King enjoys taking long, muddy walks with her dogs—otherwise known as the hairy chaos monkeys—reading, dabbling in her herb garden, and falling off horses. Just not all at the same time.

Visit her website at http://www.thenakednib.com. You can contact her at lavengra@yahoo.com.

Don't miss the beginning of the story in

BREAKING
FAITH

M. KING

http://www.dreamspinnerpress.com

Read more by M. KING in

LEGENDS OF LOVE ANTHOLOGY

http://www.dreamspinnerpress.com

Also from DREAMSPINNER PRESS

BUTTERFLY'S
CHILD

ALAN CHIN

http://www.dreamspinnerpress.com

Also from DREAMSPINNER PRESS

http://www.dreamspinnerpress.com

For more of the
best M/M romance,
visit

Dreamspinner Press

www.dreamspinnerpress.com

www.ingramcontent.com/pod-product-compliance
Lightning Source LLC
Chambersburg PA
CBHW070047030726
47506CB00002B/378